Praise for *Crimes of the Heart* . . .

"THESE 14 BRAND-NEW STORIES . . . not only take advantage of that well-known association between sweethearts and heart wounds, but by and large revel in lavishly beribboned plot twists . . . just the thing to have handy while you're cooling your heels waiting for your valentine."—*Kirkus Reviews*

"MYSTERY AND ROMANCE LOVERS ALIKE WILL THRILL TO THIS COLLECTION . . . should not be missed."—*Family*

"EACH WRITER IN THIS ANTHOLOGY IS A MASTER OF HIS OR HER CRAFT . . . Readers who enjoy a good mystery with a Hitchcockian twist will relish this notable collection."—*Gothic Journal*

CRIMES

OF THE

HEART

Edited by CAROLYN G. HART

BERKLEY PRIME CRIME, NEW YORK

CRIMES OF THE HEART

A Berkley Prime Crime Book / published by arrangement with
the editor

PRINTING HISTORY
Berkley Prime Crime trade edition / February 1995
Berkley Prime Crime mass-market edition / February 1997

The Putnam Berkley World Wide Web site address is
http://www.berkley.com/berkley

ISBN: 0-425-15674-5

Berkley Prime Crime Books are published
by The Berkley Publishing Group,
200 Madison Avenue, New York, NY 10016.
The name BERKLEY PRIME CRIME and the BERKLEY PRIME CRIME
design are trademarks belonging to Berkley Publishing Corporation.

PRINTED IN THE UNITED STATES OF AMERICA

10 9 8 7 6 5 4 3 2 1

〖 CONTENTS 〗

Foreword

Love and Kisses
Won't You Be Mine?
True Love
Could You Fall for Me?
You're a Real Treat!

It's Valentine's Day, and children across America are exchanging brightly colored bits of cardboard. Adults observe the holiday, too, with romantic cards, satin-covered boxes of luscious chocolates, and bouquets of roses. Cut-out red hearts dangle in stores. Cupid shoots his gold-tipped arrows. It's a lace-edged holiday awash in sentiment to celebrate the memory of that dear old patron of lovers, St. Valentine.

But as all detectives know (and as Jane Marple made quite clear), things often are not what they seem.

Legend has it that Valentine secretly officiated at the weddings of many soldiers and their brides despite the decree from the emperor, Claudius II, forbidding soldiers to marry. Claudius reasoned that his fighting men would be more willing to guard the Empire's far-flung boundaries if they were free of domestic responsibilities.

Legend further describes Valentine as a gardener who enjoyed sharing his blooms with neighborhood children. When Valentine was imprisoned for refusing to honor Rome's gods, the children tossed him notes of love and encouragement through his cell window. On the anniversary of Valentine's death, those who remembered his martyrdom exchanged notes, and these were soon called "valentines."

These are sweet and pretty stories, quite as nice as the valentines that have flourished since his death.

And, alas for romantics, historians dismiss them.

The truth?

The early church wished to wean its members away from the Festival of Lupercalia, an often erotic celebration of spring and fertility which occurred on February 15. How much better it was, the church fathers reasoned, to celebrate the martyrdom of St. Valentine on February 14.

So the myths about St. Valentine as a patron of lovers came into being, and, even though he's been dropped from the church calendar, St. Valentine today continues to reign as the patron of lovers in the secular world.

Valentines are still exchanged, most of them sweet and endearing, some risqué, many quite funny. Men and women reach out with lace-edged hearts, boxes of candy, and flowers.

I Love You.

Three simple words. Simple, yes, but they can be said with passion, in despair, with joy, in anger, with hope, in renunciation, with regret, in triumph.

It isn't easy to capture these feelings on candy hearts, but it's fun to try. If each author's work were to be summed up for a pink or yellow or white heart-shaped candy, these might be the mottoes:

Dorothy Cannell	Enchantment
P. M. Carlson	All for Art
Barbara D'Amato	Honor Bright
Jeffery Deaver	Forever Yours
Susan Dunlap	Top This, Valentine
Carolyn G. Hart	Listen to Your Heart
Joan Hess	Sweets to the Sweet
Margaret Maron	Naughty but Nice
Lia Matera	Be Mine

Sharyn McCrumb	Love Me
D. R. Meredith	By Your Side
Audrey Peterson	Heart to Heart
Nancy Pickard	Forget-Me-Not
Marilyn Wallace	Promises, Promises

These mottoes can only hint at what our Valentine stories offer, because it is the complexity of love—or the lack of love—that provides the inspiration for these unique and wonderful stories.

Welcome to *Crimes of the Heart*.

〚 DOROTHY CANNELL 〛

DOROTHY CANNELL'S VERY FIRST MYSTERY, THE Thin Woman, *became an instant classic. It is the all-time best-seller at Murder by the Book, a mystery bookstore in Houston, Texas. The wonderfully clever and irrepressible saga of Ellie and Ben Haskell has continued in equally original and entertaining novels,* The Widows Club, Mum's the Word, Femmes Fatal, *and* How to Murder Your Mother-in-Law. *The adventures of the world's most unlikely private detectives, the Misses Hyacinth and Primrose Tramwell, are recounted in* Down the Garden Path. *Cannell's novels and short stories have been nominated for many awards, including the Agatha and Anthony, and* The Thin Woman *was named the best mystery of the year by the Romance Writers of America. Cannell writes with warmth and wit, recalling her native England with great fondness and exuberance. A Cannell book or short story is guaranteed to lift a reader's spirits. Cannell lives in Peoria, Illinois, with her husband, Julian. Her next Ellie and Ben novel will be* How to Murder the Man of Your Dreams.

In "Cupid's Arrow," Cannell once again weaves an enchanting story, full of warmth and humor.

Cupid's Arrow

"You know what happens to wicked people, don't you, Giselle?" said Great Aunt Honoria.

"They go to hell," my ten-year-old self addressed the implacable hands on the wheel as the elderly Daimler proceeded decorously down the country road. "But surely you have to do something really bad, like murder one of your relations." I savored the prospect as a blackbird fluttered in front of the windscreen and was instantly sent into backward flight by a blast of the horn. "It was only a very small lie."

"You told me that you had been chosen to play Little Red Riding Hood in the school play." Aunt Honoria's voice deepened to a rumble that echoed the thunder that was trying to scare the car into a ditch. "It was a complete fabrication. There isn't a play. And you aren't in it."

"No, Aunt." I withdrew my gaze from her granite profile and studied my shoes.

"I always know what's inside a person, Giselle." She made this sound as though it were a special talent, like playing the piano or being able to climb a rope. While the Daimler purred on down the road, flattening out any bumps that had the impertinence to be in its path, I thought with satisfaction that she had not caught me out in my really big lie.

Aunt Honoria had asked me when we stopped for lunch in Mobley Cross if I were enjoying myself and I had told her I was having a super time. Now that was a complete fabrication! My mother had warned me that the day might not be loads of fun.

"She's a bit of an old dragon, darling! And she doesn't have a clue about children. But try to remember she is a lonely old lady with not as much money as she once had. In fact, I'm sure she's down to her last fur coat, so don't stand looking at toys in shop windows and please think small when it comes to meals."

As it turned out I didn't have to fend off the urge to gaze adoringly at teddy bears. Aunt Honoria did not take me walking past any shops. In the morning we visited the hospital where she had worked as a volunteer when she was a young woman and no one now remembered her. When we sat down to lunch at the Thatcher and Aunt Honoria ordered us each a bowl of clear brown

soup, it was hard for me to adhere to Mother's instruc-
tions and keep my lips zipped. God would not have put
fish-and-chips in this world if he had not meant them to
be eaten. And when the people at the next table started
tucking into treacle pudding, I was tempted to inform
Aunt Honoria that Mr. Rochester's mad wife may have
ended up that way because someone had starved her in
the presence of other people licking their sticky lips and
sucking on their forks. But I had smiled bravely and
told my noble lie which, if there was any justice in this
world, should have canceled out any number of bad lies,
including the Red Riding Hood story.

"I don't think I'm going to hell," I told Aunt Honoria
as a woolly gray mist wrapped itself around the car
windows and the thunder crept closer and growled more
menacingly. "At the worst I will go to purgatory for a
few hundred years."

"Nonsense. We're Church of England, so you can't
go to purgatory because we don't believe in it." She
put her foot down on the brake, brooking no argument
from the Daimler or me as we came to a barely visible
red traffic light. I was hoping we were on our way back
to my parents and the London flat. But after crawling
along for another few minutes down a lane, we passed
a building that might, or might not, have been a church
and turned onto a drive lined with evergreens. These
appeared to have been sketched with charcoal and the
house that presently rose up from the mist to greet us
also looked the product of a fevered imagination.

"Is this your house, Aunt Honoria?"

"Good gracious, no! Do I look as if I am made of
money?" She pulled down the cuffs of her fur coat and
turned off the engine with a snap. "This is Thornton
Hall, an Elizabethan house now open to the public. I
thought we might take a look at it if you will promise
not to climb over the ropes and bounce on the bed that
was slept in by Charles the Second."

"Oh, Aunt Honoria! What a treat!" I bundled out of the car and skipped around to where she stood tapping her cane impatiently on the ground. "It looks just like the house in *Jane Eyre*. And the name is almost the same."

"You're much too young, Giselle, to be reading such books."

"I did have trouble with some of the big words," I conceded, "but I looked them up in the dictionary and—"

"That's not the point," Aunt Honoria cut me off in a way that would have been considered rude in a child of my age. "You should be reading about nice people doing nice things. It's far too soon for you to know anything about illicit passion."

Rubbish, I thought. I had felt very passionate about that treacle pudding.

"Mr. Rochester had no business falling in love with Jane Eyre when he had a wife upstairs in the attic." Aunt Honoria thrust aside the mist with an imperious wag of the cane and marched without a sideways glance at topiary or sundials toward the lighted windows of the house.

"Yes, I suppose it was a bit naughty of him," I agreed dutifully, "but he paid for his sin, didn't he? I don't suppose it was much fun going blind and losing his hand in the fire."

To my relief Aunt Honoria did not seize upon this statement to continue her lecture on the well-stoked furnaces of hell. After admonishing me not to trip over my tongue, she followed the arrow signs posted along the edge of the flower beds and stalked up a short flight of steps to a door marked ENTER.

"Wipe your feet, Giselle." She gave me a poke with the cane as we stepped into the heavily beamed combination tearoom and gift shop. Oh, how lovely! China dolls dressed in a range of period costumes from stiff

Elizabethan frocks and lace ruffs to frothy Victorian crinolines were displayed among the toasting forks and horse brasses on the wall shelves. My nose twitched in appreciation of the smell of toasted tea cakes that warmed the air. But a glance at Aunt Honoria put to rest any hope that she was about to ruin my character by indulging me with butter-dripping treats.

"Is it still raining?" A dark-haired woman wearing a wool frock and a pleasant smile came around from the counter that stretched across a corner of the room.

"No, but the mist is turning to fog." Aunt Honoria spoke as if leveling a criticism of how things were run at Thornton Hall. "We could hardly see anything of the grounds so I hope"—she looked sternly down at her black leather handbag—"that we will get our money's worth here in the house."

"We only charge adults a pound for looking around the place and children are half price." The nice lady smiled at me. "Having a day out with Grandma, are you, honey?"

Before I could open my mouth Aunt Honoria set the woman straight on her mistake, then added accusingly, "You sound like an American."

"From Chicago. My husband and I have always loved England, and two years ago we decided to pull up stakes, move over here, and buy this place. It's been exciting if"—an expressive shrug—"a little daunting. The people 'round here are taking their time accepting us."

"Give them three hundred years," said Aunt Honoria, "and that may change."

"Sometimes," the woman responded with an attempt at a laugh, "I'm not sure we'll last three years. It's a lot more work running a place of this size than either my husband or I realized, and we're beginning to think we're not cut out for being cooped up with the past. Now this part of the business I do enjoy." She looked around at the tables with their yellow-and-white-checked cloths and the shelves lined with gifts. "It's cheerful in here. And my husband enjoys the gardens; he's out in the greenhouse now. But mostly we leave the guided tours to old Ned. He came with the house," she explained as Aunt Honoria raised an interrogatory eyebrow. "The man has to be a hundred if he's a day and knows the history of Thornton Hall backward and forward."

"Then I suggest we meet this treasure before I reach my centenary." Aunt Honoria's lips stretched into an attempt at a smile.

"You wouldn't like a cup of tea first?" The woman stepped toward a cast-iron cooker in the corner and held up the kettle invitingly. "And the little girl looks as though she would enjoy a toasted tea cake."

"Giselle has enjoyed lots of toasted tea cakes in her short sojourn upon this earth." Aunt Honoria looked pointedly down at my portly form. "But I have brought her here to feed her mind, thank you all the same, Mrs. . . . ?"

"Perkins." She led us through a round-topped oak door into a wainscoted hall that was bigger than the one where I suffered through ballet class, and into a room with narrow leaded windows and a great many portraits in heavy frames on the walls. A white-haired old man wearing an apron and pair of grimy leather gloves stood at a refectory table polishing away at a brass candlestick. This he set down next to its still-tarnished fellow when Mrs. Perkins ushered Aunt Honoria and me toward him.

"Ned, honey," she said brightly, "these folks would like the guided tour, and I need to stay in the shop in case we should get lucky and have a busload of people arrive all wanting tea and crumpets."

"Very good, Mrs. Perkins." The old man put down his polishing cloth, straightened his stooped shoulders, and turned to Aunt Honoria and me. "If you will kindly follow me, madam and little miss, we will get started."

"Don't let us rush you," my relation responded austerely. "By all means take the time to remove your apron."

"It doesn't make much sense to do that, I'd only have to put it back on again when I'm done with you." Ned waved a glove at the army of candlesticks, kettles, and warming pans. "The copper and brass won't decide to clean themselves."

Aunt Honoria muttered the word, "Uppity!" and, while I was hoping I was the only one who had heard her, Mrs. Perkins retreated from the room. Fixing me with a piercing blue gaze, Ned said, "Little miss, this isn't one of the really grand houses such as Chatsworth or the like, and for the admission price of a pound you don't get a tour guide with military posture wearing gold braid and silver buttons."

"I'd much rather have you," I said truthfully, because something in me warmed to his gloomy voice and wrinkled visage—*visage* was one of the words I had looked up in the dictionary while reading *Jane Eyre*. Stepping up to him I reached for his hand, but he tapped me ever so lightly on the shoulder and led us toward the fireplace with its beaten-copper surround and ornately carved mantel displaying a row of silver hunt cups.

"I gather we are about to be shown the priest hole," Aunt Honoria said, as if announcing we were to have cucumber sandwiches for tea, but I noticed a sparkle in her eyes and realized she had not brought me here for the improvement of my mind alone. Old houses, I decided, were her passion. Without making any comment, let alone saying abracadabra, Ned touched a carved rose and a section of wainscoting slid sideways to reveal a dark aperture.

"Gosh!" I whispered, feeling the stirrings of an enthusiasm that might one day transcend treacle pudding.

"It was never used to hide priests or other followers of the popish faith," Ned told us in a voice that creaked with age, as did the floorboards. Drawing a torch from his apron pocket, he shone its yellow beam into the narrow rectangle that was no bigger than my toy cupboard. "The Thornton family turned Protestant without need of the thumbscrews at the Reformation. From that time forward they were rabid opponents of the Roman church. This hideaway was used for the concealment of royalist sympathizers during the rule of the Lord Protector."

"Oliver Cromwell," Aunt Honoria informed me as if I were four years old. "I imagine we are looking at a box of tricks with a secret staircase that offered the fugitive some hope of escape should the Roundheads show any intelligence."

Ned smiled and showed us a cunningly concealed trapdoor in the flagstone floor. Our tour of Thornton Hall began in earnest with a visit to the wine cellars, which continued the merry little game of hide-and-seek by providing hidden access to a lichen-covered tunnel which exited, so our guide told us, at the far edge of the apple orchard.

"It's all so romantic!" I gave an ecstatic sigh as we trooped back up the stone steps.

"I don't suppose the royalists thought so when they were captured and sent to the Tower of London. Having one's head chopped off, Giselle, has never been my idea of a good time." Aunt Honoria tapped out an impatient tattoo with her stick, but I could tell she was enjoying herself behind her grim lips.

Ned closed off the panel to what I still thought of as the priest hole and preceded us at a stooped-shouldered but vigorous pace back to the main hall with its massive stone fireplace. The blackened oak staircase rose up forever until it was lost in a ceiling painted with an azure blue sky, banks of clouds, and golden-winged cherubs whose rosy plumpness suggested that they shared my fondness for treacle pudding and other earthly delights.

"This ceiling was painted in the eighteenth century by

Wynward Holstein, who is thought in some quarters to have influenced the work of Sir Joshua Reynolds." Ned paused for me to say, "Gosh!" in what I hoped was a suitably reverential voice. He then led us through a series of doors into rooms whose Tudor and Jacobean furniture won grudging approval from Aunt Honoria. Her stick quivered with enthusiasm when she pointed at a tapestry that depicted in finely stitched detail the Great Fire of London. It seemed to me, however, that Ned's responses to her questions concerning court cupboards and pewter platters became more perfunctory as we poked our way about those rooms on the ground floor. When I watched him open the only door we had not yet entered, I felt suddenly terribly sad.

The feeling was almost as bad as when my cat had died. And that was ridiculous because I'd had Tabitha for as long as I could remember and Ned was only a man in an apron with a face as old as time. Perhaps I only felt down in the boots because I hadn't had a proper lunch or because the rain had begun weeping against the windows to the accompaniment of wistful sighs from the wind. Perhaps Ned wasn't tired to the bone and fed up to the teeth with trotting bossy old ladies and little girls in and out of doors and up and down stairs.

The room we now entered should have brightened my mood. It was unlike any we had yet been shown. The walls weren't paneled in carved oak. They were papered in a striped ivory-and-pale-green silk that matched the scroll-armed sofas, which like the curtains were edged with rose-colored cord. The fireplace mantel was done in what Aunt Honoria whispered to me was gold leaf, and several of the delicate tables were inlaid with the same veneer of sunlight. The paintings that hung from gold cords were all of flowers—so fresh and real I was sure that if I reached up I could pluck them from their frames and gather them into a bouquet that would still be wet with dew and heady with the scent of a summer from long ago.

"Charming," said Aunt Honoria, but when Ned stood aside she did not step more than a few feet into the room. "I suppose the Perkinses did all this!" She poked at the velvety rose carpet with her cane while her lips tightened in a look of disapproval edged with something softer, and I found myself moving up close to her and wishing she would take hold of my hand. Did she feel it too, the terrible empty waiting for something or someone who had once filled this room with a happiness brighter than gold leaf or sunlight?

"Mr. and Mrs. Perkins did redecorate this room upon taking up residence," Ned said, "but they did it from an old watercolor sketch, so it now looks very much as it did at the turn of the eighteenth century when Sir Giles and Lady Thornton occupied the house."

"It's very pretty." I smiled up at him but he had already turned back toward the hall as if eager to be done with us so he could get back to cleaning his brass. Aunt Honoria did not rap him on the shoulder and demand that he give us the history of the secretary desk or the harp-backed chairs. Perhaps she had realized that Ned was also an antique of sorts and should be treated with a measure of respect. Or could it be she was growing a little tired herself? After all she was getting on in years and might now prefer a cup of tea to climbing that extremely tall staircase. I wasn't particularly eager myself, and my voice came out in a whisper that was almost lost in the wind that was beginning to sound like the big bad wolf.

"Ned, is there a ghost at Thornton Hall?"

"I never saw one, little miss," he replied, and went ahead of us up the uncarpeted stairs.

"The house must have its stories." Aunt Honoria came tapping fast upon my heels.

"It's said three of the Thornton children died in the

plague of 1665," Ned spoke over his shoulder. "And the eldest son of the sixth baronet was killed in a duel fought on the grounds."

"How awful," I said, feeling much more cheerful. The house had seen a lot in its day. Good times and sad. So some rooms, like the one now used for the tea shop, were likely to be cheerful as copper kettles, while others, like the pretty ivory-and-green room, would have their moments of melancholy. But it wasn't as though Thornton Hall was a person. Houses don't cry until they're all wet on the outside and dry on the inside. They don't love till it hurts and wish they could die, as I had done when Tabitha had to be put to sleep.

Ned took us into several upstairs rooms with enormous four-poster beds and I asked him if Charles II had really slept in any of them.

"I don't believe so, little miss, but maybe one of his lady friends did. The Merry Monarch had enough of them to fill all the beds in his kingdom." Ned smiled so that his mouth became the biggest wrinkle on his wrinkled face. And I found myself wishing I could tuck him into an easy chair and stroke his white hair until he fell asleep.

I was not a particularly affectionate child, except where animals were concerned, but I wasn't as coldhearted as Aunt Honoria, and even she seemed to be mellowing as we continued our tour. She only pointed her stick at one piece of furniture and denounced it as a blatant reproduction, and once or twice I discovered a gentle light in her eye as she looked at Ned. Goodness! I thought. Was it possible that she had fallen madly in love with him on the way upstairs and was plotting how she could lure him into having a cup of tea and perhaps a crumpet with her before we left Thornton Hall?

My head filled with romantic possibilities and calculations as to how many years Aunt Honoria and Ned might reasonably have left in which to gaze rapturously into each other's eyes. As a result I almost tripped over her cane when they stopped in front of a portrait displayed in an alcove whose gallery railing overlooked the hall.

"What a lovely girl!" Aunt Honoria voice descended to a rumble. Following her gaze I could see why she was impressed. The painted face was so alive I was sure that if we looked long enough her lips would move and she would speak to us, or that the young lady would lift the hands that held a pink rosebud and brush back the soft brown ringlet that brushed against the shoulder of her muslin gown. She was not exactly beautiful, but she seemed lit from within by a golden glow and there was a look in her eyes of such joy and—

"Love!" said Aunt Honoria. "It's in her face!" The rain slipping and slithering down the windowpane to our left was the only answering sound until Ned finally spoke.

"Wynward Holstein, who painted the ceiling in the main hall, also did this portrait. She's Anne Thornton. The only daughter, the youngest after five sons, of Sir Giles and his lady. They had that salon downstairs"— he looked down at me from under his shaggy white eyebrows—"the one you thought so pretty, little miss, decorated for her because she loved the way the sun came in at its windows. And they hung the walls with paintings of flowers because her father called Anne the sweetest blossom in his gardens."

"How old was she when this portrait was painted?" Aunt Honoria shifted her handbag up her arm and stood with both hands on her cane.

"Seventeen, Madam."

"What happened to her?" I asked Ned. "Did she get married and go away to another house?"

"She never left Thornton Hall, little miss."

"Oh!" I said, picturing a sad decline of the girl's radiant youth into years of knitting mittens for the poor and tending her parents in their old age.

"She died, Anne did, shortly after the completion of the portrait." Ned stepped away and indicated with an inclination of his white head for us to follow him down the hallway.

"Her eyes! Look how they watch you!" Aunt Honoria went tapping after him, but I lingered behind, stepping to the right and left trying to see if she was correct about the magical properties of the portrait. We had a copy of *The Laughing Cavalier* on the stairs at home, and when my cousin Freddy had come to visit I had pridefully shown him how the roguish eyes followed us whichever way we went.

"Don't dawdle, Giselle!" Aunt Honoria's voice rapped me smartly on the head and sent me scurrying after her ramrod-straight back and Ned's stooped shoulders. "How did the girl die?" she asked him. "Did she succumb in proper eighteenth-century fashion to a fever or take an ill-prompted tumble from her horse?"

"I will show you where she died." Ned opened a door set beside a tall window overlooking the rose garden and led us up a narrow stone staircase that coiled around itself in ever-narrowing circles that threatened to squeeze the breath out of me. "Here we are, madam and little miss." Ned stepped into a round tower room that was empty of so much as a table or chair under which to huddle from the wind. It came gusting in through the gaping slits of paneless windows with such force that even Aunt Honoria had to struggle not to capsize like a sailing vessel cast upon stormy seas.

"Here?" Her shadow caricatured the waggle of her cane as she stood with feet apart on the flagstone deck. "Anne Thornton met her untimely end here?"

I shivered as a spatter of rain hit me squarely in the eye. "Did she get locked in by mistake and freeze to death?"

"No, little miss," Ned said, "she was shot by Cupid's arrow."

"Rubbish!" Aunt Honoria snapped. "If you have brought us here to tell us a fairy tale, my good man, you have another think coming! I have already had quite enough of such folderol for one day!" Her baleful glance at me informed me she was referring to my Red Riding Hood story.

"Oh, please! Do tell us about Cupid's arrow!" I reached for Ned's hand, but he had already mounted the stone lookout perch that surrounded the rim of the room, very much in the way that our vicar, also an old man with white hair, might have ascended the pulpit.

"Very well, my good man! Indulge the child." Aunt Honoria grimaced up at him. "There is no peace for the wicked and I am sure if I think long and hard I will realize what I have done to deserve catching pneumonia while Giselle listens openmouthed to the Legend of Thornton Hall."

"No peace," Ned murmured. Gloved hands folded on his apron front, he shook his hoary head and began to tell us what befell the sweet-faced girl of the portrait. "Anne's parents held a masquerade ball to celebrate her betrothal to a young gentleman by the name of Roger Belmonde. The two families had been closely connected for many years and the engagement had long been hoped for by Sir Giles and Lady Thornton. Everyone of any social standing in the county was invited to the ball except"—Ned paused as if the wind had forced the words back down his throat—"except the Haverfield family, which was comprised of Squire John, his lady wife, and their son Edward, a young gentleman who was still some months from attaining his majority."

"That means he had not yet turned twenty-one," Aunt Honoria told me with a poke of her stick, which missed me by several inches, suggesting that despite her earlier protests she was becoming caught up in the story.

"Why weren't Edward and his parents invited?" I asked.

"The Haverfields were of the Roman faith," Ned said as if reading off words printed behind his eyes. "And as such the Thorntons shunned any association with them even though Haverfield House lies only a few miles from here. Sir Giles had instructed Anne when she first began to ride beyond the grounds that Edward and his parents would in less lax times have been put to the chopping block for their popish ways. He forbade her to acknowledge the lad should they chance to meet upon one of the bridal paths."

"And in those days," Aunt Honoria said for my benefit, "a young girl never set foot outdoors unaccompanied by her groom or governess. But that didn't always put a stop to misbehavior. I suspect from what we saw of her face that Anne was the darling of the household and such being the case her chaperons would not betray her to Sir Giles and Lady Thornton when she inevitably met young Edward and embarked on a budding friendship with him under the greenwood trees. One wonders"— she looked at Ned—"how he reacted to her engagement to Roger Belmonde."

"Edward came to the ball." Ned stepped down from the stone ridge and looked at us with a pensive smile further creasing his face. "It was easily done with all the invited guests masked and in costume. He slipped into the thronged hall at a little before midnight when the revelry was at its zenith. He came in the guise of Cupid with a quiver of golden arrows. He merged with the press of faceless youth in their wide silk skirts or satin knee breeches. Among the dancers, bowing and curtsying as they traced out the steps of the minuet, while the old ladies in powder and patch drank sack and the old men propped their gouty legs on footstools and talked hunting days of yore, Edward found Anne Thornton."

"A planned meeting, I presume," said Aunt Honoria.

"Most certainly, madam. Anne escaped the watchful eyes of her betrothed by telling Roger Belmonde she had left her fan in her green-and-rose sitting room. She went with Edward gladly to the tower room even though she knew she was going to her death."

"I don't understand." I wrapped my arms around myself to ward off the cold.

"Edward Haverfield and Anne Thornton loved each other," said Ned. "They had done so from their first meeting, through stolen rendezvous and the fear of discovery. He was the lamp who lit the flame of joy we saw in her face. Marriage to the man chosen for her by Sir Giles and Lady Thornton would have been for Anne a living death. And her loss unending anguish for Edward. So the lovers decided upon a means that would ensure none would ever part them. They agreed he would come to the ball in the guise of Cupid with a golden arrow in his quiver and she would go with him to this tower room. It seemed so right to Anne that after one last kiss Edward would draw his bow, piercing her heart with love's arrow, and her soul would be set free to wait for him to join her within moments on a far rainbow-lit horizon."

"Why didn't they just run away together?" I asked.

"Where could they have gone, little miss?" Ned responded softly. "Their families would have cut them off without a shilling and seen them starve in the gutter sooner than recognize their union."

"But death is so horribly final!"

"Don't babble, Giselle!" said Aunt Honoria as our shadows loomed monstrously upon the walls. "I'm sure Ned would like to get back to cleaning the brass today, if not sooner." She speared him with an eye as sharp as Cupid's arrow. "How did young Mr. Haverfield intend to achieve his own demise? Step into one of those windy apertures and throw himself off the tower?"

"That was the plan, madam, but when the moment came and he stood poised to jump, his courage failed him and his limbs locked. He closed his eyes against the dizzying drop to the courtyard below; he tried to picture Anne waiting for him with outstretched hands, but his mind was blinded by panic. He stumbled down from the aperture and crawled to where her lifeless body lay upon the floor. Cradling her in his arms, he wept over her, begging her forgiveness and praying that his fortitude would revive."

"What a rotten egg!" I pressed my hand to my mouth and my cruel shadow mocked the motion. "I don't feel the least bit sorry for him."

"Neither, little miss, did Roger Belmonde," said Ned. "That young gentleman had grown uneasy upon finding his betrothed missing when he returned to the ballroom with her fan. He was truly devoted to Anne, and a lover's instinct brought him up the stairs to this tower room. He found it locked against him and, fighting down a dreadful sense of foreboding, he summoned up the strength of angels and battered his way through the door. Picture if you will, madam and little miss, the anguish of Roger Belmonde when he beheld Edward Haverfield crooning in demented fashion over the dead girl."

"Oh, I wish Anne had loved him," I said. "He sounds ever so much nicer than the beastly Edward and I expect was heaps more handsome."

"Incensed with grief and rage Roger set upon the other man," Ned continued, "but the murderer fled the tower to lose himself in the throng of dancers still stepping daintily to the minuet. He escaped the house by way of the secret passage, the location of which Anne of the trusting heart had described to him. But do not fear, madam and little miss"—Ned smiled wryly down at my cross face—"Edward Haverfield did not elude retribution. Anne Thornton's brothers, I told you she had five, rode out in a thundercloud of black cloaks to hunt down her murderer, and when they found him skulking in the hollow of a giant oak they . . ."

"Yes?" Aunt Honoria's shadow stiffened upon the wall.

"They . . ." Ned glanced from her to me and back again. "In the manner of their times they made sure Edward Haverfield would never shoot another arrow. And afterward they bound him with cords, tossed him facedown across the eldest brother's saddle, and rode back with him to Thornton Hall. There Edward was handed over to the justice of the peace who, still flushed with an evening's worth of ale, promised a swift trial and a slow hanging."

"I think it would have been better if he had languished in prison for a long time first," I said nastily.

"As it happened he did, because his father, being a man of prominence, managed for some years to stay the execution. And so, having made a short story long"—Ned shepherded us out the door and onto the stone staircase—"so ends the story of Anne Thornton and Cupid's arrow."

"Very interesting." Aunt Honoria tested the drop between one step and the next with her cane. "You are a fine teller of grim tales, Ned. No doubt Giselle here will be afraid to close her eyes when she goes to bed tonight."

"No, I won't!" I said as the walls spun me around in ever-tightening circles. "It was awfully sad about Anne, but not creepy the way it would be if Thornton Hall was haunted because of what happened. I'd be scared to meet a ghost"—I hesitated over where best to place my foot on the narrow stair wedge—"but at the same time it would be rather exciting. And as Mother and Father say—every child should be exposed to new experiences."

"I suspect they meant that you should start helping with the washing up," Aunt Honoria breathed fiercely down my neck. "Ah, almost at the bottom! Step smartly, Giselle," she said, following me into the light blazing off the hallway walls in contrast to the gloom of the stairwell. "This is the conclusion of the guided tour, is it, Ned?"

"I'll walk you back to Mrs. Perkins in the tea shop." He looked for the flicker of a second toward the portrait of Anne Thornton before making his stooped way to the main staircase.

"Not so fast." Aunt Honoria caught up with him at the banister rail. "Here"—she tucked her cane under her arm, opened her handbag, and pulled out a black coin purse—"I must give you a little something for your trouble."

"There's no need of that." He waved a hand at her, but she pressed a two-shilling piece into the grimy palm of his brass cleaning glove. And I saw a look pass between them. I didn't think it was one of mad passionate love because I had decided when he was telling the story that his crusty old heart belonged in true romantic fashion to the memory of Anne Thornton. I sensed that the look was about tired feet and reaching a place in time where the present not the past becomes dim with age. Aunt Honoria pocketed the coin with surprising meekness when Ned returned it to her with the grunted suggestion that she take me to the old church at the corner of the lane and light a candle at St. Bartholomew's altar.

"Is that where she is buried?" I asked, but before he could answer Mrs. Perkins came panting up the stairs to announce that several carloads of people had arrived, half of them wanting tea and the rest wishing to be shown around the house before closing hour.

"No rest for you, Ned honey!" She gave him a harried smile, rippled a distracted hand through her dark hair, and bustled down ahead of us into the main hall and along to the tea shop, which was crammed with people jostling for seats at the yellow-and-white-checked tables or crowding around the gift items on the shelves. When the place thinned out by a dozen or more, Ned disappeared also. Mrs. Perkins gave us a frazzled smile as

Aunt Honoria caught up with her at the cash register to pay for our tour.

"Did you enjoy yourselves?" Her eyes stopped roving the room and came back to us when the till drawer smacked open and caught her in the midriff. But immediately her attention was demanded by a woman's voice exclaiming that if she didn't have a cup of tea and a cream cake this minute she would drop dead on the floor.

"Come along, Giselle." Aunt Honoria prodded me with her stick and headed for the door.

"But aren't we . . . ?" My longing look at the Victoria sponge sitting next to the till finished the sentence for me.

"I'm not hungry." Her lips came together in a click of false teeth. "And I can't imagine how you could eat a bite after the lunch you ate."

"I suppose I did make a bit of a pig of myself." My sarcasm was wasted on Aunt Honoria, who marched me through the grizzling rain, down the drive where the trees lined up like leaky umbrellas, to where the Daimler sat like an obedient dog who had been ordered to stay or face a lifetime without the occasional table scrap. I was about to open the passenger-side front door and climb sullenly aboard when my relative asked me how I could suppose she would waste running the engine for such a short distance.

"But we are miles from home," I said.

"And only a stone's throw from the church."

"Oh!" I stopped being cross and skipped to keep up with her. "Then we are going to light a candle for Anne Thornton! I'm glad because anyone with a bit of imagination could see Ned is in love with her portrait."

"Not just the picture, child!" The *rap-tap* of Aunt Honoria's voice kept pace with her stick as we turned left into the black ribbon of lane toward the church.

"And her story, of course! Telling it over and over

again to people like us he couldn't help falling under its tragic spell."

"Really, Giselle! It should be obvious to anyone with sense that Ned is in love with the girl herself."

"You mean"—I stumbled on a loose stone and had to grab her arm to save myself from going smack down on the ground—"you mean her ghost? But Ned told me the house isn't haunted."

"That is not what he said."

"Yes, he did!"

"He said he had never seen a ghost at Thornton Hall, but you and I saw one, Giselle."

"We did?" I stopped walking and addressed the back of Aunt Honoria's fur coat as she marched onward. "Do you mean one of the shadows on the wall in the tower room shouldn't have been there?"

"I mean," the voice came floating back to me, "that Ned is the ghost. Surely you know that Edward is commonly abbreviated in that way."

"Mr. Rochester was an Edward." I scurried to catch up with the back that had disappeared into the mist. "And Jane Eyre never shortened his name to anything except Sir. I hate to say it, Aunt Honoria," I said kindly, "but I think you are letting your imagination run away with you. The name business is just a coincidence. Ned couldn't possibly be the ghost of Edward Haverfield. He was much too real."

"As opposed"—disparaging sniff—"to other ghosts of your acquaintance?"

"And he's far too old," I persisted.

"Do you want to argue, Giselle, or would you like me to tell you why I am sure whereof I speak? Very well, I will assume you are nodding your head in agreement, not because it is loose on your shoulders." We had entered the churchyard and stood under a weeping willow that lived up to its name by dripping all over us. But I hardly noticed that I was growing damper by the minute. "If you remember, Giselle, I remarked to Ned that the eyes of the girl in the portrait followed his every movement."

"I thought you meant she was watching all of us."

"Then you need to bone up on your grammar, my girl! Did I not use the pronoun *you* when addressing him? Never mind. I pondered upon the fact that those eyes possessed a glow only to be seen on the face of a woman in love. You're too young, Giselle—"

"I'm not! I saw it too!"

"And I thought the only passion you understood was for treacle pudding! Indeed, yes!" Aunt Honoria shook her fur coat the way my cat Tabitha used to do after coming in from the rain. "I read your face at lunch with the same skill with which I read Anne Thornton's. And even you noticed Ned's feeling for her."

"He's a nice, dear man," I said, "and I don't want to believe he was ever a murderer, and a sniveling one at that!"

"He paid the price for his act of betrayal, Giselle, in the moldering cell that I imagine quickly changed him from a handsome youth to a white-haired old man. And from that time forward he has existed in purgatory."

"But you told me there's no such place," I objected.

"I said no such thing." Aunt Honoria gave the weeping willow a whack with her stick in hopes perhaps of discouraging it from dripping all over us. "I said that you and I as members of the Church of England do not believe in purgatory. Therefore we don't end up in a place between heaven and hell, but Edward being a Roman Catholic was bound by the tenets of his faith to serve out his time of penitential suffering in the manner prescribed by his faith."

"You mean polishing brass at Thornton Hall?"

"No, Giselle." Aunt Honoria began walking down the broad path toward the church. "His penance is in having to tell with agonizing truthfulness the account of Anne Thornton's death and his subsequent cowardice, day in and day out, to people wishing to tour the house and wallow in a lurid tale."

"Yes, Aunt Honoria," I said as we stood on the steps of the church, which I now saw from the posted sign was Roman Catholic. But I was still a long way from being convinced.

"You think I'm a dotty old woman." To my amazement she actually smiled, but the creaking sound came from the doorknob turning under her hand. "But Ned himself provided me with the proof that I was correct in my summations. When I put the two-shilling piece into the palm of his glove I remembered what he had said about Anne's brother's making sure that Edward would never shoot another arrow. You see, Giselle"— Aunt Honoria pushed open the church door and stepped into the light—"there was no hand inside that glove, just some soft substance like cotton wool. And"—she frowned at me—"don't go thinking you put the idea in my head by your talk of Mr. Rochester and how he lost his hand for his sins. My imagination did not get the better of me."

"No, Aunt." I smiled at her.

"And when you get home don't start babbling to your parents about any of this. Not that I wish you to lie."

"That would be wicked," I agreed.

"But there is no harm in being discreet, as Ned was when you asked him if there were ghosts. And we don't want your mother and father to get the wrong idea and not allow you to come out with me again, if you should wish to do so."

"Yes, please!" I said. "I've had a super time."

"Changed your tune since lunchtime, haven't you, child?" Aunt Honoria cleared her throat. "Well don't stand gawking. We must find St. Bartholomew's altar and light a candle for the repose of Ned's soul. I would like to think we could speed up his reunion with Anne Thornton who, if I know anything, is still waiting for him at the pearly gates." Aunt Honoria poked me toward the nave with her stick. "He was never wicked—just once young and less than heroic, and in my eyes he found honor as a man of truth. Such men are rare indeed, as you will discover when you have the misfortune to fall in love, Giselle. I don't suppose there's much hope you will develop some sense and take a leaf out of your Great Aunt Honoria's book. Thank God I never had a romantic bone in my body."

"Rubbish!" I said as her hand closed over mine and together we lit the candle.

[P. M. CARLSON]

P. M. CARLSON DECIDED THE MOST UNLIKELY AMATEUR sleuth possible would be a working mother, so she created Maggie Ryan. There are now eight books in this critically acclaimed series. Maggie Ryan books have been nominated for the Anthony, Macavity, and Edgar awards. Murder Misread was named one of 1990's ten best by The Drood Review of Mystery. Her most recent Maggie Ryan novel is Bad Blood. Carlson is now writing a series about a very different working mom, Deputy Sheriff Marty Hopkins, who appears in Gravestone and Bloodstream. As Deputy Hopkins solves vicious crimes, she also discovers deep truths about herself.

In her delightful historical short stories, Carlson features Bridget Mooney, a Victorian actress who is thrilled to meet the famed Sarah Bernhardt in "The Rosewood Coffin; or, The Divine Sarah." Earlier Bridget Mooney short stories have been nominated for the Agatha. Bridget is a survivor, saucy, clever, and endearing.

Carlson is a past president of Sisters in Crime, an international organization of mystery readers and writers, and a past national director of Mystery Writers of America. She lives in Brooklyn, New York, with her husband, Marvin.

The Rosewood Coffin; or, The Divine Sarah

"Men have died from time to time, and worms have eaten them, but not for love," said Shakespeare. But he was a wise old jake, and I reckon he also knew that love comes in many shapes. Like Jacques and Sarah's.

My dear friend Lillie Langtry introduced us. I hadn't seen her since St. Louis, so when a new tour brought her to New York I called on her. "Bridget!" she exclaimed in her impeccable English. "I plan to attend Sarah's special matinee. Do come share my box! Her son Maurice will accompany us."

Well, of course I wanted to see the famous Sarah Bernhardt! I donned a feathered bonnet that set off my red hair and a bustled dress of French blue velvet trimmed with cascades of blond lace and set off proudly for the Star Theatre.

I know, I know, you're right, of course. My Aunt Mollie would have agreed that a proper lady would not choose to be seen with these two. One could say— indeed, many did say—that Lillie Langtry was a fallen woman, and that Maurice Bernhardt was illegitimate. But Lillie remained the Prince of Wales's favorite, and Maurice was the son of a Belgian prince and a famed mother, and engaged to marry a Polish princess to boot. So don't you think a simple St. Louis girl ought to be proud to be seen with those whom crowned heads did not disdain? Yes indeed. Besides, they both had heaps and heaps of money.

I edged forward in the elegant box seat, trying to look languid instead of eager as I inspected the audience of New York theatrical luminaries in the rows below. Beside me sat Lillie, the most luminous and languid of all. She was leaning back so that the gilded fretwork partition would screen her from the multitudes. Her dress was a lovely green velvet with purple shadows, and she slowly waved her matching fan. Young Maurice Bernhardt stood behind her, a gallant young dandy. They were discussing their respective American tours, in French. Lillie, of course, had spoken French from childhood, but since I'd learned only the little I needed for the stage, it was sometimes difficult for me to follow their conversation. For all its airs, French is a rather silly language, don't you think? They use a long flowery string of words to say simple things, but then smear them all together to sound like one word, so why don't they do it the straightforward way to begin with? But there's no reasoning with foreigners. Sarah Bernhardt was about to perform an entire play in French, even though we were in New York and the play concerned a Russian princess.

But Sarah's son Maurice was courtesy itself and soon leaned closer to include me in the conversation. "Mademoiselle Mooney, you have never viewed *Maman* on ze stage, *n'est-ce pas*?"

"I have never had the good fortune to see her. I myself was on tour with Mr. Salvini the first time she was here in New York." I smiled at Maurice. "But of course I heard her praised everywhere. Did Mrs. Langtry tell you that I have had the great honor to be called 'the Bernhardt of Missouri'?"

"Missouri? *C'est charmant*!" Maurice laughed warmly. "I am all ze more pleased to meet such a delightful and capable actress."

Wasn't that charming? You can say what you want about Frenchmen, but you must admit that even in English they have a sweet way with words, although they can't quite pronounce them properly.

The curtain rose and I turned eagerly to the stage. Two men entered and nattered away in French about the dissipated Count Vladimir and about how much the Princess Fédora loved him. I had time to inspect the scenery, which represented Count Vladimir's handsome apartment in St. Petersburg, and to inspect the audience of this special matinee reserved for theatre professionals and given on a Thursday afternoon so that those of us working in shows could attend. I spotted Mr. Frohman, the famous producer, and a number of my fellow actors, many of whom were gazing at our box. No doubt they hoped to observe the renowned

Mrs. Langtry, but I made certain they also observed me.

The long conversation on stage was interrupted as the Princess Fédora made her entrance to warm applause. It was my first glimpse of the fabled Sarah Bernhardt. Sarah was a handsome willowy Russian princess, far more youthful than I had anticipated, and her singularly effective gown of lace quite dazzled the eye. Still, I thought, peering through my opera glass, she was far too thin, and her face, though intelligent enough, did not have half the loveliness of the beautiful Lillie Langtry's. Why was she known as "the divine Sarah"?

Then Sarah moved, and spoke, and lordy, I reckon my jaw almost dropped off! She seemed exotic, a creature come from the realm of spirits far away, and yet she seemed a dear friend whom I'd known all my life. I had planned to study her famed tones and gestures, and to incorporate the best into my own performances, but instead I sat transfixed. Oh, she doth teach the torches to burn bright! Her Princess Fédora was graceful as a swan, sinuous as a snake, coquettish as a kitten when she heard her fiancé Count Vladimir returning. And then, what shock when two men entered to tell her they'd brought Vladimir home wounded, what feverish suspense as the princess questioned the men to learn who had shot him, what joy when at last the surgeons flung wide the doors to admit her to her lover's sickroom, what heart-rending horror as she realized he would never again answer her tender cries of "Vladimir!" Princess Fédora began to weep. I began to weep. Never had I felt so humbled by another's genius, nor so proud to be a fellow practitioner of the thespian art. I found myself once again in love with the theatre.

The curtain fell to thunderous applause. Lillie Langtry said, "You appear to be impressed, Bridget."

"Oh, Lillie, I was mesmerized!"

Lillie Langtry, the most beautiful woman in the world, turned her violet eyes to the stage and murmured, "I would gladly exchange my reputed beauty for a tenth of Sarah Bernhardt's genius."

"She is indeed very skillful," I said lamely, for it was true that Lillie's loveliness was unaccompanied by any talent for the stage, her diligent efforts to study the art notwithstanding. Yet I knew that despite my own great talent, after seeing Sarah Bernhardt I could never again take as much pride in my own abilities. She seemed to be pure spirit, sent from the gods. Even her harshest critics admitted that she could plunge emotion like a dagger into the innermost being of the spectator. I had not been so thrilled since I was thirteen back in St. Louis, when I saw the illustrious English actress Mrs. Fanny Kemble on tour and vowed that someday I too would learn to speak correctly and become an actress.

The rest of the play became ever more intense. Sarah Bernhardt's grace was magnetic, and her voice ranged from tender to fierce so delightfully that I decided on the spot to learn more of her otherwise silly language. The play ended with a perfectly splendid death scene in which the vengeful and passionate princess takes poison and dies, writhing beautifully. I applauded until my hands tingled.

Afterward, Maurice escorted Lillie and me backstage through disappointed throngs who were not allowed to see the star. Sarah's dressing room was filled with her furs and flowers and admirers. A table laden with her jewelry, including a lovely pearl-encrusted belt, was guarded by a small gray-haired woman. In the center of the room sat the great tragedienne, wearing a rich crimson mantle trimmed with fox fur and nuzzling a brindle cat. "Such a precious little tiger," she murmured, and glanced up at her little audience. "Do you know, I rescued her from ze railroad tracks and nursed her, and zen she bit me?" I remembered that in the Franco-Prussian War Sarah had run a hospital for wounded soldiers in her theatre. The cat began to claw at her fur trim and made her laugh. "But no, I do not complain. She is fierce, like ze Princess Fédora!"

Maurice stepped forward and kissed her on both cheeks, the forehead, and the chin. *"Maman, un succès fou!"* he exclaimed.

"Here, *mon cher,* take ze little Princess Fédora." She handed him the cat, then smiled at us all. "Lillie, *bonsoir!"*

Maurice took this as a signal to begin bidding adieu to the other visitors. The little gray-haired woman aided him. But Lillie beckoned me toward Sarah and said, "I would like to present Miss Bridget Mooney, a very clever American actress. She has done me great kindnesses."

Sarah's intelligent eyes inspected me as she held out her hand. *"Enchantée."*

"Madame Bernhardt, I am truly honored. Today you were the personification of love itself."

Maurice, having got rid of the other visitors, rejoined us. "Mademoiselle Mooney is also called ze Bernhardt of Missouri."

Sarah smiled. "Missouri! Zat is St. Louis, *n'est-ce pas?* Ze land of riverboats and vaqueros?"

"Yes, madame."

"And bandits! A bandit from St. Louis once tried to steal my jewels!"

Well, hang it, I didn't want foreigners to get the wrong idea about Missouri. I curtsied, pulled her pearl-encrusted belt from my bustle pocket, and presented it to her. "Yes, madame, we are particularly proud of our bandits."

The little gray-haired woman gasped, but Sarah laughed merrily. "Lillie, *merci!* Zis young lady bandit is worth meeting. But now—" A shadow darkened her famous face.

With an angry glance at me, the little gray-haired woman fluttered to her side. *"Allons, allons!"*

"Je viens!" Sarah took the woman's hand affectionately. "Madame Guérard, she runs my life, and I must go! But first, I must ask ze advice of my dear friend Lillie about Jacques, ze poor darling."

"No doubt he is asking for money," said Lillie.

"Well, yes, but—"

"My advice is to stop being kind to him!"

"Madame Langtry a raison, Maman!" Maurice exclaimed. Madame Guérard's gray head nodded fiercely in agreement.

"Oh yes, I know," said Sarah, clasping her hands sadly. "He is cruel, yes! He makes me wish to leap from ze great Brooklyn Bridge, to die in ze cold dark waters, to plunge into ze abyss of ze unknown like your Ophelia, maddened by a mad love."

My heart was rent to hear her, and Madame Guérard stroked Sarah's pale brow with worn birdlike hands. But Lillie was not upset. "Poor dear," she said. "I myself would stay away from the man."

"Oh, Lillie, you English have such cold blood! Mademoiselle Mooney, perhaps you understand. Perhaps you have been in love!"

"Yes, Madame Bernhardt. But it was nothing compared to the love for the art of the theatre that you personified today."

"Ze performance went well, *n'est-ce pas?"* Sarah said with satisfaction.

Lillie smiled. "Now that you are feeling better, my dear, we must go and allow you to obey the good Madame Guérard. You have a performance tonight, and so does Miss Mooney."

We took our leave. Driving to tea in Lillie's fine carriage, I inquired, "Who is this troublesome Jacques?"

"Monsieur Jacques Aristide Damala is Sarah's husband."

I remembered then. A shock had gone through the theatrical world five years before when we learned that the great Sarah Bernhardt, who'd already had a long string of lovers and was too rich to require any manly protection, had suddenly married an actor, totally unknown and Greek to boot. A few stormy months later he had abandoned her and I'd heard nothing of him since. "He treated her so cruelly!" I observed. "How can she still love him? I would have tossed the fellow out long since!"

"And so would I," responded Lillie. "But we are not the greatest actress in the world. We are not even French."

"I thought they were divorced," I said. It was certainly true that Sarah's list of lovers had continued to lengthen. One of the handsome, strapping actors we'd just seen was rumored to be her current favorite. To all appearances, Jacques Damala had been just one more on the string.

Lillie smiled her luminous smile. "It is difficult to divorce husbands," said the beautiful Mrs. Langtry, who had firsthand knowledge. "And it is expensive to keep them out of one's life. You are wise not to marry, Bridget. Tell me, how is your little niece?"

"Juliet is thriving. She's learning to read, and to dance, and can almost recite the 'quality of mercy' speech. How is your Jeanne-Marie?"

"Thriving too," said Lillie, and we had a splendid tea discussing our clever little nieces.

Because I was appearing on stage myself, I was able to see only one more of Sarah Bernhardt's presentations that year, her famed revival of *La Dame aux Camélias*. Of course you know that play, the most popular of the decade! Audiences flocked to see it, Verdi based *La Traviata* on it, actresses fought like wildcats to play the heroine Marguerite. But Sarah embodied the love-struck courtesan so perfectly that none could compete. I was profoundly moved by her art and spent many hours before my mirror, practicing her finest effects in order to apply them to my own roles.

Two years later, my path again crossed Sarah's. My friend Mr. Thomas Alva Edison requested my assistance with his exhibit of phonographs and electric lighting at the 1889 Paris Exposition. "Of course I'll help, Al," I told Mr. Edison, "if you will permit me to take my little niece Juliet and her nurse. They would so enjoy seeing the splendors of Paris!"

Mr. Edison was a generous man, and besides, he was returning a favor. No, hang it, not that kind of favor, not that time! He agreed to send all three of us.

Paris was full of splendors indeed. There were broad avenues, ancient cathedrals, plane trees and chestnut trees, and best of all a stupendous new thousand-foot tower, lit by my own Mr. Edison's electric lamps, that had been built on the exposition grounds by the exceedingly clever Monsieur Eiffel. But the splendor I most wanted to see was Sarah Bernhardt. The day we arrived I tucked Juliet and Hattie into our rooms at the Hotel Terminus, donned an apple-green dress with a matching parasol, and hurried to the Théâtre des Variétés to see Sarah once again in *La Dame aux Camélias*.

But Sarah, despite her poetic movement and wondrous voice, had somehow lost the magical spark that had entranced me. She said her lines beautifully, but her soul seemed elsewhere. I soon realized what the problem was. You see, in New York, Sarah had had two excellent actors in her company to play the leading-man roles. Here in Paris, she had been able to choose from a vast number of skilled actors including those two. So why had she chosen such a dreadful leading man? He spoiled his every scene. Despite her skill, even Sarah could not completely hide her anxiety in those scenes. Surely after tonight she would fire him! The man was handsome enough, with a lovely smile and a sweet little upturned mustache, but he had a gaunt and sickly aspect, and appeared to be inebriated as well. His voice was feeble, and he had so little manly vigor that I dreaded seeing the end. Sarah had a splendid death scene in *La Dame aux Camélias*. As the dying Marguerite, she struggled upright to embrace her lover and murmur her last words. When he released her from the embrace she'd fall back dead. What an electrifying moment it was as the graceful corpse swung back, supported only by the leading man's strong arm! I winced to think of the scene ahead, because there was no strong arm in evidence tonight.

Perhaps I should do more than wince.

The curtain rose for the last act. With sudden resolution, I went outside and hurried to the stage door. A couple of guards attempted to stop me but I used my apple-green parasol to good effect and crept into the wings. The handsome leading man lay sprawled in a chair, waiting for his entrance. I stood by a door in the set. When the actress who played the maid emerged I seized her by the wrist and whispered in my carefully practiced French, "You must catch her!"

"Catch her? Who? Who are you?"

Clearly there was no time for international communication. I snatched off the maid's cap, tossed my shawl over her head, and bound it tight about her mouth. She grunted and fought like a tackled pig as I removed her dark dress and white pinafore and tied her, still thrashing, to a pipe. A couple of stagehands heard the muffled noises and began to chase me, but I hid behind some items of furniture from earlier acts, struggling out of my handsome apple-green dress and into the maid's uniform. With agitated whispers, my pursuers discovered me at last, but I dodged through a door and found myself onstage. They gasped but did not follow.

The leading man was already there. Sarah's sweet, love-struck voice never faltered, but I saw her eyes flash in surprise when the maid who usually waited across the stage came near to arrange the bedclothes quietly behind them, then clumsily dropped a pillow. The actor didn't seem to notice. He scarce had the strength to utter his lines. But Sarah did not compromise. The last exchange played sweetly, and when the moment of death arrived she collapsed, totally limp, totally artistic.

The leading man's feeble hand slipped.

Fortunately, the clumsy maid kicked the dropped pillow under the falling tragedienne's auburn head in the nick of time, then assisted the leading man as he moved the dead Marguerite gently to the bed. The curtain descended to warm applause.

"*Qui*—ah, Mademoiselle Mooney! Ze Missouri bandit!" Sarah exclaimed, as I removed the maid's cap. "I am very angry at you, you know." She looked at the pillow and added grudgingly, "But zen, you saved my poor head, I suppose."

Hang it, what was wrong? I had expected some little token of gratitude from the rich tragedienne. Instead she was scolding me, rather than the stumbling actor who was the author of our difficulties. The answer came when she turned to her leading man and wagged a finger at him. "Jacques, you poor dear, you must get more rest."

So this was Jacques Damala. I was astonished, even more when he glanced at Sarah, then slowly focused on me and said, "Mademoiselle Mooney? A bandit?" His eyes began to glow, whether from love or fever it was difficult to tell. "Mademoiselle, you are fascination itself!" He managed to bow and kiss my hand, the very soul of gallantry. Yes indeed. Sarah looked at the two of us with a peculiar expression as she gathered the cast for the curtain call. I slipped back into the wings to retrieve my apple-green dress. The hapless maid, though still in her chemise, had been untied by her colleagues, and when she saw me she burst into vehement French. I attempted to explain to her that I had just saved her employer from a dreadful accident, but she appeared to have a greater interest in tearing out my eyes. Her small plump hands were surprisingly strong. The stagehands watched us, chuckling. I was on the verge of resorting to the bowie knife I keep in my boot when the curtain calls ended and Sarah swept past us on her way backstage. *"Assez, Saryta!* Mademoiselle Mooney, do not let her tear ze costumes!" she commanded. At last Saryta ceased her attack.

Jacques Damala was eyeing me with frank delight. I realized that the maid's costume had been half pulled off in the fray. Quickly, I snatched my shawl from Saryta and covered myself. Damala said, "Mademoiselle, you are ze most charming bandit I have ever met!"

I kept my eyes on Sarah, who was looking at him oddly. At last she turned to me. "Mademoiselle Mooney, we leave soon on a tour to London. You are not traveling to England?"

"No, madame, I must remain in Paris until September. I am contracted to work at the exposition for Mr. Edison."

"Ah, Monsieur Edison! A delightful man. He recorded my voice." She glanced at Damala. "Very well, we shall return early in August. Zen, please, come to visit us. We shall be friends!"

I accepted, pleased to be considered a friend by a woman of Sarah's means. Saryta, straightening the maid's costume, pouted. But Damala caught my hand and kissed it. "Yes, mademoiselle, please visit us! It is number fifty-six, boulevard Péreire."

Sarah, Damala, and the others were soon in London, and I heard little of them, except for occasional reviews in London newspapers that expressed shock at Damala's poor performance. Confident that Sarah would soon send him packing, I turned to my own tasks. Most days I worked in the Palace of Machines, an enormous glass-roofed building that enclosed fifteen acres. Inside were countless modern machines, from railway equipment to a strange writing machine from Remington and a most peculiar carriage from Benz that was powered by gasoline instead of horses. But the Edison phonograph exhibit was the most popular of all, and those of us who demonstrated this new marvel were kept busy.

When I had the time I explored the wondrous city with my dear little Juliet and my friend Hattie Floyd. Hattie was deeply suspicious of the French. "It ain't natural to talk like that! A body can't understand a word they say!" But she agreed that their cooking was splendid, and their clothing. Before I hired her as a nurse to my niece, the voluptuous Hattie had done well enough in a rather lewd line of work, eventually joining a house that catered to the best classes in St. Louis. So it was with a professional interest that she inspected the embroidered silk stockings and lace-trimmed chemises in the shops and pronounced them most effective.

As for young Juliet James, the apple of my eye, she won over the French with ease. At seven, her blue eyes were as quick as her father's and her ear as quick as mine, and soon she was prattling in French to all who would listen: the coachman who drove the clattering omnibus pulled by three giant Percheron horses, the man who tended the carousel at the Rond Point, the baker who gave her cakes. One day I dressed her in a pretty blue frock with a lacy skirt and a big bow at the waist and escorted her up the Eiffel Tower. It took a long time to make the ascent, there being eleven thousand visitors every day, but with recourse to the packet of cakes I had tucked into my bustle pocket, she remained cheerful, especially when the balloon man strolled by and offered her a balloon in the same blue of her dress. When we reached the top platform it was a delight to look out at the cruise boats on the Seine, the cathedrals, the great glittering Palace of Machines where I worked, the exotic pavilions of the French colonies, the horticultural exhibits in the Trocadéro gardens. Juliet clapped her hands. "It's wonderful, Aunt Bridget! *Très jolie!*"

"Of course it is," I told her with a hug, "and if you continue to learn French, in a few years I'll bring you back to see the most wonderful thing in the world."

"What? What?" she demanded, her eyes sparkling.

"I'll take you to see Sarah Bernhardt perform."

That happy summer flew by. Then, early in August, Sarah and her company returned from London. Remembering her invitation, I presented my calling card at the handsome town house at 56, boulevard Péreire.

The door was opened by a nervous man with bulging eyes, a fine mustache, and a pencil behind his ear. I handed him my card and asked if madame was in good health. Oh yes, he told me in excited French, she had accepted an engagement to play the Russian Princess Fédora at the fashionable Dieppe race meeting and was deep into plans for the next season. And her son Maurice would soon be a father, so she was thrilled, he said, beaming.

"Et Monsieur Damala?" I asked.

His pop-eyed face darkened, and he whisked away with my card. In a moment Sarah herself appeared in a doorway, as sweetly sensuous as ever in ruffled white silk and beautiful ruby bracelets. "Do come in, Mademoiselle Mooney!" She took my hand and drew me into a lilac-scented salon. There was a small crowd there—Maurice, her sparrowlike companion Madame Guérard, the hollow-cheeked but handsome Jacques Damala, and even my sulky backstage acquaintance Saryta. Maurice and Damala both hastened to kiss my hand, but I was more interested in Sarah's salon.

What a breathtaking room it was! It rose two stories. Above the fronds of the potted palm trees I could see the night sky through a roof of glass. Everything in the room was the height of fashion. The rich red walls were almost hidden behind the beautiful and the exotic: Indian sabers, Mexican silver, Venetian gilded mirrors, daggers from South America, and of course numerous portraits of Sarah. Jacques Damala, who was still holding my hand, pointed out some handsome bas-reliefs. "From my country, Greece," he said proudly. "And zis rug we bought on our recent tour to Turkey."

I murmured my approval as I looked about. Dragon-headed poles supported a richly tasseled silk canopy over the divan. There were heaps of large embroidered silk cushions, furs piled and draped everywhere, and countless aromatic bouquets of flowers. I had never seen a room so beautiful and fashionable! An enormous cage stood in one corner, filled with beautiful birds that cheeped and squawked.

"Jacques, are you tired?" Sarah asked.

"Ze sight of zis fair lady has revived me!" Jacques declared.

Well, hang it, that was taking being French too far, don't you think? I'm as fond of gallantries as the next lady, but not in front of a wife, especially when the wife is as rich as Sarah. Sarah studied us an instant, then laughed merrily. "Let us dance in Mademoiselle Mooney's honor! Pitou!" she called to the pop-eyed man. He left off twirling his mustache, produced a violin, and began to play a waltz. Maurice danced with me, and I congratulated him on his impending fatherhood. But he danced the next dance with his mother, and I found myself in Damala's arms. It was very pleasant, because he was a handsome, sweet-smelling fellow and full of compliments despite his occasional stumbles, but he was not nearly as courteous as Maurice, holding me much closer than was strictly necessary. I was obliged to push him away continually as we danced, for fear that Sarah would be offended. At last I told him that I was exhausted and would like to look at the birds.

Damala smiled as I peered through the bars at the

birds. "Zey are lovely, aren't zey? Nearly as lovely as you!"

"They are indeed lovely, monsieur," I responded primly.

"In ze old days, Sarah kept her lions in zat cage."

"Lions! Oh, monsieur, that is terrifying! And is it true that she sleeps in a coffin?"

"Yes, sometimes. A beautiful rosewood coffin." He sank onto the divan, hiding his fatigue by patting the cushion next to him. "Come sit with me, mademoiselle!"

I pretended to be entranced by the birds. In fact, I was entranced by Madame Guérard on the far side of the cage, who was hissing something at Saryta and gesturing angrily at Monsieur Damala. Saryta replied indignantly, and Madame Guérard shook her gray head wearily. It was obviously difficult to manage this unwieldy household. She glanced up and almost caught me looking at her through the bars, but I quickly blew a kiss to a toucan in the cage and turned rapturously to Monsieur Damala. "I like birds so much better than lions!"

"So do I, *ma petite*," he responded. "But come, I want you to see zis fabric." Damala was patting the pillow again.

Well, I may be just a simple St. Louis girl, but it didn't seem wise to become entangled with the semi-invalid beloved of the world's greatest and richest actress. I stood as far from him as I could, snatched the indicated pillow, and took it to a brighter light. "Why, monsieur, you are quite right! The embroidered flowers are indeed the very imitation of life!"

Monsieur Damala struggled to his feet and came to stand by my side. "It is lovely indeed," he said, but he was not looking at the embroidery. He was inspecting the Venetian pearl trim at the low rounded neckline of my dress.

"Monsieur, I believe you are very weary from your travels," I said in clear tones. As I had hoped, Sarah heard and stopped dancing with her son.

"Pitou, *tais-toi!*" she commanded, silencing the violinist. "Do pardon me for a moment, Mademoiselle Mooney, I must see if Pitou prepared my husband's chamber properly."

"*Bien sûr!*" the pop-eyed Pitou reassured her. "*Madame, je vous adore!*" He followed her out, protesting his innocence.

"You ignite my heart, dear mademoiselle," Damala murmured.

I thrust the pillow into his arms and hurried toward the others. "Mademoiselle Saryta, I wish to apologize for—"

Madame Guérard touched my arm and whispered in vehement French not to give Monsieur Damala anything. I looked at her in surprise, then turned back to Saryta. "I apologize," I repeated, "for interrupting your splendid performance."

The young woman looked a trifle sulky but said pleasantly enough, "Oh, I understand. Tante Sarah is grateful to you. Now I too stand near with a pillow when she dies."

"Tante Sarah? Sarah is your aunt?"

"Yes, of course. I am ze daughter of her sister Jeanne."

"Oh, yes, Jeanne Bernhardt." I had heard that Sarah had a sister, a minor actress. "Isn't she in Madame Bernhardt's company as well?"

"She was, before she became . . . ill."

"I'm sorry to hear that."

"Some people are allowed in ze company even when zey are ill," Saryta said darkly.

I lowered my voice. "You are right, mademoiselle, it is terrible! He makes even Sarah play badly!"

"Zat is nothing new," Saryta said. "He has always upset her. Once, he had some talent for ze stage, but zat was long ago."

"Yes, I understand." I'd known some upsetting men too, like little Juliet's father.

A door opened and Sarah swept back in, surrounded by a lively band of little dogs. Princess Fédora, the brindle cat, streaked past them all and leapt onto a plant stand near the enormous bird cage, where she crouched and eyed the toucan. Pitou waited by the door twirling his mustache nervously.

Sarah went first to her husband, speaking soothingly in French, urging him to go to his room. This time he didn't object, though he did cross the room to kiss my hand politely before he left. "How I wish I had a nurse as charming as you! Will I see you tomorrow, fascinating creature?"

"Sir, I must work at the exposition," I said coolly.

"You break my heart, *ma petite*." He shuffled off, supported by the loyal Pitou. Sarah watched them go. As soon as the door closed, she whirled on Madame Guérard. The marvelous Bernhardt voice rose to berate her with the most beautifully pronounced invectives I have ever heard. Maurice tried in vain to calm his mother. A couple of the little dogs were inspired to join in with frenzied yapping.

With a flourish, Sarah held up a hypodermic syringe.

The gray-haired lady, who appeared to be used to such shenanigans, asked calmly, "*Dans son chambre?*"

"*Oui, sous le lit.*"

Under his bed. As Sarah continued to harangue poor Madame Guérard, I asked Saryta, "Forgive me, mademoiselle, but am I correct that drugs are the source of Monsieur Damala's difficulties?"

"Oh, yes, chiefly ze morphine. Others too. He promises Tante Sarah never to use it again, she allows him to come back, zen he breaks ze promise and she is furious. She screams, she rages, she beats ze pharmacist with her parasol, all for nothing." Saryta looked angry. "Tante Sarah always accuses me, because Maman was also an addict. It is not fair!"

"Of course," I said soothingly. "She should not accuse you. Nor should she accuse poor Madame Guérard." I crossed the Turkish carpet to the enraged tragedienne and begged permission to speak. "It is not Madame Guérard's doing," I explained. "Please observe what I found in Monsieur Damala's pocket while we danced." I held out a little ampoule for a hypodermic syringe.

I did not hold out the handsome hunting watch I'd found next to the ampoule.

Oh, I know, I know, a proper lady doesn't search a gentleman's pockets while waltzing. But then, he hadn't treated me like a proper lady, had he now?

Besides, the rich and brilliant Sarah Bernhardt was very interested in the ampoule. "In his pocket?" she asked.

"Yes, Madame Bernhardt," I said.

"Such a splendid bandit you are!" She seized my hands warmly. "Please, call me Sarah. And I will call you Brigitte, yes?"

"I would be honored."

"Lillie said you had done her a kindness," Sarah said, her eyes luminous. "Brigitte, would you do one for me?"

"Nothing would delight me more."

She scooped up one of the little pug dogs that was yapping at her feet and cuddled it. "Brigitte, my husband is very ill, bedridden much of ze time. Now, perhaps it is your red hair, or perhaps your exotic youth as a Missouri bandit. Whatever ze reason, he appears to fancy you."

"Let me assure you, I have done nothing—"

"Of course not! Do not think that I am jealous!" Tears filled the lovely Bernhardt eyes. "Once I was jealous, oh yes! Once I loved him with an earthly love. I think of how he tortured me, how I suffered, how I begged him to take pity on me, his slave! Every time he took a *petite amie,* I was wounded to ze depths of my soul! But all zat is in ze past. Today, my love is purer, more noble.

And I must do everything in my power to save my sweet Jacques! It is a struggle with Death itself!" She drew out a lacy handkerchief to dab at her brimming eyes. The pug licked her chin in sympathy.

"But how can I help? Wouldn't it be better to allow poor Monsieur Damala to recover from his satanic habit in a sanatorium?"

"Oh, no! Zat is impossible! Jacques is very weak, very sensitive. He cannot abide confinement in a sanatorium. No, Hamlet, you cannot abide confinement either," she said to the pug, which was wriggling in her arms. She explained, "I found zis little dog imprisoned in a box and starving, poor little thing." She kissed its wrinkled forehead.

I returned to the subject. "Perhaps Monsieur Damala has exerted himself too much on the stage."

"Mademoiselle, ze poor man needs something to live for!" she said seriously. "And what is worthwhile, but ze theatre and ze love?"

For someone who was a genius, Sarah Bernhardt was being a tangle-headed fool, don't you think? No doubt she herself lived for the theatre and for love, since she no longer had to worry about money, but it was clear to me that Jacques Damala did not value the stage enough to care about giving a good performance, and did not value love enough to refrain from romancing a new lady before his wife's very eyes. Worst of all, he did not value Sarah's amazing genius.

Still, I feared that Sarah was not yet ready to hear such truths. I said, "You are most generous to him, Sarah. But how can I help?"

"Help me to nurse him, and to keep zose dreadful ampoules away from him, and to amuse him! He takes no interest in things and sleeps much of ze day. But when you appear, Brigitte, he is ready to dance!" She nuzzled Hamlet the pug's head. "Jacques is so young, only thirty-four. If I cannot save him, I will want to kill myself!"

She gazed into space, as though contemplating a tragic and beautiful death. I remembered her obsession with her rosewood coffin and felt a chill. She continued, "So you see, I must save him. Please, help me, Brigitte!"

I was moved by her plea, but this bedridden fellow seemed a hopeless case to me. Then she placed Hamlet on a chair cushion and pulled a glittering ruby bracelet from her arm. "Oh, do not say no, Brigitte, or I will die! It will be worth your while!"

Well, hang it, how could I refuse such a splendid offer? Jacques Damala was a rotter, but she was so determined to save him that I feared she would do violence to herself if he took a turn for the worse. I dreaded the thought of a world without Sarah. And I'm bound to admit that Jacques could be charming, with his little mustache and flowery compliments that could make a young lady's limbs weak. There was also the great advantage that he was too ill to do much beyond talking. Most importantly, if we nursed him back to health he could perform his roles adequately. I even dared hope that he might leave her again so that she could once more work unencumbered at her art.

Besides, Sarah was willing to pay handsomely, and in advance. I studied the flaming depths of the rubies in my new bracelet. It would be perfect the next time I played the rich and wicked Lady Audley. Even my Aunt Mollie, that excellent businesswoman, would have approved.

So every evening, after supping with Hattie and Juliet, I came to the boulevard Péreire. I soon learned that despite the exuberance and apparent freedom in that luxurious town house, Jacques Damala was nearly a prisoner. Sarah and her household nursed him so lovingly that he could not escape. Jacques thought I was his *petite amie;* I knew I was one of his jailers. She would not leave him alone with anyone except Pitou, Madame Guérard, or me. The three of us became very efficient at blocking his efforts, although he and his unknown supplier were clever. Drugs arrived with the flowers, the potatoes, the champagne. In a few days we had a large collection of ampoules and a patient who was despondent and shaky but still wily.

"Dearest Brigitte," he murmured into my ear one rainy evening, "will you do me a great favor?"

"I would be happy to, monsieur."

"A friend of mine has left a book at the shop for me. As I cannot go out, would you bring it to me?"

"With pleasure."

I donned a cloak and went out into the summer storm to the bookseller's where Jacques' packet waited. As I entered, a small man clutching a cape to his neck came striding out. He looked somehow familiar. I fetched the book, and of course I took a peek inside the packet. Wouldn't you? And of course the book had been hollowed out inside and contained a supply of ampoules. Smiling, I delivered a different book to Jacques, although the poor man's crestfallen look after he'd opened it tugged at my heart.

He walked into the room that held Sarah's rosewood coffin and stood for a moment stroking the gleaming wood. Thunder rumbled outside. In a moment he looked up with his little charming smile. "Dear Brigitte, ze little bandit. Sarah has bribed you too, I see."

"Why, sir, what do you mean?"

"Let us be frank, Brigitte. I cannot buy anything in person because she has bribed all ze pharmacists."

That's a lot more sensible than beating them with parasols, don't you think? But Jacques did not seem to approve. He continued, "She has bribed Pitou and Madame Guérard. She drives my friends from ze house. And now she has bribed you, my last hope."

I realized what had been familiar about the man leaving the bookseller: the hand clutching the cape was Saryta's. You don't forget hands that have tried to claw your eyes out. Sarah would be very interested in this news. But I hesitated because of the despair in Jacques' eyes. "Sarah does it for your own good, sir."

"My own good." He held out a steady hand. "She has succeeded for ze moment, you see. No more trembling, only weariness. She believes I will regain my health, but she lives in a world of illusion. Zis desire will not go. You know zat, Brigitte. You are wise in ze ways of ze world."

I said slowly, "You are cured, Jacques, if you want to be."

"I will never be cured. It brings ze only joy I know." His face was bleak. "Brigitte, you are a woman of intelligence as well as beauty. You must understand!"

"Dear Jacques, I would be happy to help you!" I said, most sincerely. "But I cannot betray the greatest genius of the theatre!"

He stroked the coffin again and murmured so softly I almost did not hear him above the drumming rain, "Zen I must help myself."

I hesitated to tell Sarah about this conversation, because she thought he was better. Later that day, as she donned a ravishingly beautiful rain cloak to go visit Maurice's country house, she patted Jacques on the shoulder and said, "Dear Brigitte, you have done your work well! Jacques is much stronger. He is still disconsolate, but I will make him happy! He is asking me to give him a fine role in *La Tosca* zis fall, and I will, I will!"

There was a dreadful crash of thunder. "But Sarah," I said in dismay, "he is not yet able to sustain a role!"

"Of course I am able!" Jacques said firmly. "It will be a delight to play in *La Tosca*!"

"Why, Brigitte, I am surprised at you," Sarah said. "You know as well as I zat an inner strength comes from ze stage! It is ze best medicine in ze world!"

"Yes, that's true for you and me, but . . ."

"And true for me," said Jacques with a little smile.

Well, I knew what he meant. In the backstage confusion he would have opportunities that would never arise in the well-policed cocoon that Sarah had created for him here.

Sarah nodded, oblivious to the danger. "Of course it's true! And Jacques knows zat my love is pure and constant, and zat he can depend on his Sarah forever!" She kissed him maternally on the forehead.

I looked at them in consternation. I could see long years unrolling before me, bleak and empty of Sarah Bernhardt's art. I thought of my promise to little Juliet and suddenly understood that Jacques had won. I embraced Sarah with a sob in my voice. "It's true! You save the wounded soldiers, and the poor little pets like Hamlet and Princess Fédora, and your prodigal husband! Never have I known such a warm heart, nor a love as pure as yours! Dearest Sarah, I will always honor that love!" Both of us were overcome with tears at her nobility.

Sarah, dabbing at her eyes, left for Maurice's country house to play her brand-new role of thrilled grandmother.

Jacques Damala listlessly opened the new book I handed him and found it filled to the brim with Saryta's ampoules and a syringe. With blissful countenance he looked up to thank me but I raised a palm for silence and said, "Never again, Jacques. Do we understand each other? Never ever again." He nodded slowly.

Oh, I know, I know, a proper lady would not have given up hope for his recovery. A proper lady would have fought on bravely, like Sarah, struggling against his satanic habit, for his own good.

A proper lady might even have warned a weakened man not to use too much after a period of abstinence. But don't you think he might have done it anyway?

We called the doctors after a few hours, but they were unable to save him.

Sarah was devastated, of course. Maurice brought his mother back to the boulevard Péreire swooning with grief. She threw herself at her dead husband's feet, wailing and swearing to kill herself.

"*Maman, non, Maman!*" Maurice was frantic. At last he came to me. "What can we do? She is inconsolable! She will die for love of him!"

Did you ever hear such twaddle? My poor charming Jacques Damala died for love, it is true. He died because he loved morphine. He died because Sarah Bernhardt loved the theatre, and because I did too.

I said, "Oh, Maurice, don't be a silly goose! She didn't love him, she loved playing noble wife and nurse. Now, the first thing to do is stop being an audience for this scene." I shooed him into a corner and walked over to Sarah. She was dissolved in tears; but I knew they were not Sarah's tears. They were Marguerite's tears for her lost love, they were Phèdre's tears for Hippolyte, they were Princess Fédora's tears for Count Vladimir. I murmured to her, "Dear Sarah, difficult as it is, you must think of his funeral ceremony. It should be a splendid funeral!"

"Yes. Oh, yes!" She sat up. "He shall have a rosewood coffin, like mine! And ze ceremony shall be splendid. It shall be Greek!"

I added softly, "He will also need a memorial."

"Yes, a memorial! In Père Lachaise Cemetery! No, no, better yet in Greece, alongside ze great philosophers!" The shine in Sarah's eyes was made up of enthusiasm as well as tears. "I shall sculpt ze memorial statue myself!"

"I never heard of a truer love! And you will visit him whenever you tour?"

"Yes, Brigitte, yes!"

"Dear Sarah, you will be the noblest widow in the world!"

And she was, she was. The funeral ceremony in her great salon was presided over by the Greek archimandrite and four of his priests. Outside, the most dramatic storm yet blackened the glass roof except when the brief cold glare of lightning silhouetted the jagged palm fronds. Sarah, tearful in black, leaned on Maurice's arm for comfort, watching the glimmering embroidered robes of the priests.

A week and a half later the widow Damala played Princess Fédora in Dieppe. When she entered to find her lover dead, Sarah could not restrain her tears. The audience was thrilled with sympathy to think that she had so recently returned to find her husband a corpse. Sarah wept, and played divinely.

I sighed with relief. Little Juliet would not miss the most wonderful thing in the world.

I'm sure you've heard the rest. Sarah acted brilliantly for another thirty-three years, even after the amputation of a limb. She continued to triumph as Phèdre, Marguerite, La Tosca, Princess Fédora, as well as new roles—Joan of Arc, Cleopatra, Lucretia Borgia, Roxane, Medea. When she tired of women's roles she played men—Lorenzaccio, young Werther, even Hamlet. The last time she ever appeared on stage, at the age of seventy-eight, she played the title role in a little-known play called *Daniel*. Daniel was a morphine addict.

Sarah was the noblest widow in the world, yes indeed, and always kept green the memory of poor Jacques Damala, who died for love.

⟦ BARBARA D'AMATO ⟧

BARBARA D'AMATO IS A PLAYWRIGHT, A NOVELIST, AND a crime researcher. She has worked as an assistant surgical orderly, a carpenter for stage illusions, assistant tiger handler, and stage manager. She writes a suspense series under the pseudonym Malacai Black and On My Honor in that series was an Anthony nominee. Forensic pathologist Gerritt DeGraaf appears in The Hands of Healing Murder and The Eyes on Utopia Murders. Cat Marsala, an investigative reporter in Chicago, is the sleuth in Hardball, Hardtack, Hard Luck and Hard Women. Coming soon is Hard Case. D'Amato's exploration of the Dr. Branion case, The Doctor, The Murder, The Mystery, received the Anthony for best true-crime book. A Chicago physician, Dr. Branion was convicted of murdering his wife even though D'Amato later discovered that evidence existed that proved he could not have committed the crime. D'Amato explores this tragic miscarriage of justice.

D'Amato has served as president of the Midwest chapter of Mystery Writers of America and is currently president of Sisters in Crime. She lives in Chicago with her husband, Tony.

In "Hard Feelings," D'Amato draws on Chicago's great Valentine Blizzard of 1990 and how honesty is the best policy, even if it doesn't seem so at the time.

Hard Feelings

———————◆———————

Officer Susanna Maria Figueroa was frightened, and she hated being frightened. It made her angry. Even worse, she was sure her partner Norm Bennis felt horrible, too. Nevertheless, he had made a serious mistake, and his mistake had gotten them both into trouble.

Suze Figueroa sat on one side of the waiting room, her arms folded across her chest. Far away in the other corner—as far away from her as he could get and still be in the same room—sat Norm Bennis, feet spread, elbows on knees, hands dangling, head hanging. He looked absolutely miserable.

Hell, Suze thought, he ought to. She just hoped he felt guilty as hell, making a stupid mistake and then sticking with it. Stubborn bastard!

But they'd been together so long!

Bennis was her mentor and her friend.

The Police Academy teaches you what they think you need to know. Then the job—and your partner—teach you what you really need to know. Suze Figueroa had been assigned to Bennis just after she finished the initial on-the-job phase of working with a supervisor. She'd been afraid of what Norm would think of her at first. He looked so solid and experienced—like a walking ad for professionalism in police work for the twenty-first century. He'd been ten years a Chicago cop when she came on. He was built like a wedge, with narrow hips, a broad chest, and very wide shoulders. His square brown face, when she first saw it at that first roll call, was set in a scowl. But she soon realized that he thought it was lots of fun being mentor to a five-foot-one-inch naive female.

They hit it off immediately, and Bennis never made fun of her for not knowing whether a ten-young or a one-frank was a "disturbance, domestic, peace restored" or a "dog bite, report filed." He didn't belittle her, as her trainer sometimes had, for not knowing how to fill out a specific form. He knew the department didn't run on gas or electricity, it ran on paper, and he knew when she'd filled out a couple hundred of them, she would remember all the forms.

Bennis was sardonic, but not sour.

For her part, Suze teased him about the long series of women who took his fancy for about three weeks apiece, but she sympathized too. She was divorced. Her ex-husband called her the "affirmative-action cop." By this he meant that she was too short and too female to be any good to anybody.

Bennis thought she was just fine on the job. "You back me up better than any partner I've ever had."

"Hey, Bennis! I'm not just backup. I'm forefront."

"That too."

Suze and Norm and half the First District went to the Furlough Bar for a beer after a tour. Recently, Suze and Norm had taken to going to an occasional movie instead. It was not exactly a girl-and-boy thing, Suze told herself. They were both too embarrassed at the thought of being called just another squad car romance.

And now—now they wouldn't even look at each other.

It was 11 A.M. on February 15, the day after the incident. Two rooms down the hall, a roundtable of inquiry—four men and one woman, including an assistant deputy superintendent, a state's attorney, and the union rep—were reviewing the documents in the case. They had before them the fire department reports and the preliminary findings of the medical examiner and the detectives. But the reports from other departments only explained what happened after the incident. After the point where Norm's story and Suze Figueroa's story diverged.

Their commander, Sazerac, sat with them in the waiting room. He was as unhappy as they were. Finally he spoke.

"There's no way I can stop this. But it bothers me. I wouldn't have figured you for a shirker, Figueroa."

"What do you mean?"

"Don't you realize how they see this?"

"Yes, boss. They know that Bennis and I have two different stories about last night, and so they think one of us is improperly describing the case. So they think one of us is lying. Which would be a reprimand."

"No, Figueroa. It's not that minor."

"Minor! I've never had a reprimand and I don't intend to have one now! Uh. Sir."

Sazerac sighed. "Listen to me. We're talking separation from the department. Maybe prosecution."

"For what?"

"They think you left that man to die in the fire, Figueroa. And made up your story later to cover up. To make it seem he was dead."

Bennis groaned. "But he *was* dead, sir! Figueroa would never—"

"And they think you, Bennis, added that diagnosis later, after you realized that your story cast doubt on whether he was dead."

"That's not true. I said he was dead when I wrote it up this morning."

"Not strongly. You 'thought he was dead.' They figure that you said it more strongly later because the two of you have gotten together to save her ass."

"No. No, sir. That's just not true. Sir, Figueroa is the best officer I've ever worked with. She'd never abandon a living person."

"Are you reconsidering *your* testimony, Bennis?"

Bennis looked from Suze Figueroa to the commander and back. His face was anguished. "I can't. I'm sorry, Figueroa. I can't lie. Maybe I was temporarily disoriented by the fire. But I have to say what I know. I can't lie."

"You're lying now, Bennis," she said. "I wish I knew why."

Figueroa was seething. Bennis stared away from her at the dead plant in the corner. The commander sighed again, and then sat silent.

The door opened. A man in uniform came one step into the room. "The board is ready for you," he said.

"It was one of those nights that a lot of people call 'real Chicago weather,'" Suze Figueroa said to the board. "It had started to snow at about three in the afternoon, just as Officer Bennis and I came on duty. We knew immediately that the rush hour was going to be hell—uh, was going to be very difficult. People had started coming into town, too, for Valentine's Day dinners. By four o'clock it was snowing so hard you couldn't see across the street. By five there were already cars backed up spinning their wheels on the steeper access ramps to Lake Shore Drive and the Kennedy Expressway. Some of them had run out of gas, blocking the streets, and would be there until Streets and San made it through to tow them."

She was trying to hold in her fear, trying to put out of her mind the thought that she might be fired. Being a cop was what she had always wanted.

"It was constant from the moment we hit the street. We picked people out of stalled cars who were too scared to get out. We found several street people and ran them to shelters. We—"

The ADS, Wardron, chopped her description short. "Officer Figueroa," he said, "get to the incident."

"Yes, sir. But the weather played a very large part—"

"We know what the weather was last night. Move forward."

"Yes, sir." This guy Wardron was going to be trouble, she thought. He looked like Mike Ditka and used his voice like the blade of a guillotine. She had vibes, sometimes, when she felt sure that another cop didn't like women on the department. She didn't want to think that this guy was out to get her, personally and specifically, but she'd bet if he could prove that some woman cop had run scared, he'd enjoy doing it.

"At 2140 hours we got a call . . ."

*   *   *

"*One thirty-three,*" the radio had said. They were car thirty-three in the First District. Since Figueroa was driving, Bennis picked up and said, "Thirty-three."

"*Woman screaming for help at eight-one-seven west on Chestnut.*"

"You got a floor on that, squad?"

"*On the two.*"

"Caller give a name?"

"*Oh, yeah. Citizen. Concerned citizen.*"

"I know the guy well."

"*Gal.*"

"Whatever."

Because of the snow, all the usual city sounds around them were muffled. In fact, there were virtually no automobile noises, and they heard the dispatcher more clearly than usual. No need to repeat. Bennis said, "Ten-four."

The snow had filled the streets and was still coming down. Figueroa said, "Jeez, Bennis. It's not the traction that's a problem. It's all the abandoned cars."

"You can get around 'em here if you drive on the sidewalk."

"Right."

"Don't clip the fire hydrant."

"Bennis, please! You know what an excellent driver I am."

"Figueroa, my man, I'd trust you with my life. In fact, I do it on a daily basis."

"And you're still alive, too."

"Watch out for the dumpster!"

"Missed it by a mile."

"A good quarter of an inch anyhow."

The radio said: "*One thirty-three.*"

"Thirty-three."

"*We got a second call on that woman screaming for help. Where are you?*"

"Northbound on LaSalle. Driving's real bad, squad," Bennis said, trying not to gasp as Figueroa slewed within kissing distance of a light pole. "But I'd guess we're just two minutes out now."

"Yeah, thirty-three. Okay. By the way, the news is it's gonna keep snowing until noon tomorrow."

"How nice."

Bennis and Figueroa pulled up in front. They had entered thousands of buildings, not knowing what they'd find. They relied on each other. Each knew that the other would be there, and they even had their own shorthand way of communicating. Bennis pointed a finger to show Figueroa that it was her turn to stand to the far side of the apartment door. Then he knocked. But before he could knock again, Figueroa pointed. "Look."

There was smoke coming out around the top of the door.

Bennis felt the door to see if it was cool, which it was. The last thing he wanted was to start a backdraft. Then he backed up to take a kick at the door. But that instant it opened and a man came running out. His hair and jacket were on fire, and he was screaming. He didn't even see the two cops, but crashed frantically down the stairs.

Bennis spun and went after him, knowing Figueroa would put out the emergency call to the dispatcher. He raced down the stairs three at a time and still couldn't catch up with the terrified man until, leaping, screaming down the cement steps outside the front door, the man fell. The fire on his hair and jacket had spread. Bennis rolled him over in the snow three or four times. Then, thinking to chill the charred flesh and prevent further burn damage, he grabbed up handfuls of snow and slapped it all over the man's head and back.

There was no time to wait and see how badly hurt the man was. God only knew how many people were in the building. Bennis bolted back inside and up the stairs.

Meanwhile, Figueroa had keyed her radio. "One thirty-three, emergency."

"Go ahead, thirty-three."

"There's a fire in this apartment, and it's going fast."

"I'll get the smokies."

" 'Four."

Talking on her radio had used just six seconds. At the same time, she had been scanning the apartment. She could hardly see anything, the smoke was so thick, but she heard a woman screaming. Figueroa dropped to her hands and knees and crawled fast toward the screams.

She found herself in the kitchen, where a woman, standing up, was rushing into a broom closet, falling down when she hit the wall, rushing in again, terrified and convinced it was the front door.

Figueroa grabbed her. "Get out of my way!" the woman screamed over and over.

Figueroa said, "Hey! Stop it!"

"Get out of my way!"

Figueroa slapped her.

The flames were running along the floorboards now. The woman kept shrieking.

"Come with me, god-dammit!" Figueroa seized the woman's hand, pulled her to the floor. She put her arm over the woman's shoulder and hustled her on all fours toward the front door.

This woman was burned already, Figueroa thought. Her skin felt hot to the touch, and Figueroa could almost believe she felt blisters starting to form.

Pushing and cajoling and bullying, she got the woman into the living room. Crossing the floor, she realized she was crawling over the body of a man lying there unmoving, but she didn't have time to worry about that. She got the woman to the door.

The hall was still cool and the air in it was fresh, so she pushed the woman out and yelled after her, "Warn your neighbors!"

There was no time to make sure she did. Suze Figueroa saw Bennis coming up the stairs. She yelled, "There's a man inside."

On hands and knees she crawled back in, touching the hot wall to make sure where she was going. She found the man, but at the same instant she and Bennis heard a baby start to scream. Bennis was next to her now and he slapped the man's cheek, but the man didn't move.

Figueroa felt the man's forehead. Smoke swirled above him, but he was lifeless and cold. The baby screamed louder, from a back bedroom.

"I gotta get the kid," she said to Bennis. She wasn't sure he could hear over the roar of the fire, but then she found him following her as they crawled to the bedroom.

"How many kids?" she yelled.

There was just one crib.

Bennis stood up, grabbed a little girl out of the crib, put her solidly under one arm, and ran like a quarterback for the front door. Suze stayed to check for another child.

The fire was flashing across the ceiling now. She didn't have much time.

One crib. *Hurry up!* No other child's bed. No crying. *Hurry! It's hot!* As far as she could see through the smoke, only girl-child toys in one age group—two soft dolls, one stuffed bear, a play muffin tin, and some plastic spoons. One child.

Part of the ceiling fell.

Taking a last breath of air from floor level, Figueroa jumped up and bolted for the front door. The living room was a hell of flame, and if she hadn't memorized where the door was, she would never have made it. Her hair was singed. She could not even see the man on the floor. He was dead, anyway, and she had to warn the upstairs neighbors.

Outside, fire engines were fighting their way through streets blocked with stalled cars. They didn't arrive until ten minutes later.

"I want to point out," Commander Sazerac said to Deputy Wardron, "that Officers Bennis and Figueroa got the other tenants out of the building. Which, given the weather and the time it took for the fire battalion to arrive, surely saved their lives."

"We understand that," Wardron said, clipping his words.

Sazerac said, "The building was totally involved when the fire engines arrived. And then they had trouble getting water to it. Stalled cars were blocking the fire hydrants."

"We are aware of that."

"When the fire was finally struck at 0330 hours, Officers Bennis and Figueroa were still caring for residents, even though they were four and a half hours past the end of their tour."

"Commander Sazerac, I appreciate your attempt to help your men—ah, people—but we are interested in what happened in the Molitor apartment, not what happened afterward. We'll proceed."

Bennis said angrily, "I personally saw Officer Figueroa rescue six residents from the upper floors."

"Officer Bennis, we'll get your story later."

Commander Sazerac said loudly, "And she was burned in the attempt, Deputy!"

"Not relevant now. We'll take it into account during sentencing."

"Don't you mean *if* there is a decision to go to sentencing, Deputy?"

"Of course, Commander. This is just a preliminary roundtable. My mistake." He turned his head and addressed the four board members. "We will note Commander Sazerac has questions about this process.

However, we will take matters up in order. We are not going to use this process today as a way for the two officers involved to get their stories straight between them."

Commander Sazerac said, "They could have done that at any time in the last twelve hours. It's their integrity and their unwillingness to alter their reports to say the same thing that has caused a difference in perception to be blown up into this silly—"

"Commander! This is a fact-finding proceeding. It is an inappropriate time to make arguments. Hold them until the charges have been proven or not proven."

Wardron was in charge here, not Sazerac. Departmental structure being what it was, there was nothing Sazerac could do but sit by, just about as useful as the photo of the superintendent on the wall.

He and Wardron held each other's eyes for two or three seconds.

Figueroa said, "Sir, may I ask what the circumstances were that led up to the fire? We came into a situation midway—"

"Which is no excuse."

"I'm not suggesting that it is. But the fire obviously started in that apartment, and there were three adults inside who didn't seem to have made any effort to put it out. Why was Mr. Molitor lying in the middle of the living room floor? If he'd been shot, for instance, I would think I'd be entitled to know that. It certainly wasn't the smoke that killed him. He was down on the floor where the air was good."

"I don't suppose there's any reason not to tell you. We have a reasonably full picture, from the statement of the woman and the statements of the neighbors."

The Molitors had begun fighting in the afternoon—a husband, his wife, and the wife's brother. Fighting and drinking, and drinking and fighting. Among the burned remnants of their apartment were dozens of beer cans and the fragments of two bottles that had contained scotch.

By early evening, the neighbors were getting pretty tired of it. Judging by their observations and the wife's story, about nine the husband, who until then had been just shouting and threatening and hitting the wall with his fists, started hitting his wife. She hit back for a while, then fell, and he kicked her. She screamed for help and one of the neighbors, too frightened to go in or knock, called the police.

Meanwhile, the brother had come to the wife's defense. He attacked the husband, who by now was in a blind rage. The husband pushed the brother, who fell over the wife, and then the husband grabbed a can of lighter fluid, ran wild, spraying it along the living room and kitchen walls, and lighted it. The brother surged up off the floor. The wife, terrified, crawled to what she thought was the front door, but she was dazed from several blows, and now smoke was filling the room, and she actually went into the kitchen.

Meanwhile, the brother had picked up a chair and hit the husband over the head, hard. The husband went down.

At about this point, Figueroa and Bennis were pulling up outside. The brother's hair had caught fire. He panicked and ran out of the apartment, where he was intercepted by Bennis.

Wardron continued: "Officer Figueroa, what you should have done after Officer Bennis left with the baby was to attempt to get Mr. Molitor out. You might not have succeeded, but you should have tried."

"I knew the man on the floor was dead. He was cold."

"Officer Bennis, was he cold?"

Bennis swallowed. Figueroa fixed him with her eyes, but he didn't look at her. For a moment he straightened up, squaring his shoulders, as if he were steeling himself to take action. Then his face sagged.

"He was still warm," he said.

Commander Sazerac asked, "Isn't there a way to tell whether he was dead before the fire got to him? You should be able to test for carbon sucked into the lungs. If he wasn't breathing—"

"Commander Sazerac, we appreciate your help," Wardron said, in a tone that made it clear that he didn't. "Believe it or not, we thought of that."

Sazerac watched sourly. He knew there was something wrong with the way they were getting the picture, but he couldn't put his finger on where the problem was. Figueroa would not have left a living man to burn to death. Sazerac had been a commander much too long to make serious mistakes in judgment about his officers' characters. There *was* a problem with Figueroa, but it was the opposite. Like a lot of short female officers, she had a tendency to put herself in harm's way unnecessarily and play Jane Wayne. This charge against her was dead wrong.

Wardron added, "The entire building was engulfed when the fire department finally made it. Shortly after that, the top three floors of the structure collapsed into the basement. What was left of Mr. Molitor looked a lot like a blackened pipe cleaner."

Figueroa had been staring at the tabletop.

"Wait!" she said suddenly. She knew that wasn't the way to talk to the brass, and said in a quieter voice, "If you'll give me a minute, to go get something, I think I can explain what happened."

She got up.

Wardron said, "You can explain it right here."

"If I may leave for just a minute, sir, I can demonstrate."

"One minute, then."

Figueroa took two Styrofoam cups from the table that held the coffee urn and was back in less than a minute with two cups of water.

"Would you put the fingers of your left hand in one of these and the fingers of your right hand in the other, Deputy Wardron?"

"No. Explain to me what you think you're trying to do."

"Well maybe Commander Sazerac will, while I explain. We can always repeat it." Sazerac, intrigued, did as she said.

"One cup is hot water and one is cold. On the night of the fire, Officer Bennis had patted snow all over the brother, outdoors, and then ran back into the burning apartment. While he was doing that, I was pulling the woman out of the kitchen. She was hot to the touch and felt like she was starting to blister. When I came back, I felt along the hot wall. The instant Officer Bennis returned from outside, we both touched Mr. Molitor."

Commander Sazerac said, "I begin to see."

"Mr. Molitor was dead, but only ten to twenty minutes dead, so his skin was probably about the temperature of mine today. Commander, will you use both hands to touch my forearm?"

Sazerac did so. He smiled. "Amazing. Your arm feels warm to my right hand and cold to my left." Sazerac turned to Wardron. "The same arm," he said. "And it feels entirely different." He gestured to Wardron. "Want to try it?"

Figueroa and Bennis sat in their squad car. Bennis said, "Reminds me of this case I had once."

Figueroa sighed loudly, but Bennis knew she liked his stories.

"Guy decided to rob a fraternity house late at night, on a night when there had been a late snow. Flat, untouched snow leading up to the door. So he says to himself 'If I walk in backward, they'll think it was somebody from *inside* who stole the stuff, because there won't be any tracks leading in.' "

"Not a bad plan."

"Which he proceeds to accomplish. Picks up a lot of odds and ends, one or two wallets, a ten-inch TV, a boom box, and leaves. Kids get up in the morning, call the cops, we come in, see the tracks. Well, we'd been onto a guy in the neighborhood we knew'd been doing this kind of stuff. Go pick him up. Now he's got a problem. He wants to ask about tracks in the snow, but he shouldn't know anything about it, see?"

"Yup."

"So he says, real cute, 'You'd think you could tell whether it was an inside or outside job, snow like this and all.' "

"Real subtle."

"Yeah. Well, we said, 'We did and we knew by the tracks it was an outside job.' He says, all astounded, 'That's impossible! I faced backward, *going and coming both!*' "

Suze Figueroa giggled. "They get cute, but they never get smart."

"So you see, Figueroa, it's like this case with the fire. The way things are is all a matter of which angle you're looking at it from."

"Right, Bennis. Got it. Want to do a movie after work?"

He checked around to make sure nobody was watching and put his arm over her shoulders. "Let me take you to dinner, Figueroa. We missed Valentine's Day."

〖JEFFERY DEAVER〗

JEFFERY DEAVER IS A FORMER ATTORNEY AND FOLK-
singer. Twice nominated for Edgar Awards by the Mystery
Writers of America, he is the author of ten suspense novels
under his name and the pseudonym William Jefferies.

Deaver's most recent novel is the critically acclaimed
Praying for Sleep, which has been published not only in
this country but in the Far East and throughout Europe.
The novel, which Stephen King has called "smart, scary,
and compulsively readable," takes place over the course of
a single evening during which a paranoid schizophrenic
mental patient escapes from a state hospital to pursue the
woman who testified at his murder trial.

Other Deaver titles include Hard News, Mistress of
Justice, and The Lesson of Her Death. As Jefferies
he has written the John Pellam mystery series: Shallow
Graves and Bloody River Blues.

Deaver, who lives in Virginia and Carmel, California,
is currently at work on his next thriller.

Together

"A few people, a very few people're lucky enough to
find a special kind of love. A love that's . . . more. That
goes beyond anything that ever was."

"I suppose so."

"I *know* so. Allison and me, we're in that category."
Manko's voice then dropped to a discreet whisper as he
looked at me with his barracks buddy's grin. "I've had
a barrelful of women. You know me, Frankie boy. You
know I've been around."

Manko was in the mood to perform and all I could do

was play both straight man and audience. "So you've said, Mr. M."

"Those other girls, looking back, some of 'em were lovers. And some were just, you know, for the night. Wham, bam, that sort of thing. But till I met Allison, I didn't understand what love was all about."

"It's a transcendent love."

"Transcendent." He tasted the word, nodding slowly. "What's that mean?"

Just after I'd met Manko I'd learned that while he was poorly read and generally uninformed he never hesitated to own up to his ignorance. That was my first clue as to the kind of man he was.

"It's exactly what you're describing," I explained. "A love that rises above what you normally see and experience."

"Yeah. I like that, Frankie boy. Transcendent. That says it. That's what we've got. You ever love anyone that way?"

"Sort of. A long time ago." This was partially true. But I said nothing more. Although I considered Manko a friend in some ways, our souls were worlds apart and I wasn't going to share my deepest personal life with him. Not that it mattered, for at the moment he was more interested in speaking about the woman who was the center of his own solar system.

"Allison Morgan. Allison *Kimberly* Morgan. Her father gave her a nickname. Kimmie. But that's crap. It's a kid's name. And one thing she isn't is a kid."

"Has a southern sound to it." I'm a native of North Carolina and went to school with a bevy of Sally Mays and Cheryl Annes.

"It does, yeah. But she's not. She's from Ohio. Born and bred." Manko glanced at his watch and stretched. "It's late. Almost time to meet her."

"Allison?"

He nodded and smiled the trademarked, toothy Manko

smile. "I mean, you're cute in your own way, Frank, but if I gotta choose between the two of you . . ."

I laughed and repressed a yawn. It *was* late—eleven twenty. An unusual hour for me to be finishing dinner but not to be engaged in conversation over coffee. Not having an Allison of my own to hurry home to, or anyone other than a cat, I often watched the clock slip past midnight or 1 A.M. in the company of friends.

Manko pushed aside the dinner dishes and poured more coffee.

"I'll be awake all night," I protested mildly.

He laughed this aside and asked if I wanted more pie.

When I declined he raised his coffee cup. "My Allison. Let's drink to her."

We touched the rims of the cups with a ringing clink.

I said, "Hey, Mr. M, you were going to tell me all 'bout the trouble. You know, with her father."

He scoffed. "That son of a bitch? You know what happened."

"Not the whole thing."

"Don'tcha?" He dramatically reared his head back and gave a wail of mock horror. "Manko's falling down on the job." He leaned forward, the smile gone, and gripped my arm hard. "It's not a pretty story, Frankie boy. It's not outta 'Family Ties' or 'Roseanne.' Can you stomach it?"

I leaned forward too, just as dramatically, and growled, "Try me."

Manko laughed and settled into his chair. As he lifted his cup the table rocked. It had done so throughout dinner but he only now seemed to notice it. He took a moment to fold and slip a piece of newspaper under the short leg to steady it. He was very meticulous in this task. I watched his concentration, his strong hands. Manko was someone who actually enjoyed working out—lifting weights, in his case—and I was astonished at his musculature. He was about five-six and, though it's hard for men—for me, at least—to appraise male looks, I'd call him handsome.

The only aspect of his appearance I thought off kilter was his haircut. When his stint with the marines was over he kept the unstylish crew-cut. From this, I deduced his experience in the service was a high point in his life—he'd worked factory and mediocre sales jobs since—and the shorn hair was a reminder of a better, if not an easier, time.

Of course, that was my pop-magazine-therapy take on the situation. Maybe he just liked short hair.

He now finished with the table and eased his strong, compact legs out in front of him. Manko the storyteller was on duty. This was another clue to the nature of Manko's spirit: though I don't think he'd ever been on a stage in his life he was a born actor.

"So. You know Hillborne? The town?"

I said I didn't.

"Southern part of Ohio. Pisswater river town. Champion used to have a mill there. Still a couple factories making, I don't know, radiators and things. And a big printing plant, does work for Cleveland and Chicago. Kroeger Brothers. When I was in Seattle I learned printing. Miehle offsets. The four- and five-color jobs, you know. Big as a house. I learned 'em cold. Could print a whole saddle-stitched magazine myself, inserts included, yessir, perfect register and not one goddamn staple in the centerfold's boobs . . . Yessir, Manko's a hell of a printer. So there I was, thumbing cross-country. I ended up in Hillborne and got a job at Kroeger's. I had to start as a feeder, which was crap, but it paid thirteen an hour and I figured I could work my way up.

"One day I had an accident. Frankie boy, you ever seen coated stock whipping through a press? *Zip, zip, zip.* Like a razor. Sliced my arm. Here." He pointed out the scar, a wicked-looking one. "Bad enough they took me to the hospital. Gave me a tetanus shot and stitched me up. No big deal. No whining from Manko. Then the doctor left and a nurse's aide came in to tell me how to wash it and gave me some bandages." His voice dwindled.

"It was Allison?"

"Yessir." He paused and gazed out the window at the overcast sky. "You believe in fate?"

"In a way I do."

"Does that mean yes or no?" He frowned. Manko always spoke plainly and expected the same from others.

"Yes, with qualifiers."

Love tamed his irascibility and he grinned, chiding good-naturedly, "Well, you better. Because there *is* such a thing. Allison and I, we were fated to be together. See, if I hadn't been running that sixty-pound stock, if I hadn't slipped just when I did, if she hadn't been working an extra shift to cover for a sick friend . . . if, if, if . . . See what I'm saying? Am I right?"

He sat back in the creaky chair. "Oh, Frankie, she was fantastic. I mean, here I am, this, like, four-inch slash in my arm, twenty stitches, I could've bled to death, and all I'm thinking is she's the most beautiful woman I ever saw."

"I've seen her picture." He'd showed it to me a dozen times. But that didn't stop him from continuing to describe her. The words alone gave him pleasure.

"Her hair's blond. Gold blond. Natural, not out of a bottle. And curly but not teased, like some high-hair slut. And her face, it's heart-shaped. Her body . . . well, she has a nice figure. Let's leave it at that." His glance at me contained a warning. I was about to assure him that I had no unpure thoughts about Allison Morgan when he forgot his jealousy. He added, "She's twenty-one years old."

Echoing my exact thought he added sheepishly, "Kind of an age difference, huh?"

Manko was thirty-seven—three years younger than I—but I learned this after I'd met him and had guessed he was in his late twenties. It was impossible for me to revise that assessment upward.

"I asked her out. There. On the spot. In the emergency room, you can believe it. She was probably thinking, How d'I get rid of this bozo? But she was interested, yessir. A man can tell. Words and looks, they're two different things, and I was getting the capital M message. She said she had this rule she never dated patients. So I go, 'How 'bout if you married somebody and he cuts his hand in an accident and goes to the emergency room and there you are? Then you'd be *married* to a patient.' She laughed and said, no, that was somehow backward. Then this emergency call came in, some car wreck, and she had to go off to another ward.

"The next day I came back with a dozen roses. She pretended she didn't remember me and acted like I was a florist delivery boy. 'Oh, what room are those for?'

"I said, 'They're for you . . . if you have *room* in your heart for me.' Okay, okay, it was a bullshit line." The rugged ex-marine fiddled awkwardly with his cup. "But, hey, if it works, it works."

I couldn't argue with him there.

"The first date was magic. We had dinner at the fanciest restaurant in town. A French place. It cost me two days' pay. It was embarrassing 'cause I wore my leather jacket and you were suppose to have a suit coat. One of *those* places. They made me wear one they had in the coat room and it didn't fit too good. But Allison didn't care. We laughed about it. She was all dressed up in a white dress, with a red-white-and-blue scarf around her neck. Oh, God, she was beautiful. We were there, I don't know, three, four hours easy. She was pretty shy. Didn't say much. Mostly she stared like she was kind of hypnotized. Me, I talked and talked, and sometimes she'd look at me all funny and then laugh. And I'd realize I wasn't making any sense 'cause I was looking at her and not paying any attention to what I was saying. We drank a whole bottle of wine. Cost fifty bucks."

Manko had always seemed both impressed by and contemptuous of money. Myself, I've never come close to being rich so wealth simply perplexes me.

"It was the best," he said dreamily, replaying the memory.

"Ambrosia," I offered.

He laughed as he sometimes did—in a way that was both amused and mocking—and continued his story. "I told her all about the Philippines, where I was stationed for a while, and about hitching around the country. She was interested in everything I'd done. Even—well, I should say *especially*—some of the stuff I wasn't too proud of. Grifting, perping cars. You know, when I was a kid, going at it. Stuff we all did."

I held back a smile. Speak for yourself, Manko.

"Then all of a sudden, the sky lit up outside. Fireworks! Talk about signs from God. You know what it was? It was the Fourth of July! I'd forgotten about it 'cause all I'd been thinking about was going out with her. *That's* why she was wearing the red, white, and blue. We watched the fireworks from the window."

His eyes gleamed. "I took her home and we stood on the steps of her parents' house—she was still living with them. We talked for a while more then she said she had to get to bed. You catch that? Like she could've said, 'I have to be going.' Or just 'Good night.' But she worked the word *bed* into it. I know, you're in love, you look for messages like that. Only in this case, it wasn't Manko's imagination working overtime, no sir."

Outside, a light rain had started falling and the wind had come up. I rose and shut the window.

"The next day I kept getting distracted at work. I'd think about her face, her voice. No woman's ever affected me like that. On break I called her and asked her out for the next weekend. She said sure and said she was glad to hear from me. That set up my day. Hell, it set up my *week*. After work I went to the library and looked some things up. I found out about her name. Morgan— if you spell it a little different—it means 'morning' in German. And I dug up some articles about the family. Like, they're rich. Filthy. The house in Hillborne wasn't their only place. There was one in Aspen, too, and one in Vermont. Oh, and an apartment in New York."

"A pied-à-terre."

His brief laugh again. The smile faded. "And then there was her father. Thomas Morgan." He peered into his coffee cup like a fortune-teller. "He's one of those guys a hundred years ago you'd call him a tycoon."

"What would you call him now?"

Manko laughed grimly, as if I'd made a clever but cruel joke. He lifted his cup toward me—a toast, it seemed—then continued. "He inherited this company that makes gaskets and nozzles and stuff you'd recognize even if you didn't know what it did. He's about fifty-five and is he *tough*. A big guy, but not fat. A droopy black mustache, and his eyes look you over like he couldn't care less about you but at the same time he's sizing you up, like every fault, every dirty thought you ever had he knows it.

"We caught sight of each other when I dropped Allison off, and I knew, I just somehow knew that we were going to go head to head someday. I didn't really think about it then but deep inside, the thought was there."

"What about her mother?"

"Allison's mom? She's a socialite. She flits around, Allison told me. Man, what a great word. *Flit*. I can picture the old broad, going to bridge games and tea parties. Allison's their only child." His face suddenly grew dark. "That, I figured out later, explains a lot."

"What?" I asked.

"Why her father got on my case in a big way. I'll get to that. Don't rush the Manko man, Frankie."

I smiled in deference.

"Our second date went even better than the first. We saw some movie, I forget what, then I drove her home. Parked in front of her house. Took us an hour to say good night, you get what I'm saying?" His voice trailed off. Then he said, "I asked her out for a few days after that but she couldn't make it. Ditto the next day and the next too. I was pissed at first. Then I got paranoid. Was she trying to, you know, dump me?

"But then she explained it. She was working two shifts whenever she could. I thought, This's pretty funny. I mean, her father's loaded. But, see, there was a *reason*. She's just like me. Independent. She dropped out of college to work in the hospital. She was saving her own money to travel. She didn't want to owe the old man anything. *That's* why she loved listening to me talk, telling her 'bout leaving Kansas when I was seventeen and thumbing around the country and overseas, getting into scrapes. Allison had it in her to do the same thing. Man, that was great. I love having a woman with a mind of her own."

"Do you now?" I asked, but Manko was immune to irony.

"In the back of my mind I was thinking about all the places I'd like to go with her. I'd send her clippings from travel magazines, *National Geographic*s. On our first date she'd told me that she loved poetry so I wrote her poems about traveling. It's funny. I never wrote anything before in my life—a few letters maybe, some shit in school—but those poems, man, they just poured out of me. A hundred of 'em. She told me she really liked the ones I wrote about Florida. That's where I went on a vacation with my mom. The only real vacation I ever took with her. When you grow up in Kansas, man, seeing a beach for the first time, it does something to you. It *does* something.

"Well, next thing I knew, bang, we were in love. See, that's the thing about . . . *transcendent* love. It happens right away, or it doesn't happen at all. Two weeks, and we were totally in love. I was ready to propose. I see that look on your face, Frankie boy. Didn't know the Manko man had it in him? What can I say? He's the marryin' kind after all.

"I went to the credit union and borrowed five hundred bucks and bought this diamond ring. Then I asked her out to a movie and a burger after. I played it real cool, you know. I was going to give the ring to the waitress and tell her to put it on a plate and bring it to the table when we asked for dessert. Cute, huh?

"That day I was working the P.M. shift, three to eleven, for the shift bonus, but I ducked out early, at five, and showed up at her house at six-twenty. There were cars all over the place. Allison came outside, looking all nervous. My stomach twisted. Something funny was going on. She told me her mother was having a party and there was a problem. Two maids had got sick or something. Allison had to stay and help her mother. I thought that was weird. *Both* of them getting sick at the same time? She said she'd see me in a day or two."

I saw the exact moment the thought came into his mind; his eyes went dead as rocks.

"But there was more to it than that," Manko whispered. "A hell of a lot more."

"Allison's father, you mean?"

But he didn't explain what he meant just then and returned to his story of the aborted proposal. He muttered, "That was one of the worst nights of my life. Here, I'd ditched work, I was in hock because of the ring, and I couldn't even get five minutes alone with her. Man, it was torture. I drove around all night. Woke up at dawn, in my car, down by the railroad tracks. And when I got home there was no message from her. Jesus, was I depressed.

"That morning I called her at the hospital. She was sorry about the party. I asked her out that night. She said she really shouldn't, she was so tired—the party'd gone to two in the morning. But how 'bout tomorrow?"

A gleam returned to Manko's eyes. I thought his expression reflected a pleasant memory about their date.

But I was wrong.

His voice was bitter. "Oh, what a lesson we learned. It's a mistake to underestimate your enemy, Frankie. You listen to Manko. Never do it. That's what they taught us in the corps. *Semper fi.* But Allison and me, we got blindsided.

"That next night I came over to pick her up. I was going to take her to this river bluff, like a lover's lane, you know, to propose. I had my speech down cold. I'd rehearsed all night. I pulled up to the house but she just stood on the porch and waved for me to come up to her. Oh, she was beautiful as ever. I just wanted to hold her. Put my arms around her and hold her forever.

"But she was real distant. She stepped away from me and kept glancing into the house. Her face was pale and her hair was tied back in a ponytail. I didn't like it that way. I'd told her I liked it when she wore it down. So when I saw the ponytail it was like a signal of some kind. An SOS.

" 'What is it?' I asked her. She started to cry and said she couldn't see me anymore. 'What?' I whispered. God, I couldn't believe it. You know what it felt like? On Parris Island, basic training, you know? They fire live rounds over your head on the obstacle course. One time I got hit by a ricochet. I had a flak vest on but the slug was a full metal jacket and it knocked me clean on my ass. That's what it was like.

"I asked her why. She just said she thought it was best and wouldn't go into any details. But then I started to catch on. She kept looking around and I realized that there was somebody just inside the door, listening. She was scared to death—*that's* what it was. She begged me please not to call her or come by, and I figured out she wasn't talking to me so much as saying it for whoever was spying on us. I played along. I said okay, if that's what she wanted, blah, blah, blah . . . Then I pulled her close and told her not to worry. I'd look out for her. I whispered it, like a secret message.

"I went home. I waited as long as I could then called, hoping that I'd get her alone. I had to talk to her. I had to hear her voice, like I needed air or water. But nobody picked up the phone. They had an answering machine but I didn't leave a message. I didn't get any sleep that weekend—not a single hour. I had a lot to think about. See, I knew what'd happened. I knew exactly.

"Monday morning I got to her hospital at six and waited just outside the entrance. I caught up with her just before she went inside. She was still scared, looking around like somebody was following her, just like on the porch.

"I asked her point-blank, 'It's your father, isn't it?' She didn't say anything for a minute then nodded and said that, yeah, he'd forbidden her to see me. Doesn't that sound funny? 'Forbidden.' 'He wants you to marry some preppy, is that it? Somebody from his club?' She said she didn't know about that, only that he'd told her not to see me anymore. The son of a bitch actually threatened her!"

Manko sipped his coffee and pointed a blunt finger at me. "See, Frankie, love means zip to somebody like Thomas Morgan. Business, society, image, money—that's what counts to bastards like that. Man, I was so goddamn desperate. . . . It was too much. I threw my arms around her and said, 'Let's get away. Now.'

" 'Please,' she said, 'you have to leave.'

"Then I saw what she'd been looking out for. Her

father'd sent one of his security men to spy on her. He saw us and came running. If he touched her I was going to break his neck, I swear I would've. But Allison grabbed my arm and begged me to run. 'He has a gun,' she said.

" 'I don't care,' I told her." Manko laughed. "Not exactly true, Frankie boy, I gotta say. I was scared shitless. But Allison said if I left, the guy wouldn't hurt her. That made sense but I wasn't going just yet. I turned back and held her hard. 'Do you love me? Tell me? I have to know. Say it!'

"And she did. She whispered, 'I love you.' I could hardly hear it but it was enough for me. I knew everything would be fine. Whatever else, we had each other.

"I got back into the routine of life. Working, playing softball on the plant team—hey, you and me, we threw some balls together, Frankie. I'm a hell of a catcher. You know that."

"I'd never want to be a runner with you guarding home."

"Knock your ass clean back to third base. Am I right?"

He was indeed.

"All the time I kept writing her poetry, sending her articles and letters, you know. I'd put fake return addresses on the envelopes so her father wouldn't guess it was me writing. I even hid letters in Publishers Clearing House envelopes addressed to her! How's that for thinking?

"Once in a while I'd see her in person. I found her in a drugstore by herself and snuck up to her. I bought her a cup of coffee. She was nervous as hell and I could see why. The goons were outside. We talked for about two minutes is all then one of 'em saw us and I had to vanish. I kicked my way out the back door. After that I began to notice these dark cars driving past my apartment or following me down the street. They said MCP on the side. Morgan Chemical Products. They were keeping an eye on me.

"One day this guy came up to me in the hallway of my apartment and said Morgan'd pay me five thousand to leave town. I laughed at him. Then he said if I didn't stay away from Allison there'd be trouble.

"Suddenly I just snapped. I grabbed him and pulled his gun out of his holster and threw it on the floor then I shoved him against the wall and said, 'You go back and tell Morgan to leave us alone, or *he's* the one's gonna be in trouble. You got me?'

"Then I kicked him down the stairs and threw his gun after him. I laughed but I gotta say I was pretty shook up. I was seeing just how powerful this guy was."

"Money is power," I offered.

"Yeah, you're right there. Money's power. And Thomas Morgan was going to use all of his to keep us apart. You know why? 'Cause I was a threat. Fathers are jealous. Turn on any talk show. Oprah. Sally Jesse. Fathers *hate* their daughters' boyfriends. It's like an Oedipus thing. Especially—what I was saying before—with Allison being an only child. Here I was, a rebel, a drifter, making thirteen bucks an hour. It was like a slap in his face—Allison loving me so completely. She was rejecting him and everything he stood for." Manko's face shone with pride for Allison's courage.

Then the smile vanished. "But Morgan was always one step ahead of us. One day I ditched work and snuck into the hospital. I waited for an hour but Allison never showed up. I asked where she was. They told me she wasn't working there anymore. Nobody'd give me a straight answer but finally I found this young nurse who told me her father'd called and told 'em that Allison was taking a leave of absence. Period. No explanation. She didn't even clean out her locker. Jesus. All her plans to travel, all her plans with me—gone, just like that. I called the house to get a message to her but he'd changed the number and had it, you know, unlisted. I mean, this guy was in*credible.*

"And he didn't stop there. Next, he comes after me. I go in to work and the foreman tells me I'm fired. Too many unexcused absences. That was bullshit—I didn't have more than most of the guys. But Morgan must've been a friend of the Kroegers. I was still new so the union wouldn't go to bat for me. I was out. Just like that.

"Well, I couldn't beat him at his game so I decided to play by my rules." Manko grinned and scooted forward. Our knees touched and I felt all the dark energy that was in him pulse against my skin. "Oh, I wasn't worried for me. But Allison, she's so . . ." As he searched for a word his hands made a curious gesture, as if stretching thread between them, a miniature cat's cradle. He seemed momentarily despairing.

I suggested, "Fragile."

The snap of his fingers startled me. He sat up. "Ex*actly*. Fragile. She didn't have any defense against her father. I had to do something fast. I went to the police. I wanted 'em to go to the house and see if she was okay. But also it'd be a sign to her father that I wasn't going to take any crap from him." Manko whistled. "Mistake, Frankie. Bad mistake. Morgan was one step ahead of me. This sergeant, some big guy, pushed me into a corner and said if I didn't stay away from Morgan's daughter, the family'd get a restraining order. I'd end up in a cell. Then he looked me over and said something about did I know all sorts of accidents could happen to prisoners? Man, was I stupid. I should've known the cops'd be on Morgan's payroll too.

"By then I was going crazy. I hadn't seen Allison for days. Jesus, had he sent her off to a convent or something?"

Serenity returned to his face. "Then she gave me a signal. I was hiding in the bushes in a little park across the street, watching the house with binoculars. I just wanted to *see* her is all. I wanted to know she was all right. She must've seen me because she lifted the shade all the way up. Oh, man, there she was! The light was behind her and it made her hair glow. Like those things that, you know, gurus see."

"Auras."

"Right, right. She was in a nightgown, and I could just see the outline of her body beneath it. She looked like an angel. I was like I was gonna have a heart attack, it was such an incredible thing. There she was, telling me she was all right and she missed me. Somehow, she'd known I was out there. Then the shade went down and she shut the light out.

"I spent the next week planning. I was running out of money. Thanks again to Thomas Morgan. He'd put out the word to all the factories in town and nobody'd hire me. I added up what I had and it wasn't much. Maybe twelve hundred bucks. I figured it'd get us to Florida. Give me a chance to find work with a printer and Allison a job in a hospital."

Then Manko laughed. He studied me critically. "I can be honest with you, Frank. I feel I'm close to you."

So I was no longer Frankie boy. I'd graduated. My pulse quickened and I was deeply, unreasonably moved.

"Fact is, I look tough. Am I right? But I get scared. Real scared. I never saw any action. Grenada, Panama, Desert Storm. I missed 'em all, you know what I'm saying? I was never *tested*. I always wondered what I'd do under fire. Well, this was my chance. I was going to rescue Allison. I was going up against the old man himself.

"I called his company and told his secretary I was a reporter from *Ohio Business* magazine. I wanted to do an interview with Mr. Morgan. She and I tried to find a time he could see me. I couldn't believe it—she bought the whole story. She told me he'd be in Mexico on business from the twentieth through the twenty-second of July. I made an appointment for August first, then hung up fast. I was worried somebody was tracing the call.

"On the twentieth I staked out the house all day. Sure enough, Morgan left with his suitcase at ten in the morning and didn't come back that night. There was a security car parked in the driveway, and I figured one of the goons was inside the house. But I'd planned on that. At ten it started to rain. Just like now." He nodded toward the window. "I remember hiding in the bushes, real glad about the overcast. I had about a hundred feet of exposed yard to cover, and the security boys'd spot me for sure in the moonlight. I managed to get to the house without anybody seeing me and hid beneath this holly tree while I caught my breath.

"Then it was dues time, Frank. I leaned against the side of the house, listening to the rain and wondering if I'd have the guts to go through with it."

"But you did."

Manko grinned boyishly and did a decent George Raft impersonation. "I broke in through the basement, snuck up to her room, and busted her out of the joint.

"We didn't take a suitcase or anything. We just got out of there fast as we could. Nobody heard us. The security guy was in the living room but he'd fallen asleep watching the 'Tonight' show. Allison and I got into my car and we hit the highway. Man, *Easy Rider*. We were free! On the road, just her and me. We'd escaped.

"I headed for the interstate, driving sixty-two, right on the button, because they don't arrest you if you're doing just seven miles over the limit. It's a state police rule, I heard somewhere. I stayed in the right lane and pointed that old Dodge east southeast. Didn't stop for anything. Ohio, West Virginia, Virginia, North Carolina. Once we started crossing borders, I felt better. Her father was sure to come home from his trip right away and'd call the local cops but whether they'd get the highway patrol in, I had my doubts. I mean, he'd have some explaining to do—about how he kept his daughter a prisoner and everything." Manko shook his head. "But you know what I did?"

From the rueful look on his face I could guess. "You underestimated the enemy."

Manko shook his head. "Thomas Morgan," he mused. "I think he must've been a godfather or something."

"I suppose they have them in Ohio too."

"He had friends everywhere. Virginia troopers, Carolina, everywhere! Money talks, you know what they say. We were heading south on 21, making for Charlotte, when I ran into 'em. I went into a 7-Eleven to buy some food and beer and what happens but there's a couple of good ole boys right there, Smoky hats and everything, asking the clerk about a couple on the run from Ohio. I mean, *us*. I managed to get out without them seeing us and we peeled rubber outta there, I'll tell you. We drove for a while but by then it was almost dawn and I figured we better lay low for the day.

"I pulled into a big forest preserve. We spent the whole day together, lying there, my arms around her, her head on my chest. We just lay in the grass beside the car and I told her stories about places we'd travel to. The Philippines, Thailand, California. And I told her what life'd be like in Florida too."

He looked at me with a grave expression on his taut face. "I could've had her, Frank. You know what I'm saying? Right there. On the grass. The insects buzzing around us. You could hear this river, a waterfall, nearby." Manko's voice fell to a murmur. "But it wouldn't've been right. I wanted everything to be perfect. I wanted us to be in our own place, in Florida, in our bedroom. That sounds old-fashioned, I know. You think that was stupid of me? You don't think so, do you?"

"No, Manko, it's not stupid at all." Awkwardly I looked for something to add. "It was good of you."

He looked forlorn for a minute, perhaps regretting,

stupid or wise, his choosing to keep their relationship chaste.

"Then," he said, smiling devilishly, "things got hairy. At midnight we headed south again. This car passed us then hit the brakes and did a U-ie. Came right after us. Morgan's men. I turned off the highway and headed due east over back roads. Man, what a drive! One-lane bridges, dirt roads. Zipping through small towns. Whoa, Frankie boy, I had four wheels treading air. It was fan*tastic*. You should've seen it. There must've been twenty cars after us. I managed to lose 'em but I knew we couldn't get very far in that Dodge."

"So you split up?"

He winked. "I knew that part of the state pretty good. Had a couple buddies in the service from Winston-Salem. We'd go hunting and stay in this old abandoned lodge near China Grove. Took some doing but I finally found the place.

"I pulled up outside and made sure it was empty. We sat in the car and I put my arm around her. I pulled her close and told her what I decided—that she should stay here. If her father got his hands on her it'd be all over. He'd send her away for sure. Maybe even brainwash her. Don't laugh. Morgan'd do it. Even his own flesh and blood. She'd stay and I'd lead 'em off a ways. Then . . ."

"Yes?"

"I wait for him."

"For Morgan? What were you going to do?"

"Have it out with him once and for all. One on one, him and me. Allison begged me not to. She knew how dangerous he was. But I didn't care. I knew he'd never leave us alone. He was the devil. He'd follow us forever if I didn't stop him. She begged me to take her with me but I knew I couldn't. She had to stay. It was so clear to me. See, Frank, that's what love is, I think. Not being afraid to make a decision for someone else."

My friend Manko, the rough-hewn philosopher.

"I held her tight and told her not to worry. I told her how there wasn't enough room in my heart for all the love I felt for her. We'd be together again soon."

"Was it safe there, you think?"

"The cabin? Sure. Morgan'd never find it."

"It was in China Grove?"

"Half an hour away. On Badin Lake."

I laughed. "You're kidding me?"

"You know it?"

"Sure I do. I've lived all over the state. It must've been in the woods, on the western shore?"

"Yeah, in the woods."

"That's a pretty place."

"It's *damn* pretty. You know, as I drove off I looked back and I remember thinking how nice it'd be if that was our house and there Allison'd be in the doorway waiting for me to come home from work."

Manko rose and walked to the window. He gazed through his reflection into the night.

"After I left I drove to a state road. There, for everybody to see. Leadin' off the hounds. Here's Manko. Come and get me. I got twenty miles before they caught up with me. Was a roadblock that did it. I drove the car into this ditch and ran. Then I circled around and hid in a grove of trees. I just waited. About a half hour later this black limo shows up."

"Morgan?"

"In person. The police had the car out of the ditch by this time and Morgan comes up and looks inside then walks back toward the limo. All this time, I'm just hiding there, waiting. Finally his bodyguards wandered off.

"That's when I made my move. No sneaking up, no cheap shots. I walked out of the trees toward him. He saw me. He looked shocked for a minute but then he came right at me. I give him credit. He might've called for help. But he didn't, he just ran at me. Screaming, 'Where's my daughter? Where's my daughter?' I dragged him into the woods, away from his men and the cops, and we went at it. Man, what a slugfest! Him and me, rolling in the dirt, opening skin right and left. See this scar? Was his knuckles did that. I paid him back though, Frankie. That was his day to hurt and hurt bad. Finally I got him down and put a choke hold on him. I squeezed and squeezed. I couldn't stop myself. I felt him getting weaker, gasping for breath. I had him. Man, what a feeling!"

Manko touched the window delicately, as if sensing the temperature, then he turned back to me.

"I let him go. I could've finished him. Easy. But I just stood up, left him in the dirt. I laughed at him. A couple of his men came up and grabbed me but the police pulled them off. Morgan and I just stared at each other. I remember thinking how easy it would've been to kill him. That's what I'd been planning to do, Frank. I suppose you figured that out. Trap him and kill him. But the funny thing is, I didn't need to anymore. I knew we'd won. Allison was safe from him. We'd be together, the two of us. We'd beat Thomas Morgan—tycoon, rich son of a bitch, and father of the most beautiful woman on earth."

Silence fell between us. It was nearly midnight and I'd been here for over three hours. I stretched. Manko paced slowly, his face aglow with anticipation. "You know, Frank, a lot of my life hasn't gone the way I wanted it to. Allison's either. But one thing we've got is our love. That makes everything okay."

"A transcendent love."

A ping sounded and I realized that Manko'd touched his cup to mine once again. We emptied them. He looked out the window into the black night. The rain had stopped and a faint moon was evident through the clouds. A distant clock started striking twelve.

A solid rap struck the door, which swung open suddenly. I was startled and stood.

Manko turned calmly, the smile still on his face.

"Evening, Tim," said the man of about sixty. He wore a rumpled brown suit. From behind him several sets of eyes peered at me and Manko.

It rankled me slightly to hear the given name. Manko'd always made it clear that he preferred his nickname and considered the use of Tim or Timothy an insult. But tonight he didn't even notice; he smiled as he shook the man's gray hand.

There was silence for a moment as another man, wearing a pale blue uniform, stepped into the room with a tray, loaded it up with the dirty dishes.

"Enjoy it, Manko?" he asked.

"Ambrosia," he said, lifting a wry eyebrow toward me.

The older man nodded then took a blue-backed document from his suit jacket and opened it. There was a long pause. Then in a solemn southern baritone he read, " 'Timothy Albert Mankowitz, in accordance with sentence pronounced against you pursuant to your conviction for the kidnapping and murder of Allison Kimberly Morgan, I hereby serve upon you this death warrant issued by the governor of the state of North Carolina, to be effected at midnight this day.' "

The warden handed Manko the paper. He and his lawyer had already seen the faxed version from the court and tonight he merely glanced with boredom at the document. In his face I noted none of the stark befuddlement you almost always see in the faces of condemned prisoners as they read the last correspondence they'll ever receive.

"We got the line open to the governor, Tim," the warden drawled, "and he's at his desk. I just talked to him. But I don't think . . . I mean, he probably won't make the call."

"I told you all along," Manko said softly, "I didn't even want those appeals."

The execution operations officer, a thin, business-like man who looked like a feed-and-grain clerk, cuffed Manko's wrists and instructed him to remove his shoes.

The warden motioned me outside and I stepped into the corridor. Unlike the popular conception of a dismal, Gothic death row, this wing of the prison resembled an overly lit Sunday-school hallway. His head leaned close. "Any luck, Father?"

After a moment I lifted my eyes from the shiny lino-leum. "I think so. He told me about a hunting lodge near Badin Lake. Western shore. You know it?"

The warden shook his head. "But we'll have the troop-ers get some dogs over there. Hope it pans out," he added, whispering. "Lord, I hope that."

So ended my grim task on this grim evening.

Prison chaplains always walk the last hundred feet with the condemned but rarely are they enlisted as a last-ditch means to wheedle information out of the pris-oners. I'd consulted my bishop and this mission didn't seem to violate my vows. Still, it was clearly a deceit and one that would trouble me, I suspected, for a long time. Yet it would trouble me less than the thought of young Allison Morgan lying in an unconsecrated grave, whose location Manko adamantly refused to reveal—his ultimate way, he said, of protecting her from her father.

Allison Kimberly Morgan—stalked relentlessly for months after she dumped Manko following their second date. Kidnapped from her bed then driven through four states with the FBI and a hundred troopers in pursuit. And finally . . . finally, when it was clear that Manko's precious plans for a life together in Florida would never happen, knifed to death while—apparently—he held her close and told her how there wasn't enough room in his heart for all the love he felt for her.

Until tonight her parents' only consolation was knowing that she'd died quickly—her abundant blood on the front seat of his Dodge testified to that. Now there was at least the hope they could give her a proper burial, and in doing so offer her a bit of the love that they may—or may not—have denied her in life.

Manko appeared in the hallway, on his feet the disposable paper slippers the condemned wear to the execution chamber. The warden looked at his watch and motioned down the corridor. "You'll go peaceful, won't you, son?"

Manko laughed. He was the only one in the place with serenity in his eyes.

And why not?

He was about to join his own true love. They'd once again be together.

"You like my story, Frank?"

I told him I did. Then he smiled at me in a curious way, an expression that seemed to contain a hint both of forgiveness and of something I can only call the irrepressible Manko challenge. Perhaps, I reflected, it would not be this evening's deceit that would weigh on me so heavily but rather the simple fact that I would never know whether or not Manko was on to me.

But who could tell? He was, as I've said, a born actor.

The warden looked at me. "Father?"

I shook my head. "I'm afraid Manko's going to forgo absolution," I said. "But he'd like me to read him a few psalms."

"Allison," Manko said earnestly, "loves poetry."

I slipped the Bible from my suit pocket and began to read as we started down the corridor, walking side by side.

[SUSAN DUNLAP]

SUSAN DUNLAP COMBINES A WRY, DRY HUMOR
with a perceptive eye to create three distinctly different and
original series. Jill Smith is a Berkeley homicide detective
in eight novels, including the most recent, Time Expired.
Vejay Haskell is an amateur sleuth and meter reader in
three novels, including The Last Annual Slugfest. Private
eye Kiernan O'Shaughnessy uses her background in forensic
pathology and gymnastics to solve complex, difficult, and
deceptive cases in Pious Deception, Rogue Wave, and
the forthcoming High Fall. Dunlap's novels are remarkable
for their sense of place. She vividly evokes starkly different aspects of California. Though sharply differentiated,
Dunlap's sleuths have in common nontraditional jobs, a
disdain for pretension, and a passion for justice.

Dunlap is a past president of Sisters in Crime and has
been active in Mystery Writers of America. She and her
husband live near Berkeley, California.

Dunlap's glorious sense of humor and her uncanny
knack for capturing the absurdities of life in Berkeley make
"A Contest Fit for a Queen" a wonderful Valentine delight.

A Contest Fit
for a Queen

You can always sunbathe in Berkeley on Washington's
birthday, they say. Maybe so. But it was already Valentine's Day and it had been raining since New Year's. I
was willing to believe we'd be able to bathe in another week, but odds were it'd be with a cake of
Ivory.

Tonight, the thermometer was not ten degrees above freezing (polar by our standards). The rain pounded on the portal like a door-to-door salesman. It was a night made for staying home.

Or it would have been if one of the other tenants in Howard's house hadn't booked the living room for his club meeting. A meeting of the South Campus Respect for Reptiles Committee.

"Do they bring the esteemed with them, Howard?"

"Don't ask. But if you're going through the living room keep your shoes on." Howard shook his head. Clearly this was a topic he didn't dare dip into. The corners of his mouth twitched. He wanted to dip. His mouth opened and shut again. He was dying to dip.

I grinned.

He gave up. "It's an emergency meeting for the Reptilians, Jill. Their status in the animal rights union has been challenged. By the Save the Goldfish Committee."

It took me a moment to recall just what it was snakes ate. "May the better vertebrate win." And thinking of the fish, I added, "I suppose it's too late to make a dinner reservation."

But even before I finished the sentence, I knew the answer. You'll never starve in Berkeley. Even on Valentine's Day there is always a restaurant with an empty table for two. But while Howard insists I am his number-one love, number two (this house in which he dwells as chief tenant and lusts to own) is close behind, and he would never abandon its nurturing nooks and cavelike crannies to the Reptilians.

"Better than that!" he said, running his hand around my back, under my arm till his fingers caressed the side of my breast. "I've got an evening so romantic, a night so exotic, so Continental it should have subtitles. The lover's answer," he said, pulling me closer, "to one-stop shopping."

"Aha. Dinner in bed, you mean."

"And with a new tradition I think you're going to like."

The California-king-sized bed was covered with a spotted madras spread (we'd done dinners here before) and dotted with white cardboard cartons (Styrofoam is outlawed in Berkeley), and plastic plates from freezer dinners. Howard had bought the bed for its mission-style headboard with the four-inch-wide runner at the top—the perfect size for coffee mugs and wineglasses. (By now we had a number of spotted pillowcases.)

"Happy Valentine's Day," Howard said, uncorking the chardonnay. (White goes better with the pillow-cases.)

"And to you," I said, saluting him with a spring roll.

From downstairs came a muffled shout. I bit into the spring roll.

"Valentine's Day is a traditional sort of holiday—"

"I thought it had been created by the card companies—"

"So I propose a tradition of our own. A tradition suitable for two esteemed police detectives, like us."

"Here on the bed?"

He leaned forward, puckered his lips, opened his mouth, sucked in the rest of my spring roll. When he'd swallowed, he said, "Valentine's Day collars. Other traditions come later. What's your most memorable Valentine's collar?"

I laughed. Only Howard would come up with a tradition celebrating the best Valentine's Day arrests. I could have negotiated a prize, but as everyone in coupledom knows, no object is to be as cherished as the hard-won right to lord it over one's mate. The Collar Queen, I liked the prospect of that. "In homicide or patrol?"

"Either one. In your entire time on the force." Howard reached for another spring roll.

I could see the lay of the land here. "Oh no! You first."

"Don't you have a collar?"

"Yeah, I've got one, from when I was on patrol. But I'm no fool, Howard, and if I let you sit and listen for twenty minutes, by the time I finish talking there won't be any food left. You start."

From downstairs came a loud hiss. I preferred to think of it as a delegate's indication of dissent. As opposed to his subject's hiss of disgruntlement.

Rain splatted against the window and the wind scraped the glass with a branch of the jacaranda tree. But in here, enclosed by the warm green walls and the crisp white moldings, with the smells of Asian spices mingling with the aroma of wine, the whir of the space heater, it was turning out to be an okay Valentine's. Howard shepherded half the rice onto his plate, added a heaping scoop of vegetable satay, four chicken brochettes, and wad of eggplant with black beans. He crossed his long legs, propped his plate on one knee, and began. "This is from patrol, too. I'd already been working detective detail, but I'd rotated back onto patrol for a while. The call was on a natural death of an LOL. The LOL was in her seventies, but she looked to have been old for that age, not one of the Gray Panthers who'd stomp a mugger into the ground and walk off shaking the dust from her Birkenstocks; no, she was an LOL."

I nodded, leaning against the headboard, balancing my satay on my thigh as I reached for my wineglass.

"She lived in a four-room cottage, west of San Pablo. Hurricane fencing around the perimeter, big dog in the yard. House a square, four identical-size rooms."

"Like a sandwich you cut into quarters?"

"Right. Neighbors heard the dog barking and got concerned that he hadn't been out in that yard all day. Valentine, that was the dog's name, because he had a white heart on his rump."

I smiled. That bit of whimsy made me like the old lady. I could tell it grabbed Howard, too. "How did she die?"

"Heart attack, I think. Certainly natural cause. And fast, I think. The TV was still on. She was sitting in front of it on one of those maroon-flowered antique sofas with the buttons covered in the same material, and all of it looking too hard to sit on. Makes you understand the energy of the Victorian age."

"Had to keep moving, huh?"

"Oh no!" One of the Reptilians shouted downstairs. I glanced at the foot of the door. There wasn't a quarter of an inch between it and the jamb.

Picking up his pace and volume, Howard said, "Not much in her living room—the sofa, one chair, two end tables, a bookcase, a couple pictures on the wall, but no photos or knickknacks strewn around like you find with most LOLs."

"Maybe she didn't have anyone."

"No relatives, right. Nothing unnecessary in the kitchen or the bedroom. Looked like she lived frugally, but not desperately, like a lot of people on Social Security. She was tidy, and she knew what she liked: that Victorian stuff. If someone had told me it was *eighteen* ninety-four instead of nineteen ninety-four there wouldn't have been much to contradict it. Even her books tended to be things like Jane Austen."

I finished my satay and glanced at the carton. Despite his monologue, Howard had managed to down his portion and was eyeing the same carton. I served. "So that's it? *That's* your most interesting case?"

"Wait. I haven't gotten to the interesting part: the fourth room. You've got these three austere, Victorian-lady rooms, then the fourth. It was crammed, floor to ceiling, with the oddest collection of stuff I've come across. Golf clubs, electric trains, stamp collection, a set of something like twenty-seven drill bits, leather suitcases, a black plastic stool in which the middle of the cushion comes out, the scroungiest-looking stuffed pheasant—thing was missing an eye and all its tail feathers—with a Valentine's heart on a ribbon around its neck."

"Must have been easy to shoot."

Ignoring that, Howard went on. "Place was so full you couldn't even see the windows."

"Her late husband's things?"

"Nope, maiden lady. Neighbors said they'd never seen a male visitor. Besides, some of the stuff was almost new, a lot never used. It wasn't like mementos from the love of her life who died in nineteen forty-nine or 'fifty-two."

I put down my second spring roll. "It's all guy stuff, except the stool and that's just weird. Things like the drill bits; you'll find women who've got them, but—"

"Yeah, you can picture the owner: one of those guys who *thinks* he's going to be a handyman and his wife or kids give him the complete deluxe home handyman's set. And in this case I'd bet my last spring roll those bits had never been out of the box."

"Over by the door," a Reptilian shouted downstairs.

Howard tensed, ready to charge downstairs and defend his second love from invasion.

I put a hand on his arm. "Berkeley, the city of diversity, should create a snake run, like the dog park. It'd only take a narrow piece of land. Owners'd put their cobras and pythons on little alligator leashes to exercise them. And the best part for the sedentary snake lover is they wouldn't even have to be in good shape for the walk. Not like our burglar who had to hoist a massage chair, an arched backbend bench the size of a sofa, and enough photography equipment to furnish a studio."

"Jill, how'd you—"

I put up a hand to quiet him. The thought was tiptoeing across the back of my head, just out of reach. Something about his story . . . somethi—"The fucking pheasant!"

"What?"

"That's what his wife called it." I put down my glass. "Howard, I remember that pheasant. I took the call on the burglary it came from. On Linden Terrace. It was just an ordinary case; I wouldn't remember it at all— it must have been six or seven years ago—but the guy insisted on describing his missing pheasant. Seems it was the first thing he ever shot, and in honor of that he gave it to his wife for Valentine's Day back when they were engaged."

"She married him anyway, huh?" He dumped the satay on his rice.

"For better or worse. He even showed me a picture of it, with the red ribbon and the heart. A velvet heart with lace around it like you'd find on a box of candy."

"Probably where it came from. Guy probably gobbled the chocolates while he was waiting for the pheasant to fly." For Howard, the department's sting king, an uneven match like rifle versus wing is certainly not sport.

The warm glow of closed cases beckoned. But it had been years since that burglary. "I suppose there was no reason to confiscate pheasant and company from the old lady's house."

"Hardly. It'd've filled half the evidence room. But the pheasant, I think the neighbor took it, strange as it is to think there could be two human beings who'd want it." Howard fingered the last spring roll and grinned. "So my LOL, Rosamin Minton, was an LOF."

"Little Old Fence?"

"A fence with the worst taste in town. Or a fence who'd moved the electronics and jewelry but couldn't get rid of the rest of the junk." Howard took a bite of satay and nodded. "Still, not a bad Valentine's entry. Not so easy to top. So, Jill, what's your Valentine collar?"

I took a swallow of wine, leaned back against the headboard, adjusted the pillow—that little ledge is great for cups and glasses, but it does nothing for my neck. I picked up my wineglass, looked Howard in the eye, and grinned back at him. "You could have won by a mile, Howard. But not now. Your entry was good, a real competitive racer of a case. I was in bad shape . . . until . . . you reminded me." I lifted my wineglass in salute. I don't often win these contests with Howard—nobody does—but when I do I make the most of it. The robes of the Collar Queen were going to hang quite nicely off my shoulders. "The pheasant burglary took place, Howard, on Valentine's Day!"

Howard gave me a tentative salute. He could see he was being edged out, but he wasn't throwing in the towel yet.

"Howard, the RP, what was his name? I remember thinking it was a funny name for a reporting party—Robert Parton, that's it! He was just outraged that his bird—"

"Flew the coop on Valentine's?"

"Right. His wife did point out that it was on the mantel where he put it for the occasion. A thief could hardly miss it. Then Parton was enraged about the loss of a stained-glass lamp he'd made himself—"

"Lamp with a band of chartreuse hearts at the edge of the shade?"

"Could there be two?" I grinned wider. The lamp had propelled me to neck and neck with Howard. "And Parton was really pissed that the thief had used a couple of his old jackets to wrap the things in. His wife kept reminding him that the stereo and the TV were still there and they were worth plenty more than a bag of used clothes, a lamp, and a moldy bird. But Parton wasn't buying that. He ranted at her, at me, and even at the Chihuahua, for God's sake. Like it should have stood off the thief, single-pawedly!"

"That's it? Your whole Valentine offering? You lose! The answer's obvious. The wife did it?"

"Au contraire, my dear Howard. Mrs. Parton was out with Robert at the time of the burglary. And she's hardly the type to hire a few unemployed mafiosi. And more to the point, there were two other burglaries that Valentine's night. And the next year another three with the same MO. And three the following year, when we were half expecting them and still couldn't prevent them. Drove us crazy. And then they stopped."

"And never started again?" He meant did the thief get pulled in for something else or merely move out of town?

"Nope, nothing more. Burglary detail was keeping an eye out. Simpson there really went over those cases, but he couldn't find a link. The Bensquis were in their twenties, the Partons near forty, the Yamamotos in their late sixties. Victims were a bakery chef, an engineer, two artists, one nurse, one doctor, an airline pilot, a copy editor, a short-haul truck driver. There was no connection through their jobs, churches, hobbies, clubs—zilch. They were all in different parts of the city. Some victims had standing Valentine's plans, some went out to dinner on the spur of the moment, one couple just went out for a walk, and bingo! their darkroom was cleaned out! No prints, no suspicious characters, no vans or trucks loitering out front. Stuff never turned up in pawn shops, flea markets, or any of the normal places. Not lead one. And Parton, the doctor . . . well, if he made that number of follow-up calls to any patient, they'd die of shock." I leaned back, took a long swallow of wine, and said, "It was a very frustrating case—nine disparate couples, burgled of stuff of no particular value, and it all ends up with one little old lady who kept it sealed away from her in a back room! But, Howard, reward comes to the worthy. And thanks to your accidental discovery, you have given me an assist in winning the First

Annual Valentine's Day Collar Contest. Pay homage to the Collar Queen!"

"No you don't! This is a *collar* contest. There was no collar in your case. You, Jill, got nada!"

"Outside! Look outside!" Downstairs doors banged. Howard hesitated, clearly torn between defending his house and his contest.

"It sounds good," I said. "But I'm not using the bathroom till you make sure everyone's accounted for."

Howard headed downstairs and I cleared off the bed the remnants of the first course, preparatory to the more traditional Valentine's Day tradition.

Tomorrow, I'd track down the department's files on the burglaries. No way was Howard going to win!

What I did not track down the next morning—Monday—was Simpson of burglary detail. While Howard and I had been making our bet, Simpson had been flying off to the Bahamas.

What was waiting for me at the station was a batch of in-custodys held over the weekend. When you bungle your burgling Friday night, the city gives you free lodging all weekend. By Monday morning you are a sorry, and surly, soul. I didn't finish running the checks on the in-custodys before detective's morning meeting, and afterward ended up transporting one of the surly and sorry to San Mateo County, an hour away. In the afternoon I had a court appearance on an old 217 (assault with intent to murder) and I didn't get around to the late Rosamin Minton's neighbor till after five o'clock.

The Minton house was just as Howard described it: a square clapboard box behind a hurricane fence, in a neighborhood where shabby didn't stand out. Two scraggly trees now stood watch over the walkway, obviously the work of a newer, if not more horticulturally talented, tenant. The present neighbor, the nephew of the pheasant taker, hadn't known Rosamin Minton. He handed over the contraband bird without question. If he could have asked for a sworn statement that I'd tell no one it had nested in his house, he would have. Clearly, he was too embarrassed to ask why, after all these years, it was needed by the officialdom of his city.

I picked up the thing gingerly. Taxidermy, apparently, is not forever. The bird was not just eyeless and sans tail feathers, there were bare spots on its back, and it looked like it had used one wing to fight off its assailant. Even the lace-and-velvet heart looked like it had been slobbered over.

Robert Parton stared at the deceased bird with an expression of horror that matched my own. "It's been chewed! How could anyone—"

"No accounting for taste, Dr. Parton."

He brushed its moldy feathers. "Still, you found it! After all these years! Monica, it's still got the heart I got for you."

Monica Parton looked even more appalled. A woman of some taste, I felt.

Only the Chihuahua found merit in the miserable memento. He was running from one side of the spacious living room to the other, bouncing and lowing like he'd treed the foul himself.

"Where did you find it?" Parton asked.

"The other side of Berkeley."

"Did you get my lamp? Stained glass; took me six months to make. And my jackets?"

"Robert," Monica said, "the Salvation Army wouldn't even want those clothes. Be glad you've got your bird."

Before they could continue the sartorial debate, I opened my pad and read off a list of the other Valentine's Day victims. "Do you recognize any of these names?"

"No," Robert said, still holding the pheasant overhead, away from its other admirer.

"Mrs. Parton?"

She looked thoughtful, as if giving the list more consideration than had her booty-enthralled husband. But in the end she shook her head.

"Dr. Parton, I know how concerned you were about this burglary. In the five years since then, have you come across anything connected to it? Any motive?"

Both shook their heads. And as I left he was beaming at the bird and she was still shaking her head.

It was the next day before I had time to go over the old Valentine burglary files thoroughly enough to make a list of the losses. The stool with the hole belonged to Jason Peabody.

The Peabody house was one of those two-bedroom stucco jobs with one room over the garage. I'd been in enough of them to know that the living room would be too small for an eight-by-ten rug. The whole Peabody house could have fitted in the Partons' living room. It was just before noon when I rang the Peabody bell. And a minute or two after when the door opened.

"Mrs. Peabody? I'm Detective Smith." I held out my shield.

"Yes?" She had that you've-found-me-out look we on the force see so often that we mistake it for a greeting. "Sorry it took me so long. I needed to put Spot in the back room. Come on in."

A leather couch, matching overstuffed chair, and a coffee table made for a normal-sized room pretty much filled the space. The television sat atop the built-in bookcase, blocking the window. The dining room, too, was a space that could not accommodate one more fork or candlestick, much less a chair. I almost felt guilty as I said, "I have good news. We've found the black plastic stool that was taken in your burglary, the one with the cushion that pulls out to create a hole in the middle."

"Jason's toilet-seat chair." If she was pleased she was hiding it well.

"Your husband is incapacitated?"

She laughed uncomfortably. "No. No. When you take the center out, the chair looks like a toilet seat, a padded black plastic toilet seat."

"But it's not?"

"Oh, no. I should make you guess what it's for." She almost smiled before she recalled to whom she was speaking. I've seen that reaction often enough, too. "Jason kept the stool right there." She pointed to the side of the fireplace, next to the bookcase with the television on it.

The stool was eighteen inches square. With it in place, the Peabodys would have had to inch between it and the coffee table. "What is it?"

"A headstand stool."

Even in Berkeley . . .

"You know, for people who want to do headstands but don't want all their weight on their heads." She was eyeing my reaction, almost smiling. "They stick their heads through the hole, like they're ready to flush them." She swallowed a laugh. "Then they hang onto the legs and kick up. Jason's tall and thin. He always looked kind of like a fern in the wind with his feet waving back and forth by the mantel as he tried to keep his balance." Now she was laughing. "And the TV; it's a miracle it survived."

On duty, we are not encouraged to join in an RP's merriment, lest they later forget, or regret, theirs and become outraged about ours. With some difficulty, I waited for her to stop and said, "One of the other items you lost was a backbend bench."

She glanced at the tiny room. "Oh, jeez, you didn't find that, too, did you?"

I was going to give her the standard "Not yet, but we're still looking," but clearly that was not what she wanted to hear. "No."

She brightened. "Nor the massage chair, or the statue of Shiva?"

"Not yet." I would have noticed a leather recliner and a three-foot-tall image of an Indian god of destruction.

"Well, officer, thanks for all your effort. Who would have thought you'd still be working this case after all these years. We appreciate it. But we'll certainly understand if Jason's stuff doesn't turn up. To tell you the truth, he's gone on to other interests. I doubt he'd attempt a headstand now, even if he had the stool."

"And you'd be hard-pressed to make room for the massage chair, or even the Shiva."

It was a moment before she smiled, shrugged and agreed. But that moment said it all.

The next three victims, or wives of the bereft of golf clubs, ratty chairs, garden equipment, books of stamps barely used, aged racing bicycles, aged skis, enough exercise equipment to fill the YMCA, had clearly been warned. Their performances were not worthy of Berkeley Rep., but they'd have made the cut in many little theaters. They were delighted at our discovery, they assured me. Their husbands would be thrilled. They thanked me, thanked the burglary detail, the Berkeley Police Department, and the entire Berkeley criminal community that hadn't gotten around to fencing their conjugal wares.

I didn't believe a word of it.

Esme Olsen, a sturdy gray-haired woman nearer to seventy than sixty, looked as if my knock had jerked her out of another dimension. I found her in her basement folding gold foil carefully along the edges of a piece of teal glass cut in the shape of a tulip leaf. The sketch of the stained-glass panel she was working on was pinned

to the wall above the glass cutter and extra foil rolls at
the far end of the workbench. Irregularly shaped pieces
of glass—red, yellow, green, and three shades of purple—filled the rest of the bench and larger sheets stood
in specially made cases behind her. On the top of the
cabinet was a photo—probably fifteen years old—of her
and a white-haired man as happy-go-lucky as she was
intense.

It was almost a formality when I asked, "How would
you feel if I told you we're on the trail of your husband's
tools: the drill bits, the straight saw, the jigsaw, the
shag-toothed saws, the clamps, the hammers, and all?"

"Oh, my God! You're not bringing that junk back
here?" No Berkeley Rep. role for her! And from the
horror that lined her face as she looked around her
stained-glass studio, I could picture the room in its previous incarnation.

"Your husband didn't do much work in this shop, did
he?" It was a hunch, but a solid one.

"Work? No. Oh, he had intentions. He'd get on a
kick about building bookcases. At one time we had
six of them upstairs, more cases than books, I told him.
Fortunately, they came apart before he could find things
to fill them with. Then he thought he'd build a gazebo.
He had wood stacked in the yard for a year, and kin-
dling enough down here to cook the entire house. Then
there was the hope chest, or more accurately hope*less*
chest. For a while he bought used tables and chairs
and thought he was going to refinish them. See, he
liked the *idea* of woodworking better than the preci-
sion of it."

Some police officers never get suspects so naively
open with the police. But I've dealt with enough artists in Berkeley to know that the shift from their total
absorption in the visual takes a while, and as they cross
the bridge from right brain to left brain, good sense
can stumble over the railing. "So you gave yourself a

Valentine's Day gift. You arranged for his stuff to be 'stolen.' "

She didn't answer. She'd zoomed to the other end of the bridge. And what she found there horrified her. I wouldn't have been surprised if this was the first time it truly struck her that she'd committed a crime.

The eight coconspirators had warned each other; why hadn't they told Esme Olsen? It made me a whole lot less sympathetic to them. I wanted to reassure Esme Olsen, but I couldn't do that until she answered the questions everyone who'd worked the case had. How did the nine conspirators know each other? We'd been over every possible connection between them. Where did they meet to conspire? Did they get together for afternoon tea and complaints, or drive to bars to map out their burglaries? And Rosamin Minton, how had she come to have the loot stashed at her house? "The police department takes a very dim view of false reporting."

Esme Olsen took a step back and actually looked even smaller than she was. "I didn't mean to get the police involved, honestly, Officer. I thought Harry would have left dealing with the police to me. I thought I'd just *tell* him I reported his stuff missing."

"Give me the names of the other women you planned this with."

She took another step back.

"Ms. Olsen, you have broken the law. The police department has spent tens of hours investigating. We've had patrol officers, sergeants, and inspectors on this case. This is a serious matter. The names . . . ?"

She looked tinier, paler, older than at any moment since I arrived. In a small voice, she said, "I don't know."

"You planned an elaborate heist that took place over several years, Valentine's Day after Valentine's Day, and you're telling me you don't know the names of your coconspirators?"

"Yes." For an instant I thought she was going to explain that. Then she shut her mouth tight, like a little kid who'd rather be sent to her room than rat on her friends.

Friends who didn't deserve her sacrifice. "I'm afraid I'm going to have to take you to the station."

Her face scrunched in panic, but her question was not what I would have expected. "How long will that take?"

"Till your lawyer bails you out, Mrs. Olsen."

Her face fell. She really did look horrified. I wondered how long she had been hidden away down here, away from the realities of society.

"I've got to be back by quarter to four," she insisted plaintively. "I've got an appointment at the vet at four."

I'd seen everything from Airedales to Chihuahuas today. I realized now that this was the first house I'd visited where I hadn't been greeted by a dog. I hadn't even heard one barking in a back room. "I didn't see a dog?"

"When he's healthy he'll greet you at the gate. He's sick. On antibiotics. Oh, the vet says he'll be fine; and I believe him. I'm probably worrying for nothing, but my old dog died suddenly two years ago and I just don't want to take any chances now."

Now it all fell into place. I loved the idea of nine average Berkeley women who'd taken their spousal clutter into their own hands. A little service for each other. Personalized burglaries—we go to the address provided and steal only what you don't want. No wonder the televisions and compact disks, computers and diamond rings had been untouched while the wily "thieves" made off with aged hacksaws and headstand stools. Now I realized why her friends hadn't warned her. They hadn't seen her today. I smiled. "You weren't lying about not knowing their last names, were you?"

"Oh no. I wouldn't lie to the police."

"You all met at the dog run, right? And your dog was too sick to go out today."

She nodded.

"You could tell me the name of every one of their dogs, right, but you don't know their owners' names?" I knew enough about dog walking to understand that phenomena. By now, after years in the conspiracy, Esme Olsen might be able to call the humans by their first name, but she wouldn't have a clue about last names. "You can skip the women, just tell me what the dogs were called."

She looked puzzled, but so relieved she didn't question my demand. "Let me see, Lucy is the black Lab, and Sacha's the poodle. Then there's Emmet the yellow Lab pup, and Emily, she's mostly Tibetan terrier. And Hannah, the basset, and Sierra, he's a Chihuahua, and—wait a minute—oh, yes, MacTavish, the Scotty."

"And Val is your dog?"

She smiled before she realized she'd exposed her connection to Rosamin Minton.

Then she took me upstairs to see the whiskered brown mongrel with the white heart on his rump. He was a dog definitely on the mend.

"You went to a lot of trouble planning the burglaries. Why didn't you give the stuff to the Salvation Army?"

"Couldn't. That's where Harry shopped for the furniture to refinish. We never thought we'd be endangering Rosamin. She swore she didn't need that extra room. And she *did* need the twenty dollars a month we each gave her. And, Officer, it really did comfort her to know one of us would take Val when she died."

I smiled at her. We were still in the shadow of Valentine's Day, when acts of love are expected. And, I had to admit, there were a few items of Howard's for which I'd have hired Esme and colleagues. For his tenant's snake I'd have given them a bonus. Besides, the city wouldn't want to look ridiculous in court.

There'd be some paperwork and formalities with this case later. And after that I'd accept Howard's concession in the First Annual Collar Contest. But for now, I scratched Val gently behind one floppy ear, said, "Okay, Val, I'll leave you your mistress. Consider this your Valentine's gift," and smiled magnanimously.

Because, after all, magnanimity is a fitting quality for a queen.

[CAROLYN G. HART]

CAROLYN G. HART WRITES TWO SERIES. THE LIGHT-
hearted Death on Demand series features the detective duo
of Annie Laurance Darling and her husband, Max. Annie
and Max discover that murder isn't confined to the shelves
of Annie's mystery bookstore. The eight Death on Demand
titles include Agatha and Anthony Winner Something
Wicked, Anthony Winner Honeymoon with Murder,
and Macavity Winner A Little Class on Murder. Hart's
ninth Annie and Max, Mint Julep Murder, will be
published in September. Hart's Henrie O series features
Henrietta O'Dwyer "Henrie O" Collins, a retired news-
paperwoman with a zest for life and a talent for trouble.
Henrie O appears in Dead Man's Island, an Agatha
Winner, and in Scandal in Fair Haven.

Hart is a past president of Sisters in Crime and a past
national director of Mystery Writers of America. She lives
in Oklahoma City with her husband, Phil.

In "Out of the Ashes," Henrie O smooths the path of
young love by investigating an old crime.

Out of the Ashes

Don Brown, my favorite homicide detective, lounged
against the kitchen counter, watching me with an odd
expression.

"I never think of you as a cookie maker, Henrie
O."

I squeezed out pink icing to make the final curve of
the *e* on a heart-shaped sugar cookie. I tilted my head.
The inscription—*Love*—was a bit uneven but readable.
"Don't be chauvinist, Don."

His face squeezed in thought. "Yeah. You're right. Sorry."

I let it drop, though I could have ragged on him a bit more. No, after almost fifty years of newspapering and a second career in teaching, I don't fit the stereotype of a dear little grandma whipping up goodies. But I am a grandmother and I do enjoy cooking, although it's definitely not one of my talents—I paused to swipe up some icing that had overshot its mark—but I resent pigeonholing. I like making cookies, hammering nails, outwitting malefactors—don't try to put me in a mold. Anybody's mold.

I studied the last two cookies on the sheet of waxed paper, nodded, and squeezed out a capital *E* on the first. This would be Emily's cookie. Dear Emily. My daughter. God's greatest gift to me. Then I traced a *D* on the last cookie. I folded a napkin, put the cookie on it, and handed it to Don.

"Valentine's Day." Don's tone was morose. He stared at the cookie, the skin of his face stretched tight over the bones.

Don isn't the kind of guy who attracts attention. He's average height and slender, with a carefully blank, unresponsive face, nondescript sandy hair, and an even, uninflected voice. It's easy to miss the sharp intelligence in his weary blue eyes, the dry, wry curve of his mouth, the athletic wiriness of his build.

And something was terribly wrong with my young friend this gray February afternoon.

I got down two mugs, poured coffee, and gestured to the kitchen table.

Don joined me. But he didn't pick up the mug, and he put the heart-shaped cookie down on the table, untasted.

"Henrie O . . ." He looked at me with misery in his eyes.

Now it was my turn to make judgments, but I had no

chauvinist intent. The sexes do differ. Markedly. And it's damn hard for men to admit to emotion.

"Tell me what's wrong, Don." My voice was much gentler than usual. I am customarily cool and acerbic.

But not always.

I reached out and touched his arm.

It was such a young arm. Strong. Lean. With—God willing—so many years yet to live. I silently wished him the best of life—and that includes both passion and pain.

"Everything. Nothing." He gripped the coffee mug. "Hell, a cop shouldn't get married anyway."

"Yes, a cop should. Especially this particular cop." I gave his arm a final squeeze, picked up my own cup. "Any woman with taste would know that."

He didn't manage a smile. If anything, his face was even bleaker. "The hell of it is, she loves me. I know she does. But, damn it . . ." He hunched over the table; his anguished blue eyes clung to my face. "Henrie O, you're a natural when it comes to crime. I swear to God, sometimes I think you can smell it, pick it up like a cat sniffing a mouse."

I lifted an eyebrow. "What does crime have to do with love?"

He told me.

You don't see many happy faces at the courthouse. You're on reality time here, much as at a hospital. Pain, suffering, and despair mark these faces. I don't know whether it's worse in summer or winter. Now the marble floors were mud scuffed and the smell of wet wool mingled with the occasional whiff of forbidden cigarettes.

The DA's offices were on the third floor. I found the cubbyhole assigned to Assistant DA Kerry O'Keefe at the end of the hall.

I knocked.

"Come in."

She was on the telephone, a slender, quite lovely young woman with blond hair and an expressive, intelligent face. She gestured for me to take a seat.

" . . . arraignment is scheduled at ten A.M. tomorrow. We'd be willing to reduce the charge to . . ." Her clear voice was clipped and businesslike.

I sat in the hard wooden chair that faced Assistant DA Kerry O'Keefe's gray metal desk and looked at the young woman who was breaking Don's heart.

Kerry O'Keefe wasn't knockdown gorgeous, but hers was a face with a haunting, unforgettable quality, camellia-smooth skin, almond-shaped hazel eyes flecked with gold, a vulnerable mouth, a determined chin.

" . . . see you in court, Counselor." She hung up, looked at me politely. "May I help you?"

"I'm Henrietta O'Dwyer Collins. A friend of Don Brown's."

She had a sudden quick intake of breath, those gold-flecked eyes widened, then her face closed in, smooth, impervious. "I'm terribly busy this morning. I'm due in court." She reached for a brown manila file, grabbed it.

"How do you weigh evidence, Miss O'Keefe?"

She pushed back her chair and stood, holding the folder against her as if it were a shield. Anger and misery flickered in those remarkable, pain-filled eyes. "Evidence? In one of my cases?"

I stood, too. "Yes, Miss O'Keefe."

The tension eased out of her body. "I don't understand . . . why are you asking me about my work? What does that have to do with Don?"

"Everything."

She shook her head and her honey-bright hair swayed. "I study the record. I look at the physical evidence. I interview witnesses."

"When you interview witnesses, what are you looking for?"

"The truth, of course." Her tone was impatient.

"Yes, of course. The truth. Tell me, Miss O'Keefe, how do you know whether people are telling you the truth?"

She wasn't quite patronizing. "It comes with experience. You can pick up when people are lying. Lots of little tip-offs. They sound too earnest, look at you too directly. Sometimes they'll talk too fast. Sometimes they won't look at you at all."

I smiled. "It takes a lot of intuition."

She tucked the folder under one arm, ready to walk out, terminate this interview. "You can call it that."

"You have to have confidence in your own instincts."

Her eyes blazed with sudden understanding. "Oh. So that's why you're here. Look, I told Don, it's no use. No use at all."

"Please, Miss O'Keefe. Let me finish."

She took a step toward the door, then stopped and stood quite still.

Was it respect for my age? Or was it deeper, a pain-filled heart's desperate reluctance to make an irrevocable decision?

I made my bid. "Don believes in your instinct. He wants you to look at what happened one more time, one last time. And this time, listen to your heart. This time, begin with the premise that Jack O'Keefe was innocent."

"The premise . . ." She began to tremble.

I knew then that no matter how much Kerry had suffered, she'd never questioned the facts as they had appeared—even though every fiber of her being rebelled at acceptance.

Her eyes bored into mine. "But there's no reason to think he was innocent. Is there?"

"Yes. Oh, yes. You, Kerry. Your heart says your dad couldn't have done it. Just as your heart says Don is the man for you. Come on, Kerry, give your heart a chance."

*   *   *

The icy wind moaning through the leafless trees sounded like a lost child's cry.

Kerry O'Keefe stood with her hands jammed deep into the pockets of her navy cashmere coat. She didn't wear a scarf. Her cheeks were touched with pink from the cold. She stared at the ruins, her face empty, her eyes as dark and desolate as the blackened remnants of the chimney.

She spoke rapidly, without emotion, as if this were just one more report of one more crime. "The fire was called in at ten past midnight on Friday, January fourteenth, nineteen eighty-three. A three-alarm blaze. It took almost two hours to put it out. The firemen didn't find the bodies until almost dawn. They had to let it cool. Three bodies. My father, Jack O'Keefe. My mother, Elizabeth. My sister, Jenny." She half turned, pointed toward a well-kept two-story Victorian frame house clearly visible through the bare trees. "My grandparents live there. They thought we were all dead, that they hadn't found my body yet." She shivered. "I'd spent the night with a friend. I came home about nine. I saw our house— smoke was still curling up like mist from a river—and I ran up the drive to my grandparents' and burst in. My grandmother screamed. She thought I was a ghost." Kerry once again faced the ruins. "I didn't know what had happened until after the day after the funeral. That's when the story came out in the newspaper saying the fire was set with gasoline and autopsies revealed traces of a narcotic in the bodies." She saw my surprise. "Yes. Percodan. A prescription for my grandmother. For back pain. They said Dad must have dropped by her house, taken the stuff that day. Only a few tablets were missing. But it wouldn't take many. It's very strong stuff. That was in the newspaper. But the rest of it never came out in the paper."

I waited.

She faced me. "But people knew. Everybody knew. The bank examiners found two hundred thousand dollars gone. Dummy loans. Made by my dad."

Kelly turned up the collar of her coat, hunkered down for protection against the bite of the wind. Her voice was as cold as the wind. "I heard my parents quarreling that night. Just before I left. Mother's voice was—I don't know—stern. Determined. She said, 'Jack, you've got to face up to it. You don't have any choice.' And Daddy"— her voice wavered—"Daddy sounded so, so beaten. He said, 'Liz, how can I? How can I?' "

Kelly crossed her arms tight against her body. "I can still hear his voice. But what I don't understand, what I'll never understand, is how could he do it? How could he kill Mother and Jenny?" Her tormented eyes swept from the ruins to my face. "And me. I would have died, too. He must have thought I was in my room, asleep. It was just a last-minute thing, the call from Janet. She asked me to spend the night. I ran down to the kitchen and asked Mother and she said okay and I hurried up to my room and packed my overnight bag and went down the back stairs. Janet picked me up in the alley."

I was familiar with these facts. Don had brought me the fire marshal's report, a copy of the autopsy reports, and the file from homicide.

Because, of course, it was not simply arson, it was murder.

The official conclusion: The bank examiner discovered the dummy loans. Jack O'Keefe, facing disgrace and probable prosecution, drugged his family, waited until they were asleep, then splashed gasoline throughout the downstairs portion of the house. He lighted a candle, wrapped a string around its base. The string led from the kitchen through the dining room to velvet drapes that were also doused with gasoline. O'Keefe hurried upstairs and went to bed. There were traces of Percodan in his body, too.

Was he already groggy when he slipped beneath the covers?

Was he asleep before the blaze erupted in sudden, demonic fury?

Although his body and the bodies of his wife and daughter were badly burned, the cause of death was asphyxiation from the smoke that roiled up from the blaze below.

Now, twelve years later, wind and rain and sun had scoured the ruins, but thick deposits of carbon on the remains of the chimney still glistened purplish black in the pale winter sun.

Despite the tumbled bricks, the occasional poked-out timber, I could discern the outline of the house, imagine the broad sweep of the porch and the jaunty bay windows, estimate the size of the living room and dining room, glimpse a bone-white remnant of the sink in the kitchen.

I looked thoughtfully toward the substantial Victorian house that belonged to Jack O'Keefe's parents.

The ruins would be visible from every window on this side of the house.

I pointed to my left. I could see the roof of a house over a brick wall. "Who lives over there?"

"Uncle Robert and Aunt Louise. My dad's brother." There was no warmth, no fondness in Kerry's voice. "They built the wall a few months after the fire."

I wasn't sure I would blame them for that. Who would want an ever-present reminder of that violent night?

Who did want an ever-present reminder?

"Why are the ruins still here?"

Kerry's face was icily determined. "Grandmother. Then me."

"Why?"

"I don't know what Grandmother thinks. I don't believe anyone's ever known. I remember her, before the fire, as bright and cheerful and fluttery. But she's like a ceramic piece. The color is all on the surface, a surface you can't get past. All I know is she wouldn't let anyone touch any of it—not a piece, not a scrap."

"Didn't the neighbors complain? Don't they now?"

"No. Oh, they might not like it. I suppose a lot of them don't. But it's been so many years now, most people don't even notice. You see, we're the O'Keefes. *The* family in Derry Hills. For good or bad. The richest. The most powerful. Even though Grandad sold the bank a few months after—after the fire. But Uncle Robert's on the board of directors. And so am I. Uncle Robert's president of the country club. Last year he headed up the community drive. And no one would want to talk to Grandmother about the ruins."

"You said the ruins stood because of your grandmother—and then because of you."

"Uncle Robert was the executor of the estate. He did what Grandmother told him to do."

But he built a wall. Brown winter tendrils of ivy clung to it.

I glanced from that wall to Kerry's face. "You own the property now. Why don't you have the ruins knocked down?"

Her pale face was stubborn. "Then it would be green and grassy—and I might forget."

Abruptly, Kerry turned, headed back toward my car.

I caught up with her.

She slammed into the passenger seat.

I slid behind the wheel.

She glared at me. "This is stupid. Stupid. And it hurts too much. Because I thought my dad loved me, loved all of us. He was my best friend, the greatest guy I ever knew. When he laughed . . ." She swallowed harshly and stared out the winter-grimed window of the car, stared out at ruins and heartbreak. When she spoke again, her voice was dull, exhausted. "I was wrong about my dad. So how can I ever believe in . . . anything."

That was why she'd told Don she wouldn't marry him. That was why these grim ruins stood.

If Jack O'Keefe was not the man she'd believed in, how could Kerry be sure about Don?

About any man?

About any person?

Ever.

Her face streaked with tears, Kerry grabbed the door handle.

"Wait, Kerry. Answer one question. Just one. You spent the night at Janet's. How did you sleep?"

She struggled to control her ragged breathing. "Oh God, I hate to remember. I don't want to remember! We were having so much fun. We stayed up all night and talked and talked and talked. That's why I slept so late—"

"You stayed up all night?"

She heard the excitement in my voice.

"Yes. You know how it is—"

"You weren't tired? Fighting off sleep?"

Her mouth opened. Her eyes widened. She turned, stared at me. But she wasn't seeing me. "Oh, my God. If I wasn't sleepy—because I should have been, shouldn't I? If Daddy intended for all of us to die, I should have been drugged, too! The police believed Daddy took the Percodan from Grandmother's house and ground it up and put it in our drinks at dinner." Then the eagerness seeped out of her face. Her lips quivered again. "But it could have happened after dinner."

"How?"

"Cocoa." Her lips quivered. "It must have been in the cocoa."

"Cocoa?"

"It was a family thing. In the winter, we always had cocoa at night, sitting around the fire in the living room." She glanced toward the chimney, a sentinel against the pale blue winter sky.

"But you weren't there that night. And, if your dad planned for his family to die, it would be very important to him to be sure you drank the cocoa. But, if he was innocent and you didn't come downstairs for cocoa, it wouldn't matter, would it? He'd simply think you'd already gone to bed. Am I right?"

Kerry's hands came together tight and hard.

She wasn't listening.

She was thinking.

I gave her a moment, then I laid it out.

"If Jack O'Keefe didn't doctor the cocoa, someone else did."

Her eyes locked with mine.

Then I looked back at the ruins of the house, the once-substantial, old, and comfortable house. In a little town, back doors often aren't locked.

It could have been even easier, someone dropping by that winter afternoon. I envisioned a gloved hand lifting the canister lid, dropping in the finely ground powder, giving the canister a shake. Cocoa would better hide the bitter taste, too.

"You see, Kerry, if we're right about your father, then it was terribly, critically important to someone to be sure no one woke up when the fire broke out."

While I waited to see the president of the Derry Hills National Bank, I considered who might have doctored the cocoa.

Happily for Kerry, I was confident I could exclude several names immediately.

The cocoa wasn't doctored by anyone in the house.

How could I be certain?

Because Kerry lived.

The police had accepted the idea that Jack O'Keefe preferred to die and for his family to die rather than to face disgrace.

But that tortured reasoning made no sense, fulfilled

no logic, unless everyone died. The police assumed Jack
O'Keefe simply didn't know Kerry was gone for the
night.

But on that fateful evening, Kerry's father, mother,
and sister knew Kerry had drunk no cocoa.

If one of them were the murderer, he or she could
easily have brought a cup of cocoa upstairs to Kerry.
Once it was realized that Kerry was absent, the macabre
plan would have been delayed until the next night when
Kerry, too, would have been home.

So, I didn't put Jack or Elizabeth or Jenny O'Keefe
on my list of suspects.

If the dead could not be blamed, who could?

I intended to find out.

The office door opened and Ray Vickery, the president of the Derry Hills National Bank, walked toward
me. An eager smile touched Ray's always-genial face.
His handclasp was strong and warm.

"Henrie O, it's good to see you. Always good to see
you." His eyes said even more.

I had occasion in the past to be of service to Ray and
his wife, Eleanor, and their gratitude continues.

I could count on Ray.

He welcomed me into his office, offered me a comfortable red wing chair. He sat in its twin.

I came straight to the point.

"Ray, were you with the bank twelve years ago—
when Jack O'Keefe and his family died?"

His mobile face was sorrowful. "That was awful. Yes.
The bank belonged to the O'Keefes then. I'd been here
about seven years when it happened." He shook his head
slowly. "I still have trouble believing it."

"Why?"

"Jack O'Keefe—well, he was a fun guy, loud, always
joking. A big, good-looking man. Blond, blue eyed, with
a grin bigger than Texas. And later, everybody agreed
he'd never really settled down, worked like he should,

like his father and brother thought he should. Jack was too busy sailing or mountain climbing or building a glider or hiking with his girls or white-water rafting on the Colorado. But he was a fun guy—I couldn't believe it when he set the house on fire. His wife, the girls. And only Kerry left and that just by a stroke of luck. They say it's made Kerry a real loner. Her grandmother worries about it. She won't let anybody get close to her. If Jack had just thought . . ." Ray sighed.

"So Jack was a flake. What made him a crook?"

Ray shrugged. "Who's to know? I mean, it was such a shock. To all of us. But there wasn't any doubt about it. Two hundred thousand missing, and fake loans signed by Jack. The family hushed it up, of course. Old Man O'Keefe made up the losses. But it knocked the stuffing out of him. He sold the bank soon after. It wasn't six months later they found his skiff dumped over in the lake. His body surfaced three days later. He drowned. But I thought he did it on purpose. He was crazy about Jack."

"Who was in the loan department besides Jack?"

"Robert, Jack's brother." He frowned in thought. "And I think Gordon Evans was in loans then, too."

I took my notebook out of my purse. "Ray, some new evidence has turned up. Jack O'Keefe didn't set that fire. And that makes me wonder if he stole the money. Could someone else have signed his name to the fake loans, made him a patsy?"

Ray's mobile face reflected his response: shock, rejection, uncertainty, consideration. He rubbed his cheek thoughtfully. "It would have taken some doing. But, sure, it could have been done. Because Jack was such a loose guy and spent so much time out of the office."

"What happened to the evidence?"

He looked blank.

"The bank examiner found these dummy loans. Where would those papers be?"

It took three hours, and we didn't find the originals. But the yellowed Xerox copies in the dead files in the basement suited my purposes just fine.

Ray Vickery agreed to my plan. I knew he would. "I owe it to Jack," he said simply.

I called Don. He heard me out.

"Henrie O, it could be dangerous."

"I don't think so. But I'll be careful."

"You promise?"

"Yes."

"Henrie O, thanks."

I stopped first in Gordon Evans's office.

Evans was a lanky, somber-faced man about ten years younger than I. His handshake was limp and his mustache dispirited.

But he wasn't stupid.

When I finished speaking, he leaned forward, his gray eyes cold. "Anyone in the bank could have used Jack's office. Not I alone. And I resent the implication that I might have been involved." He reached for a sheaf of papers. "Now, I have matters—"

"Of course, there's a simple solution. Mr. Vickery has agreed to make a search of the bank's dead files tomorrow. He will then submit the papers to a document examiner along with samples of Jack O'Keefe's handwriting. If the signature is not that of Jack O'Keefe— if his name is forged on those documents—we will be sure of his innocence." I smiled. "You won't object to providing a sample of your handwriting, will you?"

"I shall do nothing of the kind. Good day, Mrs. Collins."

Alma Hendricks scooted her chair closer to mine in the bank's employee coffee room. She poked her thick-lensed glasses higher on her beaked nose and glanced uneasily around, then spoke rapidly. "Nothing ever came out in public, but everybody in town knew. I felt so awful for the family."

"You did Jack O'Keefe's secretarial work?"

"Yes. You could have knocked me over with a feather." Her green eyes stared at me earnestly.

"Did you like him?"

Sudden tears filmed her eyes. She swung away, grabbed some Kleenex, swiped under her glasses.

So. "Some new evidence has surfaced, regarding the fire. Now there is some question whether Mr. O'Keefe actually stole that money."

She listened intently as I described the search that would be made of the dead files.

Antiques, brocaded chairs, and a variety of small tables jammed Iris O'Keefe's living room. The smell of rose potpourri mingled with a violet cologne. But neither could quite mask the sweet thick scent of bourbon.

We were about the same age. An ormolu-framed mirror reflected us. Funny how we often see what we wish in the quick early morning scan of a mirror. Intellectually I know I am old. But it always surprises me—shocks me—to see the lines in my face, the silver in my once raven black hair.

We were a contrast, no doubt about it. I always look impatient. I *am* impatient. My eyes are dark, my face strong boned, my body always poised to move.

Iris O'Keefe's white hair straggled, though it looked as if it had been ineffectually brushed. Her blue eyes peered at me muzzily, but that was alcohol, not age. A heavily veined hand plucked nervously at the unevenly tied white silk bow at the throat of her wrinkled navy dress.

" . . . will exonerate your son. We'll know definitely tomorrow when we look at the documents."

Her shoulders sagged. Slowly, wearily, without saying

a word, her face drawn, she struggled to her feet and walked unsteadily across the room, habit steering her safely past the bric-a-brac-laden tables.

After a moment, I rose and followed her.

She stood by the one window with the drapes full open.

Not a tree, not a shrub marred the view of the burned-out house.

She shuddered, long, slow, deep shudders.

"Mrs. O'Keefe—"

"Leave. Leave now. Leave me."

"That's all over. Over!" Louise O'Keefe's hair curled in obedient, glistening waves. Her patterned black-and-russet silk dress was stylishly short, but Louise O'Keefe still had the figure to display her legs. She had the glisten of wealth, that unmistakable patina created by fine clothes, expensive cosmetics, superb hairdressing, exquisite jewelry (gold shell earrings and a gold pin crusted with rubies), and the confidence money buys.

Skillfully applied makeup softened the sharpness of her features. Her face was long and thin (thin, of course), her gray eyes remote, her mouth tight.

"No, Mrs. O'Keefe. It isn't over."

"It was twelve years ago." She smoothed back a wisp of hair. "Jack was a thief. And he couldn't face up to it."

I rose, but I kept my eyes on hers. "Whatever he was or wasn't, Mrs. O'Keefe, we're now certain he was not an arsonist—and thereby a murderer. Whether he was a thief will be determined tomorrow, when we study the documents."

She stood by the Adam mantel, one heavily beringed hand clutching it. "We—who is we? What right have you to make these accusations?"

I gave her a cool smile. "There are no accusations yet, Mrs. O'Keefe. But tomorrow . . ."

*   *   *

I waited patiently outside the door to the men's grill. If you want to find sexism alive and thriving, try your nearest country club. The grill was a fitting background for men of wealth: paneled walls, hunting prints, elegant Oriental rugs, and walnut card tables. The cardplayers were sixtyish men in argyle sweaters, fine wool slacks, and Italian loafers.

Often at this time of the day, I was hard at work in my office at the *Clarion*. The newspaper is produced by the journalism department at the college, but it serves the town of Derry Hills. I was op-ed editor this semester. It was strange to contrast the pulsing, scarcely leashed tension of the *Clarion*—of any daily newspaper office— with the muted, relaxed bonhomie here.

The contrast reminded me that life has infinite variations, and it's unwise to assume your pattern is all that exists.

Finally, my quarry laid out his hand, then rose from the table near the fireplace. Robert O'Keefe had thinning blond hair and a petulant face. He might once have been attractive, but his stocky body was flabby with a paunch that even good tailoring didn't quite hide.

When he came through the doorway, I stepped forward. "Mr. O'Keefe, may I speak with you for a moment?"

He took me to a petit-point sofa in an alcove off the main reception area.

His face didn't change as I spoke, but the long slender hands in his lap gripped each other tightly.

"... sure you'll be delighted if we can clear your brother's name when we find those files tomorrow."

Slowly his hands relaxed. Eyes as shiny and unreadable as blue marbles slid across my face, flicked toward the grandfather clock in the corner.

"Interesting." His voice was bored. "Too bad poor Kerry's going to be disappointed." He pushed back his chair, stood. "Got to get back to the game. Good to talk to you, Mrs. . . . uh—"

"Collins."

"But the truth of it is, Jack took the money."

And he turned and walked away.

The phone call came at six the next morning.

But that was all right. I was already drinking my second cup of Kona.

I picked up the receiver.

"Henrie O, Christ, it worked!" Don was pumped up. "So what do we do now?"

Ray Vickery agreed to loan me the boardroom at the bank.

"I'd say this is bank business." His voice was grim.

"Thank you, Ray." I hung up the phone, made my calls in quick succession. It was an invitation no one quite dared to refuse. I set the meeting for 11 A.M.

I arrived ten minutes early.

Don was waiting in the parking lot.

He opened my car door, his face grim.

"Henrie O, I got word just a few minutes ago. Those signatures on the dummy loans—they're Jack O'Keefe's." Despair etched deep lines in his face. "The examiner's sure."

I'd considered that possibility already. And thought it through. There was nothing to say about it. Now.

Instead I asked briskly, "But you brought the video-cassette?"

"It's in the car. But what difference—"

"Get it, Don."

Don stood by the oversize television. It was equipped with a videocassette player. He held a cassette in his hand.

I was at the door of the boardroom.

Kerry O'Keefe arrived first. She looked gorgeous in a black-and-white rayon suit with red trim, but her face was pale and strained and the glances she sped at Don alternated between hope and uncertainty.

Don's somber face offered her no encouragement.

Gordon Evans walked in, his body stiff, his face resentful. "I am here under protest." The gray pinstripe did little for his sallow coloring. It was a rack suit, the trousers not quite long enough to break.

I raised an eyebrow. "Surely you'd like to know the truth of what happened with those loans—since you worked in that area, too."

"I do know the truth."

"Perhaps. And perhaps, Mr. Evans, you will discover that certitude sometimes does not cover a multitude of sins."

He took a chair in the far corner, crossed one leg over the other, and watched me with distaste.

Don shot me a curious, puzzled look.

Kerry jumped up from her chair. "Grandmother!"

Iris O'Keefe wavered unsteadily, but with dignity, in the doorway. "Kerry, my dear. You're here, too?"

Kerry took her grandmother's arm and carefully shepherded her to a chair beside her own.

Iris O'Keefe hunched in the chair. Her thin fingers plucked at the pearl necklace at her throat.

Alma Hendricks hesitated in the doorway.

"Come in, Alma. I'm so glad you could join us."

"Good morning, ma'am, Mrs. O'Keefe, Miss O'Keefe." Alma slid into the chair opposite Kerry's.

Angry voices rose in the hall.

We all looked toward the door.

Robert and Louise O'Keefe, their faces flushed, stepped inside and abruptly stopped talking.

The instant of silence was full of tension.

"So what are you staring at?" Louise demanded sharply, her angry eyes snapping from face to face.

"If you'll take your seats . . . ," and I motioned to two empty chairs with a direct view of the television set.

Robert O'Keefe glowered at me. Louise tossed her head. But they sat down.

"First, I want to be sure we all know one another."

Robert crossed his arms. "Mrs. Collins, certainly we all know—"

Sometimes I don't mind being rude.

This was one of those times.

I interrupted. "Yes, of course, you know the family members, the bank staff. But, Mr. O'Keefe, I don't believe you've met Don Brown. Don, I would like for you to meet," and I introduced them, swiftly in turn, "Robert and Louise O'Keefe, Iris O'Keefe, Gordon Evans, and Alma Hendricks, Lieutenant Don Brown of the Derry Hills Police Department homicide unit."

Robert O'Keefe's eyes widened.

Louise O'Keefe drew her breath in sharply.

Iris clutched her granddaughter's arm. "Homicide? Homicide? What does that mean?"

I closed the door to the conference room and turned to face my audience. "Ladies and gentlemen, in the public mind, Jack O'Keefe is guilty of theft, murder—by arson—and suicide. I propose to prove that Jack O'Keefe was innocent on all counts."

Kerry leaned forward, her chin cupped in her hands, her heart in her eyes.

"The original police investigation, following the arson, discovered that two hundred thousand dollars was missing through fake loans signed by Jack. When Percodan was discovered in the bodies, the police concluded that Jack stole his mother's prescription, doped his family, then arranged for the fire because he couldn't face disgrace. Kerry O'Keefe's escape was believed to be simply good fortune. While it certainly was that, Kerry's escape was the first proof of Jack's innocence. You see, Kerry wasn't drugged."

Iris pressed trembling hands against her cheeks. "What do you mean? What are you saying?"

"I mean that someone took the pain prescription from your house, ground it into a powder, then dropped by Jack's house and mixed the drug into the top level of the cocoa canister, knowing that the Jack O'Keefe family drank cocoa every night.

"But Kerry drank no cocoa. Jack would have known that, would have had to know it, if he planned to kill his family that night while they slept. So Jack didn't do the drugging. Nor did anyone else in the house because, once again, it would have been a twisted response to disgrace and the intent would be for all to die, and Kerry wasn't there.

"So, someone came by and left without knowing that Kerry would not drink cocoa that night."

"This is absurd." Robert stood.

"Sit down, Mr. O'Keefe. You don't want to miss the main event."

His glance locked with mine. Slowly, he sat down.

Louise's face flushed. "This is so insulting. I demand—"

"To know the truth. Good. Don, please begin."

Don lifted the remote. The television turned on and then the VCR began to play.

Darkness.

I began to speak. "Everything hinges on whether Jack O'Keefe dummied those loans."

Nothing but darkness.

"I spoke yesterday with two men who could have arranged the theft to look like Jack's work, Jack's brother Robert and Gordon Evans."

"I object. I object—"

"Quiet, Mr. Evans. I merely said you had the opportunity. I also spoke to Alma Hendricks, both because she could have stolen the money and because she would spread the word of my search to others in the bank, and the fact that the documents would be unearthed today."

The video picture was black, but door hinges squeaked.

"I alerted Iris O'Keefe and Robert's wife, Louise. And finally I arranged for a video camera to record if anyone came to the basement dead files here in the bank last night."

A light came on. The grainy picture flickered, then came into focus on a row of filing cabinets in the dimly lit room.

A figure dressed in black hurried to the cabinets, pulled out the drawers in quick succession, scanning the folder tabs. It didn't take long. Not quite nine minutes. Then a folder was snatched up, the searcher whirled and hurried to the door, the light went out.

The film continued to whir.

Robert O'Keefe jumped to his feet, his face convulsed. He stared down at his wife. "You fool. You stupid fool."

"I had to get them. You—"

"Goddamn it, Jack signed—"

He broke off.

"Yes, Mr. O'Keefe? Won't you continue? Please tell us how you persuaded your brother to sign the false loans that you had prepared." Because Robert was right. Handwriting comparisons proved the papers were indeed signed by Jack. But I knew that Jack didn't kill his family. So he must not have been the creator of those dummy loans—even if he did sign them.

"Oh, my God," Louise moaned. "I thought—"

"Shut up, for Christ's sake," her husband ordered.

"Yes, Louise, why don't you tell us about it?" I asked.

"Louise, don't say a goddamn word."

I looked from husband to wife. "Not much communication in your marriage. Right? But Louise knew who would take money—and it wasn't Jack. I don't suppose the two of you ever talked about it. What did you think, Robert? Did you really believe your brother killed him-

self and his family? Or was it such an enormous stroke
of luck for you that you never permitted yourself to think
about what really happened?"

Tears slid down Iris's withered cheeks.

"Or why don't you tell us, Iris. You've always known,
haven't you? That's why you wouldn't let anyone clear
away the ruins from the fire. You wanted Robert to see
it day and night. But he built a wall."

"Jack was gone. I couldn't lose Robert, too. But I
knew Jack didn't take any money and he'd do whatever
Robert asked him to do. I knew that's the way it must
have happened, Robert bringing in the loans, spinning
Jack a story, asking him to sign the papers. But even
knowing it, I couldn't lose Robert, too. I couldn't." She
buried her face in her hands.

"Mother, Mother." Robert's voice shook. "Mother, I
didn't do it! I swear before God, I didn't do it. Not the
fire. I didn't."

Iris's hands fell away. She stared at her older son.

He hurried to her. "Mother, I swear to you."

She looked into his eyes, then she made a noise deep
in her throat as her head swung toward her daughter-
in-law.

"That's right, Iris." I spoke clearly. "Robert took the
money. But Louise drugged the cocoa and set the fire."

It bothers Don a lot that we could never prove murder
against Louise O'Keefe. All we had was circumstantial
evidence. We were certain, but that isn't enough in a
court of law, of course.

She could claim she went after the files because she
was trying to protect her husband. Not true, of course.
She was trying to protect herself. That was always her
goal, to protect the life and social position and security
of Louise O'Keefe. And she was willing to destroy a
young family to save her husband and her elegant way
of life.

Everyone ultimately gets what they deserve.

Louise O'Keefe is no exception.

And neither is Robert. He has a great capacity for not accepting reality. He should have known that Jack didn't drug the cocoa or set the fire. But he didn't want to think about it, refused to think about it. If he had thought too hard, he would have known the answer.

When he finally knew what had happened, he jettisoned Louise.

And there were no thefts to prove against Robert at this late date, the money long since made good, the statute of limitations long since past.

Louise and Robert are divorced now.

She got quite a nice settlement. She's living in the Canary Islands, a hard-faced, wealthy woman.

But what has her crime gained her?

Oh yes, Louise will get what she deserves, is getting it, has gotten it.

What matters, what really matters, is love.

And love triumphed here.

Kerry and Don's wedding will be in June.

I wouldn't miss it for the world.

〔JOAN HESS〕

MURDER ISN'T FUNNY, BUT JOAN HESS DEFINITELY is. Hess first tried her hand at novel writing in the heyday of romances (everybody was making a fortune), and she is the coauthor of a romance (with recipes) which she swears is absolutely unavailable. But her career as a romance author foundered because she kept writing books with plots. An agent said, "Why don't you write a mystery!" Since Hess had never read a romance novel and was an inveterate mystery reader, it seemed like good advice. It was. Hess has now published more than twenty-two acclaimed mysteries. Her Claire Malloy and Maggody series, based in Hess's native Arkansas, serve up hilarious social comment along with tightly plotted and action-packed mysteries. Hess's Theo Bloomer books, written under the pen name Joan Hadley, are equally funny and occur in exotic locales. Hess has won the Agatha, American, and Macavity awards. Her most recent books include Tickled to Death *(Claire Malloy) and* Martians in Maggody *(Arly Hanks).*

Hess is active in Sisters in Crime, the American Crime Writers League, and the Whimsey Foundation. She lives in Fayetteville, Arkansas, with her two children.

In "All That Glitters," Hess wryly charts the course of true lust and what happened to one box of Valentine candy.

All That Glitters

Welcome to the home of Remmington Boles and his mother, Audrey Antoinette (née Tattlinger) Boles. It is a small yet gracious house in the center of the historic district. At one time it was the site of fancy luncheons and elegant dinner parties. There have been no parties of any significance since the timely and unremarkable demise of Ralph Edward Boles. I believe this was in 1962, but it may have been the following year.

Remmington, who is called Remmie by his mother and few remaining relatives, is forty-one years old, reasonably tall, reasonably attractive. There is little else to say about his physical presence. It's likely you would trust him on first sight. He has never been unkind to animals or children.

Audrey is of an age that falls between sixty and seventy. She was once attractive in an antebellum sort of way. In her heyday thirty years ago, she was president of the Junior League and almost single-handedly raised the money for a children's cancer wing at the regional hospital.

At this moment, Audrey is in her bedroom at the top of the stairs. Although we cannot see her, we can deduce from her vaguely querulous tone that she is no longer in robust health.

"Remmie? Do you have time to find my slippers before you leave? It seems so damp and chilly this morning. I hope there's nothing wrong with the furnace."

Her son's voice is patient and, for the most part, imbued with affection. He is not a candidate for sainthood, but he is a good son.

"There's nothing wrong with the furnace," he says as he comes into her bedroom. "Let me raise the blinds so you can enjoy the sunshine."

He takes two steps, then pauses as he does every morning. The microdrama has been performed for many years. Very rarely does anything happen to disrupt it, and there is nothing in the air to lead Remmie to suspect this day will be extraordinary.

"No, leave them down. I can't tolerate the glare. Oh, Remmie, I pray every night that you'll never face the specter of blindness. It's so very frightening."

Two steps to her side; two squeezes of her hand. "Now, Mother, Dr. Whitbread found no symptoms of retinopathy, and he said you shouldn't worry. The ophthalmologist said the same thing only a few months ago."

Her eyes are bleached and rimmed with red, but they regard him with birdlike acuity. "You're so good to me. I don't know how I could ever get along without you."

"I'm late for work, Mother. Here are your slippers right beside the bed. I'll be home at noon to fix your lunch." He bends down to kiss her forehead, then waits to be dismissed.

"Bless you, Remmie."

Remmie Boles goes downstairs to the kitchen, rinses out his coffee cup, and props it in the rack, then makes sure his mother's tray is ready for her midmorning snack: tea bag, porcelain cup and saucer, two sugar cookies in a cellophane bag. The teapot, filled with a precise quantity of water, is on the back burner.

He enjoys the six-block walk to Boles Discount Furniture Warehouse, and produces a smile for his secretary, who is filing her fingernails. She is not overly bright, but she is very dependable—a trait much valued in small business concerns.

"Good morning, Ailene," Remmie says, collecting the mail from the corner of her desk.

"Some guy from your church called, Mr. Boles. He wants to know if you're gonna be on the bowling team this year. He says they'll take you back as long as you promise not to quit in the middle of the season like you did last year." Having been an employee for ten years, she feels entitled to make unseemly comments. "You really should get out and meet people. You're not all that old, you know, and kinda cute. There are a lot of women who'd jump at the chance to go out with a guy like you."

"Please bring me the sales tax figures from the last

quarter." Remmie goes into his office and closes the door before he allows himself to react.

Ailene has made a point. Remmie is not a recluse. He has dated over the years, albeit infrequently and for no great duration. Alas, he has not been out since the fiasco that was responsible for his abandonment of the First Methodist Holy Rollers in midseason.

Yes, even Methodists can evince a sense of humor.

Lucinda was (and still is, as far as I know) a waitress at the bowling alley. He'd been dazzled by her bright red hair, mischievous grin, and body that rippled like a field of ripe wheat when she walked. She agreed to go out for drinks. One thing had led to another, first in the front seat of his car, then on the waterbed in her apartment.

The very idea of experiencing such sexual bliss every night left Remmie giddy, and he found himself pondering marriage. After a series of increasingly erotic encounters, he invited Lucinda to meet his mother.

It was a ghastly idea. Lucinda arrived in a tight purple dress that scarcely covered the tops of her thighs, and brought a bottle of whiskey as a present. In the harsh light of his living room, he could see the bags under her eyes and the slackness of her jowls. Her voice was coarse, her laugh a bray, her ripple nothing more than a cheap, seductive wiggle. He quit the bowling team immediately.

Back to work, Remmie.

He ignores the message and settles down with the figures. At eleven, he goes out to the showroom to make sure his salesmen aren't gossiping in the break room. He is heading for the counter when a woman comes through the main door and halts, her expression wary, as if she's worried that ravenous beasts are lurking under oak veneer tables and behind plaid recliners.

If Ailene hadn't made her presumptuous comments, perhaps Remmie would not have given this particular customer more than a cursory assessment. As it is, he notices she's a tiny bit plump, several inches shorter than he, and of a similar age. Her hair, short and curly, is the color of milk chocolate. She is wearing a dark skirt and white blouse, and carrying a shiny black handbag.

"May I help you?" he says.

"I'm just looking. It's hard to know where to start, isn't it?"

"Are you in the market for living room furniture? We have a good assortment on sale right now."

"I need all sorts of things, but I don't have much of a budget," she says rather sadly. "Then again, I don't have much of a house."

To his horror, her eyes fill with tears.

Remmie persuades her to accept a cup of coffee in his office, and within a half hour, possesses her story. Crystal Ambler grew up on the seedy side of the city, attended the junior college, and is now the office manager of a small medical clinic. A childless marriage ended in divorce more than five years ago. She spends her free time reading, gardening, and occasionally playing bridge with her parents and sister. She once had a cat, but it ran away and now she lives alone.

"Not very exciting, is it?" she says with a self-deprecatory laugh. "It's hard being single these days, and almost impossible to meet someone who isn't burdened with a psychosis and an outstanding warrant or two."

"Mr. Boles," Ailene says from the doorway, "your mother called to remind you to pick up syringes on your way home for lunch."

"Is your mother ill?" asks Crystal with appropriate sympathy.

"She was diagnosed with diabetes the year I graduated from college. It's manageable with daily insulin injections and a strict diet."

"It must be awfully hard on you and your wife," she begins, then gasps and rises unsteadily. "I'm sorry. It's none of my business and I shouldn't have—"

"It's perfectly all right." Remmie catches her hands between his and studies her contrite expression, spotting for the first time a little dimple on her chin. "I should be the one to apologize. You came here to look for furniture, and I've wasted your time with my questions. I do hope you'll allow me to help you find a bargain."

Crystal is amenable.

Remmie smiles thoughtfully as he walks home for lunch. There is something charmingly quaint about Miss Ambler. She is by no means a hapless maiden awaiting rescue by a knight; when she selected the sofa, she did so with no hint of indecision or tacit plea for his approval. But at the same time, she is soft-spoken and modest. He's certain she would never wear a tight purple dress or drink whiskey. He doubts she drinks anything more potent than white wine.

He's halfway across the living room when he realizes something is acutely wrong. His mother never fails to call his name when he enters the house. It is an inviolate part of their script.

"Mother?" he calls as he hurries upstairs to her bedroom. The room is dim; the television, invariably set on a game show, is silent. The figure on the bed is motionless. "Mother?" he repeats with a growing sense of panic.

"Remmie, thank God you're here. I feel so weak. I tried to call you, but I couldn't even lift the receiver."

"Shall I call for an ambulance?"

"No, I simply need something to nibble on to elevate my blood sugar. If it's not too much trouble, would you please bring the cookies from this morning?"

"You skipped your snack? Dr. Whitbread stressed how very vital it is that you stay on your schedule. Maybe I should call him."

"All I need are the cookies, Remmie." Despite her avowed weakness, she picks up the clock and squints at it. "My goodness, you're almost an hour late. Was there an emergency at the store?"

"A minor one," he murmurs.

Remmie calls Crystal that evening to make sure she is pleased with her selection. She shyly invites him to come by some time and see how well the sofa goes with the drapes. Remmie professes eagerness to do so, and suggests Saturday morning. Although Crystal sounds disappointed, she promises coffee and cake.

The week progresses uneventfully. Whatever has caused Audrey's bout of weakness has not recurred, although she has noticed a disturbing new symptom and broaches it after the evening news is over.

She holds out a hand. "Feel my fingers, Remmie. They're so swollen I haven't been able to wear any of my rings. Perhaps you should take all my jewelry down to the bank tomorrow morning and put it in the safe-deposit box. If it's not too much bother, of course. It's so maddening not to be able to do things for myself. I know I'm such a terrible burden on you."

"I'll do it Saturday morning," Remmie says. "I have some other errands, and I'll be in that neighborhood."

"Errands? I hate to think of you spending your weekend driving all over town instead of having a chance to relax around the house. You work so hard all week."

"I enjoy getting out." He picks up her tray and heads for the kitchen.

Saturday.
Remmie grimaces as he pulls into the driveway. His mother's jewelry is still in the glove compartment, and the bank closes at noon on Saturdays. His mother will spend the weekend fretting if she finds out about his negligence, but there's no reason why she will. A good

son does not cause his mother unnecessary concern.

He sits in the car and replays his visit. Upon opening the door, Crystal hadn't thrown herself into his arms, but she'd held his hand several seconds longer than decorum dictates. Their conversation had been lively. They'd parted with yet another warm handshake.

He locks the glove compartment and goes inside. And freezes as he sees his mother slumped on the sofa, her hands splayed across her chest and her eyes closed.

"Mother!" he says as he sinks to her side. "Can you hear me?"

"I'm conscious," Audrey says dully. "I was on my way to the kitchen when I felt so dizzy I almost fell."

"Let me help you back to bed, and then I'll call the doctor." Remmie picks her up and carries her to her bedroom, settles her on the bed, and reaches for the telephone.

"No, don't disturb Dr. Whitbread. He's entitled to his weekends, just as you are. If I'm not better on Monday, you can call him then."

"Are you sure?" asks Remmie, alarmed at the thinness of her voice.

"It's very dear of you to be so concerned about me, Remmie. Most children put their ailing parents in nursing homes and try to forget about them. The poor old things lose what wits they have and spend their last days drooling and being tormented by sadistic nurses."

"This is your home, Mother. Why don't you take a little nap while I fix your lunch?"

"Bless you," she says with a sigh. He's almost to the door when she adds, "There was a call for you half an hour ago. A woman with a trailer park sort of name said you'd left your gloves at her house. I tried to catch you at the bank to relay the message, but they said you hadn't come in. I hope they weren't your suede gloves, Remmie. I ordered them from Italy, you know."

"I know." He urges himself back into motion. Had he subconsciously chosen to leave his gloves at Crystal's house so he'd have another excuse to call her? He ponders the possibility as he washes lettuce and slices a tomato.

Audrey is strangely quiet all afternoon and declines his offer to play gin rummy after dinner. Remmie finally breaks down and tells her about Crystal Ambler.

"She sounds very nice," says Audrey. "She lives in that neighborhood beyond the interstate, you said? Your father and I made a point of never driving through that area after dark, even if it meant going miles out of our way." She pauses as if reliving a long and torturous detour, then says, "What exactly does this woman do?"

Audrey listens as Remmie describes Crystal's job, her clean, if somewhat Spartan, house, her garden, even her new sofa. "She sounds very nice," is all she says as she limps across the dining room and down the hall. "Very nice."

Sunday, Sunday.
Remmie calls Crystal while his mother is napping. After he apologizes for leaving his gloves, he invites her to meet him after work on Monday for a glass of wine.

Monday.
Remmie tells his mother he'll be working late in preparation for the inventory-reduction sale. He uses the same excuse when he takes Crystal to dinner later that week. On Saturday afternoon, he makes an ambiguous reference to the hardware store and takes Crystal for a drive in the country. Afterward, he feels foolish when Audrey not only brings up Crystal's name, but encourages him to ask her out. He admits they have plans.

"Dinner on Wednesday?" murmurs Audrey, carefully folding her napkin and placing it on the table. "What a lovely idea, Remmie. I'm sure she'll be thrilled to have a meal in a proper restaurant."

"Would you like me to see if Miss McCloud can sit with you while I'm out?"

"I wouldn't dream of bothering her. After all, I'm here by myself every day. I'm so used to being alone that I'll scarcely notice that you're out with this woman."

"I'd like to meet your mother," Crystal says as they dally over coffee in her living room. "You're obviously devoted to her."

"My father left a very small estate. My mother insisted on working at a clothing shop to put me through college, then used the last of the insurance money to finance the store. Before her illness grew more debilitating, she came down to the showroom at night and dusted the displays." Remmie smiles gently. "I'd like you to meet her. She's asked me all about you, and I think she's beginning to suspect I might be . . ."

"Be what?"

"Falling in love," he says, then leans forward and kisses her. When she responds, he slides his arm behind her back and marvels at the supple contours. Their kisses intensify, as do Remmie's caresses and her tiny moans. His hand finds its way beneath her sweater to her round breasts. His mind swirls with deliciously impure images.

Therefore, he's startled when she pulls back and moves to the far end of the sofa. For an alarming moment, she looks close to tears, but she takes a shuddery breath and says, "No, Remmie, I'm not going to have an affair. I shouldn't have gone out with you in the first place. I'm too old to get into another pointless relationship. I'd rather get a cat."

Remmie bites back a groan. "Crystal, darling, I'd never do anything to hurt you. I don't want a pointless relationship, either."

"Then take me home to meet your mother."

He frowns at the obstinate edge in her voice. "I will when the time's right. Mother's been fretting about her blood pressure lately, and I don't want to excite her more than necessary."

"Maybe you'd better go home and check on her," Crystal says as she stands up. However, rather than hurrying him out the door, she presses her body against his and kisses him with such fierce passion that he nearly loses his balance. "There'll be more of this when we're engaged," she promises in a warm, moist whisper. She goes on to describe what lies in store after they're married.

The constraints of the genre prevent me from providing details.

Time flies.

"Does your friend drive an old white Honda?" Audrey asks Remmie while he's massaging her feet to stimulate circulation.

He gives her a surprised look. "Why do you ask?"

"Someone who matches her description has driven by here several times. It most likely wasn't her, though. This woman had the predatory gleam of a real estate appraiser trying to decide how much our house is worth." Audrey manages a weak chuckle. "And of course I can barely see the street from my window these days. It's all a matter of time before I'm no longer a burden, Remmie, and you'll be free to get on with your life."

"Don't say that, Mother," he says as he strokes her wispy gray hair. A sudden vision of the future floods his mind: his mother's bedroom is unlit and empty, but farther down the hall, Crystal smiles from his bed, her arms outstretched and her breasts heaving beneath a silky black gown.

He realizes his mother is staring at him and wipes a

sheen of perspiration off his forehead. "Don't say that," he repeats.

Several more weeks pass, and then back to Boles Discount Furniture Warehouse we go.

This morning Ailene is typing slowly but steadily. "Crystal called," she says without looking up. "She said to tell you that she can't go to the movies tonight."

"Did she say why?"

"Something about baby-sitting for her sister. Oh, and your mother called right before you got here. She wants you to pick up some ointment for her blisters. She said you'd know what kind and where to get it."

Remmie closes his office door, reaches for the telephone, and then lowers his hand. Crystal has made it clear that he's not to call her at the clinic. But this is the second time this week she's canceled their date to do a favor for her sister. Last week she met him at the door and announced she was going out with some friends from the clinic. Remmie had not been invited to join them.

Can he be losing her? When they're together on the sofa, her passion seems to rival his own. Although she continues to refuse to make love, she has found ways to soften his frustration. She swears she has never loved anyone as deeply.

He collapses in his chair, cradles his head in his hands, and silently mouths her name.

When Remmie comes into the living room, he is shocked. He is stunned, bewildered, and profoundly inarticulate. The one thing he is not prepared to see is his mother sitting at one end of the sofa and Crystal at the other. A tray with teacups and saucers resides on the coffee table, a few crumbs indicative that cookies have been consumed.

"Crystal," he gasps.

"Remmie, dear," his mother says chidingly, "that's no way to welcome a guest into our home. Have you forgotten your manners?"

Crystal's smile is as sweet as the sugar granules on the tray. "I was in the neighborhood, and it seemed like time to stop by and meet your mother. We've been having a lovely chat."

"Oh, yes," says Audrey. "A lovely chat."

Remmie sinks down on the edge of the recliner, aware his mouth is slack. "That's good," he says at last.

Audrey nods. "Crystal and I discovered a most amazing coincidence. It seems her mother used to clean house for Laetitia Whimsey, who was in my garden club for years."

"Amazing," Remmie says, glaring at Crystal. He's angry at her effrontery in coming, but she refuses to acknowledge him and listens attentively as Audrey reminisces about her garden club.

Out on the porch, however, Crystal crosses her arms and gazes defiantly at him. "This meeting was long overdue," she says, "and you've been stalling. Well, now I've met her. She seems to like me well enough, and I'm sure we'll get along just fine in the future. We do have a future, don't we?"

"Of course we do," he says, shocked by her vehemence. "I was only waiting until Mother . . ."

"Dies?"

Remmie steps back and clutches the rail. "Don't be ridiculous. She's experiencing numbness in her lower legs and feet, and the doctor recommended tests for arteriosclerosis. Mother is always distraught about going into the hospital."

"And then what, Remmie? Will she have problems with her kidneys? Will her blood pressure fluctuate?"

"I don't know, Crystal. Her condition is very delicate, but the doctor seems to feel that in general her prognosis is good."

"Then what's the delay?" she counters. "I believed you when you told me that you love me. Otherwise, I would have broken off our relationship long before I became emotionally involved. There are plenty of women who'll sleep with you, Remmie—if that's all you want."

He stares as she marches down the steps and across the street to her little white car. He remains on the porch even after she has driven away without so much as a glance in his direction.

"Remmie?" calls his mother. "Could you be a dear and help me upstairs? I wasn't expecting any visitors, and now I'm exhausted. There's no rush, of course. I'll just sit here in the dark until you have a moment."

January proves to be the cruelest month.

Crystal allows Remmie to take her out several times, and permits him a few more liberties on the sofa, for which he is grateful. On the other hand, he senses a reticence on her part to abandon herself to his embraces. They both avoid any references to Audrey, who continues to encourage him to go out with Crystal.

Remmie begins to feel as if he's losing his mind. He's obsessed with Crystal; his waking hours are haunted by memories of how she feels in his arms. His dreams are so explicit that he awakens drenched with sweat and shivering with frustration.

The obvious question arises: Why does he not propose marriage? If he could answer this, he would. For the most part, Crystal is the girl of his dreams (if he and I may employ the cliché). She has shown a flicker of annoyance now and then, but she is quick to apologize and kiss away his injured feelings. She has joined his church. On two occasions she has brought Audrey flowers and perky greeting cards.

When Audrey mentions Crystal's name, Remmie listens intently for any nuances in her voice. He's perceptive enough to anticipate a petty display of jealousy, but thus far he has not seen it. Audrey maintains that she is fond of Crystal, that she enjoys their infrequent but pleasant conversations.

Why is he incapable of proposing?

Mercifully, January ends and we ease into February, a month fraught with significance for young and old lovers alike.

"Does Crystal have a brother?" asks Audrey one morning as Remmie is straightening her blanket.

"I don't think so."

"How odd," she says under her breath.

"Why would you think she has a brother, Mother?"

"It's so silly that I hate to confess." Audrey sighs and looks away, then adds, "I called her house yesterday morning to thank her for the romance novel she sent. A man answered the telephone, and I was so unnerved that I hung up without saying a word. It was quite early; you'd just left for work."

Remmie is aware that two days ago Crystal canceled their plans for dinner, saying that she needed to work on files from the clinic. He has not spoken to her since then, although he has left messages for her to call.

"It must have been a plumber," Audrey says dismissively. "Would you check the thermostat, dear? I can hardly wiggle my toes."

As Valentine's Day approaches, Remmie becomes more and more distracted. Crystal denies having a brother; he's too embarrassed to say anything further. He feels as if he's driving down a steep mountain road, tires skidding, brakes smoking and squealing, gravel spewing behind him.

He is staring at the calendar when Ailene comes into his office.

"Here's the candy," she says, putting down a plain

white box that has come in the morning mail. "You should get a medal or something for going to all this trouble every year. It must cost twice as much as regular candy."

"It's one of our little traditions. I've told Mother she can have sugar-free chocolate all year, but she says it's sweeter because it's a Valentine's Day gift."

"You doing something special with Crystal?" asks Ailene, who has been monitoring the relationship with a healthy curiosity.

Remmie comes to a decision. "Yes, I am," he says without taking his eyes off the white box.

Late in the morning, he calls Audrey and tells her that he is unable to come home to prepare her lunch, citing the need to run errands. She wishes him a profitable hour and assures him she will have a nice bowl of soup.

Remmie goes to the bank and gains access to the safe deposit box. The jewelry is in a brown felt pouch. He spreads it open and finds the diamond engagement ring given to his mother fifty-odd years ago. If he wished, he could buy a bigger and more impressive one, but he hopes Crystal will accept this as a loving tribute to his mother.

At the drugstore, he buys two heart-shaped boxes of candy. One is red, the other white, and both have glittery bows. He finds a sentimental card for his mother, who will reread it many times before adding it to the collection in her dresser drawer.

When he returns to the office, he opens the white box and dumps the sumptuous chocolates on Ailene's desk. He then refills the box with the sugar-free chocolates made especially for diabetics, writes a loving message to his mother, and tucks the card under the pink ribbon.

Gnawing his lip, he dials the telephone number of a cozy country inn that is a hundred miles away. He makes reservations for dinner for the evening of February 14.

Despite a sudden dryness in his mouth, he also reserves a room with a fireplace and a double bed.

Crystal agrees to dinner. Remmie does not mention the room reservation. He will wait until they are sipping wine and savoring whatever decadently rich dessert the inn has prepared for the event, then slip the ring on her finger and ask her to marry him. He feels a warm tingle as he envisions what will follow.

"How romantic," murmurs Audrey as he describes the plans he has made, although he alludes only obliquely to what he hopes will transpire after his proposal. He's aware that she disapproves of sexual activity outside of wedlock, but he is over forty, after all.

He realizes he is blushing and wills himself to stop behaving like a bashful adolescent. "I'll call Miss McCloud and ask her to stay with you. That way, if you feel dizzy or need extra insulin, she'll be there to help you."

"Don't be absurd," she responds curtly.

"But I'll worry about you if you're here alone all night."

"I can take care of myself—and don't call her against my wishes. If she shows up at the front door, I'll send her away. Now please stop dithering and bring me another blanket. My feet feel as though they're frozen."

He goes to the linen closet in the hallway. As he takes a blanket from the shelf, he hears a peculiar thump. He dashes to his mother's bedroom and finds her lying on the floor like a discarded rag doll.

"Did she break any bones?" asks Crystal.

Remmie puts down his coffee cup and shrugs. "No, she just has some bad bruises. They kept her overnight at the hospital for observation, but Dr. Whitbread insisted she'd be more comfortable in her own bed. I took her home after I got off work."

"And left her alone?"

"Of course not," he says, appalled that she would even ask. "Miss McCloud stopped by with a plant, and I took the opportunity to come see you for a few minutes." He looks at his watch and stands up. "I'd better go."

Crystal stands up but does not move toward him. "Does this mean our Valentine dinner date is off? If you're afraid to leave your mother for more than thirty minutes, I'd like to know it right now. There's a new doctor at the clinic who's asked me out a couple of times. He's single, and he doesn't make plans around his mother."

"We're still going," he says hastily.

She goes to the door and opens it. "You'd better go home, Remmie. I hear your mother calling."

Oddly enough, Remmie almost hears her, too.

Audrey is unable to sleep because of her pain. At least once a night she calls out for Remmie, who hurries into her room with a glass of water and a white pill. Each time she apologizes at length for disturbing him.

"Do you know who Crystal reminds me of?" asks Audrey as Remmie pauses. He is reading the newspaper to her because her eyesight has worsened. It has become a new addition to their evening ritual.

"Who?"

"That woman from the bowling alley. They both have a certain hardness about their eyes. Not that Crystal is anything like . . . what was her name?"

"Lucinda," supplies Remmie. He zeroes in on a story concerning a charity fund-raiser and begins to read.

Too loudly, I'm afraid.

*   *   *

Valentine's Day.

Remmie hands his mother a notebook. Names and telephone numbers are written in a heavy black hand; surely she can make them out should an emergency arise. "It's not too late to call Miss McCloud, Mother. She said she will be delighted to stay with you. If you prefer, she can stay downstairs and you won't even know she's here."

"Absolutely not."

"If you're sure," he says. He has already made his decision, but it is not too late for Audrey to change the course of her destiny. He looks down at her. Her lower lip is extended and her jaw is rigid.

He realizes that when next he sees her, she will be at peace. Blinking back tears, he bends down to brush his lips across her forehead. "Good-bye, Mother," he whispers.

"Good-bye, Mrs. Boles," Crystal says from the doorway. She is holding something behind her back and scuffling her feet as if she were a small child. She gives Remmie a conspiratorial smile. "Aren't you forgetting to give your mother something?"

Remmie's face is bloodless as he takes the white heart-shaped box and presents it to Audrey. "I didn't forget," he says. "Special candy for a special person. Don't eat so much you get a tummyache."

"Don't condescend to me," Audrey says coldly, but her expression softens and she reaches up to squeeze his hand. "I love these chocolates almost as much as I love you, Remmie. One of these days you won't have to go to all the bother to order them just for me."

Remmie stumbles as he leaves the room, brushing past Crystal as if she were nothing more substantial than a shadow.

Unamused, she follows him downstairs to the kitchen, where a second box of chocolates sits on the table.

"Did you order them just for me?" she says, mimicking Audrey's simpery voice.

The trip has not started on a happy note, obviously. Remmie curses as he fights traffic until they are clear of the city, and only then does he loosen his grip on the steering wheel and glance at Crystal.

"You look nervous," he comments.

"So do you." She opens the box of chocolates and offers it to him.

He recoils, then regains control of himself. "Maybe later," he mumbles unhappily.

"Are you worried about your mother?"

"Of course I am. What if she has a dizzy spell and takes another fall? She could break her hip this time and be in such pain that she's unable to call for help."

"She'll be all right," Crystal says as she selects a chocolate and pops it in her mouth. A surprised expression crosses her face, but Remmie is in the midst of passing a truck and does not notice.

In fact, he is so distracted that he fails to respond when she comments on the scenery, and again when she cautions him to slow down as they approach a small town.

She finally taps him on the shoulder. "What's the matter with you, Remmie? Do you want to turn around and go home to check on your mother?"

Sweat dribbles down his forehead. His breathing is irregular, his lips quivering, his eyes darting, his hands once again gripping the steering wheel so tightly that his fingers are unnaturally pale.

"Remmie!" Crystal says, suddenly frightened. "What's wrong?"

He pulls to the shoulder, stops, and leans his head against the steering wheel. "I can't go through with it," he says with a whimper. "I thought I could, but I just can't do it. I'll have to find a telephone and call her before it's too late—even if it means she'll hate me for the rest of her life." He begins to cry. "How could I have betrayed her like this?"

"What are you talking about?"

"I switched the candy. The sugar will put her in a diabetic coma, and it's likely to be fatal unless she gets emergency treatment. I have to call her. If she doesn't answer, I'll call Dr. Whitbread and have him go to the house." He sits up and wipes his cheeks. "Maybe it's not too late. We've only been gone half—"

"It's not too late," Crystal snaps, "and you don't need to call anyone, especially this doctor. You'll be confessing to attempted murder. I doubt the jury will feel much sympathy."

"I don't deserve any sympathy, and I don't care what happens to me. We've got to find a telephone."

She reaches over to take the key from the ignition. After a moment of reflection, she says, "Your mother is not in danger. While I was waiting in the kitchen, I opened both boxes and figured out what you'd done. I switched them back, Remmie. Audrey is contentedly eating sugar-free chocolates."

"She is?" he says numbly.

Crystal's nod lacks enthusiasm and her smile is strained. "Yes, she sure is. I knew you couldn't live with yourself if you did something so terrible."

Remmie finally convinces himself that she is telling the truth and his mother is not in danger. "I suppose I'd better take you home."

"Why?"

"You must loathe me."

"I'll get over it," Crystal says, shrugging. "What I think we'll do is have our dinner and spend the night at this inn. Tomorrow morning we can go to the local courthouse to get a marriage license, and find a justice of the peace. Audrey will be surprised, of course, but she'll get over it more quickly if it's a done deal."

Remmie is more surprised than Audrey will ever be. "You want to get married—knowing that I tried to murder my mother? Don't you want some time to think about it?"

"I assumed you were going to propose this evening, and I'd decided to accept. I've already given my notice at the clinic so that I can stay home and take care of your mother."

Remmie attempts to decipher the odd determination in her voice, but finally gives up and leans over to kiss her. "I brought a ring to give you over dinner," he admits. "It's the one my father presented to my mother on their second date."

"How thoughtful," she says. "You really must call your mother as soon as we check in and reassure yourself that she's perfectly fine."

And so Remmie and Crystal dine by candlelight and make love under a ruffled canopy. The following morning, a license is procured and a justice of the peace conducts a brief ceremony. The witnesses find it remarkably romantic and are teary as the groom kisses the bride.

Only later, as Remmie catches sight of the white heart-shaped box on his mother's bedside table, does he ask himself the obvious question: how did Crystal know to switch back the chocolates?

He does not ask her, however. He is a good husband as well as a good son.

And there is always next year.

⟦ MARGARET MARON ⟧

MARGARET MARON WENT HOME TO HER NORTH
Carolina roots to write her ninth novel, Bootlegger's
Daughter, her first to feature Judge Deborah Knott. The
result was publishing history. Bootlegger's Daughter
made a unique and unprecedented sweep of the top mystery awards, winning the Agatha, Anthony, Edgar, and
Macavity for best novel. Deborah Knott's adventures continue in Southern Discomfort and Shooting at Loons.
Maron is also the author of seven exquisitely crafted and
beautifully written Sigrid Harald novels, which are now
being reissued. Coming soon is her eighth Sigrid Harald
novel, Fugitive Colors. A nonseries novel, a prequel to
Bootlegger's Daughter, is Bloody Kin.

Maron is a past president of Sisters in Crime and a
past national director of Mystery Writers of America and
is active in the American Crime Writers League. She lives
on the family farm near Raleigh, North Carolina.

Maron again visits Colleton County and Judge Knott in
this delightful and oh-so-southern tale, "With This Ring."

With This Ring

"Detective Bryant," said Dwight's voice when he finally
picked up his extension at the Colleton County Sheriff's
Department.

"Can you still button the pants of your army dress
uniform?" I asked.

"Say what?"

"I was out at your mother's last week." I let a hint of
mischief slip into my tone. "She said that picture of you
at the White House was taken only three years ago, but I

reckon you've put on a few pounds since you came home and started eating regular."

As if a district court judge has nothing better to do with her time than call just to needle him about his thickening waistline, Dwight bit like a largemouth bass suckered by some plastic feathers and shiny paint.

"Listen," he said. "I bet I can fit into my old clothes a lot better'n you could fit into yours."

I reeled him in. "It's a bet. Loser pays for the tickets."

"Wait a minute. You want to back that mule up and walk her past me again?"

"The Widdington Jaycees are putting on a charity ball for Valentine's Day," I explained. "I know you don't own a tuxedo, but—"

"You and that Chapin guy have a fight?" Dwight growled. "Or don't he know how to dance in a monkey suit?"

For the life of me, I can't understand Dwight's attitude. It's not like Kidd's the first man he's ever seen me with, and it's certainly not like he's interested in me himself. Our families have known each other five or six generations, and Dwight's always treated me like he's one of my older brothers. One of my *bossy* older brothers. Unfortunately, small-town social life resembles the Ark—everything two by two. So when I need an escort and don't have one on tap, I just call Dwight, who's divorced and still unattached. By choice, he says.

Yet ever since I met Kidd Chapin down at the coast last spring, Dwight's done nothing but snipe at him. Dwight's a chief of detectives; Kidd's a game warden. Both like to hunt and fish and stomp around in the woods. Wouldn't you think they'd mesh together tight as Velcro?

Oil and vinegar.

I've decided it's a guy thing and nothing worth bothering *my* pretty little head with.

"Kidd has to be at a conference down in Atlanta that weekend. Look, if you don't want to come dancing and help me act the fool, fine. I'll call Davis, see if he's free that night."

Davis Reed's a good-timing, currently unmarried state representative from down east, and Dwight hates his politics. (Hey, I'd never actually sleep with a Republican, but that doesn't mean I won't let one buy me dinner.)

"Act the fool how?" Dwight asked cautiously, and I knew I had him flopping in my net.

"It's a bridesmaids ball," I said. "Everybody's supposed to wear something we've worn in a wedding."

"What's so foolish about that?"

"Dwight Bryant, have you ever *looked* at one of those dresses?" I was torn between amusement and exasperation.

Men.

But that's not fair. Why should I bad-mouth men when it's women that keep putting four to eight of their best friends into some of the most ridiculous dresses known to polite society?

Was it a man who thought it'd look really darling to send us down the aisle one Christmas wearing red plaid taffeta over enormous hoop skirts and carrying tall white candles?

Lighted white candles that dripped wax all down the front of our skirts?

No, that was Missy Randolph.

Was it a man who put us in skin-tight sheaths of bright pink satin so that the bride looked like a silver spoon surrounded by six Pepto-Bismol bottles?

No, that was Portland Smith.

"What about this one?" said Aunt Zell as we prowled the far end of her unheated attic, where several long gowns hung like ghosts from the rafter nails, each Cinderella fantasy shrouded in a white cotton sheet.

"You girls were just precious in these picture hats."

"The hats were okay," I conceded, shivering in the February chill, "though that shade of lavender made me look downright jaundiced. It was the scratchy lace mitts. My wrists itched for a week. And Katy's parasol kept poking all the ushers in the eye."

"Such a pretty garden wedding," Aunt Zell sighed as she pulled the sheet back over that gown. "Too bad they split up before the first frost. Now where's the dress you wore when Seth and Minnie married? You were cute as a june bug in it."

"That was a flower-girl dress," I reminded her. "And have you ever seen a flower girl who *wasn't* cute as a june bug?"

Here in Colleton County, if a groom has a sister, she *will* be in the wedding even if she and the bride despise each other. For the record, I never exactly despised any of my brothers' brides (some of the boys got married before I was even born), but scattering rose petals can get awfully tiresome after you've done it four or five times.

The attic was too chilly for lingering, and I quickly narrowed my choices down to two.

The ball committee promised us prizes in various categories. If total tackiness were a category, surely the dress I'd worn in Caroline Corbett's wedding would be an automatic winner: moss green lace over a moss polyester sateen that had already started mutating toward chartreuse before the first chord of Mendelssohn was ever played. The neckline dipped so low in front that only a cluster of green chiffon roses preserved our maiden modesty. Droopy shoulder flounces were tied up with dangling sateen ribbons that had tickled my arms just enough to keep me slapping for a fly or a mosquito. Accessories included a floppy picture hat big as a cartwheel and a wicker basket filled with more chiffon roses. What finally decided me against wearing it to the ball were the tiered net petticoats that shredded panty-hose and legs indiscriminately.

Besides, the frosty air made bare-armed summer frocks look even more inane than usual. I was drawn instead to a wintry blue velvet concoction.

Janelle Mayhew's idea of Victorian began with a high, tight white lace collar, descended to pouf sleeves that had to be stuffed with tissue paper to hold their balloon shape, and was topped (or should I say *bottomed*?) by an enormous bustle. The white plumed fan had barely begun to molt and it ought to amuse Dwight. Besides, the dark blue velvet, bustle and all, actually flattered my sandy blond hair and turned my blue eyes sapphire. As a thirty-something judge, maybe it'd be more dignified to go for pretty instead of comic.

More politic, too, because Janelle and Glenn Riggsbee were Widdington Jaycees and certain to be at the ball. Their restaurant has prospered over the years, and they contributed to my last campaign by hosting a big reception for me out there in the country.

The old-fashioned dress had been a little on the loose side twelve years ago; now it needed a whalebone corset with power lacing. Even with a girdle, I was going to have to sit up straight all evening and remember to laugh no harder than Queen Victoria.

When Dwight came to pick me up that Saturday night, he was wearing a borrowed black tuxedo and the fuchsia sateen cummerbund and clip-on bow tie that had been dyed to match the bridesmaids's dresses when he ushered for a friend in D.C.

"Aw, and I was really looking forward to your sword," I teased.

"Mama could've let out the pants," Dwight said sheepishly, "but she said she'd rather pay for the damn tickets herself than try to get that dress jacket to fit."

Before he'd write me a check for the cost of the

tickets, he rousted Aunt Zell from upstairs where she and Uncle Ash were watching the news and made her swear she hadn't added a gusset of blue velvet in my side seams.

"No gloating, okay?"

"I *never* gloat," I told him, tucking the check away in my beaded evening bag.

He and Aunt Zell both snorted.

Widdington's about thirty-five minutes east of Dobbs, and we drove over with Avery and Portland Brewer. Portland is Uncle Ash's sister's daughter and therefore Aunt Zell's niece by marriage, which makes us courtesy cousins. Not that a family connection is needed. We laugh at the same things and have been friends since junior girls class in Sunday school.

When Dwight opened the rear door of their car, she twisted around in the front seat and said, "Oh, shoot! I told Avery I just *knew* you were going to wear that pig-pink thing Mother made y'all buy for our wedding."

She had a winter coat draped over the droop-shouldered horror of Caroline Corbett's green lace. In Portland's case, the polyester underlining had gone past chartreuse, right on into an acid yellow. "I'm competing in the 'Most Unusual Color Combination' category," she giggled.

"Where's your hat and garden basket?"

"In the trunk," said Avery. "The brim's so wide she couldn't fit in the car."

Before the interior light went off, Portland noticed my pearl earrings. "I thought we wore red-and-blue rhinestone hoops with that dress?"

"We did. That's why Elizabeth thought you stole the ring, remember? When she caught a flash of sparkling stones in your hand?"

"She just said that to throw suspicion off herself," said Portland. "I still think she's the one who took it."

"They never did get it back, did they?" asked Avery

as he waited for a pickup to pass before pulling away
from the curb.

"Huh?" said Dwight.

"Oh, that's right," I remembered. "You were probably
stationed in Panama or someplace when Janelle Mayhew
married Glenn Riggsbee. This is the dress Portland and I
and their three sisters wore in their wedding."

"All five of you?" he asked dryly. "No wonder you
can still squeeze into it."

I fluttered my ostrich-plume fan under his chin. "Why,
Rhett, honey, you just say the sweetest *thangs*? Don't
y'all pay him no nevermind," I told Portland and Avery.
"He's still pouting 'cause he couldn't get into his little
ol' dress uniform?"

"You said you never gloat," Dwight reminded me.
"What ring?"

Avery sailed through the last stoplight in Dobbs and
headed east along a backcountry road. As we drove
through the cold winter night, stars blazing overhead,
we took turns telling Dwight about Janelle's god-awful
engagement ring and how it disappeared in the middle
of her wedding to Glenn Riggsbee.

"It all began with Elizabeth and Nancy—Glenn's two
sisters," said Portland. "Both of them wanted the ring he
gave Janelle."

Dwight might not've gone to college, but he knows
about Freudian complexes. "Isn't that a little unnatu-
ral?"

"We're talking greed, not Greek," I told him, "and
strictly speaking, it really began with Glenn's great-
uncle."

Glenn Riggsbee was named for his mother's favorite
uncle, a larger-than-life character who ran away from
home at fifteen and went wildcatting in Texas back in the
twenties. Unlike most kids who go off to seek their for-
tunes and slink home a few years later hoping nobody'll
notice their tails dragging in the mud, Great-Uncle Glenn

hit a gusher before he was eighteen, married a flashy dance-hall blond before he was twenty, and lived high, wide, and handsome for the next fifty years.

He and his wife never had children, so when she died and the big money ran out, he came back to Colleton County, bought a little house next door to his niece, and settled down to bossing Glenn and his sisters around like they were his own grandchildren. Portland and I never even heard of him till our good friend Janelle Mayhew started dating Glenn, but we heard plenty after that because Janelle was terrified of him.

With good reason.

True, he'd been a Daddy Warbucks to Mrs. Riggsbee and her children when he had lots of money, lavishing her with expensive treats and setting up trust funds so Glenn and his two sisters could go to college in style. And yes, he continued to be generous with the dregs of his fortune, helping Glenn buy a first car, for instance, or doling out to the girls some of his late wife's gold and silver baubles.

But in old age, he was just as opinionated and short-tempered as he'd been in his youth. Any help he gave was on his terms and any gifts he gave came with stretchy elastic attached. For such a renegade, he had a surprisingly wide streak of conservatism.

He had expected both of Glenn's sisters to become schoolteachers and to stop work once they had babies. When Elizabeth majored in accounting and had a chance to buy into a new insurance brokerage firm soon after graduation, he refused to help. Said it wasn't fitting for an unmarried woman to be in a position to boss around married men.

The same thing happened when Nancy wanted to become a minister. A woman preacher? The very concept shocked him to the core. "Be damned if I'll bankroll such blasphemy!" Somehow he found a legal loophole that let him tie up Nancy's college trust fund until she tearfully promised not to take any theology courses.

As a male, Glenn was, theoretically, free to major in whatever he wanted, but you can imagine Great-Uncle Glenn's reaction when he finally realized that Glenn planned to use his shiny new degree in restaurant management to turn an old dilapidated farmhouse into a restaurant.

"A restaurant out in the middle of the country? Stupidest damn thing I ever heard of," he snorted. "Don't expect me to help finance it."

In vain did Glenn point out that I-40 was going to dot the county with housing developments full of wage-earning commuters happy to pay someone else to fix supper.

Nor did it open Great-Uncle Glenn's wallet when he heard that Janelle was taking cooking courses at the local community college. Indeed, he took to wondering audibly if she was good enough for young Glenn. After all, what kind of trashy mama did Janelle have that wouldn't teach her own daughter how to fry chicken and make buttermilk biscuits?

While it's true that the Mayhews were even poorer than the Riggsbees, they were by no means trash, and Janelle was always a hard worker. She also has lovely manners and yes-sirred and no-sirred Great-Uncle Glenn till, when Glenn said he was going to ask her to set a date, the old man went to his lockbox at Dobbs First National and gave Glenn the platinum-and-diamond ring he'd bought to woo his dance-hall wife.

We'd never seen anything quite like it: a huge rose-cut yellow diamond surrounded by forty tapered baguette diamonds, sapphires, and rubies in a ballerina mount.

"What's a ballerina mount?" asked Dwight.

"Picture a big yellow golf ball surrounded by a red-white-and-blue-ruffle," I said.

"Sounds sort of ugly to me," he ventured.

"It was beyond ugly," Portland assured him.

"But the diamond was what they call a flawless fancy yellow and was supposed to have been insured for eighty thousand dollars," I recalled.

"Supposed to be?"

"That's why I'm sure Elizabeth took it," said Portland. "Where else did she get the money to buy a partnership?"

"Circumstantial evidence," Avery murmured. Like Portland, he's an attorney, too.

"Not entirely," she argued. "See, Dwight, Elizabeth hadn't bought in with Bob McAdams yet, but she'd been working there a couple of years and she was supposed to have written up a policy for the ring once it went from Great-Uncle Glenn's lockbox to Janelle's finger—"

"But Elizabeth assumed the Mayhews had household insurance," I said. "And since Janelle was still living at home to save money for the restaurant, Elizabeth thought that would protect it up to the wedding."

"That's what she *claimed*," said Portland, "but even if the Mayhews did have insurance, no piddly little renters' policy would ever cover an eighty-thousand-dollar ring. Uh-uh, Deb'rah. She knew there'd be hard-nosed investigators swarming all over the place if Janelle filed a claim for eighty thousand. No policy, no claim. No claim, no serious investigation."

"No policy?" asked Dwight from the darkness beside me.

"Elizabeth dated it to take effect at twelve noon, which was when the ceremony took place and when Janelle's residence would officially change from her parents' house. The last time anybody saw the ring was at eleven-thirty when Janelle stuck it in her makeup bag in the choir robing room next to the vestibule."

I took up the tale. "And before you ask, no, nobody was seen going into that room between the time we finished dressing until after the ceremony. Miss Louisa Ferncliff directed the wedding and she was right there in the vestibule the whole time, making sure the ushers knew whether the guests were bride's side or groom's and then sending us down the aisle spaced just right. If anybody'd gone back in, she'd have seen them."

"Who was last out of the robing room?"

"Janelle and me," Portland answered. "Her sister Faye was maid of honor and I was matron of honor. Deb'rah went first, then Nancy, Elizabeth, Faye, and me. The room was empty after Janelle and I went out to the vestibule and I pulled the door shut."

"So who was first back in?"

I shrugged. "All of us. There was a receiving line with the parents right after the recessional, then we all went to put on fresh lipstick for the formal pictures and that's when Janelle discovered the ring was gone."

"And the only ones in the robing room the whole time were you six?"

"Are you kidding?" said Portland. "Both mothers were in and out, as well as Miss Louisa, the photographer, the minister's wife—"

"Don't forget Omaleen Grimes," I said. "She was dating one of Glenn's ushers, and she acted like that gave her a right to stick her nose in everywhere."

"But between the time Janelle took off the ring and the time she realized it was gone?"

Portland and I had to admit it. During the crucial time, there was just us five bridesmaids, Mrs. Mayhew, Mrs. Riggsbee, and Janelle herself.

Everybody had been sweet as molasses pie, but Portland and I and seventeen-year-old Faye Mayhew had hovered protectively around Janelle because Elizabeth and Nancy still had their noses out of joint. Glenn Riggsbee was damn lucky to find someone as fine as Janelle, but in their minds—particularly Elizabeth's— their brother was marrying down. The Mayhews were too poor to own their own home, Janelle hadn't gone to college, and on top of that, she had somehow dazzled

Great-Uncle Glenn into parting with the last substantial piece of jewelry in his possession.

Both sisters had been allowed to wear the ring on special occasions in the past, and each had hoped that Great-Uncle Glenn would leave it to her someday: Elizabeth because she was the oldest, Nancy because she was the baby of the family and had already been given his wife's garnet necklace. No matter how nice Janelle was to them, it was all they could do to maintain a polite façade, though a stranger wouldn't have known it for all the "sugars" and "honeys" being thrown around the choir robing room that morning.

A moment or two before eleven-thirty, Mrs. Mayhew had set the veil on Janelle's hair. When Janelle lifted her hands to adjust it, the gaudy ring flashed in the pale January sunlight.

"Don't forget to take that ring off before you start down the aisle," said Mrs. Mayhew. "Your finger needs to be bare when Glenn puts on your wedding band."

As if in chorus, Elizabeth and Nancy both offered to hold it for her.

"That's okay," said Janelle.

She slipped the yellow diamond into the same worn gray velvet box Great-Uncle Glenn had given his wife sixty years earlier. It was so old, the domed lid no longer closed with a tight snap, but she tucked the box into her makeup bag. Her eyes met ours nervously in the mirror. "Glenn's ring! Por?"

Portland waggled her thumb and there was the wide gold wedding band that Janelle would slip onto Glenn's finger in less than an hour.

At that instant, Miss Louisa stuck her head in and hissed, "Sst! Mothers! Places!"

The clock above the mirrors said 11:31.

We'd been primping and preening since ten o'clock, so you'd think we could have sat with our hands folded quietly and discussed the weather or something, wouldn't you? Instead we all dived back into our own makeup bags, touching up mascara and lipstick, adjusting our bustles, adjusting Janelle's veil, reminding each other how to hold the white plumed fans at identical angles, then a final spritz of hairspray before Miss Louisa herded us all out into the vestibule.

Afterwards, none of us could say who had or hadn't touched which makeup bag.

But that was later, when Sheriff Poole questioned us.

At the beginning, Janelle was sure the ring must have somehow worked its way out of the loose-lidded velvet box and slipped down among her cosmetics. Then, that it must have fallen out while we all made last-minute touch-ups. Surely on the floor, beneath the dressing table, under a chair . . . ?

Nothing.

"Somebody's taken it!" Portland said dramatically.

"Don't be silly," said Janelle, anxiously uncapping all her lipsticks, as if that ring could possibly fit inside a slender tube. Her sister Faye was down on her hands and knees searching beneath the choir robes. "We were the only ones here and . . ."

Her voice trailed away as she saw Portland and me staring at her new sisters-in-law.

Elizabeth and Nancy both turned beet red.

"If you think for one minute—!" Elizabeth huffed indignantly. "You can search me if you like."

"Me, too!" said Nancy.

"Don't be silly," Janelle said again.

"Girls, girls!" Miss Louisa stood in the doorway. "The photographer is waiting."

"Miss Louisa," I said. "Did anybody come in here during the ceremony?"

"No, of course not, dear. Why do you ask?"

Janelle broke in. "Miss Louisa, could you please tell the photographer we'll be right there?"

As Miss Louisa tottered away on her little high heels,

Janelle twisted her brand new wedding band nervously and said, "Look, if one of you took it as a joke . . ."

Instant denial was on all our lips.

"It's okay if it's a joke," she continued doggedly. "Let's go out like nothing's happened, and if whoever took it will just drop it on the floor, that will be the end of it, okay?" Her voice trembled. "Just don't tell Glenn or our folks, okay? It'd spoil our wedding day. Please?"

Subdued, we promised to keep quiet.

Without looking around, Janelle swept out to the sanctuary and we trailed along after. During the next half hour, as the photographer grouped and regrouped various components of the wedding party, Janelle managed to send each bridesmaid back to the robing room alone. Would Elizabeth fetch her lipstick? Would Nancy be a dear and find a comb? A tissue, Faye? Oh goodness, Por, she'd forgotten her blue garter!

Before she could invent a task for me, the photographer decided to take a shot of the newlyweds' hands, and Great-Uncle Glenn said, "Take me one with her engagement ring, too."

"I'll go get it," I said brightly, absolutely positive that I'd find the stupid thing back on the robing room dressing table.

Wrong.

Nor had it been dropped on the floor as Janelle suggested. I searched every square inch.

After that, a bit of discreet hell broke loose. Mrs. Riggsbee managed to keep Great-Uncle Glenn reined in till after the reception was over. Fortunately, it was only punch and wedding cake in the church's fellowship hall and as soon as the cake was cut, Janelle and Glenn pretended to leave in a shower of rice. Actually, all they did was drive over to their new apartment, change clothes and sneak back into the church robing room where Sheriff Bo Poole was questioning the rest of us.

"I'm surprised I never heard anything about this,"

Dwight said as we entered the outskirts of Widdington.

"They pretty much hushed it up when it was clear nobody was going to confess," said Portland. "Janelle insisted that someone had to 've sneaked into the robing room while Miss Louisa was watching the ceremony because there was no way that a sister or friend could have done her that shabby."

I smoothed the plumes on my fan. "Great-Uncle Glenn was furious, of course."

"But Janelle faced him down," Portland said. "She told him it was her ring and she was the one who'd been careless with it and it was her loss, not his."

"Remember his face when Elizabeth admitted that there was no insurance? I thought he was going to hit her with his walking stick."

"So what happened next?" asked Dwight.

"I think Sheriff Poole put a description on the wire, but I never heard that anything came of it," said Portland. "Great-Uncle Glenn died a few months later, and when Janelle and Glenn got back from the funeral, they found the ring in their mailbox. All the little diamonds and sapphires and rubies were still there, but the big yellow diamond was gone."

"No one ever confessed?" asked Dwight.

"Not that we ever heard," we told him.

What we left unsaid was the suspicion that maybe Janelle thought Portland or I had taken the ring because after that, we were never quite as close again.

"I don't *care* what happened to it!" she stormed when Portland pressed her about the theft a few months later. "If one of y'all needed the money that bad, then that was a better use for that darned old ring than on my finger."

Portland had called me the minute she got back to Dobbs. "She thinks you or I took it."

"She probably heard about our new mink coats and all our trips to Bermuda," I said dryly.

So we dropped it after that. Janelle was still friendly with us when we saw her, but as time passed, those occasions were less frequent. She and Glenn threw themselves into the restaurant, which took off like a rocket from opening day, and Portland and I were both caught up in our own careers back in Dobbs. Anyhow, loyalties always realign when you marry outside your own crowd. Janelle had made her bed among Riggsbees and from that day forward, it was as if Elizabeth and Nancy had never acted ugly to her. Or stolen from her and Glenn.

"Well, one good thing came out of it," Portland said, paralleling my thoughts. "Elizabeth was so grateful to Janelle for understanding about the insurance mixup that they became real friends from then on."

The Widdington Jaycees were holding their ball at the new Shrine club and as Avery drove into the parking lot, laughing couples streamed toward the entrance.

Heaven knows there was plenty to laugh at. I haven't seen that much organdy, chiffon, and taffeta froufrou since I helped judge a Little Miss Makely beauty contest last year.

Inside, the club was decorated in valentines of every size and jammed to the walls, but friends had saved space at a table for us. While Dwight and Avery went off to fight their way to the bar, lights played across the dance floor and I saw a lot of familiar faces.

And one familiar dress.

Nancy Riggsbee was much heavier now. The seams on her blue velvet had clearly been let out and her bustle rode on hips even more ample than mine, but she beamed with seeming pleasure when she spotted me and came right over.

"Deborah Knott! How you been, lady?"

We kissed air, and half screaming to be heard above the music and talk, I said, "Where's your fan? And don't tell me Elizabeth's here in this same dress, too? And Faye?"

"No, Faye's living in Boston now and Elizabeth's little girl came home from school sick with the flu yesterday, so I'm here on her ticket. In her dress. Mine was cut up for a church pageant years ago. Mary and one of the Magi, I think. The fans went for angel wings."

So Elizabeth had porked up a bit, too, since I last saw her? Mean of me to be smug about it. To atone, I told Nancy I'd heard about her getting a church out in the country from Durham and how was she liking it after so long in Virginia?

It was too loud for small talk though, and after a few more shouted pleasantries, Dwight and Avery came back with our drinks. I introduced Dwight to Nancy, who said she was going to go find Janelle and tell her we were there.

Fortunately someone got the band to turn down their speakers about then and conversation became possible again.

"So she got to be a preacher after all?" Dwight asked.

I nodded. "After Great-Uncle Glenn died, the others encouraged her to go to divinity school. It was a struggle because he didn't leave much, but Janelle and Glenn pitched in. Elizabeth, too, even though she was scraping every penny to buy into the firm about then."

"Notice Nancy's ring if she comes back," Portland told him. "After the ring came home without the yellow diamond, Glenn had the diamond baguettes set into a sort of engagement ring. They gave Elizabeth the sapphires and Nancy the rubies. Janelle told me that's pretty much what they would've done anyhow if he'd left both girls the ring—sell the big stone and make two rings out of the little ones. In the end, it made three."

I was tired of that stupid ring. The band was playing a lively two-step and I wanted to shake my bustle. Despite his size, Dwight dances surprisingly well, and I didn't mean to waste the music talking about something over and done with. We moved out onto the dance floor and were soon twirling with the best.

A couple of slow numbers followed, then the spotlight fell on the emcee who announced the first category of the evening: Heart and Flowers, i.e., fussiest dress. To the strains of "Here Comes the Bride," nine women glided across the dance floor, as if down an aisle, to a makeshift altar behind the emcee. The clear winner was a stiff yellow net covered with row upon row of tight little ruffles.

Amid the laughter and applause, I felt a light touch on my arm and there was Janelle smiling at Portland and me. She gave us each a hug and said to me, "Nancy said you signed up in the prettiest dress category? I'm so flattered. It *was* a beautiful wedding, wasn't it?"

She herself was wearing ice blue satin from her sister-in-law Elizabeth's wedding. "That's the only time I was a bridesmaid," Janelle said regretfully. "I was always big-as-a-house pregnant when everybody else was getting married."

One of the Widdington Jaycees dragged her away to help with something, and she made us promise we wouldn't leave without speaking again.

The next category was My Funny Valentine for the most unusual gown, and it was a tie between a Ronald McDonald clown (the bride managed a local franchise) and a gold lamé jumpsuit (the skydiving bride and groom were married in free-fall).

Portland didn't win the Purple Heart Award (the most unusual color actually went to a hot-pink velvet bodice, orange organza skirt, and lime green sash), but she was persuaded to enter Kind Hearts and Coronets for the most accessories and won handily with her huge picture hat, arm-length lace mitts, and wicker basket full of chiffon roses.

In between, as groups of contestants were assembled for their march down the mock aisle, we danced and chatted and filled several bedoiled sandwich plates with the usual array of finger foods found at a typical wedding reception: raw vegetables and herb dip, cheese straws, cucumber sandwiches, tiny hot rolls stuffed with ham and melted pimiento cheese, salted nuts, and heart-shaped butter mints.

Despite all the laughter, wearing the dress brought back memories of Janelle and Glenn's wedding; and seeing Nancy around the room in the same garb only emphasized the feeling. I knew Portland was flashing on it, too, because she kept going back to the missing ring. Faye, Nancy, or Elizabeth. Who had taken it? (Loyally, we'd each long since cleared the other.)

If Faye had eventually lavished money around, we'd never heard of it.

It had to be Elizabeth or Nancy.

"Nancy's a preacher," Portland said.

"That wouldn't have mattered," I argued. "They both felt entitled to the ring. Don't forget, she came up with tuition to divinity school."

"Elizabeth helped her though. And so did Glenn and Janelle. Janelle didn't buy any new clothes for three years, till long after Elizabeth bought a partnership with Bob McAdams. Where did Elizabeth get enough money if not from pawning the ring?"

"I thought Glenn cosigned a loan with her?" said Avery.

"Yes, but—"

"You gals have gone at it all wrong," said Dwight. "From what you've told me, there's only one person who could have taken the ring without being caught or even suspected."

I hate that superior air he puts on when he's being Dick Tracy, but all of a sudden, I realized he was right.

"Who?" asked Avery.

"The woman who directed the wedding, of course."

"Miss Louisa Ferncliff?" Portland exclaimed.

Dwight lifted his glass to her. "The only person alone out in the vestibule while everyone else was taking part in the ceremony. Anybody ever take a look at *her* lifestyle after the wedding?"

Avery cocked his head. "You know something, ol' son? I sort of remember when she died, Ed Whitbread was the one who drew up her will, and when he came over to file it at the courthouse, seems like he said he was surprised how much money she did have to leave that sorry nephew of hers down in Wilmington."

Portland was looking doubtful. "Miss *Louisa?*"

I spread my fan and drew myself up in a most judicial manner. "It's unfair to slander the name of a good woman who can no longer defend herself, but"—I used the fan to shield my voice from the rest of the table—"one thing's for sure. Miss Louisa Ferncliff directed just about every single wedding at that church for years. She sure would know that brides take off their engagement rings and leave them somewhere in the robing room, but that was the first ring really worth taking, wouldn't you say?"

"I'll be damned," said Portland. "Miss Louisa!"

She jumped up from the table. "Come on, Deb'rah! Let's go tell Janelle."

Protesting that we had no proof, I followed her around the edge of the dance floor until we found Janelle, who, as one of the ball's organizers, had just presented the Heart of Carolina prize for the most denim or gingham in a bridesmaid's dress.

Quickly, we maneuvered her into the lobby where it was quieter and Portland laid out Dwight's theory and my supporting logic.

Janelle was flabbergasted. "Miss *Louisa* stole my ring?"

"She certainly had plenty of opportunity," I said cautiously, "but I don't see how you'd ever prove it. She left everything to that sorry nephew and what he didn't sell off, he either burned or threw out."

"I don't care!" A radiance swept across Janelle's sweet face and she hugged Portland. "We never once thought of Miss Louisa. I can't wait to tell Glenn. If you could know what it means that we can say it was her and not—"

She broke off and hugged us both again, then whirled away back into the ballroom.

"Well, I'll be blessed," said Portland, standing there with her mouth hanging open. "Not you or me after all, Deb'rah. She really did think it was one of Glenn's sisters."

"Or they could have accused her own sister," I reminded her. "For all they knew, Faye could have been the thief."

"Oh, I'm so glad Dwight finally figured it out. Let's go buy him a drink."

"You go ahead," I told her.

The band was playing a suburban version of "Hometown Honeymoon" when I caught up with Janelle.

"You and Glenn went to New York on your honeymoon, didn't you?"

Surprised, she nodded.

"Is that where you sold the diamond?"

"What?"

"The biggest diamond market in the country's right there on Forty-seventh Street. You'd have gotten better money for it there than anywhere here in North Carolina."

There was a door off to the side and Janelle pulled me through it into an empty office, the club manager's by the look of it.

"You said Miss Louisa must've taken it."

"I said she had lots of opportunity," I corrected. "You had the most though."

"That's crazy! Why would I steal my own engagement ring? It wasn't even insured."

"I think that's exactly why you did it," I said. "You're not really a thief and you wouldn't have pretended it was stolen if it meant the insurance company was going to be defrauded of eighty thousand dollars. But the ring was legally yours, you and Glenn needed money, and that was the simplest way to get it without ticking off his uncle. All you needed to do was go through that charade."

Janelle was shaking her head. "No, no, *NO!*"

"Oh, get real," I told her. "How else did you and Glenn have enough to get the restaurant off to such a good start? How'd Glenn have enough collateral to cosign a loan for Elizabeth's partnership so quick?"

"Uncle Glenn—"

"Uncle Glenn didn't leave that kind of money. I was nosy enough to look up the records when his estate was settled even though I never put two and two together. The house went to Glenn's mom and what was split between Glenn and his sisters wouldn't have bought a partnership in a hot dog stand at the fair. That's why we were so sure one of them took it."

Her eyes fell.

"It was mean of you to let Portland think you suspected us all these years."

Janelle threw up her hands in exasperation. "I didn't want to, but it was the only way I could make her quit talking about it. I was afraid if she kept on, she'd finally figure it out."

That dog-with-a-bone tenacity makes Portland a good lawyer, but it's a real pain in the neck for some of her friends, and I couldn't help grinning.

"Are you going to tell her?" Janelle asked.

"And spoil the fun she and Dwight are having, thinking Miss Louisa did it?"

Janelle giggled and I had to laugh, too. "You know,

I bet Miss Louisa would love it if people remembered her for pulling off a slick jewel theft."

Better than not being remembered at all, I judged, and clasped Janelle's hand. We both looked down at the circle of diamond baguettes that sparkled modestly above her wedding band.

"It really was the tackiest ring in the whole world," she said.

"Something that trashy deserved to get itself stolen," I agreed.

As we stepped back into the room a few minutes later, someone yelled, "Here she is!" and immediately pushed me into the final lineup of the evening. Queen of Hearts. The prettiest dress of weddings past.

Nancy, in her sister's dress, had entered this category, too, and there was a truly gorgeous Scarlett O'Hara confection of pale green organza, plus a couple of sophisticated black silks, but none of them had a fan of white ostrich plumes and none of them was as shameless at working a crowd.

The prize was a five-pound, red satin, heart-shaped box of chocolates.

I won by a landslide.

[LIA MATERA]

LIA MATERA'S SLEUTHS, FORMER RADICAL WILLA
Jansson and tough litigator Laura Di Palma, are San
Francisco lawyers who confront moral and ethical dilem-
mas. Matera's fiction clearly reflects how the unrest in
the 1960s has affected American mores. Her novels have
twice been nominated for the Edgar and three times for the
Anthony. The New York Times selected Prior Convictions as a notable book of 1991 and described the protagonist as "one of the most articulate and surely the wittiest
of women sleuths at large in the genre." Matera's titles,
Where Lawyers Fear to Tread, A Radical Departure,
The Smart Money, Hidden Agenda, The Good Fight,
Prior Convictions, a Hard Bargain and Face Value
led Newsweek magazine to say that she was "poised
for a breakthrough." Kirkus Reviews predicts she is "on
the verge of bestsellerdom."

Matera is a member of Sisters in Crime and has had
short stories in the Sisters in Crime and Deadly Allies
anthologies. She lives in Santa Cruz, California, with
her son.

In "Do Not Resuscitate," a second wife faces a fateful
decision.

Do Not Resuscitate

She awakened with a prickle of dread like sharp-nailed
fingers up her side. Then she closed her eyes again,
closed them tight. One of her inner voices, sweet and
coaxing, usually reserved for Hank, her husband of five
years, chastised: Oh honey, don't squish your face up. If
Hank's watching, he's going to think you look like one

of those dolls with dried apples for heads.

Not that Hank would think any such thing. But she always made sure he couldn't think anything crueler than she'd already thought herself: that way, she was dejinxed, protected. No matter that she didn't need protection.

She'd married Hank, seventy-three to her fifty-one, because he was absolutely devoted and uncritical of her, a big leathery old cowboy with a quick smile and a generous nature and, until his hard stroke three years ago, a wonderful body for a man his age. Even with the stroke, his good conditioning and can-do attitude had brought him most of the way back. It had been a hellish few years, but except for kind of a pinched look on the left side of his face and some stiltedness in his walk, he was still her lean, mean ranching machine.

Just thinking of him soothed her unattributed anxiety on this chill November morning. She reached a plump, languid arm across the bed, feeling for Hank. Nothing. She fanned the arm as if making a snow angel. How odd: the sheets were cold. Whyever would the sheets be cold?

In fact, her whole body was cold. That was the sensation she'd translated into prickling apprehension.

She realized she was uncovered. "Hank?" She could hear panic in her voice. This was too much like three years ago, when his middle-of-the-night stroke had sent him sliding off the bed, dragging the satin comforter with him.

She'd awakened then to find him on the floor, murmuring vaguely and disjointedly about having rolled off. But she could tell by the temperature of the sheets that he'd rolled off much earlier in the night. And besides, why hadn't he gotten back up?

She'd dialed 911 with trembling fingers, seeing that his right side was frozen into a fetal curve. And that he'd wet himself. And that half his face had collapsed into a slack mask.

She'd been scared to death, of course, scared of losing him. Hank was the only one in her endlessly dreary life who'd loved her right. Not that it had been perfect. Not that she hadn't cried rivers over his first wife, whom she couldn't bear to hear about even for a second. Not that she hadn't offered to let him go the time that cute neighbor was making a play for him, or the time that his ex-sister-in-law was bawling on his shoulder because her boy got shot.

Every time she saw him with a pretty woman it was torture. He was so good and so wonderful. And she wasn't much; no, indeed. Not much on looks, not much on brains, disorganized, bad with money, always buying shoes that turned out not to fit or antiques that turned out to be fakes. And she didn't get Hank's jokes sometimes. And she couldn't keep track of politics even when they affected ranch business.

It was like her brother always used to say: if she was a fish, anybody would throw her back. She used to try to tag after her big brother, she loved him so. But he'd play with anybody anywhere anytime to get away from her, and he took every chance to let her know she was ugly and stupid and boring. And her parents, though they tried to give her love, couldn't help but love her brother better. They showed off his report cards and athletic trophies, and they laughed at his quick wit, and later when he became a magazine writer, they kept a leather scrapbook of his stories.

They'd been good folk. It wasn't their fault they couldn't find anything to admire in their dumbish lump of a daughter who kept living at home even into her forties without much to say for herself, bringing round one mean-tempered boyfriend after another who used her for sex with one eye out at all times for a cuter prospect.

And then, just when things seemed hopeless, she'd met Hank. A temporary secretarial agency had sent her here to this sprawling house to help him catch up on his bookkeeping and paperwork.

She'd fallen for him at first sight. He had lines of good temper leathered right into his face. He was ranch scruffy and unpretentiously willing to sit and listen to her chatter. He even laughed at her lame jokes. And he told her the first time he heard her say it that she was absolutely wrong about being fat; he thought she looked just right.

From their very first date, she'd felt guilty. Oh lord, she was wasting his evening. She'd look around the restaurant and see all the women her age who'd kept their figures and had the most refined expressions on their faces, and she'd think, He should be with her, not me. She deserves him. If he wasn't with me tonight, someone better would have him.

She brought it up a few times, but it seemed to make him mad. He didn't understand at first how hard it was for her.

For instance, at first, he used to talk about his dead wife. They'd gotten married when they were nineteen and stayed married thirty years, until she was killed in a car crash. He'd never gotten over it, he told her.

She'd burst into tears. He'd thought then that she was just tenderhearted, but it wasn't that. It was that Missy, the first wife, should still have him. She was clearly so far superior that it wasn't even right she should be living in Missy's house or riding in the four-wheeler Missy had bought.

Every time he mentioned Missy, it tore her apart. She would cry in secret for days. She would try to harden her heart toward Hank so that the relationship would die out and he could be left with the memory of that deserving woman instead of the reality of stupid, inadequate her.

When it finally dawned on Hank what was happening, he tried to talk it over with her, insisting that it didn't lessen his feelings for her to have loved someone else once. But when he said that, it was like cold steel in her heart. She only wanted to pack her things and flee. She could see he tolerated her out of kindness, and that that must be torture to a heart that had known the love of Missy.

For a while, he was angry at her. He'd been married thirty years, he cried. Was he supposed to never mention anything that happened in all that time because it involved Missy? That was silly. That was unfair to him. She needed to get over it.

He sounded just like her brother when he screamed at her that way. "Leave me alone, fatty! Tag after someone else for a change! Get a life!"

It hurt her even more when Hank finally accepted she'd never be able to deal with it. He stopped speaking Missy's name. Talked about his past only in ways that made no hint of Missy's presence. It was so artificial and obvious, it just about killed her. She'd wrecked part of his joy and happiness by being stupid about things. Knowing that was constant hell. And yet she couldn't get past it; couldn't hear Missy's name—or not hear it when it should have been mentioned—without turning inside out.

She'd had some bitter cries over the years, wanting desperately to find the strength to release Hank, to give him the chance to find a saner, nicer woman.

Every time they met a woman she liked, in fact, it hurt her terribly: she should let Hank go, and she knew it. She didn't deserve him.

And yet, selfishly, she was grateful he ignored her altruistic outbursts. But she watched him grow more and more wary of them, more and more careful of what he said and how he acted in company, because the least show of social warmth made her sure she should step out of his life right now. And feeling that way, she'd get all fragile and crazy, secretly searching his pockets and papers, or crawling to her corner of the bed and not letting Hank near her.

After Hank's first stroke, when she had to nurse him and help him, and it seemed like another woman might not want to, then they'd finally found some happiness. For a long time, his speech had been slurred, so he hadn't been able to blunder into emotionally mined territory. She'd helped him in every way she could then, feeling a ferocious sympathy for his torment. He'd always been so active, poor darling, riding the ranch, splitting the wood, mending the fences. It had been torture for him, a year in a wheelchair, another year with a walker. He'd only put his cane aside last month.

And now here she was, lying uncovered on the bed again. And she was scared, too scared to move. Because he'd begged her: if it ever happened again, she mustn't let them save him. At his age, he'd never be able to come back to anywhere near the point he was now, not again. And he couldn't survive the immobility, not again. For him, it was the worst claustrophobia.

He'd had a lawyer write him up a piece of paper saying if he ever got to the point where he was too sick to live productively, he wanted to die naturally. He didn't want machines and chemicals keeping his body alive if he couldn't use it.

In the abstract, she understood. She felt that way about herself too. Especially after seeing all poor Hank had suffered, with a tube up his nose for food and liquids, and a catheter in him, and bruises on his body, and sores under his eyes because they teared uncontrollably.

But on the other hand, with her to help him, he'd made it back the first time. And for once, she'd felt really useful and special. Almost worthy of his love and company.

All this went through her mind in a flash when she made her snow angel arm sweep and felt the bed cold and empty. But maybe it was just a knee jerk of dread to ward off the jinx. She always did think the worst thing first, to get it over. Maybe Hank was okay, maybe in the kitchen having early oolong.

But this time it didn't feel like she was just being silly. Nearly frozen with cold and fear, she scooted her size forty-two pink pajamas across the bed, peering over the edge as if over the cliffs of hell.

Her heart felt like a hot rock in her chest: There he was on the floor.

"Hank! Oh, Hank!" Her voice bled.

She slid down beside him.

He looked so old, her wonderful Hank. His eyes were half-shut and his mouth was open with his tongue tip protruding. His skin looked yellow, settling into deep caverns beneath his stubbled cheekbones. His breaths were the shallowest rasps, his lips were turning blue. She'd never seen him look so dreadful, not even that other awful morning.

With a thin wail, she reached a multiply ringed hand toward the antique-reproduction phone by the bedside, the one that replaced Missy's pink princess, just as she'd replaced all Missy's furniture and fittings. She dialed 911, and cried for a while into the mouthpiece before she could even speak.

When she knew the paramedics were coming, she sank back beside Hank and stroked his cold face. He was barely breathing. He looked almost dead. His pupils, visible through half-open eyes, were different sizes.

Months ago, the doctors had warned her: the blood thinners he took every day since his stroke would keep Hank from having another stroke from a blood clot, but if he had the kind caused by a bleeding in the brain, the anticoagulants would make the stroke worse. The bleeding in his head would go on and on, killing more and more brain cells, leaving only random sparks of consciousness in a paralyzed body.

To Hank it was the ultimate horror story. Don't ever forget, he told her a thousand times. If the paramedics come, show them the paper in the nightstand drawer. Don't let them do anything to save me. I couldn't take it, honey; it'd be living hell. Even weak from his first stroke, he'd grabbed her shoulders tight and shaken them. Don't let them keep me alive in hell, honey. Don't let them.

She watched him now, frozen in a twilight of impending loneliness. She reached a hand to the drawer and withdrew the paper. DO NOT RESUSCITATE, it read across the top. She slipped it into her pajama pocket, lost in swirling memories of his kindness and maleness and devotedness.

"Oh Hank," she whispered. "I always loved you so so much. I always wanted you to be happy and have everything you deserved. I'll never be happy without you, Hank."

There was a sudden flutter in his breathing. "Pain," he gurgled, his voice a wet, small croak of a thing. "Gone. Can't feel body."

She knew in her heart what he was telling her, what he was begging her. Begging her to remember the paper in the drawer.

"I'll do what you asked, Hank. How could I not?"

"Missy," he choked. "Aw, look what a gorgeous girl I married."

She drew back as if slapped. What she'd always feared: Missy was the one, the gorgeous one love of Hank's life. Missy's name on his lips now! After she'd finally convinced herself he loved *her!* That her nursing had made her worthy of him.

"Coming, Missy." His voice was louder now. His eyelids fluttered open, and he stared ahead with mismatched pupils. "Coming back to you now, my beauty."

She looked down at him, frozen in her vortex of rejection. It always came back to this: every man had left her for someone. As soon as there was someone else to be with, he was gone—every man starting with her own brother.

And now Hank, too.

"Remember . . ." His speech was slurring, fading. "Dancing in Paris?"

She'd refused to go to Europe on a honeymoon because he'd been there with Missy. Everything everywhere would remind him of Missy, she was sure. So they'd gone to Florida, which he hadn't much liked because she was always too hot and tired to do anything.

" 'Member? Alps? Walking?"

He looked at her and his face, so cold white and skeletally sunken, managed to wear the faint ghost of an old happiness.

"Coming back to you, Missy . . ." Then he stopped breathing. Just stopped. Grew more pale and almost blue.

For what seemed an eternity, she watched him. She imagined his soul rising to embrace the beautiful, fun-loving, intelligent mate of his spirit, the incomparable Missy. She saw them laughing and happy and full of tears and remembrances, with not a backward glance for her.

God, how it tore at her! How wrong she'd been to tell herself she should let him go to someone who deserved him! It wasn't true. It had never been true. She didn't care who deserved him. She wanted him, fiercely and with her whole heart. And she didn't care if she didn't deserve him. He was hers. She had loved him and nursed him. She had finally earned him.

She screamed when she heard the doorbell. Then, walking as if with a twisting knife in her back, she stumbled to the doorway.

In their policelike uniforms, two paramedics stood before her. She waved her arm behind her, hot tears spilling down her cheeks.

She remained rooted in the doorway while they pushed past her with their bags and plastic devices.

She trailed behind them finally and overheard one of them mutter, "Not good!"

While his partner inserted a plastic tube into Hank's mouth, he looked over his shoulder. "We're going to try to resuscitate him. How long has he been this way?"

"Stopped breathing, oh God." Her voice was a foolish twitter. "Minutes ago. Maybe five?"

The paramedic shook his head again. "There'll be substantial deficits if he does recover. Permanent brain injuries. He could be a vegetable." It was said kindly, for all the harshness of the message. "Do you know if he has a Do Not Resuscitate order on file at the hospital?"

She stopped breathing herself for that moment. She saw him dancing in Paris with Missy. It was wrong, it was too late; he was her husband now, not Missy's. "I don't think so," she whispered.

"He doesn't have a document around here saying he doesn't want to be resuscitated in a situation like this?" The paramedic seemed to be appealing to her. Telling her Hank's fate would be a cruel one if he lived.

Her hand went to the document in her pocket. "I can't give him up." And yet she always thought she could and should give him up, give him to someone worthy of him, someone like Missy. It was he who had always insisted they remain together in spite of her "jealousies." Now it was clear: she'd hung on as hard as she could every step of the way. And she'd hang on now. "He'd want you to save his life," she said. "He'd want you to try, no matter what."

And she watched the paramedic attach a bellowslike bag to the tube in Hank's throat. She watched Hank's chest rise and fall, rise and fall until a bit of color returned to his cheeks.

There would be no dancing with Missy today. Missy was not his wife anymore. She was.

[SHARYN McCRUMB]

SHARYN MCCRUMB DOES IT ALL, FROM THE LIGHT-
est, most entertaining fiction to the eloquent, moving, and
enduring drama of her Appalachian novels. McCrumb
delights readers with social commentary in her Edgar-
winning Bimbos of the Death Sun series. She uses humor
to skewer pretension in her Elizabeth MacPherson series,
which includes Sick of Shadows, Lovely in Her Bones,
Highland Laddie Gone, Paying the Piper, The Windsor
Knot, Missing Susan, and MacPherson's Lament. Her
lyrical portrayal of Appalachia has won critical acclaim for
her more serious and literary novels, If Ever I Return Pretty
Peggy O, a Macavity Winner, Anthony nominee, and New
York Times notable book, and The Hangman's Beautiful
Daughter, winner of the Best Appalachian Novel Award,
an Agatha, Anthony, and Macavity nominee, and a New
York Times notable book. The next Appalachian novel
will be She Walks These Hills.

McCrumb has been active in Sisters in Crime, Mystery Writers of America, and the American Crime Writers
League. She lives in the Virginia Blue Ridge with her
family.

In "The Matchmaker," McCrumb explores what happens when there is no love.

The Matchmaker

"You don't look like the head of a dating service," said
Carl, nervously licking his lips.

The large woman behind the desk smiled and fingered
a lock of greasy brown hair that dangled over her glasses.
"You were expecting someone more like a game-show

hostess, Mr., er . . ." She consulted the manila folder in front of her. "Mr. Wallin."

Just as she said this, the woman looked up from Carl's file, and Carl had to pretend that he hadn't been wiping his sweaty palms on his slacks. "Did I expect glamour?" He shrugged. "I guess so. I've never been to one of these dating places before."

"Naturally not, Mr. Wallin," said the director blandly. Her expression suggested that all the clients said that, and that nothing could interest her less. "Please sit down. I am Ms. Erinyes."

Carl blinked. "Is that Spanish?" His dating preferences tended more toward northern European ancestry.

"It is Greek. Ancient Greek, as a matter of fact." Her jowls creased into a smile. "Now let's talk about you."

"I thought you people matched couples up by computer," said Carl, frowning.

Another smile. "And so we do, Mr. Wallin, which is why I don't look like a centerfold. I started this company with personality-matching software of my own design. So you see, my specialty is not romance or even the social niceties. I am a psychologist and an expert in computer technology."

Carl nodded his understanding. That made sense. Now that he thought about it, this Ms. Erinyes reminded him of a couple of people in his night class: the intellectual nerds. The ones whose whole lives revolved around computers. Even their friends were electronic pen pals. Of course, Carl didn't have any friends, either, but he still felt himself superior to the hackers. The one difference between Ms. Erinyes and his ungainly classmates was that she was female. There were no women in the class. Too bad; then he might not have needed a dating service. But, after all, the community college course was in electronics. Carl thought it was fitting that there were no women taking it.

With a condescending smile at the lard-assed misfit

behind the desk, Carl flopped down in the chair and leaned back. "So how come you wanted to see me? I filled out the opscan form, just like the girl out there told me to, but I thought some of the questions were pretty off-the-wall. Like asking me to draw a woman. What was the point of that? Does it matter that I can't draw?"

Ms. Erinyes had her nose back in the manila folder again. She was looking at Carl's drawing: a stick figure with scrawled curls and a triangle for a skirt. The penciled woman had fingerless hands like catchers' mitts, and no mouth. Her eyes were closed.

"The questions? Consider it quality control, Mr. Wallin," she said without looking up. "Computers aren't perfect, you know. Sometimes we like to check our results against good old human know-how. After all, love isn't entirely logical, is it?"

Carl wanted to say, "No, but sex is," but he thought this remark might count against him somehow, so he simply shrugged.

"Now let's see . . . Your medical form came back satisfactory, including the blood test. Good. Good. Can't be too careful these days. I know you appreciate that."

Carl nodded. The medical certification was one of the reasons he'd decided to come to Matchmakers.

"I see you had a head injury a few years ago. All well now, I hope?"

Carl nodded. "Fell off my motorcycle. Lucky I had a helmet on, or I'd have got worse than a bad concussion."

"I expect you would have," murmured Ms. Erinyes, dismissing motorcycles from the conversation. "Now, let's see . . . You are five feet nine," Ms. Erinyes was saying. "You weigh one hundred and fifty-eight pounds. You are twenty-eight years old, nominally Protestant, never married. You have brown hair and green eyes. Regular features. I'd say average looking, would you?"

"I guess," said Carl. It didn't sound very complimentary.

"And do you have any pets?"

"No. I like things to be clean and neat. I never could see what the big deal was about animals." He smiled, remembering. "My grandmother had a tomcat, though. We didn't get along."

Something in his voice made Ms. Erinyes look up, but all she said was, "I see that you were raised by your grandmother since the age of two."

"What does it matter?" Carl Wallin was annoyed. "I thought women would be more interested in what kind of car I drive."

"A nineteen seventy-seven AMC Concord?" Ms. Erinyes laughed merrily. "Well, some of them will be willing to overlook this, perhaps."

Carl's lips tightened. "Look, I don't make a lot of money, okay? I work as a file clerk in an insurance office. But I'm going to night school to learn about these stinking computers, which is what you have to do to get a job anymore. I figure I'll be doing a lot better someday. Besides, I don't want a lousy gold digger."

"Nobody does. Or they think they don't. We have to wonder, though, when sixty-year-old gentlemen come in again and again asking for ninety-eight-pound blondes younger than twenty-eight." She grinned. "We tell them to skip the question about hobbies and substitute a list of their assets."

"I don't need a movie star."

"Well, that brings us to the big question. Just what kind of companion are you looking for?"

"Like it says on the form. A nice girl. She doesn't have to be Miss America, but I don't want anyone who—" He groped for a polite phrase, eyeing Ms. Erinyes with alarm.

"No, you don't want somebody like me," said Ms. Erinyes smoothly, as if there had been no offense taken.

"I assure you that I don't play this game, Mr. Wallin. I just watch. You want someone slender."

"Yeah, but I don't want one of those arty types either. You know, the kind with dyed black hair and claws for fingernails. The foreign film and white wine type. They make me puke."

"We are not shocked to hear it," said Ms. Erinyes solemnly.

Carl suspected that she was teasing him, but he saw no trace of a smile. "She should be clean and neat, and, you know, feminine. Not too much makeup. Not flashy. And not one of those career types, either. It's okay if she works. Who doesn't, these days? But I don't want her thinking she's more important than me. I hate that."

For the first time, Ms. Erinyes looked completely solemn. "I think we can find the woman you are looking for," she said. "There's a rather special girl. We haven't succeeded in matching her before, but this time . . . Yes, I think you've told me enough. One last question: have you always lived in this city?"

Carl looked puzzled. "Yes, I have. Why?"

"You didn't go off to college—no, I see here that you didn't attend college. No stint in the armed forces?"

"Nope. Straight out of high school into the rat race," said Carl. "But why do you ask? Does it matter?"

"Not to the young lady, perhaps," said Ms. Erinyes carefully. "But I like to have a clear picture of our clients before proceeding. Well, I think I have everything. It will take a day or two to process the information, and after that we'll send you a card in the mail with the young lady's name and phone number. It will be up to you to take it from there."

Carl reached for his wallet, but the director shook her head. "You pay on your way out, Mr. Wallin. It's our policy."

He stared at the numbers on the apartment door, trying to swallow his rage. Being nervous always made him angry for some reason. But what was there to be anxious about? His shirt was clean; his shoes were shined; he had cash. He looked fine. A proper little gentleman, as Granny used to say when she slicked his hair down for church. But he didn't want to think about Granny just now.

Who did this woman think she was, this Patricia Bissel, making him dress up for her inspection, and dangling rejection over his head? That's all dating was. It was like some kind of lousy job interview: getting all dressed up and going to meet a total stranger who *judges* you without knowing you at all. He clenched his teeth at the thought of Patricia Bissel, who was probably sneering at him right now from behind her nice safe apartment door with the little peephole. His palms were sweating.

Carl leaned against the wall and took a few steadying breaths. Take it easy, he told himself. He had never even seen Patricia Bissel. She was just a name on a card from the dating service. He had thought that they were supposed to send you a couple of choices, maybe some background information about the person, but all that was on the card was just the name: Patricia Bissel.

It had taken him two days to get up the nerve to call her, and then her line had been busy. Playing hard to get, he thought. Damned little tease. Women liked making you sweat. When he had finally got through, he'd talked for less than a minute. Just long enough to tell her that the dating service had sent him, and to let her hem and haw and then suggest a meeting on Friday night at eight. Her place. It had taken her three tries to give the directions correctly.

She hadn't asked anything about him, and he couldn't think of anything about her that he wanted to know. Nothing that she could tell him anyway. He'd decide for himself when he saw her.

He was one minute early. He liked to be precise. That way she would have no excuse for keeping him waiting when he rang the bell, because they had agreed on eight o'clock. She couldn't pretend not to be ready and keep him hanging around in the hall like a kid waiting to be let out of the closet. Like a poor, shaking kid waiting for his granny to let him out of the closet, and trying so hard not to cry, because if she heard him, she'd make him stay in there another half hour, and he had to go to the bathroom so bad . . . She had to let him out . . . in.

The door opened. He saw his fist still upraised, and he wondered how long he had pounded on it, or if she had just happened to open it in time. He tried to smile, mostly out of relief that the waiting was over. The woman smiled back.

She wasn't exactly pretty, this Patricia Bissel, but she was slender. To the dating service people, that probably counted for a lot; real beauties did not need to use such desperate means to meet someone. Neither did successful guys. Maybe she was a bargain, considering. She was several inches shorter than he, with dull brown hair, worn indifferently long, and mild brown eyes behind rimless granny glasses. She offered a fleeting smile and a movement of her lips that might have been hello, and he edged past her into the shabby apartment, muttering his name, in case she hadn't guessed who he was. Women could be really dense.

Carl glanced around at the battered sofa beneath the unframed kitten poster and the drooping plants on the metal bookcase. He didn't see any dust, though. He sat down in the vinyl armchair, nodding to himself. He didn't take off his coat and gloves because she hadn't offered to hang them up for him. She probably just threw things anywhere, the slut.

Patricia Bissel hunched down in the center of the sofa, twisting her hands. "You're not the first," she said in a small voice.

Carl looked as if he hadn't heard.

"Not the first one the dating service has sent over, I mean. I just thought I'd try it, but I'm not sure it'll do any good. I don't meet many people where I work. I'm a bookkeeper, and the only other people in my office are two other women—both grandmothers."

Carl tried to look interested. "Did your coworkers suggest the dating service to you?"

She blushed. "No. I didn't tell them. I didn't tell anybody. Did you?"

"No." What a stupid question, he thought. As if a man would admit to anybody that he had to have help in finding a woman. Why, if a man let people know a thing like that, they'd think he was some kind of spineless bed-wetting wimp who ought to be locked in a dark closet somewhere, and—

She kept lacing her fingers and twisting them, and she would only glance at him, never meeting his eyes. She was so tiny and quiet, it was hard to tell how old she was.

"You live here with your folks?" he asked.

"No. Daddy died, and Mama got married again. I don't see her much. But it's okay. We weren't ever what you call close. And I don't mind being by myself. I know I could have a nicer place if I had a roommate to chip in, but this is all right for me. I don't mind that it isn't fancy. A kitten would be nice, though." She sighed. "They don't allow pets."

"No," said Carl. He thought animals were filthy, disease-ridden vermin. They were sly and hateful, too. His granny's cat scratched him once and drew blood, just because he tried to pet it, but he had evened that score.

Patricia was still talking in her mousy little whine. "Would you like to see my postcards? I have three albums of postcards, mostly animals. Some of them are kind of old. I get postcards at yard sales sometimes . . ." The whine went on and on.

Carl shrugged. At least she wasn't going to give him the third degree about himself, asking if he'd gone to college or what kind of job he had. As if it were any of her business. And she couldn't very well sneer at his car, considering the dump she lived in. And so what if his clothes were K mart polyester? She was no prize herself, with her skinny bird legs and those stupid old-lady glasses. Those granny glasses. What made her think she was so special, going on about her stupid hobbies and never asking one word about him? What made her think she was better than him?

"I have one album of old Christmas cards and valentines," she was saying. "Would you like to see that one? I keep it here in the coat closet."

She edged past him as she got up to get the postcard album. Her wool skirt brushed against him like the mangy fur of a cat, and he shuddered. Her whining voice went on and on, like the meowing of an old lady's cat, and the closet door creaked when she pulled it open. Carl smelled the mothballs. He felt a wave of dizziness as he stood up.

She was standing on tiptoe, trying to reach the closet shelf when Carl's hands closed around her throat. It was such a scrawny little neck that his hands overlapped, and he laced his fingers as he choked her. He left her there in the dark closet, propped up against the back wall, behind a drab brown winter coat.

Before he left the apartment, he wiped a paper towel over everything he had touched, and he found the dating service card with his name on it propped up on the bookcase, and he took that with him. His palms weren't sweating now. He felt hungry.

Carl was not so nervous this time. It had been several days since his "date," and there had been no repercussions. He had slept well for the first time in months. The old stifling tension had eased up now, and he smiled happily at Ms. Erinyes. He had been here before. He tilted the straight-backed chair, his mouth still creased into a semblance of a smile.

Ms. Erinyes did not smile back. She was concentrating on the open folder. "I see you are applying for another match from our dating service, Mr. Wallin. Didn't the first one satisfy you?"

Carl wondered whether he ought to say he hadn't found the woman to his liking, or whether he was expected to know that she was dead. The newspaper item on her death had been a small paragraph, tucked away on an inside page. Police apparently had no clues in the case. He smiled again, wondering if they'd ever show photos of the crime scene anywhere. He'd like to have one to keep, to look at sometimes when the nightmares came. He thought of mentioning it, but perhaps Ms. Erinyes had not seen the death notice.

Carl realized that there was complete silence in the room. He had been asked a question. What was it? Oh, yes, had he liked the previous match arranged for him? Finally he said, "No, I suppose it didn't work out. That's why I'm back."

The director set down the folder and stared across the desk with raised eyebrows and an unpleasant smile. "Didn't work out. Oh, Mr. Wallin, you're too modest. We think it did work out. Very well, indeed."

Carl kept his face carefully blank, wondering if it would look suspicious if he just got up and walked out. Slowly, of course, as if he couldn't be bothered with such an inefficient business.

Ms. Erinyes went on talking in her steady, slightly ironic voice. "Perhaps it's time we revealed a little more about Matchmakers to you, Mr. Wallin. Most of the time, you see, we are just what we say we are: a dating service, matching up poor lonely souls who are too afraid of AIDS or con artists to pick up strangers on their own. People don't want to risk their lives or their life savings in the search for love. So we provide a safe referral. Ninety-nine percent of the time that is all we do; ninety-nine percent of the time, that is quite sufficient. But sometimes it is *not* enough. Sometimes, Mr. Wallin, we get a wolf asking to be let loose among the sheep."

"Con men?"

"Occasionally. We can usually spot them by their psychological profiles. And of course we do a criminal record check. I don't believe I mentioned that to you."

"So what? I've never been arrested."

"Quite true. You are a different kind of danger to our little flock." Carl shook his head, but Ms. Erinyes tapped his folder emphatically. "Oh, yes, you are, Mr. Wallin. Our questionnaires are carefully designed to screen out abnormal personalities, and we are very seldom mistaken."

"There's nothing wrong with me," said Carl. He wanted to walk out, but something about the fat lady's stare transfixed him. She was a tough old bird. Like his grandmother.

"There's quite a bit wrong with you, I'm afraid. Not that we're blaming you, necessarily, but on this particular scavenger hunt, you come up with every single item: abuse in childhood, alcoholism in the family, lower middle class background, illegitimacy, cruelty to animals. Oh dear, even a head injury. And the answers you gave on our test questions were chilling. I'm afraid that you are a psychopath with a dangerous hatred for women. There's no cure for that, you know. It's very sad indeed."

"What are you talking about?" said Carl. "I never—"

"Just so," said Ms. Erinyes, nodding. "You never had. We know that. We checked your criminal record quite thoroughly. But the tendency is there, and apparently it is only a matter of time before the rage in you builds up past all containment, and then—you strike. An unfortunate, untreatable compulsion on your part, perhaps, but all the same, some poor innocent girl pays the price of your maladjustment. Usually quite a few innocent girls. Ted Bundy killed more than thirty before he was stopped. But how could we stop you? The deadly potential was there, but, as you pointed out, you had done nothing."

Carl glanced at the closed door that led to the receptionist's office. Was anyone listening behind that door, waiting for him to make a fatal confession? He had to stay calm. He hadn't been accused of anything yet. Besides, what could they prove with all this crap about psychology? There were no witnesses; no fingerprints. He had made sure of that. The girl had no friends. It had taken two days to find her body, and the police had no clue. Carl's palms were sweating.

The director had taken a piece of paper out of the manila folder labeled WALLIN, C. It was Carl's drawing of the stick-figure woman with no mouth. "Not a very attractive opinion of women, is it, Mr. Wallin? I'm afraid there's no way to alter your mind-set, though. We could not cure you, but we had to stop you. That's the dilemma: how do we prevent you from slaughtering a dozen trusting young women in your rage? That is always the difficult part—making the sacrifice, for the good of the majority. We don't like doing it, but in cases like yours, there's really no alternative. So, we found a match for you."

Carl sneered. "Her? Miss Mousy? I'm supposed to be a dangerous guy, and you pick her as my ideal woman?"

"Precisely. It was not a love match, you understand. Far from it. Although, I suppose it was 'till death do us part,' wasn't it?"

Carl did not smile at this witticism. He thought of lunging across the desk, but Ms. Erinyes simply nodded toward the corner of the office, and he saw a video camera mounted near the ceiling. He had not noticed it before. Still, they had no evidence. Let the stupid woman talk.

"It was definitely a match," Ms. Erinyes was saying.
"Just as we get the occasional killer for a client, we
also get from time to time his natural mate: the victim.
Patricia Bissel was, as you say, a mouse. Shy, indifferent
in looks and intelligence—and, most important, she was
suicidal. Her childhood was quite sad, too. It is unfortunate that you could not have comforted each other, but
I'm afraid you were both past that by the time you met.
Patricia Bissel wanted to die, perhaps without even being
aware of it herself. Did she mention any of her accidents
to you?"

Carl shook his head.

"She fell down the stairs once and broke her ankle.
She ran her mother's car into a tree, when she was
sober, in daylight on a dry, well-paved road. Twice
she has been treated for an overdose of medication,
because—she said—she had forgotten how much she'd
taken."

"She *wanted* to die?" said Carl.

"She was quite determined, I'm afraid, and through
her own fatal blunders, she would have managed it,
or—worse—she would have found someone else to do
it for her. If not a psychotic blind date picked up in a
bar, then an abusive husband or a drunken boyfriend.
Since the accidents had failed, but the suicidal impulses
were still strong, we concluded that cringing, whining
little Patricia was going to make someone a murderer.
Why not you?"

"Maybe she needed a doctor," said Carl.

"She'd had them. Years of therapy, all financed by her
long-suffering mother. Medicine can't cure everybody,
Mr. Wallin. Nice of you to care, though."

Her sarcasm was evident now. Carl's eyes narrowed.
He was beginning to feel himself losing control of the
interview. The tension was seeping back into his muscles, knotting his stomach, and making him sweat more
profusely. "You can't prove a thing, lady!"

Ms. Erinyes' sigh seemed to convey her pity for anyone who could be so obtuse. "Did our brochure not assure you that we had years of experience, Mr. Wallin? Years." She withdrew a half-letter-size envelope from his folder, and took out a stack of photographs. "We are not a shoestring operation, Mr. Wallin. You have been observed by a number of Matchmaker employees, who took care that you should not see them. Here is a nice telephoto shot of you entering Patricia Bissel's apartment building. A concealed camera snapped this one of you knocking on the door of her apartment. Didn't the number come out clearly? And there are the two of you in the doorway, together for the first and last time."

Carl stuck out his hand, as if to make a grab for the pictures.

"Why, Mr. Wallin, how rude of me. Would you like this set of prints? The negatives and several other copies are, of course, elsewhere. You do look nice in this one. No? All right, then. Where was I? Oh, yes, the police. So far they have no leads in the Bissel case, but I think that if pointed in the right direction—*your* direction, that is—they could find some evidence to connect you to the murder."

Carl had the closet feeling again. He knew that he must be a good boy and sit quietly, or else the feeling would never go away. "What are you going to do?" he asked in his most polite voice.

Ms. Erinyes put the pictures back in the envelope and slid it into Carl's folder. "Ah, Mr. Wallin, there's the question. What shall we do? We've spent the past week looking into your background, and there is no doubt that you have had a rough life. Your grandmother—well let's just say that some of your rage is entirely understandable. And it's true that Patricia was self-programmed to die. So for now, we will do nothing."

Carl exhaled in a long sigh of relief. He could feel his muscles relaxing.

The director shook her head. "It's not that simple, Mr. Wallin. You understand, of course, that this cannot continue. You have no right to take the lives of people who don't want to die. So we will keep the evidence, and we will watch you. If you ever strike again, I assure you that you will be caught immediately."

Carl returned her stern gaze with an expressionless stare. The director seemed to understand. "Oh, no, Mr. Wallin, you won't try to harm any of us here at the dating service. For you, it has to be passive, powerless women."

She stood up to indicate that the interview was over. "Well, I think that's all. You won't be coming here again, but we will keep in touch. You were one of our greatest successes, Mr. Wallin."

Carl blinked. "What do you mean?"

"You were going to be a serial killer, but we have stopped you. Oh—one last thing. We will keep your description in the active file of our computer. If anyone should come in with your particular problem—the urge to kill—and you happen to fit his or her victim profile . . ." She shrugged. "Who knows? You may find yourself matched up again."

{D. R. MEREDITH}

UNSUSPECTED BY HER NEIGHBORS IN A QUIET SUB-
urb of Amarillo, Texas, Doris R. Meredith lives two lives—
one as an ordinary wife and mother of two children, the
other as a paid killer. After seeing her family off to school
and work, Meredith sits down at her computer and commits
murder. Famous for the unique ways her victims are "done
in," Meredith has created two highly acclaimed series set
in the Texas Panhandle. One series features attorney John
Lloyd Branson, while the second series features Sheriff
Charles Matthews. She won the Oppie Award for best
mystery novel for The Sheriff and the Panhandle Murders in 1984 and for The Sheriff and the Branding Iron
Murders in 1985. In the Branson series, both Murder by
Impulse and Murder by Deception received Anthony
nominations. Texas Almanac has named Meredith one
of the state's ten best mystery writers.

In "One Strike Too Many," Meredith refutes the con-
ventional wisdom that little old ladies are harmless, hapless
creatures. "In my experience growing up among elderly
relatives," Meredith says, "a determined little old lady
may be the most dangerous individual on the planet."

One Strike Too Many

With a lifetime bowling average of sixty-nine, Maude
Turner was not an aficionado of the sport. If one must
play a game involving a spherical object, she preferred
baseball. Not that she played baseball herself, but she
did enjoy watching it. Which was more than she could
say for bowling. Maude had never been prone to exag-
geration, but she did admit to herself that given a choice

between watching a bowling tournament or throwing herself into the crater of an active volcano, she might reconsider her stand against self-immolation.

On the other hand, Maude firmly believed that family members had a duty to support one another in their individual endeavors even if it meant watching the Senior Citizens' Center bowling team take on the Amarillo Association of Retired Air Force Officers in the finals of the annual Valentine Day's Bowling Tournament. Her brother-in-law, Victor Jamison, was the star bowler for the senior citizens, and she was fond of Victor. Duty and fondness were powerful forces for modifying behavior.

A high-pitched giggle reminded Maude that neither duty nor fondness were altogether responsible for her sudden interest in bowling. Seated next to her on the hard wooden bench behind the scorekeeper was her ulterior motive, who at the moment was clasping her hands (with long scarlet nails) against a bosom whose dimensions and lift Maude was certain Mother Nature was only partly responsible for. Camilla Barnes had a bust like the prow of a ship: able to cleave the waves with scarcely a ripple. However much Camilla paid her cosmetic surgeon, Maude was convinced it wasn't enough.

On the other hand, however much Camilla paid her hairdresser, it was too much. A redhead was born, not tinted, and at age sixty, which Maude knew Camilla was, red hair from a bottle made a woman look more like the madam of a bargain-basement bordello than a respectable widow. Not that Maude had ever met a madam, red haired or otherwise, but if she ever did, she expected her to look just like Camilla Barnes right down to the expression of avarice in her eyes.

"Isn't Victor the cutest thing in his bowling outfit," said Camilla in a breathy voice that sounded to Maude's ears as though the widow suffered from a mild case of emphysema.

In Maude's opinion, *cute* was a word reserved for ages

three to twenty. "My brother-in-law is a fine-looking man who still has his own teeth," she said, then wished she'd lied about Victor's teeth. Perhaps he wouldn't look so attractive to Camilla if she thought he wore dentures.

"So do I," said Camilla, smiling.

So did Maude—if she didn't count an expensive bridge. "He has lost his hair though. So many men his age have. He's seventy, you know."

With a languid motion of one hand, Camilla dismissed Maude's words. "Bald is in now, haven't you noticed? It's just so sexy." She dropped her voice on the last word as though she were saying something naughty, and laid her hand on Maude's arm. "I hope my language didn't shock you. I keep forgetting that women of your generation are so Victorian."

Maude moved out of Camilla's reach. "I taught first grade for forty-five years, Camilla. Nothing shocks me anymore. And Queen Victoria was before my time."

Camilla opened her mouth, but Maude was spared whatever comment the widow was about to make by Victor's interruption. "You girls enjoying the tournament?" he asked, strolling over to the bench and grinning at them.

Maude hadn't considered herself a girl for at least sixty years, but decided to let it pass. "It's very enjoyable, Victor."

Victor raised one black, bushy eyebrow. He may have lost his hair, but his brows, lashes, and mustache were as black as the first day he came courting Maude's sister. "That's high praise from a woman who thinks rolling a heavy ball down a wooden alley at ten stationary targets isn't much of a challenge."

Camilla gasped, then rose to clutch Victor's arm against her overly generous bosom. "But bowling is such a virile sport and you're such a virile man. You have such strength and skill. I just love watching you."

Victor preened like a peacock. Apparently he didn't hear the note of insincerity in the widow's voice that Maude heard, which didn't surprise her. In her experience men took compliments about their virility at face value. Virile man indeed! Camilla Barnes wasn't as interested in Victor's virility, which was legendary according to the gossip at the Senior Citizens' Center, as she was in the contents of his wallet. Marrying for financial gain might be a practice at least as old as mankind, but it wasn't one Maude condoned. Besides, Camilla had already gained enough from the practice. She had buried three very wealthy husbands, and Maude didn't intend for Victor to be the fourth. Not that Maude believed the widow guilty of hastening her husbands' departures by artificial means—all three had been over ninety with one foot in the grave—but given her marital history, any man contemplating matrimony with Camilla Barnes might consider buying a cemetery plot along with a wedding ring.

"For goodness sakes, Camilla, let the poor man go. How can he possibly roll a strike with you hanging on to his arm," said Maude crossly.

Camilla's eyes narrowed as she glared at Maude. "The term is 'throw a strike.' If you're going to enjoy a sport, then you ought to learn the terminology." She looked up at Victor and fluttered her lashes. "Isn't that right, dear?"

Maude *hated* making a mistake, but she hated more being caught at it by Camilla. "The difference is academic. The point is that Victor can do neither one if you continue to hang on to his arm with the tenacity of a limpet."

Camilla let go of Victor and flounced back to her seat beside Maude. "If you could just hear yourself, Maude Turner. You sound like a jealous woman."

Maude was certain she sounded like no such of a thing. Her motives were entirely pure. She was only concerned for Victor's happiness—and his longevity. "Don't be ridiculous, Camilla. Not only is Victor a relative by marriage, but at seventy-five, I'm five years older than he and chasing younger men is undignified for a woman of my age."

"Don't put yourself down, Maude," said Victor, his lips twitching in an unsuccessful attempt to avoid grinning. "A man of any age would be flattered by your attention."

In Maude's experience, men always interpreted a woman's interest in the most romantic light. She supposed it had something to do with testosterone levels, but whatever the reason, she would have to tend to Victor's misguided thinking later. He was already turning away to pick his ball off the conveyor belt or whatever that mechanism was called that returned bowling balls.

Maude watched Victor hoist the ball chest-high with both hands, she supposed to aim it before going into his underhanded delivery. Except he never delivered the ball. He lowered his arms and appeared to be staring at his hands. Maude wondered if his fingers were stuck in the holes for some reason. Perhaps his joints were swelling from arthritis and he hadn't told her. Men hated to admit to any physical disability.

Letting his ball dangle from his right hand, Victor wiped his left hand on his shirt, examined his palm, then lifted his ball to study it. Finally, he turned around, his Adam's apple darting up and down as he swallowed several times before speaking. "Maude, there's blood on my bowling ball—and it's not mine!"

Maude thanked her forty-five years teaching first graders for her ability to remain calm under the most bizarre circumstances and to take charge in any situation. "Then we'd better find out whose blood it is, Victor. I may need to render medical assistance."

Judging from the condition of his skull, the young teenager lying crumpled in the service area behind the

bowling lanes required the services of a mortician rather
than emergency first aid. Maude had never imagined the
lethal effect a bowling bowl might have on a human
cranium until now. As a murder weapon, she would
give it a high efficiency rating.

The amount of blood pooled underneath the boy's
crushed skull didn't surprise her. Head wounds always
bled copiously, and this was a massive wound. Maude
suspected that the murderer didn't anticipate so much
blood, else he would have been more careful wiping the
ball with the towel she noticed lying by the body. Had
he been, then Victor would have in all innocence taken
his bowling ball home and the police would have wasted
valuable time tracking down the murder weapon.

Poor Victor. Some men never developed a tolerance
for the sight of blood. Victor had turned the color of
curdled milk and began uttering a sound like a turkey
about to have its neck wrung, so Maude had sent him to
call the police while she and Hank Wiley had remained
with the body. Maude knew she was capable of guarding the crime scene by herself, but since Wiley owned
the bowling alley, she supposed he felt an obligation
to stay.

"Who is he, Mr. Wiley?" asked Maude.

Hank Wiley wiped his forehead with a handkerchief.
Maude noticed a vein throbbing in his temple and decided his heart rate must be elevated. His face was also
flushed, but he was a redhead and redheads frequently
had ruddy complexions, so it was possible his florid
color had nothing to do with looking at a dead body.

Wiley tucked his handkerchief in his back pocket and
cleared his throat. "His name is Tommy Clark. He's
sixteen and a student at Amarillo High School. He's
been working here since September."

Maude glanced around the service area, which was
just a wide corridor that ran the width of the building
and allowed access to the various machinery that sat

pins and returned balls. "Was Tommy supposed to be operating these machines, Mr. Wiley?"

Hank Wiley shook his head. "Everything is automated."

"Then what was he doing back here? If you don't mind my saying so, it's noisy and dirty and doesn't seem the kind of place a youngster would choose to go if he didn't have to."

Wiley frowned and patted his pockets as though searching for something. Finally he located a chocolate bar and unwrapped it as he stared at the corpse. He hesitated, taking a bite of the candy before he spoke. "I don't know what he was doing here unless"—he paused a few seconds, as though picking his words— "he was using my establishment to sell drugs. You know how bad kids are these days—drinking, taking dope, shooting people. It's in the papers all the time."

"Poppycock," said Maude, a little queasy from watching him eat the candy. There was such a thing as having too much tolerance for blood. "I'm not convinced youngsters are any worse than they ever were. We just keep better statistics."

He gave her a sharp look. "This service area would be a perfect place for selling drugs, a lot better than a street corner or a parking lot. No one ever comes back here unless one of the machines goes haywire, and the door is at the end of the same hall as the bathrooms. No one would pay any attention to people hanging around that hall."

Maude hesitated, glancing down at Tommy Clark's body. If one ignored the bloody, misshaped skull, the teenager looked as if he had been a normal, healthy boy. "He doesn't look as though he took drugs. I don't see any needle tracks on his arms."

"I didn't say he *used* drugs. I said he might have been selling them."

"If you suspected him, why didn't you call the authorities?"

Now it was Hank Wiley's turn to hesitate. "I didn't say I suspected him. I'm just trying to figure out what he was doing back here, and I figure drugs is as good an explanation as any."

"I think you're jumping to conclusions, and speaking ill of the dead."

"You don't believe my story?"

Maude thought Wiley chose an odd way to ask if she agreed with him. Surely he meant to say theory, not story. Before she had a chance to correct his word choice, a gravelly voice interrupted.

"Mrs. Turner, finding you watching over a murder victim is getting to be a habit. You're a regular Jessica Fletcher."

Maude turned around. "Special Crimes certainly took its time getting here, Sergeant Wilson. You responded much more quickly during the last murder case we were involved in. I sent Victor to call you fifteen minutes ago."

Sergeant Wilson of Special Crimes, a three-county unit responsible for investigating suspicious deaths, shrugged off her criticism. "Speaking of your brother-in-law, I've seen three-day-old road kill that looked better than he does. He's sitting at the snack bar with some woman with a towel wrapped around her head."

Maude nodded. "Camilla Barnes. I was forced to pour water over her head to stop her screaming when she saw the bloody handprint on Victor's shirt. Hysterics calls for strong measures."

"You and Mr. Wiley can go up and join Mr. Jamison and his lady friend. A couple of officers are there to take your statements."

Maude bristled at hearing Camilla called Victor's lady friend, but decided to overlook the sergeant's mistake for the moment. "I'll be waiting to hear your theory about the murder, Sergeant. I have a few ideas of my own."

"The last time you had an idea about a case, I arrived just in time to prevent the murderer from adding you to her scorecard, Mrs. Turner."

Maude flushed. She didn't like being reminded of the sergeant's timely arrival. Being rescued made her feel foolish. "I'll be waiting for you, Sergeant," she replied, starting toward the door.

Hank Wiley walked beside her. "God, I've got to have something to eat."

Maude felt a chill crawl up her spine at his words. Hank Wiley might have a perfectly innocent reason for being hungry. Just because murderers were frequently hungry after killing their victims didn't mean Wiley killed Tommy Clark. And just because his office was right next to the service-area door, which allowed him to be back at his desk within a minute of dropping Victor's ball back on the return mechanism, didn't mean he was guilty. A detective should never jump to conclusions without evidence.

Maude intended to find that evidence.

She still felt the chill the next morning in Sergeant Wilson's office at Special Crimes when she signed her statement after correcting typographical errors and misspelled words. Victor, she noticed, was frowning as he read his own statement. He did have his color back, though. She had been quite worried about him last night. His face had been nearly as white as the corpse's.

"Is there something wrong with your statement, Victor?" Maude asked.

Her brother-in-law looked up. "Yes, it's incoherent."

"You *were* incoherent last night, Victor, and I understand that the police must take down a witness's testimony verbatim. Isn't that true, Sergeant Wilson?"

The homicide investigator nodded. "As nearly as possible."

"Who wouldn't be incoherent, Maude?" blurted Victor.

"I wouldn't, but then as a retired teacher I'm more familiar with blood and gore than the average person. If there's a sharp or pointed object within a hundred-mile radius of a first grade boy, he will slice, dice, or impale himself on it. I often wonder how the male sex survived childhood before the days of blood transfusions."

Victor swallowed several times before he managed to reply. "I'll never bowl again," he said, signing his statement and rising from his chair. "I'll take up checkers instead. You can't kill anybody with a checker."

"I want to talk to Sergeant Wilson before we leave." Maude removed a small spiral notebook and pen from her purse and turned her attention to the detective. "What do we know about the victim, Sergeant Wilson? Do we know why Tommy Clark was in the service area behind the bowling lanes? According to my source the machinery is all automatic."

Sergeant Wilson rested his folded hands on top of his desk while he looked at her from under bushy eyebrows. Maude noticed that his knuckles were white. He really shouldn't be clasping his hands so tightly. It wasn't good for his circulation.

"Just who is your source?" the sergeant finally asked.

Maude didn't mention Hank Wiley. Until she knew more about the victim, she didn't want to accuse the bowling alley owner. She might be wrong. Occasionally she was.

"The waitress at the bowling alley snack bar," answered Maude. She wasn't lying. She had talked to the waitress, who had added to what Wiley told her. "Tommy is—was—sixteen years old and a student at Amarillo High School. He was respectful to his elders and always on time for work, two very commendable and uncommon attributes in today's youth. In my opinion, Sergeant, he was a very unlikely murder victim. What do you think?"

Sergeant Wilson took a deep breath, expelled it in a loud sigh, then took another before speaking. His face was very red and Maude wondered if he suffered from hypertension. "I think, Mrs. Turner, that you and Mr. Jamison should go home. You've given your statements about how you came to discover the body, and you have no further interest in the case."

"Victor's bowling ball was the murder weapon," said Maude, leaning forward in her chair. "I would say that gives us a very special interest."

"Mrs. Turner, this is a homicide investigation and you're not a detective," began Sergeant Wilson.

Maude interrupted him even though it was rude. Sometimes rudeness was necessary when dealing with the younger generation. Otherwise, women her age were liable to be dismissed as little old ladies good for nothing except knitting afghans. Maude hated to knit.

"Sergeant Wilson, I realize I'm not a detective, but since my recent involvement in the so-called kite murder, I've begun reading books on criminals and criminal investigations and I feel that my newly gained knowledge combined with forty-five years teaching first grade give me special insight into human psychology that would be useful in this investigation. I believe I would make an excellent undercover consultant."

"Mrs. Turner," began the sergeant.

"My God, Maude!" gasped Victor.

Maude raised her voice to drown out both Victor's exclamations and the sergeant's attempts to interrupt. "For example, Sergeant, I could elicit more information from Tommy's classmates and teachers than you since I know the terrain. A few days spent substitute teaching and I could find out everything there is to know about Tommy Clark. Youngsters that age always underestimate old ladies, and the teachers' lounge is a veritable hotbed of gossip."

"You told me you wouldn't be caught dead sub-

stituting," interjected Victor as Maude stopped talking
long enough to draw another breath, a timely interjection
in her opinion as it prevented whatever the sergeant
seemed ready to say. At least, she presumed his mouth
was gaping open for that reason.

"I wish you wouldn't use that phrase, Victor. At my
age talking about dropping dead is tempting fate."

"I don't want to see you get your pretty white curly
head bashed in!" yelled Victor.

"I'll stay far away from anyone with a bowling ball."

The sergeant tried again. "Mrs. Turner."

"There are other weapons, Maude," interrupted Victor, the verbal bit between his teeth. "Youngsters
have changed since you taught. They carry guns and
switchblades and curse worse than sailors."

"Not in my classroom they won't. Besides, according
to the waitress Tommy was the only teenager working at
the bowling alley so he wasn't murdered by one of his
peers. The perpetrator is an adult, and furthermore, it's
an adult who is familiar with the machinery behind the
lanes. Otherwise, he wouldn't know how to remove your
ball from the conveyor belt or whatever it's called, murder Tommy, return the ball, and do it all so quickly."

"And I suppose you have a suspect, Mrs. Turner?"

Maude hesitated. Hank Wiley had the means and the
opportunity. What was missing from the equation was
the motive. Why in the world would Hank Wiley murder
Tommy Cook? Without the answer to that question, she
doubted Sergeant Wiley would accept a cold chill as a
sufficient reason to investigate a prominent businessman.

Instead of answering she flipped open her notebook. "I
have a partial list of the employees of the bowling alley,
Sergeant, but I presume you have a more complete one.
If I might have a copy, then I would know what names
to drop when speaking to Tommy's friends and to his
teachers."

Sergeant Wilson mumbled something that sounded

very like "I hate those damn Miss Marple books," but Maude couldn't be sure. Much as she hated to admit it, her hearing wasn't all that it should be sometimes.

"What did you say, Sergeant?" asked Maude.

The sergeant knocked over his chair getting up. He pointed to the door. "Out, Mrs. Turner, and if I catch you interfering in this investigation, so help me God, I'll arrest you—little old lady or not!"

That did it! No one called her a little old lady with impunity. "Come along, Victor. The sergeant doesn't seem to be in a very agreeable frame of mind this morning."

She knew it was her imagination, but she thought she could hear the sergeant shouting that he meant what he said even after she was seated in Victor's restored, candy apple red 1966 Mustang convertible.

"Amarillo High please, Victor."

"Maude, didn't you hear what the sergeant said? He'll throw you in jail, and I don't think you'd find jail a very nice place."

She patted his arm. Victor Jamison was a good man, but men of his generation tended to be overprotective of women. "Of course, I heard him. I think the entire Special Crimes office heard him, but I don't believe him. The police need what they call 'informed sources'— which are nothing more than nosy people who hear things or discover information and pass it along to the police—and I can on occasion be very nosy. But always in a good cause—and this is a good cause."

Exhausted from a week of covertly questioning Tommy's peers and teachers while masquerading as a harmless substitute, Maude sipped her Coke and consulted her notebook. It was last period and she was stalking her last prey: Tommy's biology teacher, Lance Phillips, who not only was too handsome for his own good, but possessed an overly romantic first name. Maude considered such a combination likely to warp a man's character as well as cause his female students to drool.

"Such a terrible thing that happened to the Clark boy," said Maude. "Such a promising young man with a bright future ahead of him. Ambitious, hardworking, and filled with intellectual curiosity. His only unattractive trait seemed to be a tendency to giggle when he was nervous, but I'm sure he would have outgrown it. Such a tragic waste."

Lance Phillips took a sip of his bottled water. "Who are you?"

Maude sniffed. She had only taught in the room next to his for a week. Anyone not totally self-centered would have noticed her. "I'm Maude Turner. I'm a substitute teacher."

Lance Phillips raised an eyebrow. "Oh."

"Tommy Clark was one of your students, wasn't he?"

"Yes."

"Everyone says he was a fine young man."

The biology teacher shrugged. "I suppose so."

"Everyone says he was very fond of Mr. Wiley."

Lance Phillips dropped his bottled water and stared at her.

"It's a good thing it's last period," said Maude. "I'm afraid your trousers are soaked."

He cursed and brushed at his slacks. Maude gathered up her purse and coat and left the lounge. A very interesting encounter, she thought, although she wasn't certain what it meant. Lance Phillips hadn't reacted to Tommy's name, but mention of Hank Wiley made him spill his water all over the crotch of his pants.

Maude checked her red-orange wig in Victor's rear-view mirror, then slumped down in the Mustang's passenger seat.

"Tell me again why I let you talk me into this?" asked Victor.

"Because I told you I'd follow Lance Phillips by myself if you didn't help me. Besides, aren't you curious about why he was so frightened when I mentioned Hank Wiley?"

"Just because he dropped his bottled water in his lap doesn't mean he was frightened, Maude. It could have been an accident. And we have no right to follow him. Stalking is against the law in Texas."

"We're not stalking. We're conducting a surveillance of a suspect. And Lance Phillips *was* frightened. I know what I saw."

"If you're suspicious of Phillips, you ought to tell Sergeant Wilson, and while you're at it, tell him about Hank Wiley, too."

Maude sighed. "You don't believe me, Victor, and you *know* me. What would Sergeant Wilson think? He'd think I was crazy."

"Put yourself in his shoes, Maude. You're a retired schoolteacher with no formal training in police work; you're seventy-five years old; you're running around in a ridiculous wig pretending to be Nancy Drew; and you're breaking the law! If that isn't enough to make the sergeant question your sanity, then I don't know what would."

Maude grabbed his arm. "There he is! He's getting into that Plymouth. Start the car, Victor. I don't want to lose him if you have trouble starting this antique."

"This is a completely restored nineteen sixty-six Mustang convertible in mint condition! It always starts!"

"Then do it and stop yipping, Victor. You're acting as if I insulted your manhood." Which might not be too far from the truth. Maude respected Victor's love affair with his Mustang, but she never had really understood it.

The Mustang started with a throaty roar and Victor eased into traffic behind the Plymouth. "I don't know why I could always manage to keep a tough construction crew in line when I was in business, but I can't seem to say no to you, Maude."

She patted his arm. "Don't worry about it, Victor. I'm sure you'll figure it out."

"My comment was rhetorical, Maude. I know why I indulge you. It's because I'm too fond of you to want to see you committed or arrested, so my only other alternative is to go along with you on these escapades and try to keep you out of trouble."

Maude smiled. "I'm very fond of you, too, Victor."

"I know."

The note of complacency in his voice alarmed her, but before she could warn him against reading any romantic connotations into her reply, she saw the Plymouth turn. "Quick, follow him!"

"That's an alley in a residential subdivision, Maude, and not just any subdivision, but Sleepy Hollow. There's nothing down the alley but driveways and Dumpsters, and we don't look like garbage collectors. Not only would Phillips see us, but we can't pull into a driveway to mislead him. In this neighborhood they call the cops if some strange car parks on their property, especially now. Haven't you read in the paper about the burglaries in this part of town in the last two weeks?"

"I've been too busy with this murder case to worry about property crimes, Victor. That's the police's job. Now, just drive very slowly by the alley and I'll see if I can spot his car."

"Oh, God," said Victor, but he obediently slowed down while Maude peered down the alley.

"He's gone! He must have turned into a driveway. Back up and turn down the alley, Victor. I want to see which house he's visiting, then I'll check the city directory and see who lives there."

Victor stopped the car. "I won't do any such thing, Maude. This nonsense had gone far enough."

Maude sighed. "This is a fine time to be stubborn,

Victor, but I guess I can handle this myself. Wait here."
She got out of the car and began jogging down the
alley, checking each driveway for the Plymouth. She
and Victor had only been half a block behind Lance
Phillips. The biology teacher had to have parked at one
of the houses nearest the mouth of the alley. Otherwise,
they would have seen his taillights.

Someone grabbed Maude's arm and she whirled
around, her free hand doubled into a fist. She landed a
very satisfying blow on her assailant's chin, then gasped.
"Victor!"

Victor let her go and checked his face with both hands.
"For God's sake, Maude, you ought to watch who you're
hitting. You could have broken my jaw. In fact, I'm not
sure you didn't."

"Then don't sneak up on me! You should have called
my name."

"I did! But you didn't act like you heard me!"

Maude wondered if she should have her hearing
checked after all. "Speak up next time."

"And then the people would call the police and report
a strange man chasing a strange woman down their
alley."

"You've made your point, Victor. Now, hush and help
me look for that Plymouth." She heard him mumble
something but didn't catch the words. She probably
didn't want to know anyway.

They found Lance Phillips's car parked at the fourth
house. "Bingo!" whispered Maude as she jogged past the
driveway and let herself in the back gate. "You'd think
with all the burglaries in this neighborhood that everyone
would lock their gate."

She hurried toward a square of bright light at the back
of the house and stood on tiptoes to stare in a kitchen
window. People so often failed to close window blinds
in the kitchen when the room faced the backyard. She
observed Lance Phillips in a very intimate embrace with

a petite young blonde dressed in a skimpy gown. Maude blushed. She had never worn a gown that thin even after several years of marriage. Not that she imagined that it would have made any difference to her sex life if she had. Her husband, may he rest in peace, didn't vary his technique in forty years of marital relations.

"That's done it, Maude," said Victor, following her into the yard. "Not only are you trespassing, but you're looking in people's windows like some Peeping Tom. I'm taking you back to the car and tying you down if I have to." He wrapped his arms around her thighs and hoisted her over his shoulder.

"Look out! He's got a gun!" screamed Maude, staring over Victor's shoulder into the window.

"I don't either," protested Victor.

"Not you! The man in the ski mask who just stepped into the kitchen!"

"What," began Victor when the kitchen window exploded outward and the young blonde began screaming.

Still carrying Maude, Victor jumped into the shrubbery just as the man in the ski mask dived through the broken window and ran toward the gate. "Stop, thief!" yelled Maude, pushing herself up from the ground where Victor had dropped her.

The figure turned and fired. Maude saw a flash from the end of his gun and felt something sting her earlobe. Almost instantaneously Victor grabbed her ankle and jerked her down.

"Damn it, lie still and shut up!"

It was a measure of how upset Victor was that he had cursed, even so mild a curse, in her presence. Victor never used profanity in front of a woman.

"He'll get away, Victor, and he shot me!" wheezed Maude, shivering from the cold and trying to get her breath back after a hard landing on the frozen ground. The Texas Panhandle in February wasn't the place she would choose to roll around outside.

"My God, Maude! Where are you hit?" demanded Victor, running his hands over her body.

"My earlobe," said Maude, sitting up and pushing his hands away. Her face was hot from blushing. No man had touched her bosom in years, and she had thought the nerve endings were dead. Who would have thought that Maude Turner still had a sexual response left at her age.

"That murderous villain!" exclaimed Victor as he leaped to his feet and sprinted toward the gate left open by the intruder's escape.

"You come back here!" Maude yelled after him. Victor might not have been a teacher, but he didn't lack for courage, she thought. What he did lack was good sense. Imagine his chasing an armed robber. The old fool was going to get himself killed—and it was her fault.

Maude heaved herself off the ground and ran out the gate. Security lights were coming on all over the neighborhood, and she could see the two men grappling at the end of the alley. Although Victor was giving a good account of himself, Maude knew he would lose. Not only was his age a disadvantage in a fistfight, but he was too much of a gentleman to fight dirty. Under the same circumstances Maude would have hit below the belt—way below the belt.

Suddenly the intruder delivered an uppercut that sent Victor staggering backward to sprawl on the ground. The man hesitated a moment, then turned and ran down the alley and disappeared around the corner.

"Victor!" cried Maude, running toward him. She crouched down and put her fingers against the carotid artery in his neck. "You're alive!"

Victor groaned. "Get your hand off my neck, Maude. Your fingers feel like ice."

She jerked her hand away and examined his face. Other than a rapidly swelling eye and a spilt lip, he seemed unharmed. She helped him up and dusted him off, being very careful to avoid his erogenous zones. This was no time for gestures that might be subject to misunderstanding. She tugged on his hand. "Hurry, Victor. I want to talk to Lance Phillips and that blonde, and I don't think we have much time. I don't think it would be good strategy to be in the neighborhood when the police arrive. They would just waste time asking why we were in that backyard."

Victor stopped. "Oh, no, Maude. I'm putting my foot down."

"All right, Victor, as long as you put it down in that kitchen."

"Absolutely not! You could have been shot, Maude! I could have lost you. Then who would see that the housekeeper vacuumed under the furniture and cleaned the stove? Who would drink coffee with me in the mornings? Who would devil me into getting a yearly physical?" He pulled her into his arms and kissed her cheek. "Don't you see, Maude, I love you!"

"Victor!"

He cleared his throat. "Like a brother-in-law, of course."

"Of course," agreed Maude, feeling a little disappointment. A declaration of romantic love would have been nice, but in view of their kinship, very inappropriate.

Maude stepped away from Victor. "I'm going back to talk to Lance Phillips. I wasn't killed tonight, but little Tommy Clark was and I can't forget that. I don't believe in coincidence, and I think there's something very suspicious about someone trying to kill Lance Phillips."

"It was the burglar, Maude, the one who's been terrorizing this neighborhood."

Maude shook her head. "I know what I saw. The average burglar doesn't break in when people are home, and if he discovers someone *is* home, he tries to get away. This man didn't try to duck back out of sight.

He deliberately tried to kill Lance Phillips, the man who was Tommy Clark's biology teacher and who is afraid of Hank Wiley. I'm going back, Victor. You can wait for me in the car." She turned and walked back up the alley.

"The devil I am," said Victor, catching her hand. "Come on, Miss Marple, let's get this over with before the police catch us."

Maude smiled and squeezed his hand. She even let him help her through the broken window. Men liked to feel they were needed.

"Who the hell are you?" screamed Lance Phillips when he saw Maude climbing through the window. The young blonde in his arms whimpered and buried her head against his chest.

Maude took off her wig and ran her fingers through her flattened curls. "I'm Maude Turner, the substitute teacher who mentioned Hank Wiley's name today."

"Oh, God, Lance, she knows," gasped the blonde.

Maude's eyes dropped to the woman's ring finger. "You're married."

"She's Hank Wiley's wife, Maude," said Victor, climbing through the window and coming to stand beside her. "I've seen her at the bowling alley."

"No wonder you were frightened when I mentioned Hank Wiley," Maude said to Lance Phillips. "I don't think he would appreciate your keeping company with his wife when he's not home."

The biology teacher turned pale. "Jessica's filed for divorce, but Wiley is a vicious man. He's beaten Jessica before. There's no telling what he'd do if he knew about me."

Maude glowered at them in disapproval. "Did it occur to either one of you that the honorable thing to do was wait until the divorce was final before engaging in a carnal relationship?"

"But we love each other," cried Jessica Wiley,

clutching Lance Phillips around the waist. "You're too old to understand. You don't remember what it's like to be young and want to touch all the time."

"Young woman, we had lust in my day, too, but I like to believe that a respectable woman discards one husband before jumping into bed with another. I don't believe that the modern admonition to let it all hang out should apply to the adulterous use of one's private parts. Lust outside marriage is tawdry and can provoke serious crimes of the heart. Murder, for instance. Men have killed for love before."

Lance Phillips swayed, then sank down on the floor, covering his face with his hands. "I knew it was him."

"Who?" asked Maude, although she was certain she knew. However, it was best to get the name out in the open to avoid the remotest possibility of misunderstanding.

The biology teacher lowered his hands. He looked terrified and his eyes were red-rimmed, as though he'd been crying. "Hank Wiley. The man in the ski mask. It was Hank Wiley, and he's going to kill Jessica and me, but not for love. He doesn't care if Jessica screws a hundred men—just as long as she doesn't divorce him."

"He has a peculiar view of love," said Maude, shocked for the first time in years.

"Love doesn't have anything to do with it," said Jessica, bitterness in her voice. "It's money. He doesn't want me to get any money in a divorce settlement."

"Young woman, you evidently have a very ignorant lawyer. Texas is a community property state. You are entitled to half of the property."

Jessica laughed. "You're the ignorant one. The judge has the discretion to award me half the property, a percentage of it, or none at all. I wasn't counting on much of a settlement anyway, because I knew Hank would dig up every bit of dirt on me there is to find. I'll look like such a liar, cheater, and slut when he gets through with me, then I'll be lucky if the judge lets me keep my panties."

Judging by her present attire, Maude doubted Jessica Wiley even wore panties on a regular basis. Poor Victor was beet red with embarrassment and busy looking at everything in the room but the young woman. It spoke well of his sense of propriety.

"Young lady, if appearances are anything to go by, you are a liar, a cheater, and a slut. However, much as I disapprove of adultery, I disapprove more of murder. But what I can't understand is why your husband killed Tommy Cook."

"The kid at the bowling alley?" asked Jessica with a blank stare. "What makes you think he did?"

"I have my reasons," replied Maude.

"You can bet money was at the bottom of it," said Lance Phillips suddenly. "Hank Wiley never does anything unless there's money involved."

"I don't understand how murdering Tommy would be financially beneficial to him," said Maude. "I doubt he had an insurance policy on the boy's life."

"Maybe Tommy would cost him money if he lived," suggested Victor.

Maude turned to stare at him. "What are you talking about?"

"Remember what his teachers told you about Tommy? That he was ambitious and curious?"

"He was a nosy brat," said Lance Phillips suddenly. "Leave a grade book on your desk or a drawer or filing cabinet open, and Tommy Clark would snoop."

"If he snooped at school, then he snooped at the bowling alley," said Maude slowly, looking at Victor.

Victor nodded. "And what do you suppose Tommy found at the bowling alley that Hank Wiley didn't want found?"

"The loot!" said Maude.

"From the burglaries. Wiley committed the burglaries

as a cover for a perfect crime. What better way to murder your wife and her lover and get away with it than to be able to blame it on a nonexistent criminal? But if Hank is as obsessed with money as Mr. Phillips and Mrs. Wiley contend, then he kept the property he stole—which was mostly jewelry, as I recall from reading the papers. Add stolen jewelry and a nosy young boy who likes to snoop and the sum equals murder."

Maude threw her arms around him. "Victor, you're brilliant!"

He hugged her back. "I do my best, Maude."

Maude stepped away and turned back to the lovers. "Call the police. Tell them you suspect your husband is trying to kill you and tell them about Tommy and the burglaries. They probably won't believe you, of course, since you and Mr. Phillips are so obviously engaged in an illicit relationship, and neither one of you can swear you recognized the gunman as Hank Wiley."

"I'll swear to it," said Jessica Wiley.

Maude sighed. "Don't lie, young woman. If you're caught at it—and you will be because you're not as clever as you think you are—then everything you say will be suspect. Just tell the police what I told you to, and Victor and I will take care of the rest."

"What! What are you planning now, Maude?"

"We're going to look for the jewels, Victor. Examine the situation from Sergeant Wilson's point of view. None of us saw the gunman's face, so we can't swear it's Hank Wiley. He was wearing gloves so he left no fingerprints, and even if he had, it's his house after all. Sergeant Wilson has absolutely no cause to ask for a search warrant for the bowling alley except our suspicions, and I don't think a judge will authorize a search on that basis. We have to find the jewels. Then we're informed sources and Sergeant Wilson can get a search warrant on the basis of our information. Do you understand?"

"Oh, I understand all right. I understand we're about

to risk our lives again. Maude, he saw us both—and he knows me. If we set foot in the bowling alley, much less snoop around, we're both going to end up with dents in our heads!"

"We'll wear wigs, Victor. To the younger generation, all old people look alike. He'll never recognize us."

Victor tugged on his black curly wig and scowled at the menu, then looked around the small snack area with its five leather booths and row of stools in front of the long luncheon counter. The smell of grilled hamburgers and fried onions permeated the air, and the thuds of heavy balls striking wooden pins competed with the melancholy wail of a country-and-western tune from the jukebox in the corner.

"This will never work, Maude."

Maude ducked her head behind her menu. "Don't look now, but here comes Hank Wiley."

Victor touched his eye patch. Even Maude's heaviest pancake makeup wouldn't conceal his black eye, but the patch did the job nicely. "You look like a decadent pirate," said Maude.

"I feel like an old fool."

Ignoring him, Maude peered around her menu. Hank Wiley was smiling and laughing with the few customers sitting on the stools in front of the snack bar. He glanced at the people in the booths, but his eyes passed over Victor and herself without a glint of recognition. Maude relaxed.

"As soon as Wiley wanders over to watch the bowlers, I'll search his office while you stand guard in the hall," she whispered.

"What are you doing here with *her?* You broke our date for dinner so you could take out Maude Turner? You stood me up for an old crone in a cheap wig? You're trifling with my affections, Victor Jamison, and I won't put up with it!"

It was just as Maude had always believed: a woman could always fool a man by changing her hair, but she could never fool another woman. "Sit down and be quiet, Camilla," ordered Maude. "You're making a scene."

"I certainly won't sit down at the same table with you."

"Then sit at another table, but for goodness sakes, lower your voice. Victor will explain later."

Hank Wiley sat down in the booth next to Maude. "Is there a problem?"

"Just a friendly disagreement," said Maude.

"Why don't we all go outside and talk about it?" asked Hank.

Maude shook her head. "That won't be necessary."

"Slide out of the booth, please, and don't try anything stupid like screaming," Wiley said.

Maude felt something hard nudge her in the ribs and glanced down. She gulped. "I think we'd better go with Mr. Wiley, Victor. There are a number of reasons why, and every one of them is filled with gunpowder."

Victor turned white. "Oh, my God."

"What's wrong, Victor? Why are you wearing that eye patch? What is going on?" demanded Camilla, looking from Victor to Maude to Hank Wiley.

Victor grabbed her arm and pushed her toward the back door. "Let's go outside, Camilla, and please—shut up."

Amazingly enough, she did.

Hank Wiley herded them into the parking lot. "Where's your car, lady?"

"It's the Cadillac over there," said Camilla, a snobbish note of pride in her voice.

"It'll do," said Wiley, pulling a roll of duct tape from his pocket and shoving it at Maude. "Tape up their hands, old woman, and do it right because I'll be checking. Try to cheat and I'll shoot Victor through the knee-cap. My gun's got a silencer, so nobody will hear."

Camilla opened her mouth to scream and Wiley tapped her head with the gun. She crumbled to the ground.

"There was no need to hit her," said Maude.

"I don't want her screaming. I have real sensitive ears. Now shut up and use that tape."

Maude did.

Fifteen minutes later she, Victor, and Camilla were securely bound with duct tape, both hands and legs, and were sitting in the backseat of Camilla's Cadillac with the seat belts and shoulder harnesses holding them immobile. Hank Wiley had gone back inside the bowling alley, probably to arrange an alibi. Maude certainly would have in his place.

"What are you planning to do with us?" asked Maude when Wiley returned and got behind the wheel.

Hank started the car. "Since the gal with the dye job started an argument with the two of you in front of everybody in the bowling alley, I figure everyone will think you just continued it after I booted you outside. You get in the car, still arguing, and take off. You have a wreck, the car burns."

"But I still have forty more payments to make on this car," said Camilla.

"This isn't the time to worry about your car payments, Camilla. You ought to rearrange your priorities," said Maude.

"She won't have time," remarked Wiley.

Unfortunately, Maude was afraid that was true. "Since we won't be able to repeat anything we hear, will you tell us why you killed Tommy Clark? Was it because he found your cache of stolen jewelry?"

Wiley glanced over his shoulder at her. "Smart girl. You want to tell me how you figured it all out—just to pass the time?"

"Well, Victor deserves some of the credit," began Maude when Camilla interrupted.

"Did you say he murdered that little boy?"

Maude decided Camilla Barnes had an I.Q. equal to her height and she wasn't very tall. "Yes, Camilla. Hank killed Tommy Clark and he's planning to kill us."

Camilla's eyes opened very wide, and Maude thought the widow was going to faint.

She screamed instead. She screamed like a banshee. If there had been a crystal goblet within a mile radius, Camilla's high C would have shattered it. Fortunately, Camilla was sitting behind the driver's seat, and her shrieks were uttered less than two feet from Hank Wiley's right ear.

Two feet was close enough. Wiley jerked, hit the accelerator, and plowed into the side of Victor's 1966, mint-condition Mustang. The driver-side air bag inflated.

"Air bags are a wonderful safety feature in my opinion," Maude was telling Sergeant Wilson a half hour later. "But I don't think it's safe to be holding a metal object near the face when one inflates. If Hank Wiley hadn't been trying to drive and hold a gun at the same time, he wouldn't have been knocked unconscious."

"If he hadn't been knocked unconscious, and a bowler late for his match hadn't driven up and investigated what all the screaming was about, then you and your friends would be dead, Mrs. Turner. I ought to arrest you and Mr. Jamison on general principle. Maybe a night or two in jail would teach you to stay out of police business."

Maude was indignant. "No one likes a sore loser, Sergeant Wilson. Without Victor's and my help, I don't believe you would have ever gotten the goods on Hank Wiley."

"The goods?" repeated the sergeant.

"A term from one of my crime novels."

Sergeant Wilson rolled his eyes toward the ceiling of Hank Wiley's office, which he was using as an interview room. "You two get out of here and stay out of trouble."

Maude walked out of the bowling alley. It was all

over. Tommy's murderer was caught; Jessica Wiley was safe; the jewels were recovered; and all was right with the world.

Well, not quite all.

"Victor, I want to apologize for interfering with your pursuit of Camilla. If you want to marry her, then it's your business."

Victor looked at her in horror. "Good Heavens, Maude! Do you seriously believe I could be interested in the woman responsible for wrecking my Mustang?"

〔 AUDREY PETERSON 〕

AUDREY PETERSON SETS HER NOVELS IN ENGLAND, where she spent many summers during her years as professor of English at California State University at Long Beach. In her popular mystery series, featuring Jane Winfield and her music professor, Andrew Quentin, a gaggle of opera singers, pianists, composers, and their agents get involved in crimes from teeming London to remote English villages. In her equally acclaimed second series, Peterson turns to her own field of Victorian literature, introducing Claire Camden, English professor, who goes to England to do research on her biography of a Victorian woman novelist. In Dartmoor Burial and Death Too Soon, crimes from a century ago have parallels in contemporary murders and deal with the status of women, both then and now.

Peterson has served as president of the Northwest chapter of Mystery Writers of America, has edited Books in Print for Sisters in Crime, and is a member of the British Crime Writers Association.

Peterson comes home to America for her suspenseful short story, "The Bayville Killing," which is set in Bellingham, Washington, where she currently lives with her husband.

The Bayville Killing

I hadn't been back to Bayville since the day after graduation from the state university, the day I came face-to-face with a murderer in the woods near the campus and could easily have been his next victim.

Fifteen years ago. Hard to believe. After graduation, I'd gone back home to Los Angeles, married my boyfriend Dan, had two kids, and was now into a career with a designer sportswear company. I'd only gone to Bayville on this occasion because I'd flown into Seattle to do a presentation and decided to pick up a car and drive to Vancouver, British Columbia, where I had some appointments the next day. Bayville happens to be on Interstate 5, about twenty miles before the Canadian border, and I thought I'd do a little nostalgia trip as I passed through town.

It was the third week in June, and after bone-dry Los Angeles, the drizzle that oozed out of the overcast skies was as welcome as the spectacular green of the countryside as it flashed by, fringed with groves of dark firs. To the east rose peak after peak of the Cascade range, and soon I caught glimpses of the grand snow-capped cone of Mount Baker, the local Fujiyama.

Coming into Bayville around three o'clock in the afternoon, I took the exit for the campus, passing shops, restaurants, and movie theaters that hadn't been there in my day. There were new buildings on the campus at the lower end of the hill. Only my old dorm, its natural wood blending among the tall evergreens, looked the same.

At the top of the hill, I found the campus nearly deserted between the end of the quarter and the start of the summer session. No problem parking. I locked the car and wandered over to the student union building, looking out at the spectacular view of the bay, studded with tree-covered islands. The sky had cleared, and a pale sun cast whitish shafts on the water, where sailboats floated like something done by an Impressionist painter.

I strolled back, past the library, to the central quad, where I sat down on a stone bench, musing about those undergraduate days. My first thoughts turned to my murderer. Had he killed again? Where was he now? I wasn't worried about running into him here. He'd be long gone, not hanging around Bayville, that was certain.

My mind swung back to my own problems. Nothing

like revisiting youthful scenes to bring on an attack of self-analysis. Where was my life going? Had I gone wrong somewhere?

There was no doubt that my marriage was heading for trouble. Dan was pushing forty, and it seemed to me he was already into a midlife crisis. He'd complained when I went back to work five years ago. Although I had a reliable woman who was there for the children in the after-school hours, with my mother as a backup, he implied that they were being neglected. Yet I noticed he liked the extra money. We had a bigger house, with a pool, and he had the BMW he'd always wanted, while I drove the Ford van.

"So, what's the problem?" I would ask when he scowled and groused.

Now he had another grievance. "I've told you. I don't like you traveling around alone, Debbie."

"Oh, come on, Dan. We're not in the dark ages. I only take a trip once a month or so, anyway."

"Yeah. Well, I know what these guys are like who travel on business. They've got their eye out for what's available."

I laughed. "You ought to know. Is that what you and your pals do when you make those trips to the East Coast?"

What bothered me now was that the first time I said something like that, Dan just shrugged and said he didn't have time to mess around. But later, when the same conversation took place, he glared at me and shouted, "Look, I've told you I don't go in for that stuff." And he slammed out the door.

That rang the alarm bell with me, all right.

After his last trip, I'd noticed that for several days, he would sit, gazing into space, preoccupied, not hearing what anybody said to him. If questioned, he either looked startled or flared up in anger. The children asked what was the matter with Dad but soon ran off and forgot it.

Now and then, on one of my business trips, some guy had made a pass at me, in a meeting or on a plane, and I'd felt flattered but not seriously tempted. At first, I'd told Dan with a laugh about these episodes, until he started taking them seriously. Then, when he asked if anybody had hit on me lately, I'd make some flip remark like, "No luck this time."

Now, sitting on my old campus, sharp memories of those early days of being in love surged up. We had started dating at the beginning of our senior year. He gave me a ring at Christmas, and our wedding was set for August, after graduation. I remembered how we had walked around the campus in a blissful daze, talking about our plans for a future that stretched out like a sun-dappled path with no end. Dan had signed up for a good job in aerospace in Los Angeles, and I was pleased that we would live in my hometown.

Whatever our problems are now, I thought, they can't be serious. Or can they?

I'd always felt I could rely on Dan. He'd certainly come through for me that day I encountered the murderer. The whole scenario came back to me now in vivid Technicolor.

It had happened on Squamish Hill, a wooded, spinelike ridge that towered behind the campus like a backboard. A path through the woods led from the campus along the side of the hill, and women students were warned from day one not to use the path alone, as there had been attacks there in the past. Some of the girls went that way anyhow, but I'd never needed to use it, as my dorm was on the other side of the hill.

On the fateful day, I was packing the last of my belongings when I remembered I had left a sweater at the home of a girl named Martha and decided I'd better go and pick it up. I had a few hours before my roommate Cindy and I were due to leave for her family's summer place on Orcas Island, where I would spend a few days before going home to L.A. My parents had already left for the airport, and Dan had promised to come over and help us load up Cindy's car.

I'd only been to Martha's place when somebody was driving, and I now saw that, to walk there, I'd have to go down the main campus road and then back up the steep hill at the far end to reach her house. That's when I remembered the path. It would be a shortcut to where she lived at the end of Squamish Hill, where it tapered off like the blade of a knife. A local girl, she lived with her widowed mother and a younger brother who was handicapped.

As I walked along the path, I loved the feel of seclusion, like being in a magic garden out of a childhood dream. The wooded hill rose sharply on my right and dropped down the other side in a mass of greenery, with tantalizing glimpses of the bay far below.

When I first heard sounds in the thicket of ferns below the path at my left, I thought it was probably a dog nosing around, but that didn't last long. It was soon clear that some person was there, crashing through the trees, and now I recalled the old warnings about the path.

I stood transfixed, my heart leaping around in my chest, as a tall, dark-haired man burst through the shrubbery and stopped, not ten feet away, staring at me.

He didn't look like a student, although he might have been in his early twenties. He was what my mother would have called "a nice clean-cut young man." In those days, hippiedom may have long since faded into the mainstream in many parts of the country, but not in Bayville. The guys still wore their hair long, and your jeans had better have a few strategic holes or you weren't in. This guy wore slacks and a sweater, and his dark hair, neatly clipped, grew down to a sharp point on his forehead.

But the truth is, I wasn't spending much time analyzing his place in the local demography, because the look on his face was turning my insides to yoghurt. His eyes—a sort of bluish-gray—were bugged out so you could see the whites all around. He was holding both his hands up, his fingers splayed out, and he looked at me and then at his hands and back again with a kind of puzzled, calculating expression.

He took one step toward me, and I heard a feeble sort of yelping sound come out of my throat. I turned and ran in total panic back toward the campus.

I'd always thought if something like this happened to me, I'd yell my head off, but nothing had come out except this weird little gaspy shriek as I took off along the path. After a few yards, I took a quick look back over my shoulder, thinking he must be pretty close behind me, and saw, with a huge jolt of surprise, that he was just standing there watching me. Then he shrugged and turned away, taking the path in the opposite direction.

I didn't stop running, but I could feel relief prickling through my body like water on a parched plant. By the time I got back to the dorm, I'd stopped looking back, but I was still puffing out those short gaspy breaths as I told Cindy what had happened.

We agreed I should call the police. When I dialed 911, I was put through to a sergeant who asked first if I had been injured, then noted the time and place of the incident and asked for a description of the man.

The sergeant's voice was kindly but not alarmed. "Did the man touch you or make any threatening moves toward you?"

"Well, not exactly. It's just that he looked sort of . . . well, wild. And he started to move toward me and then stopped, and I turned and ran."

"Did he attempt to follow you?"

"No, he turned the other way."

"I see. Now, Debbie, we don't want you to worry too much about this. It's possible the man you saw had simply stepped off the path to, er, answer a call of nature, so to speak, and was startled to see you."

Wanting to believe this, I politely agreed.

"Good. Then, thank you for reporting this matter, and if you think of anything further, please be sure to give us a call."

When Dan arrived, I tried to make light of what had happened, but he looked worried and said he wasn't going to let me out of his sight until we were ready to leave.

The three of us went out to get some lunch, and when we came back to the dorm, we found a policeman on the doorstep. Some boys playing in the woods had found the body of a young woman—a local high school girl—below the path in the woods. She had been strangled. No attempt had been made to bury her, but her body had been covered over with ferns.

Now the police had changed their tune. I was asked to point out the place on the path where I'd seen the man, and I was questioned for hours by a platoon of officers. They had an artist do an Identikit, but except for the dark point of hair on his forehead, there were no distinguishing features I could recall, and the result didn't really look like the man I saw.

Finally, they said we could go on to Orcas. I was pretty shaken up by this time. Dan was booked on a flight to L.A. that afternoon, but he changed it to the next day and came with us to the island. That night, he held me close, and I'd never forgotten how his voice shook when he said, "I don't want to lose you, Debbie. You mean the whole world to me."

The next day, after Dan had gone, Cindy and I were out digging clams in the low tide when the Bayville Police called. They had a suspect in custody, a transient who had been seen in the neighborhood near the path, and they wanted me to see him in a lineup. Hours later, after the ferry ride and the drive to Bayville, they had me look through the glass at half a dozen men, but I saw no one in the group who looked in the least like the man on the path.

Afterward, when I was back home in Los Angeles, I was told they had no evidence against the suspect and had let him go. For my protection, they had never released my name to the press, for which I was grateful, since I didn't want to have nightmares about the killer tracking me down and eliminating his only eyewitness.

After that, from time to time, I was asked to look at photos of possible suspects, but no one was even close. The police had learned that the girl was pregnant. Her girlfriends said she had been seeing someone she was crazy about, but they could never get her to tell who it was. When she bragged that she was going to make him marry her, they decided she was inventing the whole story, and no one had a clue to the identity of the father of her child.

It had been a long time now since I'd heard from the police, but they told me a murder case is never closed. The Bayville killing had never been solved.

Now, looking at my watch, I saw it was not yet four o'clock. Plenty of time to drive around the town. I walked back to my car, reflecting that there was actually no one to visit. Bayville was a small town and most of my friends had come from somewhere else. The girl Martha was almost the only local I'd known, and we hadn't been close. A year younger than I, she was one of a group that had pizza parties, sometimes at her place, which was how I came to leave my sweater there.

I'd always liked her mother. If I could find the house, I thought, I'd stop and say hello to her and ask after Martha, who had, after all, been decent enough to mail my sweater to me when I wrote and asked her to.

I found the house with no problem, a two-story white frame with a comfortable front porch, the walk flanked by beds of roses nodding away in masses of pink and yellow. My ring at the bell was answered by a woman who peered through the screen door at me and cried out, "Debbie, is that you?"

I saw it was Martha herself, and we laughed and went through the usual "You haven't changed at all!" and "Why didn't you call?" Over coffee, we caught up on our lives. She had dropped out of the U. before her senior year and married a guy named Joe who was already making good money at the local pulp mill and was now a supervisor. They had a son, Jeff, almost eleven. I reported on my marriage, my boy who was thirteen, and my little girl the same age as her Jeff.

I was saddened to learn that Martha's mother had died some years ago. Martha said, "I never did go out to work, Debbie. I guess I really didn't want a career. Besides, since Mom died, I've had to look after Billy. That's why we moved back here to the house, because he feels secure here."

Billy? Of course, the brother. I remembered that he walked with a limp and was what people called "not quite right in the head," but he'd always had a cheerful grin, and Martha had been devoted to him.

When she asked me to stay for dinner, I thought, why not? It was only fifty miles to Vancouver. The border crossing would take some time, but this far north it would be daylight till after ten o'clock.

With a diffident smile, Martha said, "I want you to meet Joe, Debbie. He's been so good to all of us. He treats Billy the same as his own son."

While Martha checked her casserole and set the table, I chopped the salad makings, looking out of the open window to where Billy and Jeff were playing ball in the back garden. Billy must be nearly thirty, I thought, but he seemed younger than Jeff, awkwardly chasing the ball and trying to throw it back without much accuracy.

Once, when Billy succeeded in catching the ball, Jeff

called out, "Good play!" and a proud grin spread over Billy's face.

When Martha called them in to wash for dinner, she presented them to me as if they were both children, looking proud of their good manners as they greeted me.

Then I heard the front door open and a voice called, "Hi, I'm home."

Martha's face flushed. "Oh, there's Joe."

She hurried to the entry, and I could see through the dining room the tall figure of her husband as she put up her arms for a welcoming embrace. This was no routine hug. He held her in a long kiss, then pulled back and gazed into her eyes, obviously murmuring words of affection before kissing her again.

I finally unglued my eyes and turned away, feeling a small reflex of pain. It had been a long time since Dan and I had greeted each other that way.

Now I heard Martha say, "Honey, we have a visitor," and she brought him in to where I was standing.

One look and I felt a fist clutch inside my chest.

He was the man on the path!

Not a doubt. The dark hair growing down to a sharp point on his forehead, the face I wasn't likely to forget!

He must have seen the shock on my face, for he looked puzzled while Martha made the introductions. I tried to respond normally, tearing my gaze away from those mesmerizing eyes.

The dinner was a nightmare. Martha chattered happily about how pleased she was that I dropped by. "You and Joe didn't meet back in those days, did you, Debbie?"

Joe's eyes met mine, again with that baffled look, and we both said, "No."

Martha smiled. "We were already dating that year, weren't we, Joe? But I only saw Debbie with a bunch of the girls." Then she added with pride, "Joe always liked to be alone with me, didn't you, honey?"

Joe muttered a sort of "Rrr," which seemed to satisfy Martha.

Later on, passing the salad bowl to Jeff and Billy, she said, "Have some more salad, boys. Debbie made it for us."

With a happy smile, Billy spooned salad onto his plate, spilling bits of lettuce and tomato onto the table-cloth. He looked up in distress, but Martha said gently, "It's all right, dear."

Then Martha began the story of my leaving the sweat-er at her place and how she had sent it back to me after graduation, all those years ago. "That was around the time that poor girl was found dead up in the woods. Did you ever hear about that, Debbie?"

I gulped and said, yes, I had heard something about it.

Martha sighed. "And they never found who did it."

Quickly, I turned the conversation by asking Jeff about his school, mechanically responding to questions about my own children, but I could see the damage was done.

Martha's mention of the murder had triggered Joe's memory. He studied my face, then flinched and looked down at his plate, and now I knew. *He had recognized me at last.*

Fear rose up and choked me. I pushed the food around on my plate, forcing down as much as I could, trying des-perately to act unconcerned, until even Martha noticed and asked, "Are you all right, Debbie?"

"Just a headache. It's been a long day."

"Of course." She rushed to get some aspirin, and to avoid Joe's gaze, I followed her out and dutifully swallowed the pills.

When the dinner finally came to an end, I managed to convince Martha that I must be on my way. "I need to settle in at the hotel and do my preparations for tomorrow."

To my relief, Joe shook my hand and disappeared, leaving Martha and the boys to walk me to my car.

Once back on the freeway, I began to breathe again, except that now I had to face the devastating question of what to do. If I went to the police, would they believe me? After fifteen years, they might doubt my identification. Wouldn't they need more evidence than just my word? I would be accusing a man who appeared to be a solid citizen of the community.

And there was no doubt it would destroy Martha and her family. Could I do that to her?

I wondered about Joe, trying to remember the old Psych 101 stuff about psychotic personalities. Was his devotion to Martha beyond the norm, a manifestation of twisted love? Was this true of certain types of killers? And had he killed again? If there had been similar crimes in the area, the police would probably have contacted me, but what if they were nowhere near Bayville? Joe might never have been suspected.

As I drove north, the countryside flattened out somewhat, revealing the white splendor of the great mountain, now behind me and to the east.

I had gone about half the twenty-mile distance to the border when a late-model maroon van pulled out from behind me and traveled alongside. Wondering why the driver didn't pass, I glanced over and saw the dark pointed hairline and knew it was Joe.

He turned and faced me, his eyes intense, and motioned for me to pull over to the side of the road.

Little hammer blows began a steady thumping in my chest. I stepped down hard on the accelerator, gaining on him briefly, but I soon came up behind a slower-moving car and had to drop back. Again he pulled beside me and gestured for me to stop.

I tried to think what to do. If he forced me over to the shoulder of the highway, how could I signal that I needed help? Even if I could find the emergency flasher on my rental car and turn it on, anybody who bothered to look would see his car there and would assume he had stopped to help me.

I saw a slow-moving rig ahead and pulled up behind it. There were only two lanes on the highway at this stretch, and Joe could not stay in the fast lane at that moderate speed. A car behind him blasted its horn, and he moved over to drop behind me, tailgating me so that I couldn't make a quick move to pass the truck.

Traffic was fairly light, and when there was a break, Joe pulled alongside me again, trying to push me over. I veered to the left toward his van, forcing him back, as I knew he wouldn't want to risk a collision, with other spectators involved.

We went on for a few miles in this crazy procession—the rig, then me, then Joe—when suddenly we came to an exit and the rig turned and lumbered up the off ramp. For a wild moment, I thought of following, but that would make matters worse. Off the highway, I would be completely vulnerable.

My best bet, I decided, was to make it to the Canadian border crossing. With the rig gone, I moved abruptly into the left lane and stayed there at a stubborn sixty miles an hour, letting angry drivers pass me on the right, with glares and an occasional obscene gesture as they went by.

Joe hung in behind me, and at last we passed the border town of Blaine and came up to the customs stop. There were about twenty cars lined up in each of the four lanes, and I slipped into the one at the left, closest to the buildings. I checked again to be sure the car doors were locked and the windows up. Once I got to the kiosk, I would report that a man was following me, and let the officials tell me what to do.

Joe pulled behind me in the lane, as I expected, but what he did next really surprised me. He stepped out of his van, walked slowly up to my car on the driver's side, and tapped on the window. How could he attack me in the midst of all these people? I knew he could see the terror in my face, and he shook his head, making gestures to say it was all right, don't be afraid.

Then he put his face close to the window. "Debbie, please let me talk to you. Put the window down."

Was he kidding? I shook my head.

"Look," he said, speaking distinctly through the glass. "It's not what you think. *I didn't kill that girl!*"

Now the cars in the lane moved up a notch, and I followed, Joe jumping back into his van and keeping behind me.

When we stopped, he came up to my window again. "Debbie, I can explain everything if you'll just give me the chance."

I didn't buy that for a minute, but before I reached the stop, Joe had moved to the next lane, and I saw him go through before I did. When I reached the gate and told the customs officer what was happening, he told me to park by the building and report the matter there. He stepped out and walked beside me, seeing me safely through the door.

I looked around. No sign of Joe. There were two people ahead of me in the line, and I was glad to have some time to stop shaking and get myself together. I was sure Joe wouldn't come inside.

I was wrong. I heard a voice behind me saying my name, and when I spun around to face him, I saw tears in his eyes. "Please listen for a minute. I wasn't the one who killed that girl, *but it might have been Billy!*"

That stopped me, and when he asked me again to listen, I went slowly over to a bench against the far wall, where he sat down beside me.

"I'll tell you what happened, Debbie, and then you can decide what to do."

Numbly, I nodded.

"It was a Saturday, and I had gone over to Martha's

about noon. She and her mother were out shopping, and I found Billy there, very upset and crying. It was hard to get a coherent story out of him, but what he seemed to be telling me was that a girl who lived in the neighborhood was dead. He had seen her up in the woods by the bend in the path. Then he started talking about how the girl had teased him. I gathered she pretended she wanted him to have sex with her, and then when he tried to kiss her, she laughed at him. This is my interpretation, you understand. Billy's vocabulary is extremely limited."

I nodded again, wondering how much of this story I could believe.

"Well, then I asked him when this happened, but he really doesn't understand time distinctions. I began to wonder if he was imagining the whole thing. I told him to stay in his room until I got back, and if he stopped crying, I would take him fishing. He gave me that happy child's smile, and I sprinted off along the path to the sharp bend he had mentioned.

"You know what I found. The girl was dead, all right. I was horrified. To gain a little time, I covered her body with greenery. My hands were sticky from the ferns, and I was rubbing them as I came back onto the path. Then I looked up and you were standing there!

"Believe me, I was as shocked as you were, Debbie. I started to move toward you, thinking I would tell you what I'd found, but I saw that you were terrified at my sudden appearance. I watched you run, and I was sorry you were frightened, but the important thing was to get back to Billy. I hurried back to the house and found Billy still alone, but when I tried to question him about the girl, he seemed to have forgotten about it and only wanted to talk about going fishing.

"I took him out that afternoon, hoping I could get him to tell me more, but you see, Billy is totally suggestible. If I said, 'Did you hurt her, Billy?' he would say, 'Yes, I hurt her.' But if I said, 'You didn't hurt her, did you?' he'd say, 'No, I didn't hurt her.'

"That was when I knew the police would regard anything he said as a confession. And the problem was, I couldn't tell if he *had* done it. You see, he might only have found her body and remembered she was the girl who had teased him one day.

"I never told Martha and her mother. I was crazy about Martha and was about to ask her to marry me. You can imagine what it would have done to the family if I had reported my suspicions to the police. Billy would have been labeled a killer and been put into an institution. I've watched over him all these years and never seen the least sign of violent behavior. If anyone else had been accused of the murder, I would have told the police my story.

"So there it is, Debbie. It's all up to you now."

I sat still for a while. Then I turned and looked into Joe's pleading eyes.

"I guess I'll have to think about it. I'd like to go on to Vancouver now."

Joe said, "Okay. Don't worry, I won't follow you. I'll go up to the turnaround and go back across the border."

We walked out together, and I watched as he drove into a lane that said RETURN TO U.S. Nevertheless, all the way to my hotel, I kept a lookout for Joe and his van.

No problem. I checked in, locked and chained the door, and started mechanically unpacking my bag, my mind still going around the treadmill it had been on ever since Joe told me his story.

Was I being conned? He could have planned this story from the beginning, in case he was ever accused of the murder. His manner had been convincing, but that didn't prove much. What if Joe had been that girl's mystery lover? When she told him she was pregnant and insisted he had to marry her, wouldn't he have done anything not to lose Martha?

Haunted by indecision, I phoned Dan and poured out the story. "So, what shall I do?"

There was no answer.

"Dan?"

Another pause. "I'm thinking."

We talked over the pros and cons of believing Joe's story, Dan generally taking the view that it sounded pretty convincing to him. "He sounded sincere, did he?"

"Oh, sure, but wouldn't he sound that way if he'd planned this story to cover his own tracks?"

"Well, I guess he would, but you'd have felt he was lying, wouldn't you?"

"I don't know. Another thing, what if Joe is the one who had been fooling around with that girl?"

Dan said, "Oh, I doubt that. He wasn't her type. Sounds too serious."

Before I could say any more, he cut me off. "Look, Debbie, I'm coming up there. I'll arrange things with your mother to take the kids to her place, and I'll get a flight tomorrow. Okay? I'll see you at the hotel."

Mechanically, I got ready for bed, Dan's words bouncing around in my head. What did he mean, "He wasn't her type"? Surely, he didn't know the girl, or he would have said so at the time.

Or would he?

What if it was Dan—not Joe—who got the girl pregnant? Is that why he was so eager to believe Joe's story? It would let him off the hook if . . .

No, no, I couldn't believe that. I'd loved Dan all these years. Wouldn't I have known if he was capable of something like that? My body began to shake, and I crawled into bed, only to lie with open eyes, staring at the ceiling.

What if the girl had insisted he marry her? I kept hearing Dan's voice, fifteen years ago, saying, "I don't want to lose you, Debbie. You mean everything to me."

I dozed off and on throughout the night. Half a dozen

times I picked up the phone to have it out with him, and each time I put it back. He'd be here tomorrow. Better to talk about it face-to-face.

In the morning, I dragged myself to my appointments, forcing myself to concentrate, and when I got back to the hotel in the late afternoon, Dan was there, waiting.

He held me close, then pulled back and studied my face as if he hadn't seen me for a long time.

I said, "You didn't need to come, Dan."

"I know. You can handle the situation without me. I just wanted to be sure you're all right."

I sat down, and he walked over to the window, looking out at the Vancouver skyline.

Staring at his back, I said softly, "Dan, what did you mean when you said that the dead girl wasn't Joe's type? Did you know her?"

Now he turned to face me. "Yeah, I used to see her around."

"Why didn't you say so when it all happened?"

"I didn't want to get involved. It wasn't as if I really knew her."

He saw the look on my face, and suddenly his voice shook. "Sweetheart, you don't think *I* killed her?"

Pain rose in my throat. "I don't know what I think. I'm not sure I know you anymore."

Now he came to me and took my hand. "Look, I'll tell you all I know. Some of us from the dorm used to shoot some pool downtown, and this girl—she was only sixteen—hung around the place. For a while, she talked to me a lot, tried to get me to take her out, and the guys kidded me about her.

"Then, George—remember, the one with the red hair?—started making a move on her, and she switched her attention to him. They'd leave together, and pretty soon she didn't come around anymore. I always figured George might have been the unknown father, but he'd never have killed her. And neither would I."

I felt the truth in his words and saw it in his eyes.

We flew back home the next day, not talking much about the murder. It was a month later when I got a call from a Bayville police officer, telling me that a serial killer had been apprehended in a town in Oregon, and among the murders he confessed to having committed was the Bayville killing. He gave enough detail of time and place so there was no doubt about his guilt. It turned out he was the first man they had questioned after the crime and had let go for lack of evidence.

"No wonder you didn't recognize him in the lineup," the officer told me. "The man you saw on the path must have been an innocent passerby."

One result of the whole episode of my visit to Bayville has been that our marriage got back on track again. Dan told me that when I went back to work, he'd been deeply worried that I would somehow slip away from him, maybe meet some guy who turned me on. The last time he went east, he'd met an attractive woman in a bar at the hotel. She went up to his room for a drink and spent the night.

"You see, Debbie, I thought, what the hell, some of the other guys do it, and then, if *you* met somebody else, I'd feel that I'd got there ahead of you. It was really stupid. I thought nobody would ever know. Then, I saw that it didn't work that way. You *did* know, or at least you knew something was wrong, and then I felt worse than before."

We talked about Joe and Martha, and how glad we were I hadn't reported that he was the man on the path.

I'd told Dan about the big clinch when Joe came home from work, and this became a gag routine every evening.

He would clasp me and say, "Just call me Joe," while I giggled and the kids groaned.

In the end, what mattered most to me was that my old feeling that I could rely on Dan had been restored. When the chips were down, Dan had been there for me, even if it took a murder case to make it happen.

[NANCY PICKARD]

NANCY PICKARD'S JENNY CAIN NOVELS EXPLORE what it is to be an American woman in the late twentieth century, the challenges, the pitfalls, the glories, and the travails. Jenny Cain is a perceptive, wry, and passionate protagonist. Pickard never writes the same book twice and her readers can count on fresh terrain and fascinating human drama every time. Prize winners in the series are Say No to Murder, the Anthony; Marriage Is Murder, the Macavity; Bum Steer, the Agatha, and I.O.U., the Agatha and Macavity. I.O.U. was also an Edgar nominee.

In a more lighthearted vein, Pickard has continued the series by the late Virginia Rich with The Twenty-Seven-Ingredient Chili Con Carne Murders. Her most recent Jenny Cain novel is Confession. Pickard is a past president of Sisters in Crime. She lives in Prairie Village, Kansas, with her son.

Pickard is also a prize-winning short story writer and she shows her winning form in "Valentine's Night," a funny, sexy, and sad exploration of what happens when Valentine's Day coincides with a blue moon.

Valentine's Night

Oh, yes, there really is such a thing as a blue moon.

It is an actual scientific phenomenon, caused by this and that, or something or other, but who cares about that?

That's merely science.

All that really matters is that on certain fantastical nights, some fortunate folks—who lean back on their heels and squint their eyes just so—may actually see a fabulous, delectably deep blue aura around the moon, be it full, waxing, waning, or even gibbous.

It's so strange, so beautiful, so . . . moving, somehow, that they can't stop feasting on the sight of it. They want to pluck it from the sky, to revolve it in their hands, to bring it to their nose and sniff its moonly blue fragrance, and finally to gobble it down, with blue and yellow light dribbling down their chins, as if the moon were a luscious peach bathed for that one extraordinary night in fairies' blueberry juice. It makes people greedy, a blue moon does—at least that's what some folks (not scientists) say. They claim that it makes some folks want more than they already have, more than they ever dreamed— or admitted—they'd ever need. In other words, it makes some folks crave their deepest, most secret desires. And when those desires are frustrated? Watch out! A blue moon, or so it's said, is a powerfully hungry moon, and hunger—as everybody knows—is not centered in the stomach or even the mouth, but rushes, instead, straight from the heart.

It was on such a night, the very night of Valentine's Day, that Marianne Griff—who was normally a nice, steady, levelheaded sort of woman—figured out where her husband really was.

And it wasn't where he'd said he'd be!

No, where Ned Griff really was that night was a long way from where he had said he'd be, but only a few tempting and dangerous blocks away from home.

At six o'clock that evening, when the unwelcome knowledge tore Marianne apart like dynamite exploding in her hands, the moon had only just begun its rise in the Valentine's sky, and it wasn't even blue, not yet. Perhaps that is why Marianne was forced to endure so many hours of ordinary human misery.

"Cincinnati," was what Ned had told her. "With Christy."

Well, of course, with Christy. Marianne had easily accepted that fact. Law partners frequently traveled together. It was commonplace, wasn't it? Marianne was, herself, an account executive with a telephone company; she knew she could trust herself to travel platonically with men, so it was easy for her to trust her husband to travel innocently with women, on business.

Yes, it was true that Christy was beautiful—a shiny brunette with a body sculpted by personal trainers. Oh, and yes, Christy was youngish, with seven fewer Valentine's Days than Marianne had notched in her own belt. Oh, and brilliant, to have made full partner in her early thirties. Christy Phares was, indeed, frighteningly good at cross-examining plaintiffs' witnesses in civil courtrooms. Marianne had seen her in action, and she'd felt impressed and proud, on general feminist principles, on behalf of all women.

Get 'em, Christy! she'd thought at the time.

Christy had sat at the table on the defendant's side of the courtroom, face forward to the judge (a man), with her back straight, the palms of her hands disarmingly flat and splayed upon the table, her legs crossed at her silky knees but not at any provocative angle. In the courtroom, Christy had looked alert, sleek in her black suit, like a panther with nothing to fear in this jungle, her claws sheathed, her nostrils delicately flared, her muscles relaxed but ready to spring.

Marianne's husband, Ned, had sat at the same table, but never touched his partner, never jotted a note to her, or even lifted an eyebrow in silent dialogue. They had looked the very picture of the perfectly prepared law partners. The phrase "a matched set" had occurred to some observers, though not to Marianne. The fact that Ned was every bit as handsome and muscled and well-groomed as Christy, or that every man in the courtroom had fantasized a vision of the naked breasts beneath the black suit, was irrelevant and immaterial to Marianne.

The law was all: magnificently neuter. It never occurred to Marianne—also for good feminist reasons—to suspect that Ned found less beauty in the law than he did in the lawyer seated next to him. (Even if it had just possibly crossed her mind, for one teeny second, she would have quickly shooed the treacherous thought away as being disloyal to her husband and traitorous to women.)

"We'll be at the convention hotel," he'd told her.

That made sense to Marianne; she'd doubted nothing.

But then, when she was in the bedroom changing out of her business clothes into a comfortable old gray sweatsuit, she noticed the brochure for the bar convention poking out from under some of Ned's papers that he'd left on top of the chest of drawers. Curious to see who the star-spangled speakers would be this year, Marianne drew the pamphlet—*the stick of dynamite*—toward her.

The first speaker, scheduled for 8 A.M. Saturday, February eighth, was . . .

Now the dynamite was lit.

Marianne never did learn the identity of the keynote speaker for the Ohio Bar Association Convention. Her gaze had fallen back onto the date. The eighth? For a moment, she felt confused: this was Valentine's Day, February fourteenth, wasn't it?

The flame ate the wick, drawing closer to the charge.

Yes—she glanced over at the king-sized bed—there was the Valentine's card Ned had left on her pillow this morning. It was one of those modern amusing ones that were very nearly hostile in their humor, nothing sentimental or even nostalgic about it. Still, she'd been happy to receive it. He'd signed it: *"Me."* She looked into her living room and glimpsed the dozen pink carnations in a clear glass vase on her coffee table. Yes, they'd been delivered to her office today, all right, with a note: "Guess Who?"

The eighth?!
Boom.

The intuition arrived in a blast of searing pain that made Marianne feel as if she'd splashed hot grease onto her chest.

What? she thought.

And then: *No!*

To prove to herself that it wasn't true, she walked on jellied knees to the bedside telephone to dial, with trembling and suddenly freezing fingers, the convention hotel. Crazy, she thought, to feel so frightened of the phone, the very instrument she sold in such huge and profitable numbers to other people. She wished now—as it rang once, twice, in Cincinnati—that it had never been invented (her own salary and profit sharing notwithstanding). The hotel operator graciously consented to look up the number and ring the room of guest Edward Griff. Marianne waited, wishing all the while that when Alexander Graham Bell had yelled, "Watson! Come here! I need you!" Watson had not replied. If only Bell had then thought, Oh, the hell with the damn thing, and given up on his invention that had changed the world. And was about to change her world. . . .

"I'm sorry, there's no Mr. Griff registered."

Marianne longed for the pony express, which would take days to reach Cincinnati and return with the terrible news of loss and heartache. At the very least, a telegraph might have taken hours.

She pleaded: "Are you sure?"

But no. Bad news came much more quickly in this century than it ever had before, giving you no time at all to arrange your emotions, your face, your voice, your future. . . .

"Yes, ma'am. Thank you for calling Marriott."

With one hand, Marianne gently hung up the telephone; with her other hand she pressed her chest, where all the pain was radiating like heat from a charcoal briquette, and she fell onto Ned's side of the bed and buried her face in his pillow. The scent of his shampoo was like a blow to her abdomen, kicking sobs up into her chest from deep inside of her. Soon she was gasping, weeping. So melodramatic, she thought, from some cynically observing part of herself. I'm dying, she thought, from another part of herself that was a good deal closer at hand, and suffering. I'll kill him! I'll kill her! I love him! I hate him! Caught painfully in a vise whose one side was steaming passion and whose other side was coolly ironic detachment, she felt exposed, absurd, primitive, raw and vulnerable and uncivilized and deeply, unfairly wounded.

For the next five and a half hours, until nearly midnight, Marianne paced the house she'd shared with a husband—a liar!—for fifteen years. Upstairs, downstairs, the basement, every room. She touched every wall and every piece of furniture, walking, walking, as if she could walk the pain off like a hangover, as if she could exhaust it out of herself, wring it out like a good sweat. She thought: It isn't true, it isn't, it is. She wept, she swore.

She took scissors and cut his Valentine's Day card into the shape of a heart, which she then cut—with jagged edges—down the middle. She taped both sides to the dresser mirror right where her face was reflected. Now she saw a broken heart surrounded by streaked blond hair with a reddened nose between the jagged edges and a forty-one-year-old neck and body below.

She panicked, she tried to meditate, she tried to read, she prayed, she screamed, she tried to reason herself back into sanity, she attempted to evolve right then and there into a better, higher sort of person, she tried to defend Ned against her own accusations, she tried to wait, to understand, to find another explanation.

She tried, she tried, she tried!

All to no effect, of course, perhaps because the moon had not yet risen to its fully royal blueness.

Finally, five minutes before the mark of midnight, the moon did appear outside her living room window.

Oh! It was fuzzy all around with a sort of incredible blue color!

Marianne stopped in her tracks, startled, staring. The sight of the moon reminded her that this day of Ned's unfaithfulness, of his wicked betrayal, was Valentine's Day.

Of all days! The schmuck!

That single awful, ironic, sentimental, full realization struck the final shattering blow to her sadly pummeled heart. She stared at the moon—it was almost half, lying on its back in the sky like a beautiful golden fat lady in a hammock, bathed in a blue spotlight.

Marianne felt, in that moment, desperate.

She felt as if the blood inside her broken heart was spilling into the huge cavity behind her ribs, and that now the blood was lying there, helplessly pulsing at the sight of the moon, right in time to the breathing of the lady in the hammock. Marianne felt the rhythm of the moon sucking at the living pieces of her heart, tugging at her breastbone, pulling at her blood like heat drawing spilled pieces of mercury. Like an irresistible magnet, that cruel and gorgeous moon drew her out of her home and then into her car. It pulled her along the dark streets to the house where she suspected her husband lay that Valentine's night with his lover.

The golden fat lady in her hammock reached for the front fender of Marianne's car to pull her along the road to Christy's house.

This being February, there was snow everywhere.

It was cold in the car, almost immediately, when she turned the engine off, and she sat bundled in coat, hat, gloves, boots, and muffler, breathing frost into the air inside her car. There, one house down, was the two-story, red-brick house where Christy lived with her husband, Adam Phares.

A married woman!

Illuminated by the snow and the moon, the house seemed bright among the other homes on the block, as if helicopters had their spotlights beamed at it.

There! There's where the illicit couple is hiding!

Coupling, Marianne thought, and the word was a stab into her own side. That's where they're coupling. She looked over at her passenger's seat: God only knew why, but before she left her house she'd grabbed the vase of Ned's carnations. She'd set them on the car seat and then buckled them in, as if they were a child. It was an irrational act. So was coming here.

"But I have to have proof, don't I?" she asked the moon, plaintively.

Maybe she was being ridiculous. Oh, she liked that idea very much, and she let it warm her. Maybe she was the one who was betraying Ned, by being suspicious of him. Maybe she should be ashamed of herself for jumping to such an evil conclusion, maybe she could look forward to cringing with secret humiliation whenever she looked back on this awful night. Oh, yes! She'd happily trade that little private mortification for the more public one she'd been imagining: being left for a younger woman. So banal; could it possibly be worth all this heartache?

The earth swung in its orbit, passing the moon behind a cloud, then out again on the other side. Perfidious, nomadic moon! Silently, it seemed to swing into Marianne's vision, its blue halo catching the corner of her eye, snagging her attention so that she turned her head, the exact forty-five degrees that was needed to direct her attention to . . .

Ned's car.

It was parked across the street from Christy's house

in the parking lot of a condominium complex, sneaked in between a red BMW and a vintage Mustang, as if it belonged there. Maybe it wasn't his. There were nearly as many Mercedes in the city as there were lawyers. Maybe. But no, the light of the snow from below lit the personalized license: L EAGLE (short for legal eagle). And the moon shone revealingly on the dark (sinister) gray finish of the car.

No mistake: it was Ned's incriminating car.

The moon looked bluest at that very moment when Marianne's heart pulsed so hard she thought surely it would jerk from her chest and hop down the snowy street without her, plop by bloody plop.

"Oh, God," she groaned, mostly from the pain of finding out she was right, but also from the problem of trying to use a tissue to wipe her nose while she still had gloves on. The worst of her pain was centered just inside the warm tender curve of her left breast. She pressed her fingers there, and leaned into them. *Oh . . .*

The unrelenting moon pulled Marianne's hand away from her wounded breast—like a shot bird, she was—and placed the fingers on the handle of the car door, which opened. The moon tugged her out into the street and pushed her hands to close the door with a muted *click*. It shoved her hands into the pockets of her overcoat and pulled the breath from her mouth in a white mist. It made her stand alone under a street lamp for a moment, staring helplessly, furiously, at Christy's house.

And then the moon—the plump, soft invisible tugging hand of the fat lady in the hammock—touched Marianne's chin and nudged it to the left, drawing her attention to another car.

This one—an ivory Infiniti—was parked at the curb.

She saw a man seated in it, and he was also staring at Christy's house.

The moon caught his chin and turned it toward her.

It was Christy's husband, Adam Phares.

Simultaneously, he and Marianne gasped, and then flushed with the embarrassment of being caught in the act of having their hearts broken. And then the moon, merciless creature, placed its fat blue hands on the woolly lapels of Marianne's coat and jerked her right into the passenger seat of Adam's car.

"I'll kill the son of a bitch," were his first words to her.

"Just Ned?" she retorted, in a shaky voice. "What about your wife? Where did she tell you she'd be this weekend?"

"I told her I'd be in New York."

Marianne thought about that, and then exclaimed: "You *knew?*"

"I was only suspicious. *Now* I know."

"How long do you think it's been going on?"

He shook his head. "What difference does it make if it's more than one night?"

Marianne slumped down in the seat. "It doesn't." Wearily, feeling defeated, she turned her head toward him. "So what are you going to do?"

"Make sure," he said, lingering over each word, nailing them into the night. "You want to come with me?"

"Where?" And when he nodded in the direction of the house, she exclaimed: "Over there? You're kidding!"

"It's my house—" He looked distracted. "I'm sorry, I can't remember your name."

"Marianne."

"I'm Adam."

She knew that, but they'd only met at office parties. She couldn't remember what he did for a living, she didn't know anything about him, except that apparently his wife was cuckolding him with Marianne's husband.

"Marianne," he repeated. "It's my house. I can do anything I want to."

"But what—"

"I want to see them together."

He picked up a thirty-five-millimeter camera from the console between them and held it up. "*Catch* them together."

"Oh, my God, are you sure—"

"They're *lawyers,* Marianne."

"Right." She nodded, immediately grasping the harrowing prospect of divorcing an attorney. "Okay, then I'm coming, too." As he stuck the little camera into the right-hand pocket of his overcoat, an even more frightening idea occurred to her. "But what if they hear us and think we're burglars and call the police? Do you keep guns in the house? What if they mistake us for burglars and shoot us?"

"So they call the cops, so what?" Adam Phares tightened his lips, as if to draw them in from the cold. "So they shoot us." He added, angrily, dully, "So what?"

Then they'd be sorry, Marianne thought, before she corrected herself. No, they wouldn't. She bit her lips to restrain the sob that wanted to burst from her mouth.

The moon, having done its mischievous job, ducked behind a cloud and wisely stayed there.

"Can't you sneak more quietly?" she hissed, behind Adam, as they approached the bushes in front of the back bedroom window. She'd hoped the snow would muffle their approach, but no, the ice crunched like peanut brittle. Plus, Adam seemed intent on bulling his way like a defensive end charging a quarterback: his arms swinging wide of his coat, his head jutted out ahead of his body, his boots taking giant strides, he seemed oblivious of the noise he was making. She felt as if they were alerting the neighborhood, much less the lovers. "Adam, wait!"

She ran, crunchingly, after him, catching him by his coattails and jerking him back toward her. "We'll never catch them if they hear us coming first!"

It was reassuring to her that he was behaving as irrationally as she felt that she was.

They covered the rest of the distance like cautious rabbits in the snow. Adam led Marianne smack up against a windowsill toward the rear of the house, and they stood side by side, peering in, standing on top of dead and frozen marigold plants.

The lovers hadn't bothered to close the curtains.

They'd even thoughtfully left a light on in a bathroom, and that, plus the light from the moon and the snow, illuminated them like lovers on the cover of a book.

Marianne stared at the tumble of blankets on the huge bed inside.

At first, she couldn't make out any human forms, but then a fold in the white sheets revealed itself to be a slim and shapely female arm, pale and crooked at the elbow so that the forearm lay on top of a larger pile of blankets that revealed themselves to be a curve of male chest and shoulders. Finally, Marianne could make out the tousle of two dark heads in the shadows of the pillows, two heads sleeping so close together they looked like one, a giant's.

The giant on the bed didn't stir.

"Must be exhausted," Marianne muttered, spitefully.

"What?" Adam whispered.

She didn't answer, but pointed, instead, at something inside.

"What?" he asked again.

"The mirror," she told him.

There was a mirrored double closet door directly to the side of the sleeping lovers and directly across from their spouses standing outside the window in the snow. Marianne and Adam could look in the mirror at themselves looking in at Christy and Ned. Marianne moved her own head slightly, to superimpose it on top of Christy's head: now it was she who was sleeping beside her husband. Feeling reckless, Marianne turned her face and puckered her lips: her image seemed to kiss the man on the bed.

"What are you doing?" Adam hissed, and when she shifted her glance from the mirror to him, she discovered that her lips were pointed in his direction.

"Embarrassing myself," she said.

Suddenly he put his left arm around her shoulders in a strong, abrupt motion that let her know he was trying to comfort her. "I'm sorry," he said.

"Me, too," she whimpered, and she tucked her right hand into the left pocket of his overcoat. "They look . . . happy."

"Wonderful."

She laughed a little at his sarcastic tone, but she couldn't stop staring at the bed, and neither, it appeared, could Adam. Maybe it wasn't so much that Christy and Ned looked happy—Marianne couldn't, after all, even see their faces—but that they looked warm, cozy, loving. Those adjectives added up to happiness in Marianne's personal dictionary. She and Ned hadn't slept entwined like that since before they were married, not unless one of them was a little drunk. Even after they made love, there were only a few brief moments of embracing, then a quick, rather astringent kiss, and then they turned their backs to one another, each moving to opposite sides of their bed to sleep. But Marianne knew what Christy would be feeling—if she were awake—with Ned's arm underneath her head, how big and masculine and firm Ned's upper arm and shoulder would feel, and how much heat his body would be giving off. Marianne imagined she could feel some of that heat radiating all the way outside, melting some of the snow where she was standing.

Suddenly, Adam raised his right hand and touched his glove to the storm window. Snow that had been stuck to his glove filtered down to their boots. His fingers were splayed against the glass. It was a hurt and forlorn gesture that made Marianne's heart ache for him. She pulled her hand out of his pocket and snaked her arm around to his back and patted him two or three times, as if to say, "There, there."

After a moment, she had to admit to him, "My feet are freezing."

"Okay, come on." He grabbed her right hand in his left and pulled her away from the window. Together, like linked burglars, they made their way the rest of the distance around to the back of the house.

Adam used his key to open two locks almost without any noise.

Marianne held her breath as he pushed open the door.

"We'll track snow," she warned.

"It'll melt. They'll think they did it."

She entered the darkened kitchen of her husband's lover, stepping right behind her husband's lover's husband.

There was only a light on the stove and the brightness of the night outside, but once their eyes adjusted, they could see perfectly well.

"Take your coat?" Adam asked her.

She almost smiled as she took it off and handed it to him. Christy's husband had nice hospitable instincts, even under pressure. Removing her coat seemed to Marianne to be the most daring thing she'd done so far, because it might keep her from making a clean, fast getaway. She felt as if she'd taken the big step off the high cliff.

"Boots?" he asked, looking undecided.

Boldly, she nodded, and they both removed their boots and then lined them up facing the door, as if they could jump into them in a second, like the Lone Ranger onto the back of Silver. Marianne even took off her hat and unwound her muffler and put it all, including her gloves, on top of her coat, which he'd placed on a high stool.

They looked around the kitchen, which was messy with the signs of a dinner having been recently prepared and nothing cleaned up or put away.

"She never cooks for me anymore," Adam complained.

"He never did cook for me," Marianne retorted.

It appeared that the happy couple had fixed a Valentine's dinner together, and a good one: pasta still clung to the edges of a big silver pot, and you could see where butter and bits of parsley and other goodies had been stirred in a sautéeing pan. The oven door had been left wide open, and it revealed a greasy broiling pan with a butcher knife and a sliver of steak fat still on it.

The smell of garlic permeated the air.

Adam lifted a dried string of pasta from the pot and nibbled morosely on it, while Marianne walked to a doorway and looked into the next room, which turned out to be a dining room. She crooked her finger at Adam, who came over to stand beside her. Together, they gazed in at a dining room table set elegantly for two: white china with gold bands on it, heavy silver service, candles galore, and a silver decanting rack for the red wine.

"She'll be sorry," Adam said, sounding gruff and satisfied. When Marianne gave him a quizzical look, he explained: "Christine can't tolerate red wine. Gives her migraines."

Marianne said: "I hope she throws up."

"She will, you can count on it."

"Good. Any chance it'll kill her?"

"Probably not," he said glumly, and walked back into the kitchen. He opened the refrigerator. Marianne watched him remove an orange-and-black carton and take a clean glass from a cupboard, then pour orange juice into it. He then bent over and opened the cabinet doors under the sink and began to remove various cans and bottles.

Curious, Marianne went over to watch what he was doing.

Adam took a bottle of window cleaner and sprayed

some of the contents into the orange juice. He looked at Marianne. "She drinks a glass of orange juice whenever she has a hangover. I've tried to tell her that tomato juice is more effective, but she always knows better." He set the window cleaner down and picked up a can of abrasive bathroom cleanser and shook some of it into the juice.

"Won't she taste it?" Marianne asked, feeling oddly detached.

"She'll think it's the hangover."

Marianne reached around him to pick up a plastic bottle that contained ammonia, and she poured a dollop of that into the orange brew.

"You'd think it'd bubble or something," she said.

He grunted. "It will, inside her."

Marianne laughed, and then he did, too. When they had emptied a little of everything into their witch's potion, he carefully poured it all back into the orange juice carton, and then he washed out the glass and put it into the dishwasher.

"Now it'll be diluted," Marianne said, feeling disappointed.

"No, there's not much left in the carton," Adam assured her as he returned it to the refrigerator. They looked at each other and smiled, and then they turned to appraise the contents of the kitchen again. Adam seemed to be drawn to the huge butcher knife lying sideways across the meat broiler. He slid it out of the oven and held it up in the air so that for a moment he looked to Marianne like a medieval warrior.

He glanced over at her. "What'd you think?"

She shook her head. "No, you'd be sure to get caught."

"You think?" He walked over to where there was a butcher-block table, and without warning, he violently plunged the knife into the wood, groaning with his effort. Then he backed away, and he and Marianne watched the handle of the knife quiver in the odd light in the night kitchen. She had gasped when he did it, but now she was mesmerized by how deeply the knife had penetrated the table.

Adam broke the charged silence. "Is he a good lover?"

Marianne shrugged. "If you love him."

He stared at her. "Don't you?"

"Don't I what?"

"Love him?"

"After tonight? How could I!"

"It's been done before," he said wryly. "I'm more interested in before tonight. Did you love him before tonight?"

"I thought I did. Now I don't know. Do you love her?"

Adam grasped the still-moving knife handle and tried to pull it out. It wouldn't come loose. "What's love got to do with it?" he said, and then gestured to her. "Come on."

In the dining room, Adam looked at the table and said, "Somebody's been sitting in my chair."

"And eating your porridge."

They didn't have to say the next line out loud: "And sleeping in your bed."

There was an opened gift box of designer chocolates on the table, with several pieces missing. And there were a dozen perfect pink roses in a chic black vase. And there were two Valentine's Day cards lying on the table.

Marianne took a piece of chocolate, stuck it in her mouth, and picked up the cards to read. They were as sentimental as the one that Ned had given her was not; they were as gooey as the chocolate. The handwritten extra message on one of them, in the handwriting that wasn't Ned's, said: "Darling, I love you more than life itself." Marianne handed that card to Adam, who read it and then said: "Let's find out if she means it."

Marianne felt a sudden chill of coldness, a splash of

jarring reality. She swallowed the chocolate, which felt like a marble going down. This was no game they were playing. Poisoned orange juice in the refrigerator. Butcher knife in the table. With her heart trip-hammering, she watched as Adam disappeared back into the kitchen. When he returned, there was a lump in his suit coat pocket—unlike her, he hadn't changed out of his work clothes—that he was patting with his hand.

"Adam," she said, weakly. "I don't—"

She didn't what? She didn't know.

"Come on," he said, and she followed him, like a puppy being trained. On her way out of the dining room, she picked up a couple more pieces of the chocolate.

It was easy to follow the clues to the next stage in the illicit couple's evening: a trail of discarded clothing started at the beginning of a hallway and led to an open door. Marianne and Adam found, in order: a woman's belt, man's belt, woman's blouse, man's shirt, woman's skirt, woman's shoes, hose, garter belt, black bra, black panties, and finally, a man's trousers. At the last item, Marianne knelt down. She pulled Ned's wallet from his right rear trouser pocket and removed from it the photograph of herself and the one of them together.

Adam tapped her shoulder.

When she looked up, she saw that he was holding down to her his own wallet-sized photograph of Christy. Marianne slipped it into one of the empty slots in her husband's wallet. She also pulled out all the cash and then emptied his front pockets of change.

She held the money up to Adam, offering him some, or all.

He took the bills, went back to his wife's hosiery, and stuck the money down inside one of the legs.

Nasty, Marianne thought, and smiled to herself. She put the change back in his pocket, for lack of any better—or quieter—idea of what to do with it. Now Ned might suspect that his lover had stolen his money and even had the nerve to substitute her own photo for his family pictures. He wouldn't like that, the overconfidence of it, even if he decided, as he would, that it was only a joke. And *she* really wouldn't like his idea of humor: sticking cash in her stockings, as if she were some hooker. And they could each deny it until their faces were as blue as the moon, but who else could have done it, as they were all alone in the house at the time!

As an extra fillip, Marianne stuck the two chocolates deep in the left rear pocket of Ned's trousers.

There!

She smiled up at Adam, feeling almost satisfied now.

But he was staring into the bedroom beyond her, ignoring her childlike pleasure in their petty vengeance. And he was reaching toward the right-hand pocket of his suit coat.

As he walked past her, Marianne grabbed at his coat, frantically, but it only served to pull her off balance, so that she had to scramble to keep from crashing onto the floor of the hallway. For a panicked instant, she wondered if that would have been best: maybe she should scream, warn them. . . .

Adam stepped to the door of the bedroom, and pulled out his camera.

Marianne sank against a wall in relief so flooding she thought: This must be how pregnant women feel when their water breaks. Oh, God, she'd thought it was a gun. She tiptoed to a bathroom down the hall and used it. When she returned, Adam was still standing in the doorway, the camera at his side. She took her place beside him, his companion voyeur.

There they were, sprawled, blanket coated, sleeping off the booze and lust. (Marianne refused to call it love.)

Adam leaned over and spoke right into her ear. His breath tickled her as he said: "Your husband's better looking than I am."

Into his ear, Marianne responded: "She's better looking than I am." (Particularly now, Marianne thought, knowing how red her nose and eyes must be, after the cold and so much crying.)

He leaned over again. "Yeah, but we're much nicer."

She hadn't expected that, and muffled a snort of laughter behind her hands. When she looked at him again, he was smiling at her, but his brown eyes were glistening. For the first time, she really saw him: an attractive man, possibly a little younger than she, with a broad forehead and a long, slim nose and nice eyes. It was true, he wasn't as handsome as Ned was. And she wondered if the other was true: was he really any nicer?

"I'm so tired," she confessed.

He nodded and took her hand and led her down the hall.

Silently, in total understanding, they both lay down—fully clothed—on the white chenille cover on the double bed in the guest bedroom down the hall. They held hands, each of them staring at the ceiling.

"Did you get the pictures?"

"Yeah."

"Good. I guess."

Just as she was starting to go to sleep, he said, "She's not really prettier than you are. She's just smoother. It's like she licks herself down every night, like a cat." He sounded so serious, Marianne thought, as he said these awful things about his wife. "When she sees herself in a mirror, she nearly purrs."

To keep it even, Marianne said, "He's all clothes and haircut."

Adam turned his head on his pillow, toward Marianne. "Your face is much more interesting than hers ever will be. Yours isn't just pretty, it also has character."

"After tonight it sure will."

Her tone was sarcastic, but he'd made her feel a little better.

He was almost asleep when Marianne said: "Is she your best friend?"

"I guess not."

They both fell asleep, feeling comforted by the hand they held.

In the morning, they awoke to the unmistakable sounds of their spouses making love to one another in the next room. At first, Marianne thought she would weep with the terrible sorrow and longing she experienced. But when Adam pounded his fist into the mattress, Marianne felt sheer fury. Finally, they found themselves laughing at the moaning, the groaning, at the "Oh, God"s and the "Oh, Yes"es, until they were helplessly clinging to each other, stifling each other's hysteria.

And then they heard their spouses get up from the bed.

Gather their clothes, get dressed.

"Is this your idea of a joke?" demanded Christy, from the hall.

"I didn't do that!" Ned protested. "I'd never do that."

"Well, who the hell did? Nobody else has been here! Jesus, I can't believe you'd insult me like this!"

"Christy!"

"Damn, don't yell at me, I have a migraine."

In the other bedroom, Marianne clutched Adam and whispered in horror: "Oh, my God!"

He sat up, and she saw the wild look on his face.

"Try orange juice," they heard Ned say.

"No. Adam always says that tomato juice is best."

"Oh, well, if Adam says it—"

"I believe I can make my own decision about what to do for my own hangover," was Christy's cold response to that.

Adam lay back down, grinning.

"But our coats!" Marianne hissed at him. "Our boots!"

He pointed to a chair, where Marianne saw all their

belongings piled up, and he whispered back: "I woke up in the middle of the night and brought it all in here."

"What woke you?"

"The sound of Christy throwing up in the bathroom."

Marianne buried her face in the sleeve of his suit coat and grinned, despite the tears in the corners of her eyes.

The edgy, angry voices of the lovers moved out of the hall, into the dining room.

But in a few minutes, Christy's voice was coming back at them, saying, ". . . just get it the hell out of my chopping block! What do you expect me to believe, that I walked in my sleep and stuck it there? Honest to God, Edward, I never dreamed you'd have this childish kind of practical-joke humor. I have to tell you that I am *not* amused . . ."

And her footsteps sounded in the master bedroom, followed by the sounds of slamming drawers and doors.

From the vicinity of the front door, Ned called out: "Do you want to ride with me, Christy?"

"No!" she called back. "I'll drive my own car!"

"I love you!" he yelled, angrily, at her.

"Love you, too!" she yelled back, sounding furious. And then they followed that with loud good-byes, and he slammed the front door behind him.

"Ass!" Christy said, in the next room.

She slammed her way out the back door shortly after that.

It was Marianne's turn to shoot up in bed.

"Oh, my God," she said. "Our cars are outside."

But Adam was starting to laugh again. He pulled her back down on the bed. "That's okay. She'll steam out of the driveway so fast, she'll never see mine. And he'll never think that out of all of the gray Accords in the world, that one could possibly be yours."

Marianne turned toward him. "Should we feel sorry for them?"

He thought about that. "I guess we can afford to be charitable."

They gazed at each other, and then said, at exactly the same time: "Nah." They burst out laughing in a fit that continued until Marianne fell into one last crying jag. Adam held her sympathetically, tactfully, until it ended. Then they got up, gathered their belongings, straightened themselves up, and left the house by the front door.

Before they left, however, Adam gathered up the dozen beautiful pink roses and swept them into his arms, making a lovely, if dripping, bundle of them. He presented them, with a gallant bow, to Marianne.

"Will you be my Valentine?" he asked her.

She took the flowers and cradled them. Feeling suddenly shy, she said to him, "Well, maybe next year."

Adam Phares waved his camera at her as he drove off.

Marianne waved the roses at him. Then she took the carnations, opened her car door, and dumped them in the slushy street. She placed the roses carefully in the vase, made sure it was still securely buckled in, and headed home.

Behind her, the moon, nearly invisible now, looked pale and ordinary in the morning sky. The fat lady was gone. Nobody, seeing it right then, would have guessed it had ever been blue.

〚 MARILYN WALLACE 〛

NO MATTER WHETHER MARILYN WALLACE IS writing suspense novels or police procedurals with an imaginative twist, her readers know she will provide superbly realized characters and a deep sense of the interconnectedness and complexity of even the most innocent of lives—and definitely of the not so innocent. Her first novel, A Case of Loyalties, *won the Macavity.* Primary Target *and* A Single Stone *were both Anthony nominees. So Shall Ye Reap was singled out in a starred* Kirkus *review for exhibiting "... a texture and spaciousness rare in mystery fiction; the result is not to be missed."* The Seduction *continues her exciting foray into suspense. Coming soon will be* The Devil to Pay.

Wallace is also an anthologist of renown, editing the five award-winning Sisters in Crime *short story anthologies and coediting the first* Deadly Allies *anthology.*

Wallace is now living in New York City after fourteen years in Northern California.

In "Advice to the Lovelorn," Wallace wonders at the effect of even the most well-meant suggestion in a deadly affair of the heart.

Advice to the Lovelorn

Elizabeth Fahey knew she wasn't really responsible for what had happened, but that didn't stop her from wishing she could take back the advice she'd given to Virginia. At least some of it, anyway.

"There's that look in your eyes, Lizzie. I haven't lived eighty-one years without learning to spot when a person's holding out on me. You know more than you're saying about how Virginia Hartman got into this fix." Mary O'Malley unhooked her fingers from the plush strap hanging beside the limousine window long enough to dab at her nose with a lace-edged handkerchief. "Secrets give you heartburn, you know."

The crevasses marking the landscape of Aunt Mary's face deepened as she smiled. Depending on the mood of the jury, Virginia's face might look like that by the time she drank a glass of cabernet again, wore sheer black stockings and short skirts again, opened a can of mixed grill for Cecily cat again.

"You don't have to be concerned about me repeating what you tell me." The older woman leaned forward and sniffed indignantly. "I can't recall where I put the *TV Guide* half the time. If you're worried I'll remember some sordid tidbit, you needn't. If I did, I'd probably think it was last Friday's episode of 'General Hospital.' "

Elizabeth clasped her hands together, the way she used to when she was a girl kneeling beside her bed at night. She'd said too much already, to her aunt and especially to Virginia, even though she'd only been trying to help. But her knowledge was pressing against her breastbone, forcing its way out from deep inside. "You have to promise: what I say can never go beyond just the two of us."

Aunt Mary nodded her agreement. Both women glanced away from the back of the driver's head, his hair slick and glistening as a pair of new shoes.

"It was John DeMarco's fault. He was the one who made Virginia do it. Told her the one way she could really prove she loved him was to kill someone." There. She'd said it. A small sigh of relief, like a discreetly passed bubble of gas, drifted into the overheated limousine.

"Lawyers!" Aunt Mary gasped as she opened her coat collar and fanned herself with her gloves. "I knew it was something like that," she added in a disgusted whisper.

Elizabeth patted her aunt's hand, taking courage from the outrage in her voice. "Virginia was still sort of in shock when she told me. But I could swear there was something else. Maybe a little curiosity. Maybe, God help her, the idea kind of intrigued her. Then, after she'd had time to think about it for a week, to wonder what exactly he had in mind, John said that it was Bernard Blankenship he wanted her to kill. Five partners in the firm. I wonder why John singled out Bernard."

Tight-lipped, Aunt Mary brushed back a steely curl that had edged its way from under the rolled brim of her purple felt hat. She ran her fingers along the floppy feather and cocked her head. "Well, with Father Healy officiating at the funeral, even lawyers become saints gone straight to God's side. Not many people can put together a eulogy the way Tommy Healy can. I suppose they won't be letting Virginia out to attend the funeral."

"Of course not. Judge wouldn't even set bail. You never really know people, do you? Even your best friends." Who would have thought Virginia was capable of such a thing? Elizabeth searched the dismal sky for a glimpse of sun through thick clouds that promised more snow before sunset. Virginia used to love the changing sky, the subtle differences of color and texture in the clouds that preceded thunderstorms or blizzards, the winds that blew sunshine into the Hudson valley. She'd even watched the Weather Channel the way some people watched "Murphy Brown." Maybe they had cable in the state prison. "Poor Virginia. I keep thinking that if I'd given her the right advice, I could have prevented all this. John DeMarco—a *probate* lawyer, for heaven's sake—asking her to kill one of his partners. All those families trusting him to take care of everything so that all they had to do was make sure the silver tea service was polished and their crying was done into clean hankies. *That* John DeMarco, saying that if she really loved him, she'd do anything he asked."

"Anything? Right then, she should have told him he was off his rocker. Didn't you tell her that?"

As though you could tell Virginia something when it came to John DeMarco. "You know how it was with her. John DeMarco, with those wild eyes so full of danger and those dimples. And charm. You're the one that said that wee bairns had nothing on him when it came to making people smile just for being in the light of his dancing eyes. He started all this in motion years ago. Asking Virginia to work late, telling her how much he needed her. Then things, you know, developed between them. It's not hard to see how it turned out the way it did."

"That's all common knowledge. You're not telling your secret, Lizzie. Now, then, you get to the good part of the story, and maybe when you're done I can shed some additional light." Aunt Mary folded her hands on her lap and leaned into the soft leather of the seat, the very picture of the guardian of the sundae's cherry, the margarita's lime, the Caesar's cheese.

Or was she simply teasing? When it was her turn, perhaps she would shift that innocent gaze and declare that she couldn't imagine why anyone would think *she* knew anything worth telling.

"You remember Virginia going on about how she was so much more than a secretary to John. Bragging that even with a wife at home, taking care of all the, you know, wifely things, she was the one he'd be lost without." Elizabeth stared out at the blur of passing trees, bare limbed and shivering in the cold. Oh, she could have predicted that getting involved with John DeMarco would end badly. *Had* predicted it when Virginia started canceling their standing Thursday evening date for movies, pizza, and girl talk.

But Elizabeth Fahey knew more: that Virginia Hartman had chosen not to recognize the truth until it up and bit her on the tail because she was blinded by a dangerous combination of pride and lust. The way she looked at John, at his hands and his mouth and his . . . sugarplums, indeed. Little doubt about the visions dancing in *her* head. There was Virginia, forty-two, proud of her eight years serving John DeMarco, needing to believe his promises to the very end. It took a special kind of arrogance to presume that she'd *really* get a bouquet of white cymbidium orchids, a band playing "Unchained Melody," and a five-foot-long train of satin and lace sweeping behind her down the aisle.

But you can repeat yourself only so many times before you realize you're having as much impact as a feather trying to stop a locomotive. No matter who said it, Virginia refused to hear the message: He's using you, he'll never give up such a good deal. One woman at home, another at the office, both ready to do anything for him.

Aunt Mary's voice, soft and reproachful, cut through her musings. ". . . his silver tongue. I knew John DeMarco did something to set this tragedy in motion. So, you've known all this time that he asked her to kill Bernard?"

"For six weeks. New Year's Day. We were sitting in her living room drinking leftover eggnog. Mostly brandy by then, to hide that it was two days old. Virginia started by complaining how John's demands had gotten out of hand. All those other things he'd asked her to do didn't count, he said. Before he'd leave Clara and marry Virginia, she had to *really* prove she loved him."

"John being John, she should have known he'd have a complicated plan in mind." The limousine swerved to avoid a pothole. Aunt Mary clung to the strap again and then leaned forward in expectant silence.

"She had to pass his 'final exam.' *His* word for it. As though she were a college student and he was sitting behind the desk in front of the room judging her performance. Making her work extra hard for her B."

"Well, *that* sounds like John DeMarco. That boy got a special kick out of making deals. He was always trying to get more value than he was giving. He never bought something but he didn't try to maneuver a set of complicated terms. Like the time Henry wanted to buy those fifty acres of John's, out by the edge of the swamp. First, Henry had to agree to give Sarah Hoving permission to tap the sugarbush along the fence of his north pasture. Then, of course, John turned around and made a deal with Sarah to get a gallon of syrup every single year, no matter what the sap run was. And he made her promise to deliver it right to his door, to boot. Oh, this is all so sad." A puzzled frown drove a new network of wrinkles into the older woman's face. "Is that the smokehouse? What did old man McManus do, paint it red and sell it off to city people?"

"That's not the smokehouse, it's the old railroad station," Elizabeth said gently. Poor dear, was this a sign that Aunt Mary's legendary mental acuity was becoming dulled by age?

"That couldn't be the old railroad station. The house is—"

"Aunt Mary, we're not going to the house. We're going to the funeral home. The wake was yesterday, but you didn't go because you didn't want to disappoint the children you read to in the hospital." It wasn't possible for memory to go all at once, was it? Seemed more like the sharpness would wear off little by little, imperceptible nicks flowing one into the other until all the edge was gone. By the time she got out of prison, what would become of Virginia's memories?

"You were saying. About the tests." Her fingers drumming the armrest impatiently, Aunt Mary raised her sparse eyebrows and waited for the rest of the story.

Nothing wrong with Aunt Mary's memory, not when she was interested in something. "That first year, she had to make herself available to work on weekends. At a moment's notice. Then he started timing her. How long it took to get a letter typed and on his desk. How many minutes to find a file he'd misplaced. How many weeks until she mastered the new computer system. Two years ago, he made her go out and buy Clara sexy lingerie for her birthday. Virginia knew that John and Clara no longer even slept in the same room. That *she* was the one he was . . . And then he pushed the limits. Made her sign his name to some papers. She didn't realize right away that she'd forged his name on some kind of statement saying he'd transferred shares of stock to the trustees of the estate when, in fact, he didn't do it until two months later. Put a couple of thousand dollars in his personal pockets for being custodian. I think that's the way it worked. Anyway, it wasn't legal, that much I remember.

"And then, about a year ago, he asked her to fix the books. To make it look like Bernard Blankenship was concealing income from the firm. Skimming it off for himself."

It was really Bernard's fault the firm was losing money anyway, Virginia had said, taking cases that anyone else could tell would end up with the clients skipping out without paying. Would the firm do better now, with one less attorney bringing in clients and revenue?

"Bernard! I was waiting for it to come back to him. Another deal John made . . ." Aunt Mary drifted into silence as she twisted a thread from the cuff of her coat. "But Virginia went along with John's monkey business. Why couldn't she see where it would all lead?"

"Dazzled. She was so dazzled by his promises she was prepared to do anything he asked. You said it yourself. John was a tough negotiator." Elizabeth's mouth turned up in a half smile. "He warned her to be careful that no one found out she'd made those accounting adjustments. Someone might think she'd cooked the books for Bernard."

"And since Virginia was under John's spell, she needed to believe *all* his lies and she swallowed that one, too." Impatient, Aunt Mary tugged at her coat sleeves.

"He thought he was being so slick about it. Stringing her along and all the while setting Bernard up. Using Viriginia as a pawn. And when Virginia started questioning John's promise to tell poor Clara before Memorial Day that he was leaving her, John just said it was another test. That she had to prove her love by waiting until the Fourth of July. Pretty soon Labor Day had passed and still John hadn't said a word."

"You'd think Virginia would have wised up by then. I once waited for . . . oh, never mind. You mean to tell me Clara didn't know what was going on?"

"Probably did. Maybe that's why she gave Virginia all those clothes that didn't fit anymore. Even that lingerie that Virginia had picked out. Maybe Clara was piling the guilt onto Virginia. Remember how she blew up like a balloon? Clara, I mean. Didn't go anywhere or do anything all summer except eat those cheese Danishes from the bakery in Millerton. John brought them to her, six, ten at a time, and she'd eat them all before nightfall. So Clara gave away all her clothes. Suits from Lord and Taylor. Cashmere sweaters from Saks. Tweed slacks from Anne Klein. All those clothes she couldn't squeeze herself into. Clara handed them all to Virginia. And Virginia told me she felt so bad because she was the cause of Clara's gaining all that weight, even if Clara didn't know it.

"But Virginia was determined that John had to tell Clara. If she didn't take the clothes, Clara would surely be suspicious. He swore on his mother's grave that he'd tell Clara by Halloween. Of course, he didn't say a word. Virginia told him she couldn't go on with the deception of coming to the house twice a week. Picking up papers for John and seeing Clara standing there, all frumpy and dowdy in those stretched-out old sweatpants. No makeup and no idea that her husband had not three hours ago gotten out of bed with her. With Virginia, that is. So now, on top of feeling betrayed by John, she was feeling bad about deceiving Clara."

Aunt Mary stretched and then crossed her dark-stockinged legs, smoothing the maroon wool coat so that her bony knees were covered. Telephone poles whizzed by. "But not so bad that she would walk away right then and start a life that wasn't a threat to Clara's marriage. And she could have done that anytime, attractive woman like that, isn't that right? Is this going to take much longer? I need a toilet."

"We'll be there in five minutes. Finally Viriginia put her foot down. Tell Clara by Thanksgiving, she said to John, or I will. He continued to come up with excuses, but Virginia never carried out her threat because she was afraid to lose him. You know how love can be."

Had Aunt Mary ever struggled for control of her emotions, desperate to free herself from the bonds of passion? Elizabeth blinked back a picture of the young Mary, her hair still chestnut and flowing in burnished waves behind her as she ran, hand in hand with a tousle-haired lad over green fields to their secret place. If it came right down to it, had she herself ever felt the way she imagined Virginia had?

Not enough to do the things her friend had done, that was for sure. Elizabeth trembled slightly as a shiver of fear and envy ran through her.

"Love can be like porridge," Aunt Mary said, pursing her mouth with the finality of her pronouncement.

Elizabeth laughed. "Porridge?"

"Of course. You feel a deep hunger and you fill yourself up with the stuff. It's hot and thick and makes you feel good. And then it cools so quick you hardly recognize it, and it goes all lumpy and makes you think you've got a pile of stones lying there inside you. You can sprinkle it with all the brown sugar in the world, that'll turn to lumps, too, unless you finish the whole thing before it cools. Do you know how he kept the temperature up so that Virginia's porridge stayed hot all the time?" Aunt Mary wriggled her twined fingers. "Meanness."

"Meanness? You talking about his procrastination in telling Clara?"

"You may know certain secrets, my dear, but I saw something. Neither one of them knew anyone else was around, but I saw it and it made me feel that Virginia was getting just exactly what she wanted from John DeMarco. And he was so good at giving it, yes he was, oh yes he was."

"Don't talk riddles, Aunt Mary. What did you see?"

"Actually, it wasn't seeing. I *heard* it. The office door was shut and they were in there, the two of them. I wasn't eavesdropping, mind you, just stopping by to drop off some papers John wanted me to sign, something to do with Uncle Pete's bond funds maturing and whatnot. John always kept his eye on those things, bless him. And there I was, quiet as a mouse, thinking Virginia would come right out to her own desk any minute. But the voices got louder and before I could leave, let me tell you, I was so embarrassed by what I heard that I couldn't wait to get out of there. But when I stood up, my purse went upside down and everything fell out onto the floor and then . . ." She shook her head and stared at the fogged window glass.

Elizabeth held her breath, waiting for Aunt Mary to go on. The hard brown hills, crusted with old snow, flew by as they approached town.

"I've met some men in my life who have this way of letting you know that they don't think of women as actual people, but John DeMarco," Aunt Mary said, scrunching her gloves in her clenched fist, "went way beyond them all. It was near Christmas, the one just past, and I was concentrating on the patterns of the lights blinking on that huge tree. You can always tell about someone by their tree, and his practically took up all the space in the little reception area outside his office. *And* every one of the ornaments was gold. Doesn't that say something, now? Anyway, I was watching the lights blink on and off and then I heard her voice rising. Saying, no, she wouldn't do that again."

And here she thought Virginia had told her everything about her relationship with John DeMarco. Elizabeth smiled her encouragement to her aunt.

"Her voice wasn't like her own. It sounded scared. Even when she was a little girl I never knew Virginia to sound afraid. If it were me, I'd have been angry, but she was frightened. She started talking real low. 'I'm no sweet young thing,' she said. 'Why does he want a middle-aged secretary in a black silk teddy? I don't want to wear that black thing. It makes me feel so cheap.' And then he laughed and said why should she feel cheap when she's free. I was a little shocked. But that wasn't all."

She fanned her crumpled gloves onto her lap, each empty finger pointing in a different direction. "The next thing he said took my breath away. 'It's for us,' he said in that lawyer voice of his, 'so we'll finally be able to get married. You have to do this. If he wasn't the auditor, I'd never ask. He wants fifty thousand dollars and another night like the last one and then he promises he'll be blind to what we've done. He had only two stipulations: he wants you to wear this, and this time he wants you to stay the night. Come on, honey, I promise. This is the last time, absolutely the last time.' That's what John said, and my stomach almost turned itself inside out right there on his carpet. What he was asking that poor girl— can you believe it?"

So John DeMarco not only lied to Virginia about his intentions, he also traded her—and more than once—

like a foil-boxed bottle of Scotch. For favors. For protection from the accusations of powerful men. "What did Virginia say when he begged like that?"

"It was the strangest thing. As soon as his voice turned all cajoling like it could, you know, she got hard herself. 'I think I'll wear that blouse with all those tiny pearl buttons down the front, the one you like to watch me undo,' she said, and then she laughed. 'You know how auditors pay attention to detail. He'll probably get his rocks off just waiting for me to finish unbuttoning.' And then I heard her high heels, you know how she always wore them at work. Well, I would have died if she'd thought I heard all that, so I got up and stood as though I'd just come in, and when she flew into the room, I just told her, 'Hello, dear, I'm here to see John about these papers.' But I could tell she wondered. I could just tell. Poor thing."

Elizabeth braced herself as the car veered into the long oval drive of the funeral home. Exhaust plumed from the tailpipes of the cars and limos lined up along the left side of the gravel. The parking lot was crammed with well-wishers from all over the county. Paying their respects. Needing to be seen by the remaining partners of the firm, as proof of their continuing loyalty. Just another business obligation: wasn't that what it was for the lot of them?

The driver caught her eye in the mirror. "Someone will be along to get the door in a second and to help you up the steps. It's icy out there, ma'am," he said to Aunt Mary, "so I'd advise you just to wait here until that gentleman in the gray topcoat comes for you."

Aunt Mary nodded distractedly; she leaned toward Elizabeth. "Isn't that Peter and Sarah Hoving? She's wearing *pants* to a funeral! Oh, and there's Henry and Deeny in their once-a-year ties. And Riley Hamm, wearing his uniform. Oh, and isn't that poor Clara DeMarco? Look at her, Lizzie. Doesn't she appear to be thinner?

Really, I mean, it's not just that she's wearing black."

Yes, Clara did seem thinner. Maybe even a little less pinched around the mouth. As though she'd just shaken a stone out of her shoe, maybe. Her face behind the veil more relaxed, less jowly. Not quite stylishly slim yet, but who knew what the next few months might bring?

"That look of yours is back, Lizzie. Your expression is, I don't know, guilty, as though all this were your fault." Aunt Mary clasped Elizabeth's free hand between her gloved fingers. "Well, of course it isn't. Anyone can see that. No matter what you *said*, it's what she *did* that counts."

On the face of it, Aunt Mary was right, of course. Done was done. "I was only trying to get Virginia to see that John DeMarco's a man who won't ever be satisfied. He'd push the limits. Ask for more and more. Make promises and break them. You have two choices, I said. You can prove you love him by killing someone. Or you can end the relationship."

"That Virginia always did hate being backed into a corner." Aunt Mary chuckled softly. "You tell her she has two choices and she figures out how to take them both."

Outside, the man in the gray topcoat, his expression harried, picked his way over the icy walk to the first car in the line, extended his hand, and waited while Ruth Hoving stepped onto the ice. He escorted her up the stairs, then returned to the next car in line. Opened the door. Extended his hand.

Aunt Mary stared at the tall figure that unfolded into the early morning chill, watched as he paused in front of the sign and read the announcement of morning services. "Somehow, after everything you've told me, I didn't expect *him* to be here. The man's always gracious but today he looks, I don't know, *grateful*."

"Why not? Bernard Blankenship should be allowed a moment to celebrate the fact that *he* isn't the partner being buried today." As she watched John DeMarco's widow greet Bernard, Elizabeth Fahey swore off giving advice. If Virginia, if *anyone* needed help straightening out the knots and kinks of a complicated love life, they'd have to get it somewhere else.